978-1-7773423-9-5

Also by Krista Wallace

In paperback, ebook and audiobook

Gatekeeper's Key

In audiobook

Gatekeeper's Key
Gatekeeper's Deception - Deceiver
Gatekeeper's Deception - Deceived

Audioshorts

To Serve and Protect
The Inner Light

For all the kickass women in my life, and the
awesome men who have our backs.

Gatekeeper's Deception I
Deceiver

One

Whatever It Takes

Kyer leaned forward, her back as rigid as the chair on which she sat, and watched Valrayker. The dark elf chewed the inside of his cheek. There was a slight tremble in his shoulder as he breathed deeply and forced a tight-lipped smile. He was trying to hide it, all right, but she could tell. Beneath that mask of calm the dark elf was distressed. Even the crackle of the fire was an interruption in the silence of the small chamber. Val stood before her and her four companions with such an uncharacteristically formal attitude, she forgot the full wine cup next to her.

"A week after you left on your mission," Val said, "we received a message from Bartheylen Castle." Kyer made a quick calculation. *Three weeks ago, then.* "You will note that Kien is not here to greet you, and he asked me to pass on his regrets."

Kyer felt like waving her hand to brush the comment aside. Clearly a higher concern took precedence over mere courtesies. But it wasn't her place to dismiss it.

"He returned in great haste to Bartheylen Castle upon hearing that Lady Alon Maer has been taken seriously ill."

Alarm seized Kyer's heart. "How seriously?"

"We do not know. The healers could tell us their observations but have drawn no conclusions. All we know is that it seems her life may be threatened by this illness."

The dread hung in the chamber like the deep resonance of a gong. The group waited.

Valrayker was not finished. "The other part of the problem is that Alon is pregnant. It stands to reason that if her life is in danger, so is that of the child." Here, the dark elf turned away, and Kyer saw his shoulder blades contract, controlling the emotion that surged. She scanned her friends and frowned with concern at Derry. He was nearly overcome, with his palm pressed over his mouth. As Val's captain, he had known Kien and Alon Maer for at least half his life.

"There must be *something* we can do," Kyer said. "Do the Healers not have *any* ideas?"

All five watched their leader expectantly.

Valrayker composed himself. "It is true that there is one idea."

"Well, let's have it!" Kyer said.

The dark elf contemplated her. "I confess I'm moved by your depth of feeling for a dear friend of mine, though you have never met her."

Kyer frowned away her blush. They would never understand why Alon Maer meant so much to her.

Valrayker wandered over to ponder the map on the wall.

"The healers at Bartheylen Castle are the best in Rydris. They have employed the full spectrum of their craft, all the ancient arts, their knowledge of spells and charms, all their energy and internal powers and have come up with nothing but minor, temporary remedies. They cannot even come up with a diagnosis, let alone what they need: a cure. The prime healer here in Shael suggested it, and we all agreed that in order to learn exactly what ails Alon, and to discover a cure, if there is one, we need to consult a higher power."

Valrayker looked directly at Jesqellan.

Jesqellan is a higher power? Kyer thought doubtfully. But then the mage's eyes widened in stark contrast to his dark skin.

"You can't mean that we need to consult Kayme?" Jesqellan murmured, his mouth agape.

The duke nodded gravely. "The prime can think of no other option."

Kyer looked from one troubled face to another around the room. Nobody seemed happy with the idea. *Who's Kayme?*

"No one has seen or heard from Kayme in years!" said Jesqellan. "Why, it has been at least *fifteen* years since I have heard him utter a single sound from his dark tower way up north, and even then it was a three-word declaration, 'I am busy,' that gave us all the strong message that he absolutely does *not* want to be disturbed! One does not just walk up to the tower of the most powerful wizard in Rydris, knock on the door, and ask for a casual favour as if we were asking to borrow some eggs. It just isn't done."

"It's our only hope." Valrayker sank wearily into his chair. "If you don't wish to be a part of it, I won't blame you or bear any grudge against you. It may be that he isn't willing or even able to help us. I'm merely asking you to try."

"I'll go," said Kyer without hesitation.

"As will I." Phennil nodded, though the blond wood elf spoke too confidently for Kyer to believe he wasn't afraid.

"You know I will," Captain Derry said quietly to his lord.

Jesqellan stared at the floor and said nothing. Next to him, Janak sat with his jaw crooked in a thoughtful pose and played with his beard.

"It isn't necessary to make a decision this instant," Valrayker assured them. "The situation is urgent, but I'm also fully aware of the danger you would be heading into. We'll talk further in the morning."

Kyer left the chamber as swiftly as decorum allowed. Her teeth felt numb, and no amount of elvish wine had stilled the thudding in her chest. A few hours earlier they had ridden into the city of Shael expecting celebration after their successful mission in the north. Instead she had sensed that a pall had settled over the city. Whatever she had guessed the cause might be, she hadn't imagined this.

Derry stayed in the room with his Lord awhile longer, but Phennil, Jesqellan, and Janak followed her into the back of the castle foyer. Kyer gulped fresh air, only now aware of how many hours they had been cooped up in the small chamber. It had been midday when they arrived, and now the torches and candles cast warm, flickering light into the shadows that stretched from corner to corner across the stone. The story of how they rescued the people of Nennia had taken several hours. At least two meals had been brought to them as they told their tale.

"I don't mean to sound like I'm complaining or anything," said Phennil, stretching his legs with a lunge, "but weren't you hoping we'd get to rest a bit when we got back here? I suppose we'll have to leave again in a few days."

"Of course." Kyer tried to find a purpose for her hands. "I'd leave now if I could."

Jesqellan clutched the front of his brown, travel-weathered Moabi robes. "Some of us have not yet decided if we will go at all," he said softly. "Some of us are more aware than others of the significance of Valrayker's request."

Phennil's forehead creased with concern at the mage's warning, but Kyer stood her ground. "He needs us to ask a wizard for help. How difficult can that be?"

"My dear girl, Kayme is not just 'a wizard'." Jesqellan narrowed his eyes at Kyer. "I was not exaggerating when I said Kayme is *the most powerful wizard* in all of Rydris. He is arrogant, impatient, and does not like to be disturbed." His voice remained quiet, but its increased intensity betrayed his fear. "Casual favours will not be entertained. And I shudder to think what the price will be for such an interruption."

"This is hardly a casual favour." Kyer matched his intensity with no trace of fear. "A person's life is at stake."

Jesqellan drew up his entire five-and-a-half foot height. "Many lives are at stake all over Rydris. War does that." He tapped his staff on the stone floor in frustration. "Three years ago, a small party sought his help, and he became so enraged at their temerity they found themselves scattered, separately, to the corners of the continent! No food, no horses, no weapons, nothing. Alone. It took my cousin six months to reach home again, and he very nearly perished." A gusty sigh escaped his lips. "Yes, a life is at stake. Nevertheless, no life is worth the risk of summoning the wrath of Kayme upon myself."

Janak's grunt inserted itself between his two comrades. "I'm deciding nothing until I've slept in a bed for one night." He opened the door to the tower stairs. "Val said an instant decision wasn't necessary—" He darted a backward glance at Kyer, his deadened left eye baleful. "—so, unlike some, I'll not make one." He bumped into the doorframe as he shuffled his dwarven bulk into the stairwell. Jesqellan nodded to Kyer and Phennil and went after him.

Kyer did not follow. Earlier she'd have given almost anything to drag her exhausted, travel-weary body upstairs to her cosy guest room in Shael Castle. Instead, the dark elf's announcement had dispersed her fatigue. There was something she had to do before she would sleep tonight.

Smouldering, she stalked across the stone floor into the shadows of the castle foyer. Granted, she didn't know this Kayme person; perhaps she ought not to be hasty. Would extra consideration change her mind? Janak knew better than the others how she had been affected by her previous hasty actions. He had every right to caution her about her decision making. This time, though, Kyer's impulsive choice was not a reckless one, no matter how it came across to her companions. *I don't need to justify my "instant decision" to any of them.* She hopped up the first few stone steps of the broad staircase that curved its way up to the second floor.

She stopped partway up and turned to face the massive oak doors that both provided and denied entrance to the keep. Raising her eyes above the doors, she beheld there the image she had wanted—no, *needed* to see.

The painted version of Lady Alon Maer stood next to her jet black horse, healthy, dignified, her palm resting on her sword hilt. Beautiful and deadly. How many had she killed? How many of those were duels in which the lady had been forced to make a snap decision? *How many*, Kyer sucked in her breath, *were cold-blooded revenge against the direct order of her superior?*

Kyer had killed six men since coming into contact with Valrayker. Two had been in self-defence during an attack in the woods. Two had been in Nennia, in defence of her friends. The other two had been one-on-one. Face to face. The first was a duel in which a blackguard named Simon had cheated. He would certainly not have been content to accept his defeat had she left him alive. The other . . . Kyer gripped the balustrade as the tempest of emotion swirled around her again.

In her report to Valrayker a couple of hours ago, Kyer had admitted to killing Ronav Malachite. She couldn't have avoided telling him. But what she had left out was the manner in which she had killed him. Ronav had made himself her enemy. He had beaten her, flogged her, and very nearly mutilated her. He had done unspeakable things to a village full of innocent people. Oh yes, he deserved to die. And though she had promised Derry she wouldn't take matters into her own hands, she had disobeyed his direct order because *she* wanted to be the one to kill Ronav.

There was no glory in it.

Derry had been angrier with her than she had ever seen him. But eventually he had, she thought, understood why she had done it.

Kyer's vision cleared and she stared at the Lady, a warrior to whom this kind of struggle must not be foreign. Kyer nodded, certain that the Lady's gaze forgave her. She renewed the vow she had made a short time ago.

"I'll do it alone if I have to."

She was startled by the sound of a throat clearing softly. "You won't have to do it alone, Kyer. Derry and I volunteered, too, remember?"

Phennil's light-footed steps had traced hers. She had forgotten he was there. He stood at the bottom of the stairs, eerie and ghostlike in the dim light of the dozen or so half-burned candelabra around the stone walls of the foyer. He looked up at her cautiously, politely not intruding upon her space.

She blinked a few times, and a grim smile finally eased the tautness in her forehead. He took it as an invitation, and leapt, two steps at a time, to join her. Kyer sat and waited for him to ask the question she knew was on his mind—the same question Val had already raised. She braced herself.

"What do you think?" He plopped down next to her. "Will they join us?"

She was surprised; that was not the question she expected. "Do you doubt it?"

"I don't know. Jesqellan seems awfully hesitant, and Janak—"

"Won't say no to a mission that I've said yes to," finished Kyer. "Janak and I . . . we reached an understanding," she said thoughtfully. "I imagine things won't have changed that much." She rested her elbows on her knees.

"What about Jesqellan?"

Kyer's jaw jutted out thoughtfully, and she breathed in the faint odours of coal, wood, and stone. "If I've learned anything about Jesqellan, it's that he needs to know he's useful. He'll know we need him on this mission."

Kyer looked sidelong at her friend. Janak and Jesqellan thought she had been impulsive again. Here was Phennil, in perfect position to suggest the same thing, and he hadn't. Somehow that decided it. Kyer peered up through the darkness to the enormous portrait that was the focal point of the foyer, right above the oaken front doors. The subject of the painting was barely visible in the candlelight, but Kyer knew it by heart. "How well do you know Alon Maer?" The Lady looked down at them out of her exquisitely painted eyes, her pale high elven face surrounded by thick, multihued dark hair.

"I've only met her a couple of times," Phennil admitted. "I think Jesqellan and Janak are both ahead of me." He turned a puzzled eye to Kyer. "But I've met her a couple of times more than you. What made you volunteer? You even beat Derry."

There it was. The question she'd expected.

Kyer didn't answer straight away. Instead she rose and studied Alon's portrait with the same admiration she felt the first time she'd seen it. The sword, the marvellous detail of the Lady's leather cuirass that reminded Kyer of her own, unequivocal substantiation of something special Kyer shared with her. The Lady's hand on her hilt revealed the muscles in her wrists and forearms. Kyer clenched and released her fists, sensing her own strength concealed there. This was what Kyer had needed to do before she could retire to bed.

"Phennil," she began, and her throat tightened. "Remember the first time I entered this castle? It was, what, a month ago? And you had to come and get me from this very spot so we could go meet Kien."

Phennil nodded. "I had to call you about three times."

"I have never met another woman who is a swordfighter. A *true* fighter. Soldiers, troopers, yes, but—" She took a deep breath as she considered whether or not to speak her next words. "I studied the *wæpnian*, Phennil, I don't know if you knew that."

He whistled low. "That would explain a few things."

"Back home in Hreth, I used to train with another girl my age, but she didn't take it as seriously as I did. People used to call me a freak and names a lot worse. They'd whisper and stare at me. They'd do everything they could to avoid me." Kyer pointed at the portrait. "She is a warrior, one of the best. She is—" Kyer's throat caught as she realized what she was about to say, "—*living* proof a woman being a fighter is not freakish." She sat back down. "I have more in common with the Lady Alon Maer than I have ever had with any other woman. That means more to me than I can possibly explain."

Kyer focussed on the wood elf's startlingly blue eyes. "Phennil, I know I have never met her. I never will, if she dies."

———

Valrayker shook Derry's hand. "I want you to know how much I appreciate your success in Nennia. It means a lot to me, I'm sure you understand that."

"Yes, absolutely." Derry looked at him hopefully.

Val refilled their wine. "Very few injuries, and fewer fatalities, excepting the perpetrators. What was it, two?"

Derry shivered, though the room was warm. "Three," he said with reluctant honesty.

"Unfortunate." Valrayker made himself comfortable in his armchair and gazed thoughtfully at the landscape painting that hung above the fireplace. "I am disappointed not to be able to question Ronav; he'd have been able to provide us with invaluable information."

I knew it, Derry said to himself. Aware of what Valrayker's wishes would be, Derry had given Kyer a direct order to bring Ronav to him. Instead she had obeyed some crazed instinct of her own and killed him. Derry had been infuriated with her. "Kyer was the last one to speak to him." It was hard to keep the bitterness out of his voice. "Perhaps you ought to ask her—"

"And that's another thing," Valrayker nodded gravely, and Derry exhaled in relief at being able to finally speak of what he saw as his biggest failure on the mission: his lack of control of his own people—well, of Kyer—and the resulting death of Ronav at Kyer's hand.

His lord's next words let him down. "Tell me again about Kyer's sudden reappearance. She was gone for how long?"

"All day." He unhappily, but dutifully, switched topics. "Taken by his men at sunrise, and full dark when she appeared at our camp."

"And there was no way she could have known how to find you?"

The captain shrugged, himself baffled by the strange affair. "We had travelled throughout the day and had not followed our planned route. I don't see how she could have known where we were."

"And she was immobile?"

Derry cringed at the memory. "They'd beaten and flogged her nearly senseless. There was absolutely no way she rode a horse in that condition. She simply reappeared out of nowhere."

Valrayker rested his chin in his hand and tapped the air with his foot. He stared ahead at some point in the middle distance, as if searching his mind for something to grasp. His jaw was tight, and he gave his head a small shake, dismissing some possible conclusion. Then he sat up straight and smiled. "Very interesting, indeed. Was there anything else?"

Taken aback, Derry opened and closed his mouth. He wanted to say, *I was hoping you had something else to say to me.* He wanted to ask if *this* time he had done enough to satisfy Valrayker's exacting criteria.

"No, my lord." He added hopefully, "Unless you had anything more—"

"Nothing, Captain, except to say again: Thank you for freeing those villagers from a horrific fate."

Derry rose awkwardly, confused and more than a little frustrated by his lord's interest in Kyer's reappearance but not her killing of the man responsible for that abominable manipulation of Valrayker's people. Also frustrated by the abrupt dismissal, he bowed and exited.

Kyer sat on the stairs for a few minutes after saying good night to Phennil. She stared up at the portrait of Alon Maer. "Whatever it takes."

She descended the staircase and walked around behind it to the little door that led up the tower stairs. As she passed the door to the meeting room, it opened and she was nearly blindsided by Derry. Upon seeing her, his face turned stormy as he carefully pulled the door to.

"Did you have a nice talk?" she asked.

"Oh, very nice," he said sarcastically and went through the stairwell door.

"What does that mean?" She hustled to keep up with him on the stairs.

"It means even with the success of that mission, even though we eradicated a problem that would likely have spread throughout all other duchies, even though we saved those poor people from mindlessly killing each other—" His voice caught as his intensity increased.

She ran to catch up with Derry's long strides. "What about it?"

"I thought I had done it this time. Everything he wanted of me. I thought surely this time I had impressed him."

"Of course you impressed him. You saw his face."

Derry stopped on the landing at the second level. "Not enough, Kyer. He did not offer me a knighthood." He continued the climb.

Kyer rolled her eyes and followed. "He's hardly had time to take a breath since we told him everything that happened. Plus, he's got Kien and Alon Maer on his mind. Maybe tomorrow, or the next day—"

"I doubt it."

"He's your mentor. Can't you ask him why?"

Derry flung open the door at level three and stopped again. He didn't look at her as she caught up to him. He gripped the door handle. "I know exactly why. He didn't offer me a knighthood because I'm not good enough, because he wanted me to bring the perpetrator to him for questioning. And we both know why I didn't do that, don't we?"

It would have been less painful if he kicked her in the gut and knocked her down the stairs. He went out and slammed the door, leaving her alone. His bootsteps echoed down the corridor. Val hadn't given Derry a knighthood, and it was her fault. Kyer sank against the stone wall.

To Chart's mind, there were two kinds of fear: the fear of things you know, and the fear of things you don't. He wasn't even sure which category this situation fit into.

He stood at the end of a row of five servitors, three men and two women, and felt small and insignificant in the massive black chamber. Most of his weight was on his left foot, and he hung his arms at his sides. Surely he at least looked unperturbed. *I'm not as convincing as* he *is, though.* His neighbour to the left had placed his hands on his hips. His jaw was slack, as if he had been here before and had nothing to fear. He oozed defiance, as if demanding to know why he'd been Gated here.

Chart had a strong inkling of why he'd been Gated here. He had failed in his assigned task. Time had run out. He couldn't count on his lordship showing mercy.

Three other beings shared the space. One was an uncommonly tall man, whose height was less imposing the way he sat in his armchair. His long legs were crossed, the top foot on the table in front of him, while his head, dark hair contrasting the odd pallor of the face, was propped against the chair's winged back. His elbows rested on the arms of the chair, and his hands were clasped loosely on his belly, thumbs toying with a shiny button on his black waistcoat. On the whole he was a good deal more at home than the five men and women who stood before him. He kept glancing down at a game board on the table, contemplating his next move.

The second being was also a man, dressed in a loose-fitting robe that would have appeared informal, but for the fabric which shimmered like spun gold. The shiny black floor mirrored gold beneath him as he stood before them. His hands clasped behind his back, he appraised each of the servitors in turn.

The third being was a dragon.

"Your reports are . . ." The man in gold thought for a moment, doubt on his lean face. "Satisfactory, at best. I prefer excellence. Lieutenant?" Lord Dregor turned to the seated figure. The golden glow from the floor shifted with him, rippling like moonlight on a lake.

"My lord?" The lieutenant's expression was all innocence and mild curiosity. It, more than the stern expression of his superior, sent a shiver down Chart's spine.

"These hirelings are under your command, are they not?"

"That is so."

"And therefore, is it not your responsibility to see that they carry out their duties as per your direction, which is an extension of the orders given by me?"

"It is my responsibility to relay your orders to them, my lord. It is their responsibility to carry them out." He picked up a game piece and twiddled it around in his fingers.

Chart shifted his weight to the other foot and frowned. The others also adjusted their stances, and Chart was comforted knowing they were trying as hard as he to hide their fear.

Lord Dregor eyed his lieutenant suspiciously. Chart had the impression, not for the first time, that a game of one-upmanship was being played before his eyes. The lieutenant was called Golgathaur. Though Lord Dregor was the elder, the more powerful, as far as Chart could tell, and without question the one in highest command, Golgathaur had a mind of his own, and Chart didn't think Lord Dregor fully understood what went on inside it.

"Are you saying," Lord Dregor peered out at Golgathaur between his eyelids, "that you take no responsibility for your underlings?"

"Not at all, my lord," Golgathaur answered with a smile. "I am saying that I take no responsibility for their failure to carry out your orders, as delivered to them by me." He started to place his game piece then changed his mind and drew it back. One thing Chart was sure of, if his lordship was ever dissatisfied with the lieutenant's words or performance, it was unlikely to be the lieutenant who would suffer the consequences.

Lord Dregor turned back to the five retainers. "Well then." He glared at each one. "Let them explain to me why certain goals have not been met."

His frown settled upon Chart, who shifted so his weight was evenly distributed on both feet. He hoped it might lessen the trembling in his knees. The piercing gaze of the dark lord penetrated Chart's defences. His blood chilled. His body grew heavier until it was a mass of iron on legs of wicker. No longer able to hold him upright, the wicker gave out, and Chart fell to his knees, a jolt of pain shooting up his back. The dark lord's stare drew Chart's jaw downward toward his chest until his head was bowed.

"My Lord Dregor," Chart found himself saying. "I serve you with my heart and soul and will give of myself, breath and bone, until death takes me." The words tumbled out of him unbidden. Chart could not clamp his mouth shut, try as he might. Fear simmered inside him as he surrendered control over his mind, and panic bubbled up his throat until he was shouting. "I failed, my lord! Yes, it's true! I was to cause a disruption in the city of Shael during the Springrites festival, to put fear in the hearts of the Southern Alliance. I was to have completed the task by midnight of the full Swan Moon. I was not able to find an opportunity; I did not make an opportunity. I failed and yet to you I continue to pledge my life and devotion, my Lord Dregor, Lord of All."

Chart's body jolted as the dark lord yanked the probe out of his mind. His muscles liquefied and he flopped to the floor. Lord Dregor had moved on to the next man, who now assumed the same humiliating posture. Chart heard words, though only in pieces, as if he were hearing them from under water. "I failed, my lord! ... gather two dozen ... Guarded Realm.... nineteen who were willing to leave their families ... devote their lives ... We were run out of Prost … was killed."

The black marble floor felt harsh and cold beneath Chart's cheek. Of the others, he heard only faint, faraway cries, as if they were calling from the far side of a valley. All he saw were the reflection of gold in the mirror-like black floor and, farther away, the red that shone off the patiently waiting dragon.

The aroma of steam filled the air, mingled with a faint scent of lavender.

Chart shook uncontrollably. How did Lord Dregor punish failure?

What felt like moments and hours later, strength returned to his limbs. He drew his knees under himself and pushed up onto his elbows. *Please, can't I just stay down here?* But no, he could not.

Standing again, though shakily, Chart glanced at Golgathaur, who still sat infuriatingly at ease in the armchair wearing an interested smile.

"I have heard your stories," Lord Dregor said. "I trust you will do better from now on."

"Yes, my lord," they murmured, and Chart nearly sighed with relief.

"And to help you remember …" Lord Dregor held out his hand.

Without warning, something seized the man next to Chart around his middle.

"Wha—what? No!" screamed the very man who had feared nothing. His legs propelled him forward under some other power. Chart's heart choked him as he watched the man trying to fight off the invisible hook that drew him across the floor. Chart saw where he was headed and quaked.

Greok lay with his enormous head resting on his forepaws, claws curled underneath. His vertical eyelids were closed, though one eyebrow was raised expectantly. The victim came within reach of Greok's claws. Despite his struggles, he was pulled closer until he stood immediately before the gigantic reptile, whose reflection glowed like embers. The man knew his fate. Fear of the unknown had become the fear of the all-too known, and Greok tortured the poor human by making him wait. Chart crammed his fingers into his ears against the screaming.

Finally, Greok opened one eye and lifted one forepaw, twisting it the way Chart would turn his hand to pick up his beer. Greok's great maw opened a touch, enough to show his ghastly fangs dripping saliva. The screaming intensified. The paw moved slowly behind the human's body, then drew him swiftly into the awaiting teeth. As the mouth closed around him, his screams stopped, filling the chamber with an even less bearable silence.

Lord Dregor lowered his hand and brushed a bit of lint off his golden robe.

"Lieutenant?" he suggested.

Golgathaur, still smiling as if nothing had happened, bowed where he sat and nodded four times. A shimmering gateway appeared in front of each of the remaining hirelings. "Until we meet again, good people." He finally placed his game piece.

Each servitor shuffled through a doorway, back into the life he or she had given over to Lord Dregor. They took with them the reminder of what happens to those who fail. Just before his door closed behind him, Chart heard Golgathaur's voice.

"It's your turn, I believe."

Sleep, when it finally came to Kyer after she had seethed into the wee hours, did not help her conclude all her ruminations on Derry's knighthood. Had Val actually told Derry he was not yet worthy of a knighthood because he hadn't brought Ronav back to Shael? She had admitted to Val that she was the one who had killed Ronav; Kyer had a hard time believing that the duke would blame Derry. The duke hadn't seemed interested in the details during her share of the report, and certainly the captain had had ample opportunity to explain more after she and the others had left the room last night. Kyer had a nasty feeling that no such conversation had taken place.

Derry, upset over not achieving his goal, needed someone to blame. And that someone was her.

Fine. It hurt, but she trusted that Derry was merely angry and would get over it soon enough.

What she had not admitted to Valrayker was that her act was utterly, unequivocally premeditated. There was no self-defence involved. She sought Ronav out and she killed him in a cold and calculated fashion. That act was unbecoming of a *wæpnian*-trained warrior, and it was *that* which she needed to confess to Val.

Valrayker, exiled duke of Equart, was one of two people in Rydris whose good opinion truly mattered to her. If she confessed to him and he no longer wanted her in his company, she would—well, she didn't know what she would do. When morning came, she resolved to tell him, and she would live with the consequences.

Sleep had not altered Kyer's frame of mind about the mission either. She opened the door to the chamber from which they had withdrawn so late last night. It was the same room wherein Kyer had met Val's best friend, Duke Kien Bartheylen, a month ago, before their mission. Now it was Valrayker's centre for handling Kien's affairs while the other duke was tending his wife at Bartheylen Castle, three weeks away in one of his two other duchies. And this morning, as well as providing the privacy the small company needed to discuss the business of the day, it had become the breakfast room.

Kyer's four friends were attacking the food with desperate appetites cultivated by a month without decent fare. She spared a glance for Derry, but he didn't look up. It was just as well; she couldn't have guaranteed a civil response. Janak's head was tilted to one side so he could peer directly at his plate with his good eye. He ignored her presence. Purposefully? Jesqellan was also totally absorbed in eating. Kyer wasn't about to let them get away with it.

"Well, you've slept on it. Are you coming or aren't you?"

Janak looked up then and glared at her as if she'd insulted his mother. Jesqellan just sniffed.

"Well, you have to make a decision sometime." She heaped her plate with ham, eggs, chunks of melon, and bread.

Valrayker entered whistling, his long, black hair freshly combed and tied back neatly, his moustache and short beard trimmed. His grey eyes twinkled at Kyer as he sank into a chair opposite her. This was not the time to bring up anything morbid with him. Though he certainly was not behaving like someone who thought her actions reprehensible.

"My, it's good to have you all back again." He heaped blueberries into a bowl.

Derry eyed his lord quizzically.

"I have proceeded with your travel preparations, if only for the benefit of the three who have already committed their involvement." He said this without glancing significantly at anyone. "Further to that, we are expecting one more guest for breakfast." He poured cream, which turned blue as it washed off the powdery bloom.

"Who is it?" Derry asked. The captain's curiosity seemed forced. Kyer had a feeling he hadn't slept well. *It's only fair that it wasn't just me.*

"Your newest travelling companion. I met with him last night, and he has agreed to join the company on this mission. I've discovered him to be an excellent archer, as well as possessing several other talents that will no doubt be of valuable service to the group. You'll ask yourselves how you managed without him in the past. He's truly a unique find, and I'm very pleased that he accepted with no pressuring on my part."

Kyer took a mouthful of ham and studied the dark elf. Valrayker had a knack for plucking suitable members for his company out of unexpected settings, herself not excluded. Their eyes met and Val winked at her.

The door burst open and she jumped. The newcomer paused ever so slightly to get his bearings then rushed forward in a brightly coloured blur. A small figure planted himself before Kyer, to her utter astonishment. She turned to Val, open-mouthed, begging him to tell her he was playing a horrible prank, but he was too busy splitting his face from ear to ear. She gaped at the vision of outlandishness in front of her.

"Dear lady, we meet again! And under circumstances such that I cannot adequately express my joy! Travelling companions! To be able to gaze upon your countenance, to begin each new day with you in my immediate vicinity, and your face to be the last thing I allow to enter my sight before I fall into slumber filled with dreams of you!" The creature knelt grandly next to her as he finished his speech and, bowing his head, horrified her further.

Hand on his heart, he recited poetry.

"Such a beauty is Kyer

Shimmering gold lights up her hair

Her eyes, deep green, like shadowed lair

Never was there one so fair

As my lady, my true love, Kyer."

He then scampered around to perch on the seat next to Valrayker.

Kyer's gaze remained transfixed upon Skimnoddle. *Has Valrayker gone insane?*

"You'll have to tone down your orations if you're going to gain credibility with this lot," Valrayker murmured to the halfling, who bobbed his head and adjusted his cravat. To the rest of the group, Val said, "I believe most of you have met Skimnoddle."

Kyer looked daggers at Valrayker. Oh, she'd met Skimnoddle, all right. Twice. Once during her lunch at a local inn, when she had caught him trying to steal her purse, and she had forced him to return all the items he had stolen from her fellow patrons. And secondly, the same evening during his performance at the Springrites festival, when he had seen her in the crowd and presented her with the flowers he'd been juggling. Valrayker well knew the circumstances of those encounters because he was there for the second one. She thought at the time that he had enjoyed himself far more than was becoming of a duke. Val had shown on many occasions that he was no ordinary duke. He smiled smugly over his companions as if he had just won the war for them all.

This baffling, annoying halfling was to travel with them to visit the most powerful wizard in all of Rydris?

She glared. "Val, are you out of your mind?"

The dark elf just beamed.

As soon as she'd scooped the last spoonful of egg into her mouth, Kyer fled the chamber.

The bell above the apothecary's door jangled as Kyer stepped in. The thin-necked man behind the counter was busy with another customer. It was Derry. He said hello and the apothecary looked up, saw Kyer and blanched.

"How soon can the fenugreek tincture be ready?" Derry asked, snatching the man's attention. "We may have to leave in a few days."

"Oh, I er . . . Perhaps the day after tomorrow. I can't be . . . But if that is everything . . . ?" The flustered man tried to regain his composure.

Derry paid him and put the items in a shoulder bag. The man came around the counter, ostensibly to show Derry out, which Derry resisted.

"Are you picking up your—?"

"Yes. He's all right," she told the man.

The apothecary hesitated but acquiesced. Then he locked the door.

He squinted at Kyer as if she had a disfiguring disease and disappeared into his back room.

"You getting stuff for your kit?"

Derry nodded, leaning both elbows on the counter. Then, "You must be anxious to catch up on the news with your halfling friend after a long month of separation."

"Hilarious."

"You'll be unable to keep away from him once we leave."

"All the more reason to keep away from him now." She rolled her eyes. "My hair isn't even gold. It's *brown*."

Derry smirked. "I'm picturing you two heaped on the floor of the Harvest Moon with your dagger on his cheek."

He spoke genially but if he was trying to make up for his comment the night before, he'd failed.

"And then, in the crowded square, he kneels before you with a bouquet of flowers. I can't remember now: Did he actually propose marriage?"

"You're going to have to deal with the little bugger while we're travelling," she warned. "I'll try to be civil, but don't expect me to keep my mouth shut."

He looked sidelong at her. "No, I would never expect that."

Afraid of betraying how that stung, she clamped her teeth. *Bastard.*

At last the apothecary came back with a sack under his arm.

"Did you have it hidden in an underground cavern behind a massive door with seventeen locks guarded by a six-headed dragon you had to tame before you could get in?" Kyer asked.

His throat bobbed and he glared at her as he opened the sack. He drew out the wooden chest that had become Kyer's after she killed Simon Diduck.

In a hushed voice, the apothecary said, "I don't ask where you got this. Any thief would be well-rewarded for its procurement."

"What is it?" she asked. Its previous owner had hinted only vaguely at its purpose before he died.

"It is a shield of a powerful nature. It has. . . additional properties. I have created instructions. I wouldn't have written them, but for my fear that the device could be misused."

A low murmur of anxiety thrummed in her chest. "I think it was going to be misused before," she muttered.

"The instructions are hidden within the lid of the box. Now take it away from here, and *keep it under lock and key.*"

"What do I owe you?"

"You may remunerate me by getting it out of my shop."

He practically booted them onto the street and shut the door, bell jangling. The street was alive with people and horses headed for the square, where the mayor was due to make an announcement. Kyer adjusted the chest under her arm and wrapped her cloak around her.

Derry said, "You'd better get back to the castle with that."

"You think?" she said sarcastically. She glanced around furtively, planning her route.

Derry put a hand on her arm. "What did you mean when you said it was going to be misused?"

Kyer shook her head. "Something—Ronav said, that's all."

A family with a passel of children veered around the pair, stepping into the dirt road. The mother swept a youngster out of the way of a rider.

"I thought it was Simon's."

"No, he was only Ronav's delivery man. Listen, I'll see you—"

"But what did Ronav tell you? You should tell Val—"

"Derry." She looked at him squarely. "I will decide what I tell him."

Several emotions flashed across the captain's face before he settled on one. "Naturally."

With a whiff of aloofness between them, Derry bowed curtly and disappeared, weaving through the throngs of Shael citizens. Hot with annoyance, Kyer frowned and stepped into the current heading north toward the square then stopped herself. With an enormous crowd gathering to hear the mayor's speech, the square was hardly the place she wanted to traverse with a bulky box containing a vastly expensive and dangerous magical device. Instead, she crossed the street to head east.

"Kyer Halidan."

She stopped short and peered into the dimness of the narrow space between a shoemaker's and a guildhouse. A dark figure lurked there. It beckoned. She glanced furtively up and down the road, but the people, intent on reaching the square before the noon bell, ignored her. She stepped toward the figure, fascinated, and the scent of lilacs swirled around her like the shadows.

He was uncommonly tall, entirely in black, including the hair that framed a pale face. "Kyer, do not proceed through the square. It is not safe for you at this time."

The box was well hidden; she knew it. "I had already decided not to."

"Go back to the castle as quickly as possible. Go east to Riverside before heading north to the castle."

"That's where I was going. Who are you?"

He held up a hand. "One who cares for you. Go now. Quickly."

Backing into the shadows, he vanished.

She frowned at the strangeness of the encounter. And how had he known her name? She supposed, with a degree of surprise, that Shael citizens would be familiar with Valrayker's company and that perhaps her name was now mingled with those of Derry and Jesqellan. In any event, the stranger had echoed her own conclusion. Tightening the chest against her side, she shrugged the encounter off and turned eastward at the next street, a circuit that skirted around the square by a few blocks. She hustled along.

The crowds had thinned, now that most people were already at the square. It had to be close to noontime. The mayor would appear on the steps of the City Hall at any moment now. Left onto Riverside, jostling with someone as he hastened out of a shop. She doubled her pace, clutching the chest close to her under her cloak, the safety of the castle approaching. *Take it away from here, and keep it under lock and key.*

<h1 style="text-align:center">Two</h1>

<h2 style="text-align:center">It Would Not Be an Apology</h2>

A shuffling and a whimper from the bed woke Kien, and he rushed to his wife's side, where the pillow and sheets were yet again drenched with her sweat.

"Help me!" Kien cried over his shoulder to the Healer. "This one is worse."

The Healer rushed over and scooped a small handful of fresh herbs, tossing them into the steaming dish atop the brazier beside the bed. The fragrance erupted anew, its heady scent drifting upward with the steam, and the Healer's apprentice gently squeezed the tiny bellows to waft it across the anguished body of Kien's wife.

Alon Maer's body contorted, and a groan like the hinge of a rusty gate was forced from her throat. Kien pressed his cheek against hers, clutched her hand, and whispered urgently into her ear. "Hold them off, Alon, they are *nothing*. It is Dregor's minions, that is all." Her head rocked in torment, knocking into Kien's, and he bit his tongue. He sucked back the taste of blood. Her glassy eyes flashed open then screwed shut again, blocking out some vision of horror. "You are Bartheylen, Alon Maer; you are stronger than they," he insisted, willing her to hear him. She shuddered violently and her body twisted, wringing out pain like water from a cloth.

The healer knelt on the bed and rubbed her palms together, gathering warmth and energy before placing them firmly on Alon's chest, just below each shoulder. Kien leaned down to clutch his wife's hand to his cheek. The healer chanted and hummed as the lady thrashed about in pain, struggling as if she were chained to the bedposts. The healer's voice rose to match Alon's volume in a battle to subdue the evil that was consuming her. Conquering it had so far proved impossible.

The two or three days between episodes provided false hope that her condition was improving, and the subsequent resurgence was that much harder on Kien. The duke trusted that the healers were doing all they could, but he was very much afraid it was not enough.

At last the fit subsided. Alon's cries diminished to moans, whimpers, and finally, she slept. Her body ran with sweat that the healer and her apprentice bathed away.

Kien Bartheylen breathed deeply, letting the tangy aroma of the herbs and the spicy incense do their calming work on him. They just barely masked the sickroom smell that always made him think of old skin. He drifted back from the bed and slumped into the wing-backed armchair. "How much more can she take, Roman?" He brushed his neglected steel-coloured hair away from his narrow face.

The healer barely glanced up from her task. "Oh, she's a mighty one, my lord. She'll not give up easily." Her voice betrayed her fatigue, though the strong, sweeping motion of her arms as they worked belied her condition.

"Yes, yes she is," Kien replied. "That is why I chose her." He admired Alon's sword-wielder's body, so muscular and curvaceous even as she lay so ill. One pointed ear peeked out through her dark hair, which was matted and spilled out all over the pillow. Hoarse breaths gusted through parted, cracked lips that had only moments ago been taut with pain.

Kien's eye was drawn to the trinket she wore around her neck, a necklace shaped like a serpent. It was a pretty little thing, light blue and jewelled, which he'd noticed immediately upon his return from Shael several weeks ago. The apprentice healer had told Kien it reminded Alon of him, and she had been upset at the suggestion of removing it. The corners of his mouth twitched as Kien pictured her lovely face with that thoughtful smile that had attracted him from the start, that smile instead of the creases of pain she wore of late.

The continued gradual swelling of her abdomen was a hopeful sign that all was not lost. The babe fought for life and growth in spite of the odds against him. A true Bartheylen.

"Don't forget to breathe, my lord," Roman said. Startled, he looked over at her just as she smiled and returned her focus to her ministrations. He laughed, a gentle, self-deprecating laugh, and took her advice. He filled his lungs, shaking out his hands, which had been gripping the arms of the chair like the hilt of his greatsword.

"Thank you, Roman."

"Honestly, my lord, I've enough to occupy me with this one. I don't need another to care for. You'd best be taking care of yourself."

"You're right, I know," Kien said wearily. "But I cannot—" He stopped himself.

"I know, my lord." Roman pushed herself to her feet. The apprentice held her arm to steady her; the healer had exerted a good deal of energy in this latest battle. "I know you wish to remain with her, but I beg of you to eat a hot meal and to sleep, sir. She's resting. Lord Valrayker has all your other affairs in hand. Be at peace for now."

Kien nodded in listless agreement, wondering if he'd ever again feel like the duke of three duchies. He got to his feet, his body leaden, but forced himself to his full seven-foot height. Kien Bartheylen was the strongest man in Rydris; mere fatigue cost him nothing.

"If I am to care for myself," he said to Roman, "then so are you. That is not just a suggestion."

He gave a short bow and made the kitchens his destination.

Kyer took herself to her room where she could open the chest away from curious eyes, and remembered the cedar aroma from the first time she'd opened it. The same whirr of air wafted gently at her face. The brushed pewter armband was nestled in the soft protective cushion. With its inlaid green jewel and etched lines it was a thing of beauty. This time she did not allow her palm to hover over it and feel its unnerving buzz of vibration. That could wait until she knew what the thing was. The information was hidden, as promised, inside the lid, beneath the red plush lining. Sitting crosslegged on her bed, Kyer unfolded the slip of parchment.

A device of deadly protection, the alchemist had written in a shaky hand. *Will block an attack on the wearer, but gains its power one of two ways: by stealing life force from the wearer, or by taking another nearby life, with only minimal control.* There was a bit more, about deflecting attacks, and angles and strength, but Kyer did not presently feel equal to the task of studying it. She kept the paper to look at later, but swiftly shut and locked the box, tucking the key and note deeply in her pack.

And now, what to do with the chest? It was too valuable and dangerous a thing to carry with her at this time, and she was by no means ready to wield it. Ronav would have had no misgivings about donning it instantly, prepared to sacrifice anyone around him for his own protection. He would have believed it was his right. Kyer was not willing to risk the lives of her friends. Better to leave it behind in safety, until she had had time to study the instructions. Which left her puzzling over where to keep it.

Acadia. That's who she needed. Kyer couldn't keep it in her own room because it might be used by another guest at some point. Acadia would know of a place to safely keep the box. Kyer wove through the castle in search of the steward.

"Yes, of course," Acadia said when Kyer found her in her room. She beckoned her to enter. "How's this?" A panel next to the fireplace had a hidden latch. It opened, revealing a small cupboard. "This is where I keep my few valuables, and it's unlikely someone would look for this in here, don't you think?"

"Yes, I agree." Kyer breathed a sigh of relief to have the chest out of her hands. "Still, I'll get it from you as soon as I can; it shouldn't be your responsibility."

Acadia grimaced up at her as she tucked the chest in the back of the cupboard and closed the door. "Believe me, this is the least of my worries."

She invited Kyer to sit. Acadia was the first woman with whom Kyer had had opportunity to form a friendship since leaving her friend Bianca behind in Hreth. The fair-haired steward, to Kyer's great joy, was too smart and capable to be intimidated by a woman with a sword and had put Kyer at ease almost instantly upon their meeting at the start of Kyer's first mission. The unfortunate incident between Kyer and Acadia's brother, Fredric, the former captain of Shael Castle, was the only hitch, and even that had not succeeded in coming between them. She was a woman of enormous responsibility and competance, and Kyer respected her a great deal. The two women had a few pleasant moments to catch up before they were interrupted by the bell at Acadia's door.

Acadia sighed, her blue eyes smiling. "No one can accuse me of idleness. Follow me and we can still talk." She closed the door behind them. Building a friendship within a smattering of moments was far from easy.

Kyer kept pace. "Tell me: Have you heard from Fredric?"

The brightness in Acadia's eyes dimmed just slightly, like a thin layer of cloud over the sun. "No, I haven't." Her voice contained a sort of determined pride. "My brother is out of my life." They hastened down the main staircase. "You know something? Until he'd been gone for about two weeks, I had no idea just how much of a negative influence he had on me.

Like a wicked fairy always whispering in my ear. But he's gone. I have put him behind me." She smiled, her eyes clearing.

"Still, I *am* sorry. I never meant for it to go so far."

"I hope you're not still blaming yourself. He had it coming. All you did was make the truth known." They reached the bottom of the staircase. "Now I really must get back to work, but one more thing." Acadia rounded the corner with a swish of her dark red skirt and bright eyes. "It's all over the castle that you killed Ronav Malachite. I want to hear the details about that before you leave."

The steward rushed off to her office.

Kyer froze. *Blood of Guerrin.* Derry thought he had lost his knighthood because of this, and now people were gossiping about it in all eagerness?

"Oh, this is not good." She hastened to the meeting room in search of Val. She had to set him straight before another hour passed. There was a guard outside the room.

"Excuse me. I need to speak to Lord Valrayker."

"He's busy with the prisoner."

"Prisoner?" *What in seven hells . . .* "What prisoner?"

"I'm not at liberty to speak about it."

"Fine." Kyer spun around and headed toward the stairs.

As she took the first few steps up, she heard the door to the room open. The guard stepped aside and let Derry pass.

Kyer rushed back down. "What's going on?"

Derry closed the gap between them with his long strides. "Where have you been?" He grabbed her by the arm.

She shrugged him off, annoyed. Was he her guardian all of a sudden? "With Acadia, not that it's any of your business."

He sighed, relieved. "There is no need for rudeness. I had no idea where — Thank Aidan you're safe."

"What are you talking about?"

Derry spoke in a low voice. "There was an explosion in the square."

"An explosion!"

"Yes. Not long after I left you." He looked and sounded haggard. "I wasn't right there when it happened, but I went to help, and some people had caught this fellow"—he gestured back to the room he had left—"so I brought him here."

"Who is it?"

"I don't know. Did you find a safe place to keep that chest?"

Did he think she was a half-wit? She waved over at a sideboard against the wall. "Sure, I put it down right over th— Oh no, it's gone!"

Derry tensed like a wild animal. "We've got to—" When he saw the look on her face, he checked himself, frowning, and clearly biting back some sort of rebuke.

"Of course I found a safe place for it, Derry. It's locked up someplace real special."

He looked relieved and irked. Running a hand through his short, blond hair, he might have been counting to ten. She recognized that line in his jaw. "I don't suppose you saw anything that would help in the investigation?"

"No, why would I? I was too busy getting a magic box to safety under orders from great authority." She gave a passing thought to the tall, pale stranger.

Derry opened his mouth, about to give an exasperated retort, but the door to the meeting room opened. The prisoner emerged, hands behind his back. Two flanking guards marched him to the door that would lead to the cells. The guard who'd been waiting outside followed. Any hope she had of speaking to Val now was foiled when he emerged, still deep in conversation with Governor Lyndon, and walked by without even seeing her.

The prisoner was not the strange man from the shadows, and her encounter with him was forgotten.

Captain Usher Tompkin reported to Valrayker and his company in Kien's meeting chamber late in the afternoon. Just as the mayor had begun his speech, a ball of bright, white light, like a shimmery crystal ball, had sailed over the heads of the crowd in the square, as if it had been tossed. It hovered near the mayor, and the crowd tried to back away in alarm. The ball exploded, setting fire to many people's clothing and killing at least twenty citizens, including the mayor.

Several people had seen the man who threw the ball and had handed him over, which was how he had come to be in custody so quickly. He was now undergoing "interviews" with Piper, the castle wizard, who so far had nothing to add.

Valrayker, shaken by the news of the mayor's death, did not speak, and simply stared down at his hand. He appeared surprised that he held a cup of wine. His lips were pressed in a tight line. He finally worked them open, and with a deep breath, thanked Usher for his report. "It is rare to apprehend the culprit in a crime like this so speedily. I assure you he will be tried and treated accordingly."

"I am thankful to hear he has been apprehended." Jesqellan rose and clasped his hands behind his back. "I should say at this time that the events of this afternoon have influenced, in part, my decision to join you on the upcoming mission. This incident has shown me the importance of maintaining the strength of the Southern Alliance. We need Kien, and it follows that we need Alon Maer and their child." The mage looked over their heads as if addressing an audience in a large council chamber. "I am the member of the party with the most experience dealing with wizards. My position on the wisdom of this venture remains unchanged, yet it is my hope that as a mage and a Shaman, I will be able to be of some service in the communication with the enigmatic Kayme."

Kyer listened to this speech with bemusement, and when she caught Phennil's eye, the elf gave her a wink. *Sure enough, he can't bear to be left out.*

Once Jesqellan had ceased speaking, the brief silence was broken by a grunt from Janak, who then added, "Might as well count me in. Nothing better to do."

Jesqellan looked irritated that the dwarf had stolen his thunder.

Kyer smiled. "Why can't you just admit you care as much as the rest of us?"

The dwarf threw a dirty look at her.

Before she had a chance to ask Val if she might speak to him, he excused himself and rushed out.

She headed back to her room. Just as she reached the door to the tower stairs, two young sentries stepped out of the access to the rear corridor. Their eyes lit up with recognition.

"Aren't you the one that killed Ronav Malachite?" one asked, his voice bright with admiration.

"No." Kyer's face flushed and she slammed the door behind herself.

She ran up the stairs.

Hero she was not. What had happened in the woods of Nennia had frightened her. She'd made a promise to Derry. A promise which, although it had pained her to speak the words, had made sense at the time. Then deeper emotions had taken control. She ought to have simply captured Ronav. Brought him here to Shael. Let Val give him a fair—

Kyer stopped on the stairs.

She pictured a child in shock over her father who sat in their front room with a knife through his throat. She pictured Phennil keeling over after trying to stop innocent people from killing each other. Then . . . Derry kneeling among the bloody mass that was the bodies of a teenaged girl and her baby. Kyer's chest heaved.

I wouldn't change a thing.

She had killed Ronav in cold blood. And it felt good. She could summon no remorse for what she had done. If anyone deserved to pay the ultimate price, it was Ronav. And in her heart, Kyer knew that if anyone—*anyone*—but she herself had carried out the sentence, she would have felt cheated.

She might have a confession to make to Valrayker, but it would not be an apology.

—✦—

Hunter stoked the fire that warmed neither the air nor the atmosphere of the stone chamber within the mountain he had inherited from Ronav. It was darker, danker than his room in the barracks at Shael Castle.

This one is all mine, he thought sardonically.

He set a chunk of hemlock on top of the glowing pile, adjusted it with the poker, and backed up to sit in the armchair.

A heartbeat later he was bolt upright and whirled around, poker poised to strike the person in the chair.

"You seem to have made yourself quite at home here," Golgathaur said.

Hunter lowered the poker, swallowing hard to push his heart back down into his chest. "Why can't you announce yourself?" He used more than a hint of ire.

"I can," answered the other, with an implied shrug. "How are things going?"

Hunter let the poker fall with a thud to the braided rug that hid the stone floor. He sat in the other, less comfortable, chair before deigning to answer. "Do you mean generally, or just since you put me in charge of this rabble?"

"As you wish." The man stretched his uncommonly long, black-trousered legs toward the fire. He smelled floral. His pleasant expression said,

Do go on. I'm listening.

The pleasant expressions worried Hunter more than the unpleasant ones. The new chief glared at the fire rather than aim his frustration at his . . . superior.

"The men have accepted me as well as can be expected. Whatever that means. I suppose they listen to me because you told them to."

"Then you must encourage them to listen to you on your own merit."

"I'm working on it. They still have trouble with the fact that I only got here in time to go with Ronav and the others to Nennia, and I'm the only one who returned."

"Then you must let them know there was a reason that you remained alive."

"What, because I'm so much better than they were?"

"Well, aren't you?"

Hunter considered this. His training and experience certainly placed him far beyond the strengths of the strongest of those men. And without question he was of higher quality than Ronav on a number of levels.

"Do you listen to me because of who I work for," Golgathaur asked, catching Hunter by surprise, "or for myself alone?"

Hunter's throat suddenly felt like he'd swallowed chalk. "Actually, you've . . . uh . . . never happened to mention who you work for."

The pale man tilted his head to one side. "Any ideas?"

Hunter could only nod.

"Well?"

It was infuriating that Golgathaur always demanded answers to questions that Hunter thought rhetorical. "Dregor."

"That's *Lord* Dregor to you, my good man." Golgathaur gave him a delighted grin. "Nicely done. I see we have chosen well."

Hunter said nothing.

Golgathaur clapped his hands to the arms of the chair. "Well, I just dropped in for a short visit to see how you were faring. Don't let me impede your enjoyment of the evening." He rose and his tidy black hair brushed the stone ceiling of the chamber. "Oh, by the way, I met someone today. Someone whose acquaintance I believe you may have made. Kyer Halidan?"

A pale, shimmering light flickered, and he vanished.

Hunter stared before him, blind to the bright firelight. All he saw was *her* face, glowing in the light of another fire, smiling at him mischievously, her dark green eyes daring him. Then *her* face as she humiliated him in front of his men. And then . . . Hunter squeezed his eyes closed, trying to shut out the image . . . his lord, beloved Kien, possessor of his devotion—*that* face as it handed down the sentence.

Again Hunter relived those last moments as Fredric Heyland. Shamed, cast aside, banished from the only life he had known. Hunter had left that persona behind as he rode out of Shael.

Alone with his misery in his new home, trapped in his new life, he renewed his vow.

I will kill her.

Valrayker wasn't at breakfast. Kyer swallowed fruit and wine, but she couldn't swallow the lump of desolation that had formed in the night. She resolved to find him directly after eating and steeled herself for the meeting. She had to come clean and tell him what an ignoble warrior she was, even if it meant that he might not want her to work for him any longer. She took a mouthful of wine, feeling her brows draw together as she wondered what she would do with herself if Valrayker dropped her.

"Poor thing," Janak said, making her jump. "She can't speak, she's so a-quiver over her halfling boyfriend coming along."

Kyer could muster only a mirthless grimace.

She downed the last of her wine and went to Kien's—Valrayker's, while Kien was away—study, only to find her way barred by a sentry. The duke was in a meeting with Piper and the prisoner and wasn't expected to be through any time soon.

Later in the day, she returned. A different sentry gave the same message. As she stood in the corridor, a maid arrived with a tray of food. The sentry allowed her in, but Kyer couldn't even get a peek. The only thing she learned was that the prisoner's name was Chart. She asked the sentry to please let Valrayker know she wished to speak to him, though she doubted even he would have that opportunity.

By the end of the day, with no luck at getting to speak to the dark elf, Kyer resigned herself. He had other things on his mind. She didn't need to burden him with yet another problem.

Instead, she wrote a long overdue letter. She added a short note for her parents and folded the one inside the other. She addressed the outside of the letter to *The Halidans, Care of Sendra Flack, General Store, Village of Hreth, Heath Duchy*. But the inside letter began, *Dear Nix*. It was signed *Fralyrn*, which looked like a name. Only three people in all of Rydris would know it translated as *Student*. Moreover, it was written in a language that all but those three would interpret as simple gibberish.

The next day, the stable yard was a bevy of grooms, stable hands hustling, and friends waiting to say goodbye. Derry stood with the rest of the company as they checked bags and packs and made ready to leave the luxuries of Shael Castle. Derry recalled one detail he hadn't taken care of yet. He wove through the activity and approached Jesqellan.

"Jesqellan, will you be my second, as usual?"

"Of course, Captain."

Turning back, Derry caught a glimpse of Kyer's profile. She had certainly heard the exchange, and the muscle in her jaw was clenched. *Too bad.* She can't have thought he would choose her to be his second, not now. No, Jesqellan was the most experienced. Not to mention the most level-headed. He defied Kyer to argue that.

Donnagill snorted and bobbed his head, reacting to the flurry of excitement, but the groom expertly whispered and calmed him. Derry returned to him and stroked his shoulder soothingly, and the groom continued her work, the warhorse towering over them. Derry combed his fingers through the chestnut's black mane and watched Valrayker.

The exiled duke wandered among his team, holding saddlebags open while last minute items were stowed away, or offering pleasant words and even garnering a laugh here and there. He looked tired, yet Derry saw a light of anticipation burning in his eye. The fate of his best friend's wife lay with this motley company, and the sooner they were on their way, the sooner Val could begin counting the days to Alon's recovery. Derry's resolve redoubled.

So he had not been knighted yet. Valrayker must have his reasons, and he hadn't blamed anyone, not even Kyer, for neglecting to bring Ronav to Shael; he'd merely expressed disappointment. Whatever the reason, it was not Derry's place to question him. What did it change? He lived to serve Valrayker and was all the more determined that this assignment would be the ultimate service to the dark elf: every action would be performed with Valrayker in mind. Derry would be knighted at the end of this mission or . . . or . . . Derry sighed. Who was he kidding? He had never contemplated any other goal, so he could not conceive of quitting this one. Instead he double-checked the location of his sketch book in his saddlebag and gave one final tug on each of Donnagill's straps.

"It has taken me altogether too long to thank you all properly for what you did for my people in Nennia." Valrayker positioned himself before his emissaries. The yard fell silent. "Not only did you solve the problem and help them to recover, you have restored their faith in me, which means much in these dark days. I hope I live to see the end of such times and to return to my land and my people." He looked at each of them, the steadiness of his gaze belying the emotion he fought to conceal.

Derry bowed his head.

"I promised you gifts once you returned from Nennia," Val went on. "As you know I haven't much to give. And with Kien away, I can only prevail so much upon his kindness. Besides the tent cloth I found, which has been stowed among your supplies, I managed to come up with these few tidbits." He bent down to a sack at his feet and rummaged around inside it. Derry heard faint clanking of metal and glass. Val drew something out and straightened. He held two six-inch cylinders, about the width of his thumb. One was made of a dark reddish wood, and the other was a brownish-green, the colour of dying leaves of a rosebush. "For Jesqellan. A Firebolt rod and a Dispel Illusions rod. Two uses each." He handed them to the mage, who clasped his hands on his chest and bowed his thanks in the traditional Moabi Shaman fashion.

Val reached into the sack again. He pulled out a vial of dark blue glass and handed it to Janak. "Oil of Unbreaking. Inside the top is a brush. Smear that stuff on your weapon, and it won't break in a normal battle. Lasts about a week, Piper tells me. Can't say how it would stand up against magic, though." Janak's *harrumph* sounded pleased.

For Kyer, Valrayker had a key, similar to the one that locked Kien's study. It was about four inches in length, with a grip through which Kyer could stick her little finger. Derry thought it looked like iron, yet when the dark elf handed it to Kyer, her hand reacted as if it had no more weight than a walnut. Val said it would unlock anything and would work four times. She nodded her thanks.

Then it was Derry's turn.

"Your magnificent steed, my captain, has already been newly shod."

Derry ran a hand down Donnagill's leg and gently squeezed his fetlock until the animal lifted his foot. "They're magic, of course," Val went on as Derry scrutinized the shoe. It looked like cast iron. "Donnagill won't know what came over him. He won't tire as easily, and you'll find an increase in his agility."

Derry released the foot and straightened. "Thank you, my lord." The captain felt the warmth from his master's eyes. *That's what's been missing since our return*, Derry realized.

"Thank *you*," Valrayker clarified. "And for you, Phennil . . . no I did not forget our aromatic elf." The others laughed. Derry continued to not understand what was funny about it. Phennil flushed but stuck his chin up with pride. "For you, I have this." Val stuck his hand in and produced a hat. Made of soft leather, black, with a narrow brim and dark red band. He passed it to the elf. "With your elvish footsteps, the enemy won't hear you coming. With that invisibility hat, they won't see you coming . . ." He paused dramatically with an impish half-grin, and Derry leaned forward, waiting for the punchline. Val lifted the sack and whipped out a bright orange feather. "And with that Fragrant Feather, they won't *smell* you coming either!"

He stepped over and stuck the feather in the hatband, amid gales of laughter. Even Derry smiled. Phennil went an even deeper shade of crimson but grinned from ear to ear and gave Valrayker a grand bow.

"Finally." With that single word Val requested stillness again. "Skimnoddle was not on the last mission, but I didn't want my newest recruit to feel left out." Derry immediately went in search of Kyer's reaction to this, but she was expressionless and didn't look his way.

"I have two arrows here that will explode on impact. Careful now," Val said as the halfling placed them gingerly into his quiver.

"And one more thing." The dark elf pulled out a case. "In here is a set of jewels." His voice sounded tired again. "Kien gave them to Alon upon their engagement. I have been instructed to give them to you as an offering for

Kayme."

Dumbstruck, Derry stared. *Surely not.*

"I hope it will help sway the wizard's decision to help us," Val finished.

Murmurings of protest sprouted throughout the courtyard. "If any of you has another idea, I'd be happy to entertain it." Val handed the little mahogany box to Derry.

Silence. Then Phennil spoke up. "Our journey will take us near my home at Plicatha. Why don't we go there first and ask my mother and father to help?"

That would be . . . interesting. Derry could not picture a whole family of Phennils.

Jesqellan nodded. "It would add no more than two or three days to the journey and might just be worthwhile."

"I would prefer not to sacrifice Alon's jewels if it can be avoided," Derry said. And so it was agreed. Their first destination was Plicatha, the Front City of the Donnan Forest.

The travellers made final tightenings of straps and ropes. Skimnoddle put the wrong foot in his pony's stirrup and a groom patiently prevented him from sitting backwards in the saddle.

Derry watched Kyer transfer a few items from one saddlebag to another to even things out and smiled in spite of himself at her look of disgust as she pretended not to watch Skimnoddle struggling to mount his pony.

Derry felt a hand on his arm. Val gripped the younger man's hand. "Derry."

"Sir?"

"Aidan guide you."

In his lord's eyes Derry read the urgency of the journey. And he'd invoked the blessing of the Goddess of Life. *He's worried.* Kien and Alon were like family to Valrayker. The dark elf would lose a piece of himself if Alon died. Drawing himself up, Derry replied, "We'll see you at Bartheylen

Castle."

Golgathaur was a clever one, that was certain. The only thing certain about him. He never announced himself, just popped up, without warning. The tall, stark man sent ripples of fear through Hunter such as the former captain of the guard had never experienced, not only because the fellow possessed an undefined amount of magical power and could probably cause a man to disappear out of this world with a snap of his fingers; not only because he was lieutenant to the dark lord himself, which automatically classed him as Dangerously Evil in the grand scheme of things. It was because Golgathaur was all of these things, combined with a natural charm, intelligence, and a casual sense of humour. That was what frightened Hunter most. The vampiric-looking mage was pure evil and completely at ease with it.

Golgathaur had a flair for drama and clearly took delight in watching the effect his words and actions had on those beneath him. Hunter still felt the chill of Golgathaur's sudden disappearance after handing him his title of chief. And he most definitely had not fully composed himself after the lieutenant had visited him in his chamber and dumped on him that not only was he lieutenant to the dark lord but that he'd met Kyer Halidan. Hunter stalked down the shadowy, carved-stone descent to his chamber inside the mountain. *He ought to have just stabbed me in the throat and left me to bleed.*

Four more days had passed since that last visit. Long enough for Ronav's —rather, *Hunter's*—council of cutthroats to get restless and just long enough for Hunter's innards to tighten into a terrific knot of uncertainty.

Not nearly long enough for Hunter to adapt to working for the other side.

Hunter had just sent the rowdier of his men out to bring in more meat.

He had no idea how long they'd have to wait before he'd receive instructions.

Not long.

He opened his chamber door to see Golgathaur sitting in the chair he'd occupied on his previous appearance.

"How is the new chief doing today?" He gave Hunter an irksomely cheerful smile.

Hunter grimaced at being spoken to like a child but responded promptly. "My men are growing restless, waiting for something to do." The knot gave another good twist before settling into the anticipation of action.

"Well, I have just the thing for you and your men." Golgathaur slapped his knees playfully. "I am not sure if you are acquainted with someone named Kien Bartheylen?"

Fredric said nothing. Golgathaur knew full well the answer.

"If you are, you might also know his wife, Alon Maer?"

Fredric grunted in reply.

"If perchance you are acquainted with her, it might interest you to know that she is dreadfully ill. To the point where she just might die, she and the child she carries."

Fredric sat down, hard. In spite of his self-control, there was no preventing the pallor that took over his face. He could pretend all he liked that he hated Kien, that he had left his former life behind of his own accord, but he could not hide the truth from himself. And Alon Maer was blameless in Fredric's conflict with Kien; he had no reason to have lost his love for her.

"Die?" He pushed the word out hoarsely.

Golgathaur crossed his legs and, resting one elbow on his knee, tapped his lip with his index finger in a thoughtful fashion and nodded. "Now, here is the concern that my Lord Dregor has: This divided loyalty. I assured Dregor, and I am absolutely certain you would back me on this, that your one and only goal is to please our master, is it not?"

Once again, he actually waited for an answer.

A stab went through Fredric's heart as he thrust out the words. "Of course."

"Ah, you see?" Golgathaur held out his hands toward Hunter. "I told him there was nothing to worry about. 'Hunter is the right man for the job,' I told him. And I was right.

"Now, there is the problem: your history as a knight is causing you to display this gallant sense of caring for the lady. Almost as if you . . . had a *fondness* for her and her husband." Fredric put a hand to his belly. "I know it isn't really necessary, but I shall, just for the record, remind you that Kien Bartheylen, all his friends, and all his kin, are the enemy. The *enemy*, Hunter. Do you understand? So any display of care or concern for them is not called for. In fact, it would be decidedly frowned upon by my lord."

Hunter dragged a mask of stone across his face.

"So, here's the thing," the terrifyingly friendly evil man said. "Right now, some people are on their way to find a cure for the lady's illness. Among them are a few I have no doubt you have met before. Derry Moraunt. Does the name ring a bell? And Kyer Halidan."

No need to feign the hatred that gripped him at the mention of that name.

"They are headed for Plicatha, the Front City of the Donnan Forest. Their plan is to continue on to the tower of the wizard Kayme, to learn of a cure.

"You are charged with the duty of stopping them," Golgathaur said. "Their mission must fail." And the lieutenant abruptly vanished to allow the implications of the instruction to sink in.

Fredric just sat.

He struggled for two hours to find the strength to appear before his company and explain the new orders to the entire group.

With his background, presenting himself as their leader would pose no problem. The tricky part was to muster a tone of authority for a situation in which he had not a shred of eagerness. Eventually he strode up the dim passageway toward the hall, imagining he was still the captain of the guard at Shael Castle. His confidence had been genuine, there.

"All right, you blackguards," he yelled. Men stopped whatever they were doing and heads turned his way. "Leave off scratching yourselves. We have a job."

Three

What Better Way to Infiltrate

The bell on the door of Hreth's depleted general store jangled, calling Sendra Flack in from the back room. The bell seemed noisier these days, with so little stock on the shelves to absorb its sound. The large front room had a cold hollowness to it, like a cave with a wooden floor. The stranger who'd entered appeared to think so too, as he revolved in bewilderment.

"Sir?" Sendra said to the back of his grey-flecked dark brown head, attempting her usual storekeeper cheer. "Is there something I can help you with?"

"Oh, uh, yes." As he rotated to face her, Sendra saw the insignia of Drakenmoor embroidered on the cap and cloak of his dispatch rider's uniform. That city was nearly a week away. "What's happened here?" he went on. "Fire? Earthquake? Dragon?"

"Fire certainly." Sendra began rearranging the rolls of rick rack and lace to keep her hands busy. "But not from natural causes."

"Is it true, then? What I heard in Fri? An attack?"

Sendra's hands stopped moving. "You mean, you hadn't heard of this in Drakenmoor? The news hasn't got farther than Fri after *three months*?"

"And even then it was put across more or less as a rumour." He ambled to her counter, lifted the lid of the licorice tin, and replaced it, disappointed at the void inside. "People didn't think it was possible, and I admit I agreed with them. Why would Dregor attack such a crummy—sorry—little place as this? I mean, what's even here?"

"Practically nothing, now." Conscious of her unkempt, apathetic appearance, she leaned back against the shelf with what she hoped was nonchalance to get a better look at the man. Not much beyond her own forty-five years, she reckoned. Broad shouldered. Standard dispatch rider's broadsword at his right side. Dark beard and bushy eyebrows enlivening the weather-dried face. A seasoned face. "Used to be a thriving farming village. Little bit of mining, too, west yonder in the mountains. That's why we hoped word would have got 'round to outlying areas. Most of our crops were destroyed, most everything we had to trade or sell is gone. We need supplies to last until we can rebuild." Sendra opened her arms wide. "Just look at my store." She shook her head: the empty barrels on the floor, the two remaining bolts of fullcloth, a few sacks of flour and beans in one corner; the scattered remains of a brisk business illustrated her point better than words could. His brown eyes followed her movement, and the eyebrows contracted in sympathy.

She was lucky, she told him. The invaders had only battered her front windows and kicked in the front support post, causing one section of the roof to collapse. The width of the main road had saved her haven from the fire that had destroyed the entire northwest quadrant of the village. The man's gaze didn't leave her face as she talked. Embarrassed by her display of intensity, Sendra reached under the counter for a rag with which to dust the shelves. Perhaps the attempt to bring some life back into the shop was futile, but she decided right then and there that she had not given up.

"It's funny, you know." She mindlessly swiped the rag across an empty shelf. "It wasn't that long ago that a lot of people in this place didn't even believe Dregor existed. We had young people training to defend the village, and the older set clicking their tongues and thinking the young folk were too imaginative, caught up in the thrill of adventure and heroism. Now the unbelievers are the loudest whiners."

There was no shortage of customers, a seemingly endless stream of despondent villagers, leaving just as disappointed as when they came in. In spite of Sendra's efforts, twenty sacks of flour went only so far and her credit was already being pushed to the limit in the nearest villages and towns. Not much stock and too few villagers with coppers to pay for what little there was. She passed her credit on to her neighbours whenever she could, but not one of them could guarantee payment within a limited time. And they tossed blame about like chicken feed. She added, 'Least helpful, most helpless,' my mother used to say."

"Look, ma'am, I'm really sorry. I'll tell them when I go back through Fri to send as much help as they can." His dark eyes spoke sympathy and kindness. It had been years since a man had looked at her like that. Her hand involuntarily straightened any stray hair.

He tilted his head, puzzled. "Have you had no help from the duke?"

Sendra nodded hastily. Some might cast aspersions on Lord Bartheylen for lack of action, but Sendra knew he had done what he could. "Oh yes, he sent people here as soon as he heard, and him with his wife ill and all. It took over a month for them to arrive, but then they helped rebuild pretty much everything that's standing out there now. They left only a few days ago and promised to bring more supplies. But even if they bring seed corn, wheat, and potatoes it'll be too late in the season for planting."

"Like I said, I'll pass on word."

"That's good." Sendra brushed her chapped hands down the front of her apron and wished she hadn't run out of salve. "Did you come all this way just to confirm rumours?"

"Oh, no, of course not." He reached into an inside pocket of his cloak and pulled out a brown envelope. "I have this."

He flipped it over to examine the inscription on the front. "Are you

Sendra Flack?'

"I am." Sendra's shoulders tensed with alarm.

"This says it's for the Halidans, care of yourself."

Sendra must have gasped at the name, and she was sure her face had paled.

"Are you all right, ma'am?" He looked poised to spring over the counter to assist her.

She brushed a hand across her face and moved to take the envelope. "I'm fine, it's just—" It looked so official. *Bad news?* She glanced at the inscription before turning it over and felt her eyes widen. The bright green Bartheylen seal. *Why would Lord Bartheylen write to the Halidans, unless . . .* "Where did this come from?" Her voice trembled.

"It came all the way from Shael, ma'am."

It's about Kyer, Sendra thought. *It has to be. In trouble?* She bit both lips in dismay. There were those villagers who would love to hear about the fruition of their predictions. *Kyer Halidan in prison in Shael.* They'd be delighted. The Halidans weren't here. What should she do?

"Ma'am? Would you be able to tell me where they live so I can deliver it, or should I leave it with you?"

"Oh, call me Sendra, would you?" she said absently. "Everyone else does."

He tipped his cap. "And you can call me Tell, if you like."

She leaned her elbows against the smooth wood. "To be honest, I'm not sure what to do. The Halidans' farm was the one you passed on your right as you came to the outskirts of the village."

Tell looked puzzled for a moment. Then he understood. "Oh." He whistled. "Wiped out. Are they—did they—" He stopped as if unable to speak the thought on his tongue.

"No, no, they're alive." Her voice tightened. "Some didn't make it. I'm glad there weren't more losses but it's hard. My son lost one of his best friends. At least I didn't lose my son, but Adric's father and mother can't say the same thing. Neither can—"

Movement over Tell's shoulder caught her eye, and she signalled him to silence as the door opened, the bell accentuating it unnecessarily.

The leading village gossip, short and squat Jessica Bolen entered, followed by her second, the late magistrate's tall, skeletal widow Hilary Wynn. The pair always reminded Sendra of a pot-bellied stove and its pipe. Sendra discreetly tucked the envelope in her apron pocket.

"I'll get this to them, you have my word," she said to Tell in a low voice.

"And I'll come back. With supplies." Tell bowed. "You have my word."

He tipped his cap to the ladies as he slipped by and out the door. They both turned their heads to watch him.

"Well." Jessica was not unexpectedly the first to speak. "What is a dispatch rider from Drakenmoor doing here? Did he bring supplies?"

"No, not this time." Sendra realized belatedly that she hadn't tipped him.

"Then why did he bother coming a'tall?" Jessica said, her lips pursed in a polite sneer.

"Perhaps as a dispatch rider, he had a message to dispatch," Sendra said dryly.

"Well, did he?"

"If he did, it wasn't for you, Jessica."

Sendra felt happier than she had in weeks. She conducted the hens' business efficiently and sent them on their way. Uplifted by the dispatch rider's promise and, admittedly by the way her heart fluttered as he looked at her, she recalled a recipe to make her own salve for chapped hands using herbs, a bit of lard, and beeswax.

She also, in that moment, knew what to do with the letter. She put her *Closed* sign on the door early and left to walk the few blocks to Brendow's little cottage in the southeast end of the village.

The near-summer sun glimmered lazily through the late-afternoon clouds. The wood smoke smell that had hung perpetually in the air for weeks had begun to dissipate at last, to be replaced with a freshness reminiscent of the spring air they'd missed. The outlying fields that had been blackened by the fires were sending green shoots up out of the earth. With things turning green again, Sendra found it much easier to believe the village of Hreth would be all right.

But Sendra, like Jessica and Hilary and every other villager, had continually asked herself why Dregor would choose to raid a place like Hreth. Just to annoy Kien Bartheylen? She couldn't see it. Nor could she give a second thought to the ridiculous notion put forward by Jessica that young Kyer was connected with the attack, that she was some sort of spy.

Dregor's soldiers had asked some strange questions, or so she had been told. And they had destroyed buildings systematically, as if looking for something—or someone. Sendra had one idea, but she didn't dare voice it to those two gossiping ninnies. Could she defend Kyer by disclosing distrust of the girl's friend and mentor? No, she could not. It just made more sense to Sendra, though, that Lord Dregor would not randomly choose Hreth, but that he would send his men here for a specific reason. And the only reason she could think of was that Brendow lived here.

Few *Wæmniars*, the masters of the warrior arts known as the *wæpnian*, remained in the duchy of Heath. Her own son Tarqan had spent years training with him, alongside Kyer, young Adric, Bianca, and some others. Nobody knew Brendow's complete history, but it was said he had travelled all over Rydris and had done his fair share in the battles alongside Dukes Bartheylen and Valrayker. That could easily make him a target for Dregor.

She had to admit the one flaw in her idea: Brendow's house alone had remained untouched when the rest of the village had been all but flattened. Many villagers decided that meant he was in league with Dregor, just as Jessica had decided about Kyer.

Shortly after the attack, a group of villagers had taken it upon themselves to visit Brendow's tidy little unscathed cottage carrying axes, clubs, and torches. Strangely, they had not been able to find it. Odder still, they could not recall their purpose and had wandered about aimlessly before ending up back at the tavern in confusion over their makeshift weapons.

Sendra didn't know what to make of it.

Today she had no trouble locating Brendow's home. He sat on his front step stroking his cat, Nix. He rose as Sendra came in through the gate, spilling Nix off his lap. Even at his advanced age, he moved with the litheness and grace of a youthful warrior.

"Sendra, what brings you here?"

"I have something I thought you might be able to help me with." She drew the envelope out of her pocket and held it out to him.

"From Lord Bartheylen." He ran a thoughtful finger over the seal.

"The dispatch rider said it came from Shael," Sendra nodded. "I thought if it was bad news—about Kyer I mean—you'd want to know."

"Gareth and Della won't be back for a couple of weeks more." He studied the item he held in his fingertips.

The old man hesitated then agreed with her. He pulled open the seal and slid the folded pieces of parchment from their enclosure. "Shael Castle letter paper." Worry edged his tone. Sendra watched him anxiously as he unfolded the sheets and hastily glanced over them. She allowed herself to breathe only when a smile began to play on his lips.

"It's not *about* Kyer; it's *from* Kyer."

"Writing from Shael Castle?" Sendra asked, disbelief and pleasure vying for prominence.

"It would seem our Kyer has come a long way."

Sendra walked back to her shop with lighter feet than she'd had since the attack. The Halidan girl was not in prison, and her letter had been delivered by a man named Tell. *What a lovely day.*

Brendow closed the door behind Sendra and leaned heavily against it, clutching Kyer's letter to his chest. She had found Dunvehran.

About a week prior to her departure from Hreth, Kyer had been attacked on her way home one evening. She had single-handedly defended herself against eight men, going far beyond what he had trained her to do. She had come to him later and showed him a medallion she wore, asking if he could tell her anything about it. He couldn't. When she told him it had flared with warmth during the fight, he felt uneasy.

He decided she was ready to leave anyway, to go out into the world and learn, as had been her goal for years. He did not mention his possibly baseless disquietude to her but breathed easier when he saw her safely away. The attack on the village so closely on the heels of her departure was not indisputable confirmation of his fears. Still, he couldn't help but thank the gods she was not there. He carried on, living, reading, training other young people, but all the time Brendow wondered if she had found him. How could she find what she didn't know she sought? Yet Brendow could not tell her for fear of word getting around that someone was looking for the exiled duke of Equart. He also had to protect his own identity. So, giving her his sword both as a well-deserved gift and as a message to Valrayker, Brendow sent her to Wanaka, a place he knew the dark elf often met with people who worked for him. And he waited.

To finally learn, after all these months, that she had found him, that she was safe, was a soporific for all his apprehension. He sighed as he sank into his chair, giddiness bubbling a chuckle out his throat.

He smiled fondly at the hand that could make even the flowing cursive of Dark Elvish look like it was written by a goblin.

Dear Nix,

I am certain G and D will pass this on to you and I have taken the agreed upon precautions, but who would have guessed that within three months since I last saw you I would be offered the use of this particular seal? This letter will travel under the Dukely protection of the high elf's personal messengers, though I don't put enough trust in them to write in Rydrish. I am sitting in the library at the second largest castle in the continent, of all places, and am about to embark on a second journey for someone who says he knows you: a man about whom you taught me all I know; evidently your information was closer to first-hand than you let on.

I'm not dead. You'll want to know that, although it's not for want of people trying to make me so. When you said you'd taught me all you could, and that it was up to me to learn the rest through living, you couldn't have been more right. You trained me well, my friend, for which I am thankful, but admittedly there are some aspects of this lifestyle for which there is no training. There are always consequences for standing up for what you believe in. Did you know you can make enemies that way? When you make that first kill—even when it was in self-defence—and wind up being pursued relentlessly, captured, beaten . . . you have to continually question whether you'd do the same again if given another chance. Not things you could have taught, which I guess you knew.

It all sounds melodramatic now. To think on it, none of it seems important anymore. At least, it has taken on a dream-like quality in my memory, rather than the vivid nightmare it was at the time. Anyway, I feel at home here, and safe. Of course no place is completely safe. Only this afternoon a magical device exploded in the city square, killing the mayor and several others.

I'm putting off saying the one thing I need to say; the main reason I am writing. I tried to meet with our mutual acquaintance but he is busy with the aftermath of the explosion. I need to tell someone: I killed a man in cold blood. I hated him and I believed he deserved to die. So I killed him. I'm not proud of it, and yet I know in my heart I would do it again if given the chance. What does that say about me? Would my hero still want me to work for him if he knew? I'm afraid of the answer. I hope telling you eases my conscience for the next journey.

When we've accomplished what we set out to do, perhaps I'll be able to come home for a visit. Be sure to let certain old bats know who my new friends are!

I imagine you're sitting in your chair by the window, sipping tea as you read this, a ball of purring fur on your lap. Perhaps you've just come in from working with some more trainees like myself. I imagine that the village is quiet, sleepy as ever, with the biggest excitement being the height of the corn and how many mice the cat dragged in. Has Sheska snatched up Tarqan now that I'm gone? Do Tarqan, Adric, and Bianca still train with you?

I have made some fast friends, and in spite of everything I'm happy. I think of you often.

Very truly yours,

Fralyrn

Brendow folded the letter and stared unseeing out his crosshatched front window. The early blooms in his window box were merely a colourful blur at the bottom of his frame of vision. Her letter was thought provoking in many ways, not the least of which was her confession. Yes, she would not function well with that on her shoulders, and yes, she would be able to carry on now.

The main point that struck him about her letter was something Kyer had not intended. *She does not know about the attack on the village.* He scratched gently under Nix's chin. Kien knew about it, or else he could not have sent aid. This likely meant Val knew about it, too. Nix purred and Brendow nodded in understanding.

Brendow tucked the other letter—the one meant for her parents—into a book. He leaned his head back and sighed, noticing a shift in his unease. He looked sidewise at the chair that Kyer used to occupy so regularly.

It was not Kyer's tendency to go halfway with anything. "Try not to learn everything the hard way."

Kyer rode at the head of the party with Phennil. Derry's voice came from the rear, calling the elf's name. Kyer turned around and looked past Janak and the halfling to the captain atop his warhorse. "How long until a suitable camp spot?" Derry said.

"If my memory serves me correctly," Phennil replied, "there is an excellent spot not far from here. Maybe another half hour."

"You don't mean another of those two-hour half hours, do you?" Janak bellowed. "I'm tired of those."

"Ha!" the elf tossed back at the dwarf and spoke to Kyer. "You'd think I underestimated the distance every night, the way he goes on."

"Well, once seems like an accident. Twice was pretty careless. If you do it a third time, nobody's going to believe you grew up around these parts."

Phennil returned her smile. Reaching up, he held a cedar branch out of her way and winked at her as he let it snap back to nearly unsaddle Janak. The dwarf's curses echoed through the trees.

Nine days ago they'd crossed the border out of occupied Equart, after weeks of furtive travel, into Phennil's homeland, the Guarded Realm. Kyer's only education about the area had come from the village schoolteacher, who had said it was "a wasteland of godless ne'er-do-wells living in anarchy." Phennil confirmed Kyer's suspicion that this was myth. Though the Realm was not governed by any one individual or group, there was organization. Everyone's ultimate goal was the same: the Guarded Realm was the home of the Tree of Life, and it must be protected.

The Tree's protectors were allies to Kien Bartheylen, and as the group moved farther from enemy territory, its lightheartedness returned. In

Phennil's case, it meant he talked more.

In the past few days, the fair-haired elf had chattered so much that Kyer thought she'd never last all the way to Plicatha, let alone to the Plains of Kalkamar, where Kayme's tower stood.

"As I was saying . . . *four times* I had to tell him I was joking before he stopped slamming my head into the ground and let me go," Phennil carried on.

And on and on, Kyer said to herself.

Glancing back between the hemlocks, she saw with dismay that there was no hope of rescue from the rest of the party.

Janak was similarly entangled with Skimnoddle. And there was no way she wanted help from the halfling; Behind them Derry was absorbed in a conversation with Jesqellan, towering above the short man, whose bare feet kept sinking in the needle-strewn earth.

Kyer forced her attention back to Phennil.

". . . youngest, the one they're the fondest of. Me, I'm just Phennil, the irritating brother who was too young to be involved in their important discussions, but too old to be sent off to play. Not that they didn't try."

Kyer felt a pang of guilt for using the word "irritating" so many times to describe her friend. Though he sounded cheerful as ever, she could tell there was a good deal of bitterness beneath the humour in his story.

"I think that's why I became a tracker, you know," he said introspectively. "I kept my mouth shut but my eyes and ears open."

She nearly snorted at that but caught herself. It was probably true. The elf's chatterbox nature likely emerged full force when he wasn't at home. It was an honour, then, that he felt companionable enough with her to talk non-stop and trust that she wasn't going to gag him.

Kyer suddenly realized that all was still, apart from the murmurs of the others' voices and the buzzing of flies amid plodding hooves. Phennil had stopped talking. She drew her brows together when she saw that her friend's lips were pursed and his countenance bore an atypical pout.

"Hey, Phennil," she began. He turned his head and in that brief moment, she saw a strange flash in his vivid blue eyes. He faced front again.

"I just don't understand why we haven't seen any scouts. This close to the city, I'd have thought . . ." He fell silent again.

"Phennil, are you . . . nervous? About going home, I mean."

He exhaled loudly. "Nervous? No way, this is going to be great. I can't wait to show you my house, and introduce you . . ."

And he was off again. Kyer didn't believe for a second that he wasn't nervous.

For nearly three weeks, Kyer and her companions had trekked on eggshells through the enemy-occupied duchy of Equart, staying away from populated areas whenever possible. Kyer had admired the humble majesty of the Deserat mountain range; the vast beauty of the rolling plains, coloured vibrantly with late spring blooms; the inviting blueness of the Gulf of Tarash distant on the eastern horizon as they'd finally crossed the border into the Guarded Realm at the foothills of the Craighon Mountains. The richness of the landscape had often made Kyer's throat ache with longing to return it to Valrayker's keeping. But Val would have to wait; first they must accomplish the task he'd set for them.

Being unified against a common enemy had shoved Kyer's anger at Derry to a sideline. But she had not forgotten, and she hadn't felt completely at ease in his company since they'd left Shael.

They'd had only a few skirmishes, and no one had been seriously wounded, but they had breathed a collective sigh of relief at crossing over into the Guarded Realm. Now they travelled through the Donnan Forest, at the north end of which they would find the city of Plicatha. The road through the hemlocks and cedars of Donnan had at one time been well-travelled, though in the past year or two, undergrowth had been spared the trampling of many hooves and feet. Sword fern and bracken did their best to blot out the path, while gentle deer fern lined it, in its polite way of indicating what the more gregarious plants tried to conceal. Jesqellan had to magic some fallen conk-covered logs off the path then got wet up to his knees when they forded the serpentine stream that criss-crossed the trail once in a while. Skimnoddle occasionally dashed off the trail to pick herbs, wild ginger, onion, and mushrooms to enhance his cooking. Derry exclaimed with more subdued eagerness each time he happened upon another variety of fungus or plant specimen for his physicker's kit.

The part of the forest in which they now travelled was particularly close. Overhanging branches dipped across the travellers' faces, and Derry especially, on his warhorse, could be heard cursing as he dodged the low-hanging growth.

Kyer looked over her shoulder at him, smirking at his predicament. At one point Derry drew his sword and hacked at a branch.

"No!" Phennil cringed in horror as if the weapon had been drawn against him.

Derry arrested his action. "What?"

"Sorry, Captain, but I'm a wood elf. If you hurt the trees, I can feel it."

"What do you suggest I do, then?"

"If a person is in your way, do you simply cut them down? No, you say, 'excuse me,' and the person moves aside. If they've got any sense of etiquette, anyway. Same thing with trees, only they take a bit longer to react. Just shift them aside, and they'll remember that this is a road, and they'll stop being so greedy about the space."

Derry stiffly apologized. Kyer suspected he wasn't entirely sincere.

"It's obvious nobody's come this way in a while," Phennil said, more to himself than to anyone else. "The trees don't usually forget so easily."

"How do you mean?" Kyer said.

"It's just strange." His voice was quiet, thoughtful. "I'd have expected . . .

"But never mind." Phennil broke into the Elvish tongue. "Are you still glad you came along?"

Kyer had taken advantage of every opportunity to practice her Elvish in an effort to grasp Phennil's fluidity and outgrow the staccato human accent she'd learned from Brendow. The first time she'd spoken in his tongue, Phennil's face had lit up in surprise. He was delighted and more than happy to help her master the unusual inflections of his particular dialect.

"What? Oh, on the journey," she said, picking up the language. "Yes, of course. I just want to get to Plicatha so I can feel like we're doing something. All this riding doesn't feel like progress."

"It won't be long," the elf replied. "We're not far."

"Are you sure your father will help us?"

"Of course. My father is the Lord of Donnan and a citizen of the Guarded Realm; any chance to aid the allies in the south is another thorn in Dregor's side. Here!" He called back to the others and drew Leoht off to the side of the trail. "See? I do know my homeland."

They set up camp in a glade of hemlocks, its floor spongy with eons of needles, dotted with symmetrical bunchberry flowers. The company rubbed down the horses and fetched firewood. Jesqellan spread his Tracking Confusion spell over the last leg of the day's journey, and Skimnoddle worked his own magic.

Even Kyer was forced to admit that Skimnoddle was handy to have around. The halfling was a most excellent cook. If this was what Valrayker had been referring to when he'd said the company would wonder how they'd managed without him in the past, Kyer didn't know; the halfling was passable with a bow, but if he had any other indispensable talents, he hadn't demonstrated them yet. No matter: for now the cooking was enough. It took him no time at all to employ his little blow-dart to deprive a rabbit family of a couple of relatives, and soon they were pivoting happily on a makeshift spit.

While the meat roasted, the drippings making pleasant cracking and hissing sounds as they plopped into the flames, the others erected their shelters of tent cloth. Skimnoddle prepared a side dish of wild strawberries and miner's cabbage. Kyer took a few vessels to fill with water and tore herself away from the smell of rich, roasting meat that tantalized her nostrils and made her drool.

She followed a tiny streamlet down through the trees and knelt by a pond. As she raised her head from the crystal-clear pool, Kyer was surprised by what she thought were tiny flashing lights in the air above her head. When she looked where she had seen them, they were extinguished. She stared into the darkening forest for a moment and shook her head; they must have been either fireflies or her imagination. When she returned to the camp, she mentioned the lights to Phennil.

He looked puzzled. "They sound like sylvan sprites." He shook his head. "But that doesn't really make sense. I've never seen them in our forest before. We're so close to home; there's no way Father would allow anything hostile to spend much time this close to the city."

Kyer detected a tautness in these last words, a conviction that she didn't think was entirely necessary. "The sprites are hostile?"

"No."

She opened her mouth to question him further, but the skin on the back of her neck prickled. She felt eyes peering at her from the shadowed woods and shivered. At the same time, the horses began to fidget, and Donnagill snorted tetchily. The party, alert now, moved calmly but automatically into their standard defensive positions, drawing weapons and making ready for whatever it was. Skimnoddle, who had been facing the fire, tending the rabbits, turned around, giving his eyes as much time as possible to adjust to the dimmer light. His very short recurve bow was already in hand.

"What is it? Where?" Derry whispered, his armour glowing in the firelight.

"Over there." Phennil indicated the darkness off to his left. "I see two of 'em."

"Two of what?" Derry squinted in the direction Phennil had nodded.

"Cats of some kind," the elf replied. "About sixty feet away. They must smell our dinner."

"They'll be hard-pressed to get it," Skimnoddle said. "They'll have to pass through me, first."

"I imagine they would just go over you," Kyer remarked dryly, gripping her bastard sword and peering into the shadows.

"There's another one over here." Janak scanned the darkness on the other side of the fire. This one was much closer and approached quickly. Kyer circled closer to the dwarf, and by that time it was near enough to identify.

"Looks like a cougar," Janak said, "though it's an awful big'un."

An arrow whizzed past Kyer's head, and she glanced back to see Skimnoddle fitting another one to his bow. The first one had merely shaved a short strip of the animal's fur, catching its attention but causing it no damage. Angry now, it bounded, deftly avoiding fallen logs and low-hanging branches. Kyer's sword arm twitched, yet she hesitated to injure such a graceful, fluid creature. She was jolted out of her admiration when the cougar took a running leap from fifteen feet away and knocked sturdy Janak into one of the shelters. The cloth entangled him as he brought it to the ground. Kyer swiped at the animal, drawing blood from its hind leg, giving Janak a chance to roll over it and out of the mass of cloth. One fork of his beard took on a red hue. Her sword flew up again.

The other two cats had reached the edge of the glade. One of them had an arrow sticking out of its side, but it hardly seemed to deter the creature. Jesqellan's hand pointed to the other cat and let fly a lightning bolt that nearly missed its mark, singeing the animal's flank. It hissed in pain and fury.

"Careful Jesqellan or you'll have the whole forest up in flames!" Phennil tossed his bow aside to take up his bastard sword.

The mage had better success with his second lightning bolt, but not quickly enough to prevent the ferocious animal from gashing four parallel rents down his robe.

Derry wrenched his weapon out of the foreleg of Phennil's cat, after frustrating its attempt to hook its claws into the elf's arm. He raised the glinting steel for a second strike but was startled by a crash. An enormous black cat had dropped onto Skimnoddle from above, knocking over the spit and sending the rabbits right into the fire. The halfling cried out, struggling, and Derry was there, sword aimed at the creature's neck. He stabbed the sleek animal's deceptively tough hide. At the same time, Skimnoddle took the arrow he had intended to let fly, and thrust it with all his might into the beast's snarling maw. Derry dragged the sagging cat off the halfling's supine form and offered him a hand up.

Janak's hammer bashed a bloody dent into his wildcat's head. With Janak on top of the creature, Kyer could not slash downwards from above. Instead, she dropped to her knees and thrust her sword low to the ground, avoiding Janak's knee and piercing the cat through the ribs.

They fought, panting and swearing amid feline yowls and screeches.

As suddenly as it began, all sound ceased.

Kyer lost her balance and nearly fell over as she missed the animal who had fallen out from under her sword's path. All four beasts had simultaneously dropped dead. Their massive bodies were sprawled around the camp as if they were lazing in the sun. Kyer's eyes darted, trying to focus on the tiny flecks of light that hovered over the glade but weren't still long enough for her to perceive whether they were real or not.

"Look!" was all she managed to utter before they had vanished again. Kyer breathlessly wiped sweat from her eyes and looked around the clearing at the dead animals. "What in Death's name just happened here?"

Skimnoddle had scuttled to his feet and, despite the rising lump on the back of his head, grabbed his tongs and used them to right the spit. He removed the rabbits from the fire, murmuring, "hot hot hot hot!" to himself as he tried not to burn his fingers.

"I do believe these are done to a turn," he announced proudly. "The meal could not have been cooked closer to perfection if I had planned it this way. Those of you who like your meat rare shall have a slice from this end, and for the others, there is a mouth-watering selection of slightly crunchy bits from this side!"

Derry scowled, ignoring him. "Why does there appear to be three different species of wildcat?" He was right: there were two of a tan colour, the black one, and one with spots.

Phennil nodded, his teeth clenched. "Working together."

"In what seemed very much like a *planned attack*!" Kyer could not believe her eyes or her own words.

Jesqellan moved over to the animal nearest him and held his palm over it.

"I wouldn't have been surprised—well, as surprised, anyway—if they had all been cougars," Phennil picked himself up, gingerly touching a deep scratch on his thigh, "because we're near the base of the Grey Mountains, and they do tend to wander around. Cougars, panthers, and jaguars working as a team? It's crazy."

"A bit on the big side too," Janak threw in, picking bits of sticky fur off his war hammer. He was still bleeding from somewhere beneath all his hair.

"Exactly." Jesqellan moved to another dead cat. "I would surmise that Dregor has dipped his fingers into the Guarded Realm in a dangerously subtle way." He held both hands over the animal. "I'm feeling magic in these creatures, and I would be willing to wager that all four have been subjected to a dose of Lord Dregor's power. What better way to infiltrate a territory than by using animals that are indigenous to that area? They are not quite twice the size of their unaffected brethren which—"

"Now hold on just a minute!" Phennil slapped his hand on the rock he had conscripted into use as a chair. "My *father* is lord of this forest! There is absolutely no way he would allow Dregor to get his filthy tendrils into any of it, by any means whatsoever! He would know about it, and he would wipe it out. That's it."

There was a long pause as Phennil's eyes challenged the mage to add more details to his hypothesis. Finally Jesqellan lowered his slender hands and shrugged, joining Skimnoddle at the fire. Phennil folded his arms and scowled.

Derry slowly resheathed his sword, cleaned of jaguar residue, and spoke in a low voice. "Phennil, how long has it been since you were home?"

"Five years," the elf replied crossly.

Derry left it at that.

Four

I Always Said She Was Trouble

Skimnoddle filled tin plates with meat and vegetables, which had remained undisturbed in their pot and were only slightly beyond the point at which he would have proclaimed them to be ready. Derry wouldn't eat until he had tended to the group's cuts and scratches. He fetched his kit and worked on Janak's cheek, the most serious of their injuries.

"Misjudged the distance of the damn thing," the dwarf said. "Damn eye." He had the decency to look abashed, as if the words had slipped out unbidden. Kyer thought it best to leave it alone.

As she blew on a spoonful of dinner, Kyer voiced the thing that had been on her mind more than the influence of Dregor on the animals.

"Did anybody else notice the flashing lights, or was it just me?"

"Yes, I saw them too," said Jesqellan.

"Oh good, 'cause I was a bit concerned about my sanity." Kyer grinned.

"Dear lady," Skimnoddle orated, "regardless of whether the quality of your mind was in doubt, I would without question remain your most humble servant, ever sustaining you with unparalleled devotion." He bowed.

She looked up at him without raising her head. "That's . . . that's great. But that's hardly the point, is it? I want to know what they were and how much of a part they played in killing those damn cats." She gave her attention to Phennil. "You mentioned sylvan sprites before?"

"Well, yes." Phennil sounded cross. "They abhor evil of any kind; it would be natural—" The elf clamped his mouth shut. Then he turned abruptly to Skimnoddle. "This is really good, Skimnoddle, once again."

Kyer had to agree, but she would never say so. Rather, she observed Phennil as he rose and wandered around the camp. Conversation resumed, but Kyer was not so rapt that she did not notice Phennil examine each of the animals, under the guise of nonchalantly preparing them for burial. She watched him out of the corner of her eye and saw him put more than one tiny item into his pouch. Samples of the animals' fur? She said nothing.

Two mornings later, Phennil scrabbled out of his bedroll and his long stretch became a little jig as he announced, "Friends: that was our last night sleeping on the ground, for a few days at least. We'll be at Plicatha, the Front City of Donnan, by late afternoon."

Janak grunted. "Terrific. Then we'll be surrounded by countless elves as noisy and malodorous as you."

"Absolute rubbish," Phennil cried. "No one in Plicatha is as malodorous as I."

Kyer counted in her head. By the time they reached Plicatha, it would have been a full week since they'd stayed in an inn and she'd had a hot bath. A horrifying thought struck her.

"Phennil, do they even have baths in Plicatha?"

He threw a startled look at her, but when he saw the twitch in the corner of her lip, he casually bent and picked a cluster of salal berries, and flung them at her.

Hunter fell with ease back into the authoritative tone he had habitually used when issuing commands to his soldiers at Shael Castle. Each time he gave his new company an order, he was reasonably sure his words were impressive enough. He tried to be vague about their task, giving himself room to be less than specific as they neared their mark. Unfortunately Golgathaur had prepared for that eventuality.

Hunter had asked for a dozen men. Hew was the first to volunteer. Formerly Hugh, he'd earned the nickname from his way of carving up his opponents, even after they were dead. Hunter would have to watch himself with that one. But Hew was nothing. Of the dozen men he'd requested, he got eleven. The twelfth person was a woman, a mage-assassin who called herself Misty. She and her twin brother, a double-shortsword-swinging fighter named Juggler, had only days previously returned to headquarters after a trip west on an undisclosed errand.

They were the creepiest pair he'd ever encountered. The way they looked at him with coal black eyes made him uneasy, and the way they talked in whispers all the time, their dark, curly heads bent toward each other. They understood each other's thoughts without speaking and smiled identical little knowing smiles at each other every time he gave an order, as if they were just humouring him. To ignore them was impossible. To confront them was out of the question.

After a couple of weeks of travelling, Misty and Juggler approached him as he curried his horse. Misty did all the talking. Her willowy beauty was witch-like and unnerving.

"Chief Hunter." Her childish, sing-song fashion was bizarrely juxtaposed by her low-range voice. "My brother and I must speak to you."

"I suppose I should feel honoured?" Hunter replied more bravely than he felt.

"We'll see if you still feel that way after I've finished." She smiled coyly. "We just had a visit from our old friend, Golgathaur. You know him, of course." She stroked his horse's flank. Hunter could not imagine why that made him so nervous. "He informed us that he more or less sees us as seconds. That means second in command where we come from. Now, we should make sure you know the significance of being a second, shouldn't we Juggles?"

Juggler did not even have the human sensitivity to flinch at the pet name.

"I think I'd like you to look right at me when I say this to you, Hunter, so I know you've understood things." He obliged, yet he could not keep his eyes from darting back to where she caressed his horse. He wished she'd remove her hand.

"Our job as seconds is to make sure you do your job as chief. Does that make sense to you? Golgathaur will give you instructions, and you will pass those instructions on to the rest of our little party. We know your background, so if at any time Juggles and I feel that you might be withholding anything from the group or misleading us or casually 'misinterpreting' Golgathaur's instructions, we can go speak to him. Isn't that lovely? And you can't even accuse us of insubordination because it's part of our job. And here's the piece I like best: once he's decided on a course of action, we will be the ones to carry it out. Juggles and I really like that sort of thing, don't we Juggles?"

Juggler did not respond. Hunter wasn't foolish enough to think him a half-wit. He was all too aware of the two short swords at the quiet one's waist. One smooth and razor-sharp, the other jagged like a saw on both edges. Fredric had watched him practice with them, making a blur of motion like the wings of a hummingbird, tossing them in the air and catching them, throwing them to impale a squirrel against the trunk of a tree. Fredric did not relish the notion of being anything like that squirrel.

"Chief Hunter, we will help carry out Golgathaur's orders in every way we are capable of." Her tone lost its sing-song style and became virtually toneless. "And one of those ways is ensuring that you do not forget your allegiance.

"There. Do you still feel honoured?"

Fredric felt sick to his stomach. When they'd gone and he finally turned back to his horse, he saw what she'd done. Somehow, with her hand, she'd shaved a diagram into his animal's hair: the chevrons, stars, and tree of the Bartheylen crest, with a thick X through them. Hunter had to sit down.

Now they were only just over a week away from Plicatha. Hunter's hope of deceitfully thwarting the group's efforts had vanished. All that remained was his lust for Kyer's blood. He could taste it, even as he had tasted the wine on her lips. The vision of her deep, mysterious eyes as they caressed the shadows in the candlelight of his room altered to become the expressionless eyes that looked through him as he was handed his fate from his beloved lord. The only vision that made him smile now was that of the life draining from those eyes as she fell on the point of his sword. He clutched that vision.

Soon.

Phennil was as much unlike his father as Kyer could have imagined. She had assumed he would be the spitting image of his senior. So when she followed Derry into the giant red cedar meeting room, the spicy aroma of the wood curiously fresh, the contrast between the old elf and his third son surprised her. She glanced around the room looking for someone else, but there was none other who could possibly be the Lord of the Donnan Forest.

Lord Fyrhen's eyes were deeper set than Phennil's and a bit too close together, making his face look squashed and severe. When he stood to greet them he smiled a little, and it was as if someone had grabbed both his pointed ears from behind and stretched them back, spreading his face apart. He was shorter than his son by several inches, and heavier, with a thickness around his neck that could have been attributed to either his considerable age or the plate of sticky buns at his elbow.

The only similarity Kyer noted—and it was a subtle one—was the tendency of both men's hair to be bushy. Lord Fyrhen's was longer, though, the weight of it reducing its volume, whereas Phennil's was jaw-length and sprang up, adding to his boyish appearance. The father's hair was darker, too, more like red maple, rather than Phennil's paper birch colour.

"It is a joy to see you again, my son." The lord embraced him, rather stiffly, Kyer thought. "I hope your journey was a pleasant one. You appear to be in good health; that is something to say for you. Please introduce your friends. Some faces I believe I recognize; others I do not."

Phennil spoke with uncommon formality. "Our captain, Derry Moraunt, whom you have met before. He has been Lord Valrayker's captain for several years."

Derry gave a courtly bow and moved to the side. Was it Kyer's imagination, or did he give her a look that said, "If not for you, I would have been introduced as 'Sir Derry' as I ought to be." She frowned and tried to shake her crossness by the time her name came up. When Phennil said Kyer's name, she perceived a slight rise in the pitch of his voice and wondered if he was worried about her behaviour or his father's. The lord squinted at her.

Kyer did not like him.

He looked her up and down, and she watched him make a mental note of her armour, her weapons, her boots, even her hair, which couldn't possibly be a pretty sight after weeks of travel. Kyer was reminded of the way the cranky schoolteacher in Hreth used to look at her before flinging something at her head. The old teacher was all geniality in comparison to Lord Fyrhen.

"Welcome all of you to Plicatha, the Front City of Donnan, on behalf of Lady Fyrhen and our household." Lord Fyrhen's apparent opinion of Kyer was set aside and replaced with something resembling friendliness. "I trust you shall enjoy your sojourn, and I would be delighted if you would share this evening's meal at my own family table. Until then, my servants will direct you to your chambers." With that, the old man turned to go.

Kyer stared at his exiting back. *I highly doubt that man is capable of 'delighting' in anything.* Then Phennil was at her side, and he walked with her out the side door and through the lamplit trees. Two servants accompanied the others in front.

"I'm sorry, Kyer," Phennil said in a low voice. "I have no idea what the appraisal was all about."

"Don't worry about it, Phennil. I'm used to creating some sort of disturbance every time I enter a new room. It's getting a little tiresome, but for you, I can tolerate it." She gave him a friendly slap on the back.

The trees were like a rooftop overhead, so thick it would take an exceptionally heavy rain to penetrate it. Lamps resembling small metal houses hung from branches about fifteen feet off the ground. The roof of each one was a large, flat cone-shape to protect the flame from rain and the tree from the flame. They cast shadows that were at the same time cheerful and eerie. It was a strange sensation, this feeling like she was indoors yet knowing she was not. The trees wafted gently in a breeze that was undetectable to her, and they seemed to murmur amongst themselves. Kyer's skin crinkled but she adopted what she hoped to be an affable appearance, to stay on the trees' good side.

She caught glimpses of several shelters nestled among the trees, at ground level and above, the higher ones accessed by sturdy looking circular staircases. Kyer followed Phennil into a long, low building and her eyes had to adjust to a new kind of dimness. This time the light source was candles, dozens of them on sconces of shiny metal that protected the log walls from the flames. The floor was wooden planks, covered with the same organic materials that naturally occurred outdoors: hemlock and pine needles, sword ferns, strips of cedar bark, and scaly cedar leaves all softened their footfalls so even the sturdiest of dwarves could walk almost noiselessly through this corridor. Doors lined the hallway, half a dozen on each side.

"Why doesn't this whole place go up in flames?" Kyer asked.

"All the materials are kept green magically," Phennil replied. "Besides, we use all the plant life with their permission, so they don't actually die once we've cut 'em."

Kyer stopped for a second then carried on. "How . . . do you get their permission?"

"We ask them, of course. See you at dinner."

Kyer entered the hall for the evening meal and hesitated in the twined-cedar-bough doorway, breathing in the pungent scent of the tree of which the room was fashioned. Instead of a ceiling, the room came to a point, beyond which was the cedar trunk and boughs, as if they were *inside* the tree. Kyer thought the wood elves must have asked this tree very nicely.

Her friends already had found their seats. A bright-eyed girl with red cedar-coloured hair rose and waved her over. Kyer approached.

"I'm Kendra Fyrhen." The girl invited Kyer to sit in the empty seat next to her. "Phennil's younger sister." She looked not much younger than Kyer, though Kyer was unsure what the equivalent of twenty-three was in elven years.

Kyer sat and switched to the Elvish tongue. "Do you have any embarrassing stories about Phennil you can share?"

Kendra laughed and Kyer saw the resemblance to her brother. The elf pointed out all the siblings. Rupi, the eldest, with his distinguished demeanour, already looked fit to be Donnan Lord, in his turn. Next to him was his handsome partner, Tristan. Then came Paullin, the second Fyrhen son, with dark eyes and mahogany-coloured hair.

"Can you guess which of the elder sisters is which?" Kendra asked playfully.

Kyer considered. "Those two are Shellot and Nena, but I don't know which is which. But that," she nodded at the woman next to Phennil, "must be Marlo." Kyer remembered that Marlo was the one Phennil was closest to, and from across the room, Kyer almost would have taken them for twins. They were practically identical, right down to the eyes and hair. Marlo even kept hers short like Phennil's, though it was tidier.

"Well done! I suppose that's sort of two out of three. Light brown is Shellot and auburn is Nena." Finally Kendra pointed out Darken, the youngest, a quiet youth who lived up to his name, with dark hair like his eldest brothers, and about twelve, by human standards.

A golden-haired elf came around pouring wine into each goblet, though when she reached Janak, the dwarf's deep voice cut through the conversations. "I thank you, but no, I would prefer a mug of the palest ale to a cup of your richest wine." The girl's jaw dropped but she recovered herself and murmured something, to which he replied, "I only say that because I've heard none but the best report of Donnan ale." She blushed and spoke to a passing server who sailed out of the hall.

Nice recovery, Janak, you rude bastard, Kyer thought with a certain fondness.

"Oh, and here's Mother." Kendra sat up straighter.

Kyer had assumed correctly, after all: Phennil *was* the spitting image of his senior. Phennil's mother was stately and slender, several inches taller than her husband, with long, wavy hair of the same white blonde as Phennil's. Her face was narrow and soft, a kind face that seemed to smile perpetually, even if the corners of her mouth were not turned up. Kyer now saw where Phennil had inherited his bright blue eyes. Lady Fyrhen's were azure blue and shone out all over the entire room. Kyer liked Lady Fyrhen at first glimpse. A bit of weight appeared to lift off even Lord Fyrhen's shoulders in the presence of his wife. Her grace and ease of manner cast a warmth over the company.

As they commenced the first course, Kyer nudged Kendra. "How do you get used to all these people? Remembering everyone's names and all."

The girl shrugged with a crooked smile. "I don't know. I was born into it, so it comes naturally, I suppose. Don't you come from a large family?"

"Nope. Just me and my parents. Makes for really quiet family gatherings."

The conversation centred around Phennil and his experiences during the past five years since he was at home, the last two of which were the most interesting because that was when he had joined Valrayker. He told the story of meeting the dark elf, and one other involving Jesqellan and a horde of giant slugs. The rest of the group helped him tell of their recent mission to Nennia, and the important role they each had played there. They emphasized Phennil's archery skills for the benefit of his family.

Kendra leaned closer to Kyer. "Did he really stop those people from killing each other?"

Kyer nodded. "I don't know how else we'd have stopped them." She smiled to herself at the younger girl's wide-eyed admiration of her brother.

"Well, my son," said Lord Fyrhen. "I am pleased to hear that although you are not using your talents to aid your people directly, you are at least putting your skills to good use for others."

Phennil beamed quietly at the praise. It gave him courage.

"Actually, Father, perhaps this is a good time to talk to you of our current journey." He nodded to Derry, who was the spokesman for the party.

Lord Fyrhen grunted. "I had a feeling you might have another reason for coming home since seeing your family does not usually figure largely in your plans."

Kyer frowned. Phennil's face reddened slightly, and he shrank in his chair.

Derry stepped in. "Our journey brought us in this direction, and I know I would never have passed up an opportunity to bask in Fyrhen hospitality." Derry raised his goblet and toasted his hosts by way of thanks for opening their home, and, Kyer suspected, in an effort to smooth over whatever feelings might have been wounded by the lord's comment. It didn't work on her. She was less and less impressed by his lordship.

Derry set his goblet on the table. "As Phennil introduced to you, there is a small piece of business that also contributes to our detour in this direction.

"We are on an errand for my Lord Valrayker, though it is moreso for Lord Bartheylen. His wife, the Lady Alon Maer, is pregnant with their child, and yet, I regret to report, gravely ill." Lady Fyrhen placed a hand over her heart. "As even Heatha's best healers have been unable to find a remedy, we are on our way to visit Kayme—" Several intakes of breath were heard around the room. Lord Fyrhen's creases lengthened. "We are hoping that Kayme will be not only willing to perform a spell to identify the illness but perhaps provide a cure. We know we are taking a great chance with our boldness, but we have no other options."

"And what is it you want of me?" Lord Fyrhen asked without enthusiasm.

"We were hoping, Father and Mother, that you might be kind enough to donate a few items that we could offer Kayme as gifts. We have some things Kien gave us, but we don't know if it will be enough."

"To gain Kayme's favour?" Lord Fyrhen said.

Derry cleared his throat. "We thought it presumptuous to assume he would be willing to address the problem without some sort of recompense."

Lord Fyrhen considered the matter, pouting as he wiped the condensation off his goblet with his fingers. "I wonder if you could tell me why I ought to be involved."

Jesqellan said, "It must come across as if we are taking advantage of your hospitality, asking you to extend it this far. Believe me, we have thought long and looked for other possible options along our journey. But everyone in Rydris is suffering because of the wars, and few people have anything of value, let alone items they are willing to give up."

Phennil spoke up again. "It is ultimately for the sake of Rydris, Father. Not simply because the lives of Kien's wife and heir are at stake; I know you are more concerned about the Guarded Realm than you are with the lands to the south. But in troubled times like these, is it not fitting to make a show of goodwill for our neighbours and friends with whom we share a common enemy?"

"I knew this 'common enemy' talk would come up eventually." Lord Fyrhen gave a dismissive wave. "This has nothing to do with that; it is about Kien Bartheylen. Alon Maer's health does not concern me."

Lady Fyrhen's voice spoke with warm clarity. "It does concern *me*. Alon has always been a good friend, and I am saddened by your lack of care."

Her husband looked at her darkly and picked up his fork to eat his last mouthful of fruit pie. It occurred to Kyer that the lord's grand words of opposition might just be an act, so it didn't look as if he were giving in too easily. On the other hand, it could have been that his lordship had other reasons not to accommodate them. She was puzzled by his apparent disregard for the "common enemy" topic.

The old man swallowed and casually dropped his fork with a clatter onto the plate and leaned back in his chair. "Very well." He sniffed. "If it will make my wife happy to support a friend during a difficult time, I will not say no. I will think on it and try to provide you with something. But I have to say I don't know offhand what to give the great wizard who already has everything."

Kyer rubbed the back of her neck, and wondered at the sarcasm in his tone.

Lady Fyrhen sipped her tea and said in a gentle low voice, "Hardly everything."

The conversation at breakfast meandered around to the affairs of the world. Kyer observed how leisurely the Fyrhens were able to speak about this topic with their father not present.

"Is there danger of Lord Dregor seeking you out during your journey?" Tristan glanced at Rupi as Lord and Lady Fyrhen came through the doorway.

"I have gathered a few items for your use," His Lordship announced as he sat. "Some jewels, a decorative dagger, and a helm of some value that belonged to my great uncle. It will have to suffice, for I can find nothing else."

Derry rose and bowed. "I thank you for your generosity, on behalf of us all."

"Thank you, Father, Mother," Phennil added with sincerity.

His father replied with a curt nod. His mother's smile was apologetic, as if she wished she could provide more.

The conversation soon resumed, albeit a bit more self-consciously.

"To answer your question," Derry said to Tristan, "of course, this mission is not directly influenced by Dregor's movements, but he is on our minds at all times."

"You must gain intelligence, I suppose, no matter where you travel, that may influence Lord Bartheylen's decisions." Paullin said with a hesitant glance at his father.

"Yes, it is so," Jesqellan nodded. "Certainly coming this far north is a risk, our confidence and faith in the strength of our allies in the Guarded Realm notwithstanding." He nodded toward Lord Fyrhen. "We hope to remain as inconspicuous as possible, but if anything, it would be nice to learn something that will be of value to the dukes upon our return."

Lord Fyrhen's face took on a grimmer countenance as the discussion progressed. Rupi's jaw was set, as if the eldest son struggled to hold back. Tristan placed a hand on Rupi's. Paullin studied his tea. The others ate wordlessly, and avoided any eye contact.

Kyer could no longer resist. "What steps are you taking, Your Lordship, to prepare for any action on the part of our common enemy?" To anyone else, it would seem an innocent enough question. "It must worry you that the Guarded Realm is now sandwiched between enemy territories." She widened her eyes to appear as curious as possible. She avoided Derry's gaze, though it bored into her like a termite into wood.

"You all keep mentioning this 'common enemy,'" Lord Fyrhen began. *We're getting to the crux of it right away*, Kyer thought with satisfaction. "My common *sense* tells me that the best way to make an enemy of Lord Dregor is to provoke him. In my view, it is best to remain unnoticed."

Jesqellan said quietly, "Do you not regard him as the one enemy of all, Your Lordship?"

"He is evil, to be sure," the elven lord replied. "But like poking a hornet's nest, he need only be an active enemy to those who choose it."

Rupi's elven pallor took on a pinkish hue. Shellot stopped chewing and Kendra passed the fruit bowl to Darken. Nena stirred her eggs around on her plate. Marlo rested her fingertips on the edge of the table.

"I don't understand what you mean, Father," Phennil said cautiously. "You make it sound as if it were a viable choice to *side* with him. Are you saying that Dregor was somehow *elected* to the position of enemy by those who oppose him?"

Kyer was reminded of a conversation with Brendow, wherein her trainer pointed out how war would not happen if nobody ever opposed their oppressors. No one would die in defence of their homeland if they simply stepped aside and allowed invaders in. For most, that was not an option.

"I'm not talking about siding with him; I'm talking about the other choice: not taking a side. Those who stand up to him only escalate the problem. My point, dear boy" —Kyer felt Phennil cringe from the other side of the room— "is this: Dregor is far more likely to focus his attentions on those whose presence and motives are obvious than those whose actions are more discreet and inconspicuous." He pressed his forefinger into the table for emphasis.

This pronouncement was, Kyer assumed, for the educational benefit of this particular party, considering the prominence in Rydris society of both Kien and Valrayker. Neither was a figure hiding in the shadows. She had not allied herself with the subtlest lot, she was well aware, but at least she could be proud of her involvement. Her spine stiffening, she warned herself to be careful what she said. This was Phennil's father, even if she didn't feel altogether warm toward him. She took a deep breath, even as she noticed Derry's glance telling her not to say a word. *What? Does he think I'm incapable of speaking with diplomacy?*

"What discreet action will you be taking, then, sir?" Kyer said, hoping he would tell them something useful that would prove his support of the force against Dregor. "Espionage, perhaps? Any information from within—"

"At this time I will do nothing," he replied. "It is an unnecessary risk to the lives of my people."

Kyer leaned forward. "With all due respect, Lord Fyrhen, isn't that just a little bit short-sighted? To ignore such a threat as Lord Dregor?"

"I would argue that, young lady. He's not a definite threat. Clearly he has other interests than the Guarded Realm."

"The Tree of Life is in the Guarded Realm." She thought, *What're you all guarding if not that?* If the elves refused to take up arms in the Tree's defence ...

"Donnan is but one province of the Guarded Realm. The Tree's protection is the responsibility of all provinces, not solely mine. Yet, if Dregor were truly interested in taking the Tree, why did he not enter and take it? Why did he plot his course to circumvent us and *take Equart*? I will not risk the lives of my people for a mere *potential* threat. We can stave him off indefinitely if we tread carefully."

Kyer jammed her heel on the floor to stop her knee bouncing. "I can't speak for Dregor's motives, but I would have thought that being surrounded would be *more* worrisome, not less. Would it not be prudent to prepare?"

"Kyer—" Derry began.

"Yes, Father," said Phennil, coming to her support. "Were we not attacked only two days ago by wildcats on the perimeter of Donnan? Wildcats that weren't wild by any traditional sense of the word. Jesqellan, didn't you say they were magically enhanced?"

The siblings shared quick glances of alarm. Their mother's blue eyes flashed at her husband.

Kyer was astonished at Phennil's admission that his father may have been negligent when he had been so quick to defend him at the time.

Jesqellan had time only to nod before Lord Fyrhen spoke again, his volume and pitch rising with the effort to grip his patience.

"The young lady cannot speak for Dregor. Nor should you judge my tactics. I say this is all the more reason to remain calm and quiet, not stirring things up. *That* would be prudent, as you outspokenly put it, as opposed to those who gallivant around the countryside making spectacles of themselves and drawing all his attention. Though perhaps I ought to be grateful to such fools: their carelessness draws Dregor's eye away from my people."

Kyer's blood boiled. *Carelessness?* He relied on everyone else to sacrifice themselves to protect his people and called them careless for their efforts.

"I may not call Valrayker 'My Lord,'" said Janak in an uncharacteristically civil tone, "but I work for him because I am doing my part to beat down Dregor on behalf of my people. I will not wait for Dregor to come to me."

"Make no mistake, sir dwarf, if—and it is only an if, mind—it becomes necessary to take action, I will do so. But not until then." His word was final. So he thought.

Janak never said much, and when he did, it was almost unheard of for him to agree with Kyer. Though he sounded reasonable, and less angry than she felt, she was fuelled by his support, and her anger gained momentum. "That's wonderful, but what has to happen for you to decide it's necessary? Have you done any travelling, Lord Fyrhen? Have you not seen how Dregor uses people and flattens whatever stands in his way? If Dregor wants the Tree of Life, or if he wants the entire Guarded Realm for that matter, he's not going to forget about it just because you sit here quietly minding your own business and not stopping him."

Derry broke in. "There are obviously many points of view," he said awkwardly but with a stern look at Kyer, "many interpretations of the enemy's actions, and a variety of methods of counteracting them—"

"Yeah, like hiding in the trees while he burns down the forest," Kyer said crossly.

The room quaked as if the cedar tree that formed its foundation and walls were in pain. Elves shrieked or gasped, and several slapped hands over their ears. Paullin looked like she'd punched him in the gut. Rupi clutched his heart, and Tristan clenched his eyes shut. Lady Fyrhen simply looked shocked. Kendra cringed and tears had formed in Darken's eyes. It was as if Kyer had thrown an axe at Phennil.

"She didn't mean it!" Phennil leapt to his feet, crying out to the branches that surrounded them. The room groaned and shifted, then stopped.

Dead silence took over the room. Half the stunned faces were on Kyer, and the other half were on Lord Fyrhen.

"What did you just say?" His lordship's voice was barely audible.

Kyer closed her eyes in shame. Never mind that she had accused Lord Fyrhen of cowardice with the word "hiding." She couldn't care less about him. She opened her eyes and immediately locked gazes with Phennil, who looked as if she'd struck him.

"You didn't mean it," he said firmly, yet his eyes expressed a plea that he wasn't wrong.

She shook her head. "No. I didn't mean it." So much for being affable to the trees. She looked around the table, where every eye watched her and every ear waited. She had crossed the line and regretted her temerity. "I can't believe how thoughtless that was. I wish I hadn't said it. I am truly, humbly sorry." She bowed and left the room.

I guess Derry's right: I am incapable of diplomacy.

Skimnoddle had found a twist in a ceiling branch that looked remarkably like his bedroll as it hung from his pony. He looked up at it rather than trying to decide where else to look as the family members fidgeted. He heard Janak sigh and glanced over at Phennil, who sat down and stared into his empty cup, bereft of words. Derry and Jesqellan held each other's gaze as if helping each other think of how to move on from here.

"Well, I must say that my esteem for Valrayker has been shaken if this is what I am to expect from his company," Lord Fyrhen said finally.

Derry let out a tiny growl. "Lord Fyrhen, please do not let the words of one individual impair your good opinion of my Lord Valrayker. Lord Kien as well. Their good works for all of Rydris are evident. Kyer's behaviour is quite separate from them." Skimnoddle's brows clenched ever so slightly to hear Derry throw Kyer under the cart in front of everyone.

"Our friend is known for her forthright words, yes, but also the heartfelt emotion behind it," Jesqellan said. "She joined us not even three months ago, and we are making an effort to train her presence of mind to better express what is in her heart. You may be sure she regrets this."

"You make excuses for her?" Lord Fyrhen said.

"No, sir. Explanation," the mage said.

"She did apologize," Phennil said dully, and Skimnoddle was happy the elf had said it before he did.

"Sometimes an apology is not enough," Derry said firmly, as if annoyed that Phennil should defend Kyer. "The damage here is irrevocable. She deserves some form of punishment."

Skimnoddle opened his mouth to protest, but he was interrupted.

Phennil's mother spoke for the first time. "It was apparent to me that Kyer did indeed regret her words, and I believe her apology was sincere. If it was a foolish mistake to speak her thoughts aloud, her honesty at least is commendable, and she is obviously intelligent enough to learn from such an error. I accept her apology."

Skimnoddle nodded.

"That's well enough," Lord Fyrhen said gruffly. "It was not your leadership that was under attack."

"No, indeed, it was not." She took the last bite of her meal through pursed lips.

Lord Fyrhen rose and exited.

"I hope we may all put this unfortunate incident behind us," Lady Fyrhen said graciously and left the room.

"I always said she was trouble," Janak said.

An hour later, Phennil knocked on the door of his father's study in response to a summons.

"Enter," came the gruff voice on the other side of the door.

Phennil entered. "You called for me, Father?"

His father looked up at him from beneath his eyebrows without lifting his head. He didn't lower the quill in his hand but arrested its motion mid-sentence. "I have changed my mind," the old man said. "You may thank that outspoken snippet you choose to engage with in spite of your superior upbringing."

Phennil shook his head. "What do you mean?"

Lord Fyrhen snorted. "Clearly travelling has not demuddled your head. I mean, I am withdrawing my offer. There will be no gifts."

Phennil's jaw slackened in disbelief. "But what about Alon Maer? Mother—"

"That high elven snob is no concern of mine."

"Father, this isn't just about Alon Maer. What about keeping good relations with other domains in Rydris? What if in the future—?"

"Oh, are you now going to cast aspersions on the way I govern my people? You've been cavorting with the wrong crowd for too long. I should forbid you to—"

"You can no longer forbid me to do anything."

They exchanged a glare, both surprised that Phennil had said such a thing.

"Kyer is my friend, just the same as Jesqellan and the others. They may be better at concealing their feelings than she is; it is not to say they disagreed with her." Phennil fought to keep his voice low and stared at the man to whom he had never been close but who had been at least partly responsible for shaping him into the person he was now.

"She's a troublemaker and owes me an apology."

"She already gave you one." Phennil's eyes flashed. "At least she's willing to stand up for what she believes is right. You won't even think about what is right, let alone stand up for it."

"Now you call me a coward?" Lord Fyrhen looked like a snake about to spring.

"I call you unrealistic."

"I ought to flog you."

Phennil waved his arm. "I used to fall for that threat; not anymore. You're looking for a way to prove your power. The better way to do that would be to take a stand against Dregor."

Lord Fyrhen slowly rose out of his chair and glared at his son through icy eyes.

Phennil held his ground. He could hardly believe his own courage in doing so. His heart thudded against his ribs, but his voice was barely above a whisper. "I don't know what has been going on since I last left, but something has changed. I used to fear you, but I still admired you. Now I just fear for our people."

For a moment he was afraid his father would hit him.

But Lord Fyrhen merely stood there, clenching and unclenching his fists at his sides. "Get out, Phennil," he said finally. "And you may as well not come back."

"I will. But before I go, let me give you these." Phennil carefully opened his pouch and closed his fingertips delicately around some tiny silver items. He laid them on top of the book in which his father had been writing. "These are arrows, Father. Arrows from the bows of sylvan sprites. I took them from the hides of the animals that attacked us in *your* forest only two days ago. I am sure I don't have to tell you this, but just in case you've forgotten, sylvan sprites *only* show themselves when evil is about. They would not have helped us kill normal beasts." The young elf looked at his father and sighed with just a hint of sadness. "I defended your honour to my friends that night."

He left the room.

Lord Fyrhen remained standing for some moments, his teeth gritted, glaring at the door that closed behind his son. He finally forced himself to lower his eyes and acknowledge the minute arrows glittering in the afternoon sunlight that filtered through the window. He hesitated, as if touching them would make them more real. Eventually he picked them up and rolled them between his thumb and fingertips. A gust of breath emitted from his throat, and he dropped onto his chair. He snapped the arrows in a tightly clenched fist.

Five

Are You Prepared to Pay?

"All I'm saying is that he is our host; you shouldn't have opposed him so openly." Derry leaned against the mantel in the guest sitting room.

"How silly of me," Kyer said sarcastically. "I thought we were having a *discussion*. You ought to have warned me that when Lord Fyrhen's opinion is on the table, nobody is permitted to bring up any other facet of the issue." She had thought her friends were off hunting with Phennil's brothers, and she'd hoped to be alone. She felt bad enough after hearing Phennil's news without Derry adopting his captain role and taking it upon himself to admonish her. She crossed her ankles on the low table, displaying a more relaxed attitude than she felt.

Derry let out a sigh of exasperation. "It wasn't so much what you said as how you said it." She raised her eyebrows at him, and he sat in the chair opposite. "I saw the look on your face. You knew what you were doing, asking that question about his preparations. You were *trying* to provoke him."

"Someone had to. He's completely naïve. I merely brought it up to force the discussion he didn't want to have."

"I do not think that was an appropriate role for you to play."

"Whose is it, then?" She sipped her wine.

"His peers'," Derry said. "His family's. It was shabby of you, especially after his kindness."

She snorted, nearly spitting wine everywhere. "Oh, very kind! He wouldn't have agreed to anything if his wife hadn't let him know it would be socially unacceptable not to. Besides," she added insistently, "I think I showed remarkable restraint given the ridiculousness of the conversation."

"Yes, Kyer, but you have to admit that when you restrain yourself is when you finally come down to everyone else's level of 'overwrought and disrespectful.'"

"Everyone agreed with me! You know they did. I admit I went too far at the end, and I took responsibility for that."

"By the gods, Kyer, you're working for Valrayker! You are always an ambassador for him; your behaviour needs to reflect that, or it speaks ill of him."

"Oh, don't throw that 'ambassador' shit at me, Derry." She pointed a finger at him. "I haven't dedicated my life to him. *You* have and I'll thank you to not keep imposing your Knight's Code of Ethics on me. I'm never going to be you, and the sooner you accept that into your thick head, the sooner we'll arrive at a better understanding."

He said nothing but she saw his wounded pout out of the corner of her eye.

"Anyway, the purpose was served," she went on with an effort at a civil tone. "Maybe now he'll do a little bit of thinking."

"Just like you're going to think about the wisdom of your actions?" he said.

She looked at him coolly. "Okay, speaking of taking on inappropriate roles, *my lord*."

He stiffened and had the decency to look a bit guilty for his patronising manner.

"Are you telling me I'm wrong?" she asked.

His eyes softened. "To feel that way, no. To speak it aloud, yes." His elbows rested on his knees, and he placed his chin on his clasped hands.

She stared at the cold heap of ashes in the fireplace. "You're probably right, damn you."

"And now Fyrhen's not going to give us what we asked for," Derry said bitterly. "That could mean the difference between success on this mission or none. I don't need to tell you this is life or death."

That did it. She stood up. "Okay thanks, Derry," she sneered. "I promise to take all the blame when the mission fails."

Taking her wine cup with her, she swept out of the room and went to her chamber. *Ambassador for Valrayker.* Now Derry had another story to tell him, another strike against her. She wracked her brain for a way to make amends.

Skimnoddle shrank back against the wall outside the sitting room door as Kyer flew out in the other direction. He had hoped to find someone to teach his favourite dice game to. Having overheard the better part of their conversation, the halfling found it very interesting that Derry actually let Kyer call him out for superciliousness. Skimnoddle couldn't imagine anyone else getting away with it.

Teatime found captain, mage, dwarf, and halfling sharing tea, biscuits, and fruit in the sitting room. Phennil and Kyer had declined the invitation to join them. It was the first opportunity they'd had to discuss their options, now that they had none. Skimnoddle rolled dice and counted between bites of biscuit.

"I still say good for her," Janak harrumphed.

"Why Janak, I do believe you are siding with Kyer." Jesqellan smiled.

The dwarf's good eye glared at him. "It's not personal; it's the principle."

"Ah good, I would hate to think that your distaste for Kyer were all just for show. That is the one thing I have come to count on all these many weeks."

Derry frowned into the fire. "I confess I don't quite understand it. He didn't want to give us anything in the first place, but then he agreed to it to please Lady Fyrhen. Doesn't he still want to please her?"

"You mean, why would he stop wanting to help his wife's friend just because of Kyer?" Janak said.

"Well, yes. It comes off like he was looking for an excuse not to give us anything."

Jesqellan cocked his head. "That could be. Maybe we rubbed him the wrong way from the outset. We came in here as guests, prevailing upon his hospitality. Then we prevailed upon his generosity by asking for a favour, and then we insulted him—"

"I like the way you keep saying 'we,'" Janak said. "*We* were quite polite. *She* was less so."

"Ah, there's the Janak we've come to know and love." Derry poured himself more tea.

"I agreed with what she said, but just remember when Kayme refuses to help us that it wasn't my fault," the dwarf said.

Skimnoddle continued to play dice, listening intently. Something about the discussion bothered him, but what precisely he couldn't say. He knew the others did not take him seriously yet, being so new to the group, so he wanted to be sure of himself before speaking. The dice rattled on the table. He was up to 8,500 points in only twelve turns.

"I just can't bring myself to blame him," Jesqellan carried on. "I think if

I were in his position, I, too, would not want to bestow any favours on us."

Derry picked up a jam-covered biscuit and leaned back, crossing his booted ankles. "I would to Aidan that Kyer would learn to use her head and keep our mission at the forefront of her thoughts. I appreciate her ... her energy, but she's got to learn to harness it. And Phennil encourages her by leaping to her defence," he added in a mutter, and Skimnoddle glanced at him.

Jesqellan leaned over and touched the captain's elbow. "Perhaps there will yet be something we can offer," he said hopefully. "Some service we can provide."

Skimnoddle's resounding tones made the others jump.

"I find I must object to this chastisement of my lady," he announced, having discovered what was bothering him. Derry's mouth hung open, the biscuit poised.

"It irks me to hear such blame being placed on Kyer for this apparent loss of offering to Kayme," the halfling went on. "It was my impression, upon embarking on this journey, this adventure, that our ambition was not to find a gift for Kayme, but to find a cure for the Lady Alon Maer. We have not yet failed in that. I see no need to attribute culpability to anyone until such time as true failure occurs. That is all."

They stared at him, speechless.

Derry thoroughly chewed the biscuit and swallowed before nodding and saying, "Thank you, Skimnoddle, for putting things back into perspective."

Phennil's book lay in his lap. He hadn't slept well. Unable to concentrate, he let his mind wander, communing with the ancient trees outside the window of his bedroom. He had come and gone and come again, but those old friends were always there. So dependable. They never let their emotions get the better of them. They did not promise one thing then change their minds just because someone offended them. Their feelings could be hurt, certainly, and once in a great while, they even were moved to anger. Even in their worst moments, the Old Folk were always better at communicating than any person Phennil had ever known. They never minded when he talked their ears off, *so to speak*. They could always be relied upon to give their honest opinions with tact and diplomacy, caring for the feelings of those who lived among them. *Much moreso than we two-footers do for each other*, the elf thought dejectedly.

A rap on his door drew him away from the window. "Yes?" he called. The door opened and noiseless feet stepped in. "Mother!" He smiled and straightened his slumped body, tossing the book onto his side table.

"Phennil, my son," she said warmly, "I hope I am not interrupting?"

"No, of course not, Mother! Where you're concerned, anytime is a good time." He rose and put his arms around her slight frame.

"I'm sorry I haven't been in to see you before now."

"It's all right. I'm glad you came by. There's so much to tell you! I've tried to remember each and every thing I've done so I could share it with you. I don't even know where to begin."

She smiled, and sat on his bed. "I am always overjoyed to see you, Phennil, but there is ever an underlying sadness, knowing it is only for a short time and that you must leave again."

"I know," he said. "I never know whether it's a good thing to come home for these short visits or if I'd be better to stay away."

"No! Never that." His mother laughed. "Staying away would not do at all. I should become bored to self-destruction if I didn't have your visits to look forward to, short or not. You're the only one in this family who ever does anything interesting. Who would tell me stories of distant lands and fill my dreams with exciting adventures and heroes and heroines? And for the gods' sake, who would let me know what's really going on in the world? Your *father* certainly does nothing to find out!"

Phennil stared. "Mother!"

He saw the twinkle in her eye, and they both laughed.

"Honestly, Phennil, he's been driving me crazy lately." She sighed. "He does worry about Dregor, you know. I think he feels his choice is truly what is best for our people. Many of the elves do not agree, including Rupi and Paullin." She saw the look on Phennil's face. "Oh yes, your brothers are not blind. They won't let this go on."

"I went and talked to him last night." Phennil told his mother what he'd said to his father. She tilted her head in surprise. "He told me not to come back," Phennil finished glumly.

"Well, that's rubbish. Don't you listen to him." Phennil looked a question at her. "I was Lady of the Donnan Forest long before he was lord of it," she said with a smile. "I have always left military decisions up to him, but he does not have absolute power and cannot decide things of that nature on his own."

Phennil grinned and placed his hand on hers. Though his was slightly larger, they had the same shape and dexterity.

"Your friend Kyer is very beautiful," she said suddenly.

"Well, yes," he said, taken aback.

"How long have you known her?"

"A couple of months, I guess. Valrayker met her in Wanaka and asked her to join us."

"You're glad he did."

"Well . . . sure." He smiled shyly.

"You admire her?"

Phennil shrugged then nodded because in that moment he knew she was right.

"She seems to be of good character. Are you sure there isn't even a little bit of elf in her?" she asked thoughtfully. "Have you seen her ears? And surely you've noticed her fluidity of motion."

"Oh, Mother, I doubt it," Phennil chuckled, shaking his head. "That's just wishful thinking. She has no elven qualities that I can see. That hot temper and stubbornness clearly mark her as a human through and through."

"Still, I have no objection to humans. Your father may feel differently, but I've already pointed out that he may not be of sound mind at the moment. It is widely known that half-elves possess many remarkable qualities."

Phennil laughed. "Oh, Mother, are you suggesting I pursue Kyer as a partner?"

"Why not?"

"Ha! You're only saying this because she's the first woman you've seen me with since Merribell left me high and dry."

"And even if I am, I say again, why not?"

"For the simple reason that Kyer Halidan knows her own mind better than I know the shape of my hand! If I were on her list of desires, she'd already have me."

"Don't brush off the idea completely, my son. A woman who knows her own mind is quite capable of changing it."

Phennil threw his head back and laughed, hugging his mother. "Thanks for looking out for me."

"You could start trying to get into her good graces by taking a bath," she suggested with a crooked smile.

"No way! The easiest way to scare a girl off is to be too obvious. If I bathe, I run the risk of chasing her away forever."

"Oh, Phennil, it's so good to see you."

"You too."

"But that isn't the only reason I wanted to see you today."

"Oh?"

"Your father may have overturned his promise of aid for your venture, but I have not. Here." She handed him a small bundle wrapped in a piece of deep red cloth.

Phennil unwound the cloth. Inside was a silver bell so tiny that he could have concealed it in one hand and so bright that he was afraid to touch it lest it tarnish before his eyes. As if reading his mind, his mother said, "Don't worry; you can't spoil it; it's magical."

Phennil's eyes widened. "Where did you get this?"

"It was a wedding gift from a former suitor. It's magic but I never had a chance to use it. I was told that its ring can be heard for miles around but only by those that are trusted by the bearer. They will be able to follow the sound and locate it. It could be quite useful for an adventurer like yourself."

"Then I ought to keep it myself and not give it to Kayme. But, Mother, are you sure you want to part with this?"

"Oh, well, one shouldn't have such an attachment to *things*, should one? Anyway, if it can help your cause, it will be worth it. I've never had a use for it, and it's going to waste in my drawer. Besides, I know it is something that will . . . catch Kayme's attention. Try giving him your other things first because if you don't have to give it to him, you may as well keep it and I hope you find it handy someday. But if those other things don't suffice, this certainly will."

"You're so sure of this?"

His mother sighed and smiled gently. "Kayme was the one who gave it to me."

Kyer's conscience gnawed at her even as they lost sight of Plicatha behind them. It wasn't that she wished she hadn't said anything to Lord

Fyrhen. It was just that a part of her saw Derry's point: they were on a peaceful mission, nothing related to Dregor and the allied strategies. It might have been a different story if they had been seeking Lord Fyrhen's participation in the war effort and he'd refused on the grounds he stated. This visit was not the time to discuss such things.

She should apologize to Derry. *But I just can't bear to hear that smug tone of his again.* It wasn't as if he needed to be told he was right. Kyer stared at the road ahead of her, every moment expecting Derry to try to break the silence by asking her what was on her mind. *He knows. He's waiting for me to say it.*

The road through the forest was a trade route, servicing Plicatha's connection with towns beyond the forest. This morning the company had taken the northern fork that headed for Trosh, bypassing the eastern turnoff for Prost. The dense forest had thinned as though it had been sifted, giving way to maples and pines, and the wider road allowed them to ride side by side along the wagon tracks. Occasionally they had to sidestep out of the road for a buggy or cart to pass in the opposite direction. The traffic was helpful in hiding their trail, but they continued to play it safe, having Jesqellan toss his Tracking Confusion spell every once in a while.

Kyer and Derry plodded along behind Skimnoddle and Jesqellan, who were arguing the merits of copper versus tin for the purpose of both magic and cooking.

"Look, you're right, okay?" she blurted out in an undertone. "I'll try not to mouth off every time someone irks me."

Derry chuckled softly.

Anger flared. "You don't believe me, do you?"

"Don't get so defensive. It's only that you sounded irked even as you said it."

She sighed and glared ahead of her again. *Right again, damn him.*

"Anyway," Derry continued, "it isn't that I'm asking you to change the way you feel. You might try a cautious assumption that people are on our side. Try not to get your back up so easily."

"Lord Fyrhen wasn't on our side."

He seemed about to speak then let his breath go. He shook his head. "You're missing the point."

She gave in. "No, Derry, I'm not. Really. I'll try to be more . . ." She couldn't think of a way to end the sentence.

"How about 'patient with people'?" Derry suggested.

He was smiling now, so Kyer knew things were all right.

There remained nearly a week in the journey to Kayme's tower at the base of the Black Mountains, on the eastern edge of the Plains of Kalkamar. The company camped in forest, plain, and foothill with, thankfully, no further incident of attack by wild animals, magically enlarged or otherwise. With the spring showers, they were very happy to have Valrayker's tent cloth and stout pegs. They fashioned support poles from the wood around, and though the shelter was meagre, they were grateful for it. Each night Kyer's sense of foreboding deepened as they moved closer to their destination.

Kayme lived in the Guarded Realm—likely his tower was built there ages before the Guarded Realm existed as such. He did not claim allegiance to the allied forces, any more than Lord Fyrhen. He held himself aloof from all the goings on in the surrounding world. Valrayker had said he had reason to believe, however, that the wizard would be more disposed to siding with them than with the dark lord, should the need for choice arise. Kayme's magic was, by all accounts, every bit as powerful as Dregor's, though he wasn't as demonstrative. "And considering Kayme could have already taken sides with Dregor but hasn't is something," Valrayker had said. "He is a quiet man, craves privacy, and likely just can't be bothered to take a stand against Dregor. A showdown between the two of them would be interesting to see, actually. But really, I think Kayme would find it amusing to lend his support to the underdog in a case like this."

That conviction of Valrayker's gave the group courage as they drew nearer to their destination, and discussion naturally turned toward what they might encounter.

"I will take on the task of speaker," Jesqellan said. "As second, as well as the only mage in our party, I believe it is my role. Not to mention that if he deigns to entertain our request at all, he may be more likely to do so with a fellow magic user. Not that I would never presume to be his equal," he added modestly.

"Surely he will at least listen to our request," Derry said.

"Well, we're not asking him to contribute anything to the fight against Dregor, anyway," Phennil pointed out.

Jesqellan shook his head and frowned. "I can't imagine what it will take to persuade the most powerful wizard in Rydris to involve himself in a strictly personal matter."

"I'm sure we'll be able to come up with some sort of arrangement," Kyer said. "Living all alone like that, there has to be something he wants."

The charm of the once-knight Fredric Heyland was bound to come in handy occasionally. Odd, though, that he should use it to oppose the one who trained him in it. But he banished that thought from his mind as he employed his talent in speaking with the young elven scout.

"We have been racing after Captain Derry for several days, with news to impart," he explained.

The fellow was very sorry to say that Valrayker's company had left two days ago. "But if the message is as important as you say, I wish you all speed in catching them up." The elf saluted them as he sent them north on the tracks of their prey.

Close. So close they were. Hunter could practically hear the rasp of sharp steel on bone.

Jesqellan felt the weight of responsibility, but he did not allow it to slow his pace. The company rounded the spur of the mountain, the last obstacle before the bay of grassland, at the centre of which stood the tower of Kayme, like a lone piece on a game board. The riders reined in their horses and sat silently for a moment. Jesqellan felt the bite of the stiff grass more keenly under his feet as he surveyed their destination with the trepidation of a juvenile. The westering sun cast a hard-edged U-shaped shadow to surround the tower like a claw about to enclose it in its grip and Jesqellan sympathized with it. He fully expected that grip to grasp him equally tightly the moment he entered the tower. If the wizard didn't kill them all with a wave of a dismissive hand. The mage clutched his staff to his chest and swallowed.

Dark windows stared at the group from high up the sides of the ominous obsidian structure, immeasurably deep eyes performing sentry duty for their master. "Do you suppose he knows we're coming?" Kyer asked rhetorically.

Jesqellan was certain the wizard had been watching them from afar.

Derry recovered his voice. "We will be required to relinquish our weapons." Jesqellan sensed his disquietude.

"If that is what is required, that is what we will do," the mage said to show that he, at least, would not hinder the progress of the interview, though being parted from his staff would undoubtedly leave him feeling ill at ease. It was up to him to show leadership.

They started toward the narrow, cone-shaped tower. A railing rimmed the flat apex; a perfect place to observe the stars.

"He lives in that place all alone?" Phennil said in awe.

"I have to admit I feel quite diminished down here," Jesqellan said. "I was cognizant of Kayme's vast power, but to be here, now, and see what he commands... Suddenly the Tunnel spell I am working on seems far less impressive."

The tower grew.

They rode around its west side. A small outbuilding with wooden double doors and low roof squatted next to it. A stable. Derry led Donnagill inside, fighting some protest, though the warhorse calmed down once he smelled the food that awaited him. Kyer and the others followed, their mounts seemingly reassured by the larger animal's newfound comfort. Jesqellan had no experience with the care of horses, yet even he could see that this was as well-kept a stable as anyone could ask for. Large stalls bedded with fresh wheat straw and wood chips; feed bins newly filled with hay, oats, and maize; and plenty of drinking water. Shelves and racks held all the supplies a rider could need, with brushes and combs, blankets and neatly folded cloths, saddle soap and leather oil. Their host had provided as hospitable accommodations for the animals as anywhere. Jesqellan gave a small shudder to see pails of *warm* soapy water standing at the entrance to each stall. The power behind these features was unimaginable. If the travellers were unwelcome here, at least their host did not hold the animals responsible.

The mage hovered by the door, glancing over his shoulder at the tower entrance. He ran through his rehearsed words of introduction, and entreated whatever goddess might be listening to protect him.

A short time later, Kyer gave Trig a comforting pat and they closed and secured the stable door. Derry forced confidence into the lift of his chin, and Jesqellan walked beside him, assuming his role of the party's mage and captain's second. Janak and Skimnoddle followed them up the front stairs, Janak carrying the little mahogany case containing their meagre offering.

Kyer and Phennil brought up the rear. Phennil fiddled nervously with something in the pouch at his waist.

"What have you got there?" she asked.

"Oh, it's just something I . . . nothing."

A thick, red-gold rope with a knot at the bottom hung like a dead weight next to the blackened oak door. Derry took one deep breath and pulled the cord. If it caused a bell to ring inside, the travellers could not hear it. Kyer's heart pounded out the moments, which amounted to a lot more than she thought necessary. Maybe he was on the top floor when the bell sounded? She had a vision of the wizard standing inside with his ear to the door, purposely making them wait, and chuckling to himself at the nerves he was aggravating. *But*, she reasoned, *if he has such a dim view of visitors, why have a bell cord at all?*

Finally there was a thud of wood on metal, and the door swung open, swiftly and noiselessly. To their surprise, the doorman was Kayme himself. Kyer had never laid eyes on him before, but there was no question that this was the fearsome man they hoped to call host. That wordless greeting was too aloof and self-assured for it to be anyone else.

Kyer's immediate thought upon regarding the august face was that their errand was doomed to fail. Kayme had no time for them. Sure, he had come to the door himself, but she sensed that it was less to entertain guests or their whims than for his own amusement. Kyer felt decidedly small and inferior.

Even from her lower position on the staircase, Kyer was drawn to Kayme's eyes. Blue, as startling as Phennil's, though for different reason. Where Phennil's were bright, like a cloudless summer sky, Kayme's were deep, like sapphires, almost glowing, in an age-defying face as dark as the tower in which he resided. They passed vaguely over the travellers. Apparently unthreatened by the diversified cluster on his doorstep, Kayme stepped back and held his arm out.

They filed past him. Kyer avoided eye contact and repressed a small shudder. She stopped next to Phennil in a small, square, windowless entryway, just large enough for the entire party to stand within and the front door to be closed. A candelabrum hanging from the high ceiling cast weird, soft-edged shadows on the plank floor. Kyer saw no other door. Were they going to have to make their request bunched up in here?

"Leave your weapons in the cabinet." His voice was tenor-ranged, stern yet not arrogant. The sapphires pointed out the location, and one by one, Kyer and her companions relinquished their defences, some willingly, some begrudgingly. The floor-to-ceiling cabinet had shelves near the bottom for smaller weapons and a series of hooks and clasps higher up for swords and polearms. She unbuckled her belt of sword and daggers and chose a hook for it. Then she bent and pulled out her boot dagger. It clattered in after the others onto one of the shelves below.

As the weapons thunked and clanked into place, Kyer observed their kingly host. He was not quite as tall as Derry, and not as broad across the shoulders. Those shoulders held a cloak of grey over a tunic of some shimmery fabric in a deep red that sometimes looked black. Black trousers and a black sash about his slender waist. Dark curly hair, tousled and spiked, with a few hints of grey speckled throughout. Oval face, with features that might have been a jewel setting, so well-defined and precise. And the eyes . . . The wizard was ageless: about forty and at the same time much, much older. He radiated an energy both repellent and magnetic. Kyer couldn't keep her eyes off him. *Did he dress up just for us?*

"Your staff is also a weapon, dear mage," he murmured.

Jesqellan hid his frown with a bow and placed his staff in the cabinet next to Janak's axe. Then, with no tactile assistance, the heavy metal mesh door clanged shut, sealing the weapons in their prison.

"Don't worry. Your effects will be returned to you upon your departure. None of you is capable of opening the door."

For all that Kyer would normally be tempted to try after such a speech, in this case, she believed him. He wheeled around with a sweep of his cloak, and to her surprise, a doorway had opened in the wall by the front door. She followed her friends behind him into a sitting room, larger than the entrance hall and better equipped for a discussion. Cushioned benches and sofas lined the walls, upholstered in rich greens, blues, and reds. The furniture looked comfortable, but nobody was disposed to sit. The chamber felt as homey as Kyer's mother's front room, though Della would have covered the blank wall on the left with a quilt or painting. All the walls were dark stone but possessed surprising warmth. Another chandelier hung from this ceiling, and its light was supported by the natural light from the corner window. *Window?* Kyer regarded it suspiciously. She was certain she had seen no corresponding window on the outside of the building. She moved toward it but was startled into an about-face when Kayme's voice began again.

"You must pardon my way of greeting. It isn't often I have visitors, and I'm afraid I can trust no one immediately. I never trust anyone entirely. Help yourselves to beverages." He nodded at a low, maplewood table with two pitchers, one of water and one of a dark brown liquid that steamed. There was some irony in his expectation that they would trust *him* immediately, but Skimnoddle did not seem to have noticed it. He leaned over the hot stuff, sniffed it loudly, poured himself a mug, and took a sip, pronouncing it "unparalleled." Their host looked amused and nodded his thanks for the halfling's appreciation of his brew.

The others, seeing no adverse effects exhibited by Skimnoddle, finally accepted the offer as well, and soon all held mugs of either hot or cold liquid. As Kyer replaced the water jug on the table, she glanced at the wizard. He was watching her profile with his head cocked to one side, as if waiting to get a better look. She straightened involuntarily and as his eyes fell fully upon her, they widened in surprise.

"Oh!" he said, "I haven't seen one of your kind in a long time."

My kind? Surely he had seen a woman in recent history. *Well, perhaps not, if he spends so much time alone in this dismal place.*

"Let us not waste time." His eyes shifted abruptly from her to roam over the entire group. "I know you are here to ask something of me—no, that is not a demonstration of my power. Nobody comes to see Kayme unless there is some need. I may live like a recluse, but I am no stranger to the ways and means of the outside world. Now, tell me what you want so I may reject you and get on with my work."

Jesqellan stepped forward and cleared his throat. "Lord Valrayker of Equart sent us on behalf of his friend, Lord Kien Bartheylen of Shae, Koral, and Heath. Lord Kien's wife is dreadfully ill . . ." Gaining confidence Jesqellan went on to describe her illness and their theory of how Kayme might help. The wizard looked bored, even a little annoyed, as if he had heard the same tale countless times. Even as Jesqellan spoke, the wizard's blue eyes wandered over the party to rest again on Kyer. She returned his look, but for some reason could not withstand his stare and turned away feeling somehow ashamed of her weakness.

"The healers at Heatha are highly skilled, and yet—"

"What is your name, my dear?" Kayme interrupted. Jesqellan stopped short in irritation and cleared his throat. Derry looked at Kyer as if she had committed yet another social blunder. She was tempted to tell Kayme off for his rudeness, but the wizard's voice was much gentler than she had expected from one so wise and ancient. It was soothing. The tension in the room intensified in spite of it, and her companions shifted uncomfortably.

"Kyer Halidan," she answered with her chin up in an attempt to disguise her uneasiness. She was both afraid and thrilled by the way he looked at her.

"Well. Interesting." He nodded slowly. "Welcome."

"Can you tell us about the antidote, Kayme?" Derry broke off their little exchange. The wizard snapped his gaze in the younger man's direction. Kyer felt a glimmer of disappointment that confused her.

"Can I tell you?" Kayme ambled around the chamber. "Yes, of course I can tell you. The condition from which the Lady Alon Maer suffers is one I have heard of and even seen before. Naturally I can tell you. I am Kayme." With this, he threw a glance at them over his shoulder, and his eyebrows asked if they had dared to forget the fact. "*Will* I tell you? Hmm . . . that is another question entirely."

Derry bristled.

"You cannot expect something for nothing, you know," Kayme went on with an occasional sidelong glance at Kyer. Sure she saw the thoughts forming and evolving in his mind, her belly fluttered with something less than contentment. "What is in it for me, hmm? People come and ask me for favours because they know my wisdom is unrivalled. Why should I do it? Do I ever ask others for favours in return?"

He stood just a few feet from Kyer, looking pointedly at her with an odd little smile. "For everything there is a price."

She shivered in spite of her efforts at calm and willed her gaze to stand on Phennil.

"Are you prepared to pay?" the wizard hinted.

Jesqellan broke the tense silence by clearing his throat again. "Yes, Kayme, we gratefully acknowledge the time you have taken from your tasks to speak with us and have brought these fine jewels all the way from Shael. We offer them in return for this knowledge." Alon's jewels were flawlessly beautiful but here, now that they were faced with the one who could either accept or reject them, Kyer sensed the deficiency of their gift. She silently applauded Jesqellan's attempt to heighten interest in their meagre offering. "Would you care to see them?" He gestured for Janak to bring forth the chest. The dwarf moved to do so but was stopped by a wave of Kayme's hand.

"Bah!" the wizard said with mild exasperation. "I have more jewels than I know what to do with. I'd like something . . . different."

Guilt lurched through Kyer. She was responsible for their lack of a more interesting gift.

Phennil's hand moved to his pouch again, and he opened his mouth to speak but stopped himself.

"I realize our offering is perhaps somewhat common." Derry resumed his usual diplomatic tone, aware of how easy it might be to offend the wizard. "But we've come a very long way, and we don't have much time to go on a hunt for something else. What do you have in mind?"

"Hunt?" Kayme said impatiently. "Nobody said anything about a hunt. Is it not obvious to you fools? Why, my fee is right here in this room! If she's willing."

Dumbfounded shock chilled the room as her friends gawked at Kyer, and awaited her reaction.

She just stared at the wizard, stunned. "What do you want from *me*?"

Kayme moved over to her. "Do not be frightened, my dear," he smiled. "I merely am asking for your company this evening; that is all."

She looked at him sidelong. "What does that entail, my 'company'?"

"You need an antidote. I need a companion for the evening," he said reasonably.

"Why not ask Jesqellan?" she grumbled, glancing at the frowning mage, whose eyes brightened hopefully. "I'm sure he'd love to—"

"I don't need to spend time with Jesqellan. I need to spend time with you."

Kyer had a bad feeling that the wizard would not be persuaded.

The sapphires beheld her with a quiet intensity that made moths flutter up her back. "You must trust me." The wizard's voice was silky as a rose petal.

Kyer pulled herself away and walked to the window, annoyed at the extraordinary combination of fear and attraction. "Why should I trust you?" she demanded.

"It is you who needs the antidote." Kayme sat on a cushioned seat and crossed one knee over the other. "I don't see that you have a choice."

Damn him! What did he want from her? How did he hope she'd amuse him? How could she walk blindly into the unknown with this man who could do anything he wished? He'd taken her weapons, not that they'd help her if it came to that, but how could she possibly defend herself if he tried anything . . . *magical*? Still, she debated, if that is what it would take to get the information they so desperately needed . . . And maybe this was her chance to make amends for bungling the arrangement with Phennil's father.

Derry couldn't stand the silence. "We cannot allow this." He confronted Kayme. "There must be something else we can give you."

"No." Kayme smiled, enjoying the distress he had caused.

"We simply cannot allow a member of our party to—to—*prostitute* herself." Derry begged the company for support.

"If there is a decision to be made here, it will be mine," Kyer interrupted, wheeling from the window to face him. "It is not a question of whether or not you will allow this to happen."

Derry gave her a warning look.

Kyer glared back. "If we don't leave here with the antidote for Alon Maer, we fail. Plain and simple."

"But it isn't up to you to do this on your own," put in Phennil. "This is our mission as a company, not just yours."

"You were all pretty quick to remind me this was life and death back in Plicatha," she snapped. "I took the blame for Lord Fyrhen's decision then, and I take it now. This is my chance to make it up."

"It's not necessary, Kyer," Phennil said earnestly. "We have another option—"

"Do we?" Kyer gestured over to where the wizard sat with his arms folded in patient confidence, gentlemanly enough to at least pretend he couldn't hear their discussion. "*He's* made up his mind! Do you suppose even if we were able to produce some incredible magical object out of thin air he would want it now?" They withered under her defiant gaze. "There's nothing else he will accept." She wiped her palms on her trousers.

"I'm afraid she's right." Jesqellan's jaw jutted to one side, and Kyer knew he was put out. But she did not have the time or the inclination to try to mollify him.

Derry massaged his head as if the decision had caused him physical pain.

Phennil lowered himself into a chair and stared at the floor.

Finally Kyer turned to Kayme and spoke cautiously. "If I agree to go with you now, it does not mean I agree to everything hereafter."

Kayme nodded in agreement.

She looked at her friends to see if they were satisfied.

The captain made his final decision. "Very well." Derry put a hand on her arm and whispered. "Just be on your guard."

Kyer steeled herself. "I will go with you."

Kayme smiled and bowed again. "I am deeply honoured." He then whirled around to the men. "A meal awaits you in the adjoining chamber. Then follow those stairs to your sleeping quarters." He took Kyer by the hand and led her toward the blank black wall. She gasped as a small doorway appeared in the smooth surface, and halted her footsteps. Heart hammering in her ribcage she swallowed her trepidation and stepped through.

When it clicked behind them, the door vanished.

"Great!" Derry threw up his hands. "We can't even go after them."

"I think that was the intention," Janak said dryly.

"Well, I am not comfortable with this at all." Derry paced, and rubbed his hair.

"Neither am I." Phennil laid his hand on the pouch on his belt.

"Can we go eat now?" Skimnoddle said. "I'm starving." Derry ignored him.

Jesqellan grabbed Derry's arm. "Kyer is strong," he said with warm assurance. "And she is not a fool."

Derry took one final brooding glance at the wall where the door used to be, wishing he could at least see where Kayme had taken her. But if Derry was the leader of this group, he could not let his concern overcome him.

"You're right."

He was closest to the door Kayme had indicated, so the others followed him through it into the chilly chamber that was to be their lounge for the duration of their stay.

Six

More Powerful Than You Know

Whatever Kyer had expected, it was not what lay before her.

Kayme led Kyer into a large chamber, about the size of the bailey at Shael Castle. Countless candles and wall sconces reflected off the shiny black walls, giving the space an atmosphere of elegance. Tapestries on the walls depicted scenes of castles, rivers, lakes, and forests. The images were startlingly realistic, with colours so vivid, she was fooled for a moment into thinking they weren't wall hangings at all, but windows into other worlds. The longer she stared at them, the more they came alive. Were those clouds actually moving? Was that flag on the topmost turret fluttering in a breeze unfelt by herself, with eagles soaring high above it? In her limited experience, Kyer had never seen such an artistic use of magic.

Warm rugs scattered the stone floor, and a couple of armchairs and a sofa encircled the fire in its elaborately carved stone fireplace. The centrepiece of the seating arrangement was a table adorned with an enormous vase of extraordinarily beautiful spring wildflowers: tiger lilies, foxglove, alpine lupine, honeysuckle, and their fresh scent reached Kyer and brought the outdoors within the tower so vividly that her shoulders dropped and her neck softened. The dark wood of the nearby dining table shone, but not as much as the intricately etched candelabra of astonishingly bright silver which stood in the centre. Another table held liqueur bottles and glasses. On the far wall was a glossy cherry writing desk. A golden harp stood on a rug with a chair ready next to it.

She took in the whole setting with breathless wonder. "But this is beautiful."

"Were you expecting instruments of torture?" He spoke so gently, she returned his smile.

A curving staircase climbed the far wall. Kayme gestured to it as he spoke.

"I am certain you would like to refresh yourself after your long journey. You will find everything you need upstairs in your chamber. Take as much time as you need." He lowered his arm and bowed. "I'll be waiting."

Kyer thanked him somewhat awkwardly. She was in awe of him, and this room, and the situation in which she had so suddenly found herself. She ascended the stairs, her thudding heart loud enough to echo in the chamber. She could feel his eyes on her as she climbed and glanced back down at him before opening the door at the top. He bowed to her again, and she thought of his words, *One of your kind*. She passed through the door, out of sight of that alarming gaze.

A landing gave way to another door on her right. She opened it and went up two more stairs to a large bedchamber, furnished simply but beautifully in rich, warm colours and textures. Bed, washstand, wardrobe in the corner next to a full-length mirror. A fire in the grate cast the warmth of summer over the room. A bathtub near the window steamed, and the scent of lavender permeated the chamber. A cotton robe was draped across a chair and warming by the fire. Either it had all been prepared magically—she shivered—or Kayme had lightning-quick servants.

Leaning out the window, she looked down to see how far up this room was. *Nope, I don't think I'll jump.* She craned her neck upward to see how much more tower was above her. The sunset silhouetted the building, giving it a glowing aura. Many more stories were stacked above this one. Why did one solitary man need such a huge home?

She opened the wardrobe to see if Kayme had provided her with anything decent to wear for dinner. How could she doubt him? Though she wondered at his choices: Four dresses, of red, gold, green, and blue. Kyer couldn't remember if she'd ever worn a dress.

She slipped out of her boots and stockings to scrunch her feet into the thick, soft fur rugs that cushioned the stone floor. Dipping her hand suspiciously into the bath water, she considered her vulnerability. She ought to remain on guard, yet she felt safe here. It was unlikely Kayme would kill her with a hot bath. Saving her caution for later, she peeled off her grubby clothes.

Derry suspended his suspicions at the decent meal that awaited them on the table, and no one said much while they ate. The one topic that was on all their minds already coursed heavily through the room. It made for a noisy evening. Derry wished someone would say something to drown out the reverberating thoughts in his head. "Please pass the carrots," was the best he could come up with, and it had little to no effect.

Skimnoddle was the only one who did not seem vexed by Kyer's absence. All evening he chattered about what Kyer and Kayme might be up to and if they were hitting it off to Kayme's satisfaction. Derry gave him his best warning glare, but it went unnoticed. The captain slouched in his chair by the fire.

"Any bets on which can drink the other under the table?" Skimnoddle asked.

Janak guffawed. "*That* would be a contest worth seeing."

Derry shifted, and failed to get comfortable. "I don't know how you can joke about it."

"Perhaps I see things in a different light," Skimnoddle answered. "We had nothing with which to trade for the knowledge we seek. Kyer had. It follows that if we wish to save the lady, this is the right course of action."

Phennil stepped in. "But it's wrong that she should have to sacrifice herself—"

"We hope she is *sacrificing* nothing," Derry corrected the elf irritably.

"Kayme gave his word to do nothing against her will," Jesqellan said.

Janak kicked Skimnoddle's boot. "Knowing her she might very well be willing."

Skimnoddle snorted. "Say, do you suppose there might be a problem with humans and wizards being . . . you know, *compatible*?"

"Enough!" Derry flexed his fingers and quelled an urge to reach for the halfling's throat. "Speaking of her as if she were a strumpet. We have no idea what Kayme wants or what he's capable of."

"Let's just hope he doesn't say anything to set her off," Janak said. "She's like flint in a strawpile, that one. If she spouts off to him like she did to Lord Fyrhen, we'll not get what we came for, and by the Hammer God, I don't want to imagine what he'd do to her."

"Oh, surely she won't be so foolish again," Derry said under his breath.

Kyer emerged at the top of the stairs to feel harp music billowing up and around her. She fixed one fierce resolution into her mind and her will: *Resist him.*

Kayme saw her and rose from the harp as though she'd lifted him. The notes wafted around the room for a strangely long time. In the bright light of the fire and lamps, he gazed up at her as if he'd never seen her before. And truly no one had seen Kyer like this. She had never felt so . . . feminine. The forest green gown of crushed velvet clung to her figure and gained fullness in the skirt as it fell to her feet. The scooping neckline hid her medallion, though its chain was visible, and the fabric revealed her upper body strength. Her neck and collarbones were flattered even more by her hair, which shone and was swept up, gathered loosely atop her head with a comb. Kayme's eyes met hers, and a tremor passed through her.

One hand held the green cloth out of the way of the calf-hide boots that cradled her feet with the softness of moss. The other slid down the railing to steady her as she descended the stairs. She tried to frown, to concentrate. But she was unnerved by the way he looked at her, as if he could see through her. And as a flush crept up her bare neck, her resolution wavered and she felt herself smile at him. Her lips quivered.

Could she resist him? Did she want to?

He held out his hand as she reached him, and she placed her calloused one in it. His fingers blended agility with strength, and his hand enveloped hers like a glove of the finest cloth. His touch sent tingles through her core to her limbs. She was loath for him to release it. He led her the few steps to the dining table then turned and regarded her thoughtfully.

"I thought you might choose that one."

"The dress?"

"Yes. It suits you . . . perfectly."

Kyer forced an air of nonchalance. "It's been such a long time since I've dressed this way; I don't feel like it suits me at all." She remembered her resolve and gently pulled her hand out of his. *That was noteworthy self-control.*

"Oh, believe me. It does," Kayme insisted. He had not taken his eyes off her. "You are lovely."

She had heard the words before, dozens of times, but never had she been moved by them. Never had she been charmed by a mere compliment. This was different. And she liked it. She wondered with amusement how the others would react if they saw her.

Kayme looked at her fixedly. Once again she fought back a blushing smile and failed.

Suddenly his mood shifted. He took on a more casual attitude, less intense.

"Would you agree to dine with me?"

"Yes, I will agree to that." She hadn't much choice since she was famished. Yet his behaviour was that of the perfect gentleman as he motioned her to a chair at the table and helped to seat her. She saw no reason not to trust him thus far. Still, she must not be careless.

The table, which was bare when she went upstairs, was now a dazzling display of light. The candles glimmered off the silver-lidded platters, gilt-edged plates and silverware, crystal water goblets, and silver wine cups. The luxury of it was overwhelming to the girl from the northern farming village. Her host's face glowed with pleasure, and she saw that her own reflection was not dissimilar. Kayme poured white wine into her cup.

"I assure you I have not poisoned anything." Kayme smiled cheekily.

"No, I don't suppose you would need to, you being a wizard and me completely unarmed and all."

"Ah, unarmed, yes, but not defenceless." Kyer's eyebrows shot up. His eyes twinkled at her puzzlement. "And may I add, dangerously disarming?" Raising his cup, he toasted, "To the many facets that make a woman alluring, beauty and strength among them."

Kyer had fully recovered and met his eye evenly. Then she raised her cup and drank to that.

She had never dined in so formal a manner and had been eating nothing but mushy mixtures from a tin cup for so long that she was thankful for the dim memories of Gareth and Della trying to teach her at least basic table etiquette. Even the meals she took at Shael Castle were not as formal as this. Kayme did not embarrass her by noticing when she nearly forgot to lay her serviette on her lap nor when she caught herself eating with her knife, out of habit. It was a lot to get used to, the attire and the elegant meal.

She was not the sort who easily lost her composure and did not allow these small trials to impede her enjoyment. Kyer ate strips of grilled meat in red wine sauce, rack of lamb, rosemary and mint potatoes, asparagus, and baby carrots. There were balls of melon and chunks of apple to dip in warm chocolate or caramel. And plenty of wine. Kyer's initial unease was quickly replaced with contentment. They conversed lightly about Kyer's journey north, her mission for Valrayker, and her childhood in Hreth.

When they had eaten their fill, Kayme suggested they move over to the fire.

Kyer took her cup of wine and sat on the sofa. Kayme went to the small table and poured a drink of something new for each of them. He handed her the glass and sat in an armchair. "A liqueur made from elderflowers."

She sipped. "It's good. Do you gather your own elderflowers?"

"Occasionally."

"Do you never leave here? To travel even?"

"I travelled in my youth," he told her, "but I have spent much of my life here. I have everything I need and contact with others when I desire it. And sometimes when I do not."

"Are we intruding on your privacy, Kayme?" Kyer said, just a little pertly. "You didn't have to allow us to stay, you know."

"And I very nearly did not!" Kayme replied. "But for your presence, I likely would have sent your friends away."

"Why?" She overlooked the part about her own influence on his decision. "You keep saying you live here alone. You have all the time in the world for anything and everything you want to do. So what do you have against helping people out once in a while? Are you afraid people will start to like you?" She caught her breath as she realized she might be pushing her luck with her bold familiarity.

The wizard did not respond right away, and Kyer looked into the pale amber liquid in her tumbler, awaiting condemnation. Yet as she waited, she got the bizarre impression that he was searching for the right words, as if he were equally dependent on her good opinion of him. She had no idea why the idea came to her, but she knew she was right. She sipped the sweet liquid again.

"I have no wish to be a god," he said finally. "I live alone because, for the most part, I like it this way. Though sometimes—" He cut himself off, as if about to give away more than he intended. "My purposes are much more suited to being feared and held in awe. If my reputation were to grow as a benevolent figure who would grant wishes to all and sundry, how long would my solitude last?"

"It's okay." Kyer shrugged. "I get it. Though I wish you'd made it easier in our case." Another sip and she placed her empty liqueur tumbler on the table.

"I would not say I made it difficult in your case," Kayme said quietly. "Have you found it difficult?"

Damn. She'd walked right into that one. But she couldn't lie. "No. You're right."

"It is not as if this arrangement is one I make all the time."

"Then why did you? Why me?" The question could no longer remain unspoken.

"I was curious. I wanted the chance to . . . speak with you in private. I felt that your company was something I have been waiting for."

Throughout his response, Kyer felt her skin prickle. There was something odd about this. She recalled his comment when he first saw her and felt certain his curiosity was not merely idle. "You were relying too much on someone you'd never laid eyes on before," Kyer replied. "What if I hadn't agreed to come with you?"

"Then you would all have left without the information you seek."

"And you would have spent the evening alone again," she said pointedly.

"Still, a greater loss on your part than mine, don't you think?"

"I guess that depends on why you wanted to 'speak with me in private.'"

Kayme was silent a moment. "I knew you would agree to it," he went on matter-of-factly. "You had to. You are a warrior dedicated to your mission and will do what is necessary to be successful."

Kyer frowned. "You mean you think you could suggest *anything* and I'd go for it just to get what I need?" This was a dangerous assumption on his part, and a shiver of alarm rushed through her. "What if I don't agree to everything you wish?" she said stiffly. "How far do you hope to push my dedication? Are you going to change your mind if I refuse to grant your every pleasure?" She rose, her voice echoing back to her off the black wall.

"If you're trying to coerce me to sleep with you, you need to stop. Now. This. . . arrangement," she waved her hand to include the room, "will *not* extend that far. Are we clear?"

The wizard looked alarmed and swiftly moved to her and took her hand. "My dear, you forget!" He gently drew her down next to him on the sofa. "I made a promise as well. I wish it never to be said that Kayme makes a promise lightly." He straightened his spine. "Upon my honour," he put a hand on his heart, "physical intimacy is not my object."

She looked deep into his sapphire eyes and saw no deception. She believed him. "Good," she said, without embarrassment.

"I have not asked anything of you that was unreasonable, have I?"

Kyer took a breath, and her jaw relaxed. "You're right." She shifted her focus downward to where the green gown caught the firelight, outlining the contours of her knees. She turned back to him and was taken aback. He was very close to her. And gazing at her that way again. His eyes were as deep as the sky; she might drown in them, yet they held her. Safety and freedom gleamed there. His hand reached up slowly, as if being pressed down by a weight, and removed the comb that held her hair.

"You are so much more than a wielder of a sword." Her hair tumbled down around her shoulders, and he stroked its softness with the back of his fingers. They carried on, breathing a whisper of a touch on her cheek, and she stifled a gasp. Pleasure and fear trickled down her back like drops of cold water. Some sort of force from within him pulled on something within her, and Kyer couldn't tell whether she wanted to be free of it or not. But some other energy snapped her eyes shut and weakened the connection. She held on. *Resist him.*

"Do I frighten you?" His voice was soft, emotionless, soothing like waves on a lakeshore.

Hyperventilating, she rubbed her face with one hand, frantically shaking off the desire that probed, seeking entry. She felt weakened and wondered about the potency of Kayme's elderflower liqueur. "I—don't know whether to be frightened or not. Should I be? I don't think 'frightened' is the right word." She concentrated very hard. "You have an advantage over me in more ways than one. If I had my sword, I'd still feel unarmed. You look at me . . . and can see into me. You *know* more about me than even I do, and I know nothing about you." She paused. "I feel like a prisoner here and yet, if I asked to leave, I believe you would let me go."

"Do you wish to leave?"

The tension in the room rippled like a heatwave as Kyer struggled with the strange emotions that churned inside her. When had he taken her hand?

"No, I don't." She was aware of a sensation that this was some kind of battle won for Kayme. But it was all right. She was certain that she had let him win it; her own determination had not allowed her to retreat so soon.

Kayme appeared more relaxed now. Or was he just a bit more sure of himself?

"You told me during dinner about your last mission," he said, with a lift of his previous intensity. "And you also explained why Alon Maer is so important to you."

Kyer waited.

"You risk your life and will spend several months searching to help someone you merely hold idealistically in your mind."

Kyer frowned, puzzled by the statement. Was he trying to make her feel foolish? She finished the last mouthful of wine and set the goblet next to the tumbler. Kayme rose to replenish her liqueur.

"How much time are you going to spend on this sort of thing?" He smiled as if hinting at something, though she couldn't guess what. "When are you going to start focussing on what *you* want to do?"

"What do you mean? I'm doing exactly what I want to do."

"Not quite."

A nervous laugh. She brushed her hair back behind her shoulders. "Of course I am. I studied the *wæpnian*. I am a swordfighter, working for Valrayker, for Kien, doing exactly what I trained to do. What are you driving at?" She sipped from the tumbler.

He sat down again, leaning close to her. "What of your own purpose?"

Kyer leaned away from him and said nothing.

"Come now, my dear. You know what I'm talking about. Why do you think I really wanted to talk to you tonight? Surely you understand how a bond between us would be beneficial to us both." His sapphire eyes explored deeply within her emerald ones.

She shook her head, uncomprehending. "I left home to meet other warriors," she said, as if by saying so it would become the truth.

"No, my dear, you are lying to yourself." Whatever enchantment his eyes were weaving came on full force. "What is on the end of that chain you wear about your neck?" His fingertips didn't quite touch it.

Startled, she raised her left hand to where the medallion lay on her chest, hidden by the crushed velvet garment. She tore herself away from his penetrating gaze and moved swiftly toward the fire.

"What do you know about it?" A vein on the side of her head pulsed.

He backed off slightly. "When I first saw you, I told you I recognized you."

Breathe. She tried to calm herself and slow her heartbeat. Her hand still lay upon the medallion. "I assumed you meant you hadn't seen a woman in a long time." Her voice came gruffly and sounded entirely unlike herself.

Kayme looked sincerely astounded. He leaned back against the sofa. "You mean—?" He looked at her quizzically, as if thinking through a series of questions.

Kyer had nothing to say.

Kayme rose and moved around behind the sofa, apparently in some agitation. "I assumed . . . I thought that was why you—but then, of course not, or else you wouldn't be—" He stopped pacing, having arrived at the end of his discussion with himself. He had evidently come to some conclusion.

In spite of several more sips of wine, Kyer remained discomposed. She'd lost whatever minor feeling of control she'd had at the start of the evening.

"So will you admit that you left Hreth to learn more?"

Kyer rested her hand on the mantel, reluctant to respond. "Well, yes, isn't that why people travel? I thought I might happen to pick a few things up along the way."

"'Things' seem to have fallen neatly into place, though, wouldn't you say?" He took a slow return journey to her side of the sofa. "I mean, you find yourself working for Kien and for Valrayker, two of the most learned in Rydris lore remaining alive. Two of them, but not the only ones, mind. You are given the opportunity to travel and meet a good many people, some of whom you get along with better than others because of your tendency for outspokenness—"

"How do you know all this?" She rubbed her eyes with the heel of her hand and gulped yet again from her cup.

"I know a good many things."

"You're irritating me now."

Suddenly he was right in front of her. He reached out and took the empty cup from her hand and set it on the mantel.

"And your travels brought you to me." Kayme took both her hands. "I could help you. What if I could tell you everything you wanted to know?"

"Then I would expect you to tell me and stop playing at riddles," she said crossly.

"Oh, it wouldn't come as easily as that, you know. These things take time."

"'For everything there is a price'?"

"Yes, that's it exactly." His eyes probed into her again. This time Kyer was not caught off guard, but she was getting impatient.

"You are trying to tempt me, Kayme, but you want something. What is it?"

He was taken aback. But then he smiled and spoke earnestly. "It is true. I can tell you everything." Her mouth opened in awe. "I can tell you who you are." Her breath came in short puffs. He nodded encouragement. "I can tell you *where you came from*." Kyer's jaw was slack, and she leaned forward. "Yes! I know all about you! And I can tell you all of these things!"

Was he just posturing? A little nagging voice inside her said, *Hold on!* but she wasn't listening. "You know all about my medallion?"

"Yes, I do."

Her blood quickened, pulsing with emotion, and as she stared at him, waves of music swelled around her. She broke away and sought equanimity with the flowers on the table, drawing in their scent to deepen her tremulous breaths. Then sinking to perch on the edge of an armchair, she studied its red plush upholstery. She thought hard and raised her head. "Why don't you just tell me, then? Who am I? Why was I left in Hreth?" He opened his mouth to speak, then seemed to think better of it, knitting his brow. She interpreted this as stubborn refusal. "What do you want?" she demanded.

He walked to the fireplace, gazing about him, arms out in a welcoming gesture.

"Stay with me."

Kyer stared at him in astonishment.

"What? Here?"

"Yes. Be my . . . companion."

She looked at him levelly. "For how long?"

He looked surprised. "For all our lives! *Companions*."

"Not really . . . a prisoner, then."

"Certainly not."

"But not really free either?"

"This would be your home! Safe. You've outgrown the farming village of your upbringing. This is much more suited to the Kyer you have become. The Kyer you *will* become as you grow." He had just used her name for the first time, and she liked hearing him say it. "Naturally, you could go off on a journey now and then, but this would be the home you'd return to gladly after your travels." He approached her. "Think of what you would gain," he insisted. "The knowledge! I could teach you so much. Everything I have could be yours, the tower and everything in it, all my magic!" By then he had reached her, and his trembling hands grasped hers and drew her to her feet. "Your friends do not need you so much on their journey. I'll give them the information they need, and you can stay here, knowing that the instructions will be carried out."

Her words sounded stupid even as she said them. "But—and not help with the mission? Not take the antidote to her and make sure she survives?"

"You've never even met her!" he said, wide-eyed. "Isn't it enough to know you've done your part by joining me this evening? Your friends seemed to think it was too much to ask of you; they will not begrudge your choice to bow out now, after such a deed." He reached a hand to her shoulder, and the touch sent crackles down her back as he ran it down her arm to take her hand again. He stroked it with his other.

"These hands, so strong, yet so gentle." His soft voice had the effect of the hot bath water, making her sleepy, yet she also felt the palpable intensity of his longing for her companionship. She might be overwhelmed and consumed by it, but it would also sustain her. The tiniest of steps toward him, loving the pull of his gaze. Staying here in the tower. What an opportunity! Why, Jesqellan would probably put shoes on or ride a horse if it meant he could live in Kayme's tower as long as he wanted. She would learn *everything*. And to be safe from ever handling people again? No more diplomacy. No more danger, no more enemies, no more fighting for her life. She hadn't realized how much it all had troubled her. Who would not jump at such an offer? *His eyes are so blue!* Despite her acceptance of his earlier declaration, she longed to run a hand through the dark spikes of his hair.

That glint of self-consciousness sent a shudder through her senses. "But why me?" The words burst out of her. The drawing force shunted ever so slightly, and she seized the chance to pull back. The chamber revolved around them.

"Oh, Kyer! Do you not feel it? There is such a powerful energy between us. We were meant to be together." His voice was so soothing, and oh, how it moved her! An inner calm enfolded her, a relaxation she'd only ever felt when she was at home.

"Together what *couldn't* we achieve?" he went on ardently. "We would be the ultimate partnership."

"Would we?" Clouds billowed in her head.

"I know it." He spoke softly, and took her chin in his soft, dark hand, lifting her bewildered face up toward his. "Can you doubt it?"

The clouds in her head swirled and spun. Her breath came as if she'd been running hard. *Think*, she commanded desperately. *Think! Something . . . something's wrong here.*

"Do you doubt it?" He was a bit more demanding this time.

"No!" She pulled away, anger surging. "I don't!" She put her face in her hands. "But— Oh, I have to think!"

She walked swiftly away from the warmth of the fire to the other side of the room. She needed to wake up, to snap out of it.

She touched the medallion, felt the smooth facets of the gem through the velvet, remembered sparks flying from it. There was a message there, somewhere, if she could only think what it was . . .

The answers to all her questions? Everything that had mystified her since she was a child, when Della and Gareth first told her she was not theirs. That *was* another reason she had left Hreth. She had known no one there could tell her anything about herself, but it felt less important at the time than pursuing her dream to be a fighter. Now, with almost no effort at all, Kayme was willing to tell her everything she needed to know. Her real family, where she had come from, her medallion, the language she had spoken when she arrived in Hreth and still knew.

Looking up, she saw that Kayme had not moved but that his eyes followed her wherever she went. His awe-inspiring figure seemed to have grown in stature. She was sure he wasn't even as tall as Derry when they'd arrived, yet now he loomed, filling the area by the fireplace. Just looking at him, she felt his power drawing her to him, willing her to agree with him. She couldn't think of any reason she shouldn't. But her gut told her there must be one, and she thought frantically to find it. Was he being straight with her? Or was he exaggerating his knowledge and power? She paced about until the chill helped to clear her head a little. Her heart hammered against her breastbone. What was she forgetting?

She found herself at the far end of the room, next to the harp. Reaching out, she plucked a string and was astonished at the clarity of the ring that echoed about the vast chamber. She could almost see the note reverberate through the space. A note, clear like the ring of steel when her sword clashed with another. Kayme's music versus her music.

A vague memory of dark woods and that ring of steel. Her own voice. "One. Two. Three." A dead man. Her own pain. And Val. . .

She looked down at herself, surprised to see green velvet instead of leather armour. And her hair hung down her shoulders instead of being secured back in one long braid, the way she liked it, out of the way for fighting.

Fighting. A breeze had stirred in her head to blow the clouds away. When she looked back at Kayme this time, his missile gaze deflected off her rather than being absorbed. She had wanted to absorb it; it had been strangely pleasurable. Now, the control Kayme had tried to wrest from her was returning to her own power, and the answer to the extraordinary offer he had made formulated in her mind. There had to be more in this for Kayme than he was letting on, or he wouldn't have tried so hard.

She had left Hreth as a swordfighter. True, she had felt that there was something she was supposed to do, and she had known she wouldn't find it in Hreth. But she was fairly certain that her chosen path, led by Valrayker—and Kien—was, at least for now, the right one.

She breathed deeply. Her head stopped spinning and returned to its normal state of clarity and self-assuredness. Refusing to be intimidated by him, she turned to look at Kayme. He still watched her from the fireside.

"Your price is too high," she said. "I know some might leap at the chance, and I really do thank you for the offer. Believe me, I'm overwhelmed by your attention to me. This place is not for me, though. Maybe I'm a fool, but I think I have to learn things at a steady pace and in the right setting." Kyer took a step toward him. "I'm sorry."

He floated across the stone floor to join her. His lips were pressed together in respectful concession. He was perhaps disappointed, but the sapphires told her that he yielded. He took the hand she offered, but this time he did not try to draw her toward him. Instead he examined its roughness and strength created by years of wielding a sword. He grasped it gently and bowed.

"You, too, are very wise. And you are more powerful than you know."

With his other hand, he gestured to where her medallion lay beneath the crushed velvet, adding intensity to his words, like a warning. "You don't need that."

Kyer put her hand on her chest protectively. "Of course I do." She wanted to ask what he meant, but she was suddenly very weary, and more ready for sleep than another conversation. Besides, she did not want to know what the price would be for such an answer. She smiled up at him rather fondly, and on an impulse, she took his chin and kissed him.

"I wouldn't want you to forget me when I'm gone, you know." She smiled. "Good night." Then she headed up the stairs. She did not look back.

And she did not hear Kayme when he spoke under his breath. "That is not likely."

She hung the green dress back in the wardrobe. With one final touch of the finery, she closed the door on it. Pulling a warm nightgown over her steady head, she slowly wandered around the room, extinguishing candles as she went. As each flame puffed out, her weariness grew, until she felt almost obliterated by exhaustion. Whatever battle she had just fought, she had won it.

She crawled into bed and lay there as if on a cloud. The tension, fear, and anxiety of the day melted and carried her with it into nothingness. As her mind reached the point of clarity just before falling asleep, she sat bolt upright. "He didn't tell me the antidote," she said to the bedpost. Then she flopped into the pillows and plummeted into dreamless sleep.

Seven

Their Mission Must Fail

Derry turned over again. And again. The straw mattress was too hard. It sagged in the middle, so sleeping on his front with one knee up didn't work. The wool blanket was thick but smelled of camphor. Jesqellan's meditative breathing a few feet away and Phennil's soft snores were frustrating, not soothing.

Skimnoddle had more than made up for his insensitivity by providing entertainment to pass the time. He had sung, juggled, and made them laugh with his magic tricks. Even Derry had smiled a bit. In a particularly thoughtful gesture, the halfling said, "Captain, you need something you can really concentrate on."

He pulled from his pocket a little purple drawstring bag with some gold writing on it and invited the men to join him on the floor. Loosening the string, he tipped out five dice and taught them a game.

Derry got the hang of it fairly quickly, and within three turns had reached a thousand points. Phennil, practically shredding his already unkempt blond hair, didn't manage to reach that plateau until Derry had already gained 7,850. Janak hollered curses at the stone cubes and flew past Derry in one turn. It was a tight race, and Jesqellan came out the winner in the end.

It was a good game and had taken up the captain's thoughts for a time.

When the men retired to the dark, disused-smelling chamber upstairs, he rolled onto his side and could think of nothing but Kyer.

Why had they not even *tried* to follow her? They'd abandoned her to a nameless fate. Surely Jesqellan could have attempted some sort of spell to open the door or at least to see what was transpiring behind it. Was Kayme keeping his word? Was Kyer being well treated? *I should never have let her go.* Derry did not like the way the wizard looked at Kyer and liked even less the way Kyer blushed beneath his intense gaze.

Had Kayme given her a decent place to sleep?

He sat up, throwing the blanket aside. Was she sleeping alone?

If she was not alone, was it by her own choice?

If the answer was "No" . . . Derry's guts churned with rage.

But if the answer was "Yes" . . .

Derry hardly knew which answer was worse.

The chill of the damp room penetrated his tunic and crept along his skin. He drew the covers up and lay down again, eyes staring up at the shadowed stone ceiling. But the black stone was not as dark as the pit in Derry's gut. An unfamiliar emotion had worked its way into him, like ivy roots creeping through cracks in stone. When he finally slept, he had disturbing dreams.

When Derry awoke to see stripes of daylight on the floor through the shuttered windows, he leapt out of bed, anxious to get downstairs to wait for Kyer's return. He hurried down to the dining chamber where they had supped the night before. The fire already burned brightly, as if, knowing someone were coming, it had lit itself. This time the table was laid out with eggs, meat, cheese, and fruit all looking delightfully fresh and delicious. The table was laid for six, not just five.

Derry sat down and began to eat and was soon joined by Jesqellan then the others. All but Derry, it seemed, had slept well, though he did not admit it, for fear of needing to explain it to them. They ate in silence.

The door from the entrance hall opened. In walked Kyer. Jaws dropped, chewing stopped, and Derry stood, knocking his chair over.

"Thank the gods! Are you all right?" he cried.

"Of course." She glanced over her shoulder to make sure he wasn't talking to someone else. "What were you expecting?"

She looked just the same as ever, except perhaps a little cleaner and less rumpled than when she left them. She sat down and filled her plate.

Of all the things Derry had expected, this was not among them. Tears of relief, maybe. Cuts, bruises, dishevelled hair, yes. Refreshed and content? Shocking. Derry couldn't believe it and flushed with embarrassment and annoyance that he'd wasted so much energy worrying about her.

"What happened?" he demanded. "I've been—we've been worried about you. Did he harm you or try to force you into anything?"

"Absolutely not. He was a perfect gentleman." She scooped a forkful of egg.

"What, then?"

She stopped mid-mouthful and stared at him. The others had gone back to eating. He gulped his irrational indignation and righted his chair, trying to compose himself. He sat. "Where did he take you?"

"He directed me to a beautifully comfortable bedchamber."

Derry stiffened. "And then?" he prodded impatiently.

"I had a bath."

"A *bath*?"

"Yes. A bath," she said archly. "Is that problematic for you?" she gave him a cheeky smile.

"Kyer, please. You know what I mean." Why did she have to be so contrary?

"Very well, then." She yielded and put down her lump of cheese. "After bathing—yes, that part was true—I went downstairs and we shared a very elegant meal, during which I had to try to remember not to eat with my knife. Then we sat by the fire drinking wine and elderflower liqueur, which was wonderful, and we talked. That's all. I didn't even insult him or anything," she added proudly.

"There's a surprise," Janak said.

"That's it?" said Phennil.

"Well, not entirely." She hesitated.

"What else?" asked Jesqellan.

"I wore a dress." She tossed her head. Snorts popped out of Skimnoddle, Janak, and Phennil.

"Did he tell you the antidote?" Jesqellan said after a moment.

"No." Kyer's face was troubled. "I'm certain he will."

Derry's steady gaze met hers. "We are very glad you are all right."

Kyer's smile filled him with warmth.

The door opened and Kayme walked in.

"Ah good! You've had a nice breakfast. Did everyone sleep well?" he asked cheerily and, without waiting for an answer, went on. "I wanted you to be refreshed for your journey this morning."

"Your pardon, Kayme," Jesqellan said, "but we will not leave until you hold up your end of the bargain."

Kayme looked at him quizzically. "Why, whatever do you mean?"

Derry stood up and faced the wizard.

"You know what we mean, Kayme. I hope you aren't trying to tell us you won't give us the antidote after all. Kyer did what you asked, and now we ask that you honour your promise."

"Gentlemen, gentlemen, let us be calm." Kayme leaned casually on the doorframe. "A promise made is a promise kept."

"Well then. . . ." Jesqellan raised his eyebrows in expectation.

"I have already done so!" Kayme said. "Kyer knows the antidote." All eyes shifted to Kyer, who looked shocked. She shook her head. "Yes, my dear, you do. You have but to think back to your dream of last night. It will all become quite clear once you have left here.

"Now, I came in to bid you farewell. My home is beginning to feel crowded, and even the charms of Kyer Halidan cannot counteract the effect of her friends. I expect you to be ready to leave within the half hour." And with that, Kayme left the room.

They all looked at Kyer. With her forehead resting on her hands and her eyes shut, she shook her head.

"Well? What do you know?" asked Derry.

"I don't remember dreaming anything last night." She looked up. "I slept more deeply than I ever have in my life." She got up and exited into the entrance hall.

And if he has lied, we are powerless to do anything about it. Derry snatched up a grape and flung it against the wall.

Jesqellan threw up his hands. "We have no choice but to trust him again."

Derry was certain Kyer had not told them the entire story about her encounter with the wizard. The way she had passed the evening off as nothing was too glib. He was not convinced that she was not distressed by something besides the antidote. He resolved to speak to her about it the next time they were alone.

When they met in the hall, their weapons were available in the open cabinet. As they finished refitting themselves, Kayme swept through the door to the sitting room they had conversed in last night. He shook hands with each of them in turn and wished them a safe journey as they went out the door. When he came lastly to Kyer, he took her hand and spoke in a low voice.

"May I express again, my dear, my pleasure in your company."

"You may express it all you like, Kayme, but I will not be content until I know the cure for Alon Maer."

"A determined and loyal warrior," the wizard replied. "Kien is a fortunate man. You have my word that you will know the antidote."

She nodded. He bowed and kissed her hand, reluctant to let it go. "It is not too late to change your mind." His eyes finally met hers. She shook her head.

"I will not change my mind. But thank you again for a wonderful evening."

"I want you to take this." Kayme pulled out from his cloak a single white rose. He placed it in her hand. "Keep it close to your heart." Sapphires fused with emeralds.

Perceptive of his sincerity, she nodded. "I will." She tucked the flower inside her armour, and with a final wave at the most intriguing man she had ever met, she went through the door.

"It will never be too late!" He called as the door closed.

Persistent bugger.

They rode, although they had no idea which direction to take without the specifics of the cure. Kyer could not believe Kayme would lie about it, but she couldn't help wondering if he would have been more forthright with the information if she had agreed to stay with him. She lifted her chin. *No regrets.*

"Let's head east," suggested Kyer. "We have to clear the mountains anyway, and then maybe I can think more clearly."

"I hope so," said Jesqellan.

As if I don't. Kyer felt more than a little pressured. She looked crossly back at Kayme's tower. Was that his face she had just seen at an upper window? It was gone now, whatever it was.

Within seconds of turning back, she was hit with a compulsion.

"We want to head northeast," she announced. "To the Cold Fells."

Kayme was true to his word. Kyer rode at the front of the group, alongside Phennil. About an hour after leaving the tower, she felt herself becoming mesmerized by the plodding of the horses, at Jesqellan's pace, and the expanse of plain spread out before her. Her vision clouded over, and she reined in her horse. The others came closer, curiously. As if in a trance, she related to them the images her mind showed her.

"We're in the Cold Fells. We're underground. It is very dark, but we have some kind of light. It's a cavern, I think. There is a large chamber with . . . dripping walls. The walls are covered with . . . it looks like lichen. It's called falander." She paused as the image changed. "Now we've journeyed west to the Sea of Khûn. There is a flower. It's a wildflower, tiny and white. The petals are a trefoil. We need an extract from it. It's called tahleema." The image changed again. "I see a fine sand, almost like dust. It's reddish. We're in another cavern, in . . . a place called the Indyn Caves." She stopped and turned to Jesqellan, her eyes unclouded. "That's it. Those are the ingredients. He wasn't lying."

"Tahleema and falander and dust from the Indyn Caves," Jesqellan said thoughtfully. "What are we supposed to do with them? Did your dream tell you that?"

"We're to mix the dry ingredients with the extract and some sap from the Tree of Life. That's all I know." Kyer was certain. The images had been as clear as the note from Kayme's harp.

"But where are the Indyn Caves?" Phennil asked.

"I . . . don't know exactly."

"I do," Derry said. "It happens that my lord has travelled extensively and has told me stories of his travels. Though I've never been there, I know where to go."

Kyer nudged Trig forward, uplifted by a sense of profound relief.

At midday, Derry called a halt for a meal and to rest the horses. Opening his saddlebags to dig out something to eat, he was surprised to find a good supply of food he hadn't put there. He had a package of dried meat the size of two loaves of bread as well as several pounds of fruit and cheese.

"Well, Kyer, you certainly made an impression," Jesqellan commented, exhibiting a gorgeous loaf of bread and some parsnips from his pack.

"How so?"

"I have known people to pay visits to Kayme, yet never have I heard of someone leaving with such a supply. I have only ever heard of Kayme as impatient and ungenerous. What did you say to him?"

"No idea. I guess I didn't offend him, anyway." She did not add much to the conversation while they ate. Derry thought she looked weary. The meal wasn't rushed. As they finished eating, the speculations opened about what the Cold Fells were, where they were, and what might be found there. Kyer didn't seem to be listening. It wasn't a formal discussion, such as the group might have when formulating a plan; still, it irked Derry somewhat when she got up and walked away. He was of a mind that the one person who had any details on their mission ought to have taken more interest.

Cloak flung back over her shoulders, the rope of braided hair among its folds, she took several slow, uneven steps and staggered a little, not as if she were drunk, but as if she were extraordinarily weary. His crossness shifted to concern. Her hands didn't swing at her sides, rather she had pulled them in front of herself, where he couldn't see them. Her head tipped down. She stopped a few paces away and with the same grace with which she fought, lowered herself to sit on the ground. With a mind on investigating, Derry grabbed two apples from the stash of food and went toward her.

He had suspected she'd pulled something out from within her jerkin. As he came closer, he caught a glimpse of what appeared to be a flower and she breathed its scent, her eyelids closed as if near sleep. She turned her head slightly, so he knew she was aware of his presence.

"Am I disturbing you?"

She shook her head but tucked the flower back inside and hugged her knees. "We leaving soon?"

He seated himself near her. "Fairly soon, yes. Are you all right?"

"Fine. A little tired." She took the apple from him and stared at it. The light breeze waved a few bits of stray hair like prairie grasses.

Careful not to sound interrogative, he asked, "What have you got there?"

"Oh, this." She didn't actually pull it out but peered down at it. "A lovely parting gift from my new best friend."

He smiled. "Oh yes?"

"It's a rose," she said dismissively. "He asked me to keep it near my heart."

"Literally or figuratively?"

Her turn to smile. "Both, I think."

"He made an impression on you, too, I believe."

Her eyes rounded. "You could say that." A small smile played about her lips.

Derry turned his apple in his fingers, unconsciously waiting for Kyer to bite into hers before he could do the same. The mood was too tentative and would be broken by the slightest crunch. "You seem, uh, awfully tired. Did you not sleep well?"

"Are you kidding? That was the most comfortable bed I've ever slept in.

Like sleeping on clouds! And I was utterly exhausted after—" She pressed her lips together.

What? What? he wanted to say. He waited a moment then said, "Yes?"

Kyer straightened and looked back toward the others. "I guess we need to leave soon."

Derry was incomprehensibly irritated by her evasiveness but bit back a cross word. "Yes, it would be wise."

They got to their feet. With an arm, he gestured that they should walk. Kyer didn't move. He cocked his head questioningly.

"He wanted me to stay with him." She was staring into the middle distance. "To live there with him as his companion. He said—" She swallowed. "He would share all his knowledge with me. He said we were meant to be together."

Derry's eyebrows went up.

"He said that together we would achieve ... well, I don't really know what he said, but he seemed to think I belonged there because of— something ... I don't know." She peered up at Derry, and he resumed a neutral expression. "Kayme said you all don't really need me on this mission."

Derry's mind was filled with the memory of his lousy night on a crummy bed in a dank room and that cloud of blackness in the pit of his stomach. "Well, that's nonsense. And obviously you knew it because ... you turned him down."

She shifted her gaze ahead to the others, to the horses, to the plains beyond which contained their journey. "Yes. I turned him down."

Kyer took a bite of her apple. Derry looked at his but no longer desired it.

The first night after leaving Kayme to his solitude, they camped on the northern edge of the mountain spur northeast of Kayme's tower. The ride to the Cold Fells would take at least five days if they stuck to the plan to hug the mountain range as closely as possible without tracing its every spur and angle.

Skimnoddle outdid himself as a cook with the surprise items Kayme had given them and a little help from his own unique skill as a hunter. On that first evening, he floored them all. He rummaged through the bags, taking stock of Kayme's offerings, and muttered to himself, occasionally letting out a small whoop as he discovered something particularly pleasant or rare.

"It is for this sort of selection of delectable comestibles that a culinary specialist such as myself lives." He sighed with pleasure as he tottered over to his designated preparation area with an armload of vegetables and sundry foodstuffs. He sank to the ground and eagerly sorted through his collection, squealing under his breath with delight at what he was about to create.

Janak harrumphed as he brushed the halfling's pony. "It's great that you're so happy while the rest of us do your chores for you."

Kyer scoffed. "Oh sure, you'd rather take your turn at cooking, I suppose? Because you're so much better at it than Skimnoddle?" Trig was freshly groomed and shining, and Kyer sat down to wipe her tack.

"Better than you are, anyway," the dwarf said.

Kyer laughed. She still felt tired, but the excessive weariness had faded as they moved northward, farther from Kayme's black tower.

"There's no disputing that." Phennil pointed his hoof pick at her between flicks of dirt from Leoht's foot.

"Perhaps I'm always so hungry by the end of the day that it doesn't matter to me, but I've never been bothered by any lack of quality in anyone's cooking," Derry put in.

"We can always count on you to be the diplomat," Janak said.

"Someone has to counterbalance Kyer," Phennil quipped.

"Oh good!" Kyer returned the captain's smile. "We have Skimnoddle to set off my cooking and Derry to set off my tactlessness. What more do we need?"

"My lady, if I may but suggest . . ." Skimnoddle leapt to his feet and doubled over in an elaborate bow. "The greatest contrast of all: your beauty, which can only be accurately counterbalanced by Janak."

Hoots from everyone but the dwarf himself.

"Bravely said, I must admit." Kyer wiped tears from her eyes. And then she shook her rag at Janak. "Don't you go taking revenge on him for that, either. You started all this, you know."

"I did no such thing; it was that malodorous elf. And the point of it all was that here I am, caring for the halfling's beast while he gets to sing and twitter away over something he takes pleasure in. It's wrong, I tell you."

"Yeah, well, you don't take pleasure in anything, so what difference does it make?" Kyer pushed herself up off her moss-covered log to fetch a needle to mend some stitching in her bridle.

"Except perhaps in deriding everyone around him." Phennil grinned and gave Leoht's gleaming coat a final pat.

"All right, Janak, let's hear you sing and twitter over that," Kyer laughed.

Janak harrumphed again. Through with Skimnoddle's pony, he set to circling the clearing in search of sticks for firewood, carefully stepping around a motionless Jesqellan who was deep in his meditative trance, regenerating his energies. "I thought Valrayker promised we would wonder how we ever got along without him, anyway." He nudged an elbow in Skimnoddle's direction. "Was he just referring to food, or is there something else you're good for?"

"Janak," Derry warned.

Skimnoddle stopped mid-slice and set the knife down on his cutting board. He looked thoughtful rather than annoyed or hurt. Finally he said, "I have not had occasion to put it into effect for anyone's benefit here on this journey, but mayhap this circumstance allows for it." He thought for a moment then moved to stand before Kyer again. She rested her elbows on the bridle in her lap, looking at him suspiciously.

"My lady, as you must know by now, there is nothing that fills me to repletion with joy more than your happiness. To that end, I pray thee, tell me your desire: What repast may I provide for thee that you have long since craved?"

"*What?*"

"I speak truly. Please let me honour thee by procuring a specialty food item for your enjoyment."

Kyer was silent. What could she choose that would be quite impossible to find here in the north, on the edge of the wide plain? Reminiscent of last night's meal, she said, "How about lamb?"

"For you, my lady, it is done." He skittered over to his saddlebags.

"Did you ever consider becoming a cleric?" Derry said dryly.

"You honour me, dear Captain." The halfling did not glance up as he scrabbled through his bag.

"Aren't you glad he was so much in awe of Kayme that he was silent yesterday?" Phennil whispered to Kyer as he flopped next to her and leaned against her fallen log.

Skimnoddle produced a square of cloth that looked like simple canvas and a small brush with a narrow tuft of bristles. He knelt next to the pail of water by the fire and spread the canvas on his lap. Staring into the bushes where some sort of animal shuffled around, he dipped the brush in the water and began to paint on the cloth. Curious in spite of herself, Kyer set her task aside and rose to look over his shoulder. She could just faintly see the outline created by the wet brush. Skimnoddle was apparently as adept at drawing as he was at singing; as she watched, a lamb took shape on the cloth. And when he was through, he set the brush down gently and lifted the cloth, giving it a little wave toward the bushes.

The company's collective jaws dropped in astonishment as they heard a *baa* and a grey lamb hopped into the clearing.

"How did you know there was a lamb in the bush?" Janak growled.

"How did he get me to suggest a lamb, even if he *did* know there was one in the bush?" Kyer said crossly. It pained her to be impressed with Skimnoddle.

"He did neither," said a voice that had been still for some time. Jesqellan had arisen from his meditation in time to see Skimnoddle's trick. They turned to him, the halfling looking smug. "It is a very unusual magic." He squatted down by Skimnoddle. "May I see?" He indicated the cloth, which the halfling handed to him. The image of the lamb had evaporated. "I have heard of this only once, and I have never seen it put into practice. Correct me if I am inaccurate, but I believe it uses surrounding objects, creatures, and transforms them somehow."

"That is correct."

Janak pointed at the cooking pot. "Why don't you use that and draw a picture of some gold? That'd be more useful."

"Can you turn Janak into a newt?" Kyer said.

"He'd only get better," Derry pointed out.

Skimnoddle bowed and re-rolled the cloth around the brush. "You may think, my good dwarf, that your proposal is revolutionary, or perhaps one I had never thought of myself. But I pledge to you it is not, I have, and it is impracticable. You see, the spell, as most spells, has its limitations. It may be used only for non-selfish acts and nothing that may cause bodily harm to anyone. Believe me, I have tried."

"How did you come by it?" Jesqellan asked casually.

"That is like asking how I manage to find this leaf—" He reached over to the mage's head. "—behind your ear," he finished and winked as he placed it in Jesqellan's upturned hand.

That night they ate lamb cooked on skewers with onion and tiny tomatoes, alongside pan-fried zucchini and boiled new potatoes. And Kayme had supplied them with cake for dessert.

"Well, well, well, lucky me. What a week for visitors," Kayme said dryly as he leaned against the frame of his front door.

"You don't seem happy to see me," the new arrival replied.

"I can't honestly say I am experiencing any particular emotion at all," the wizard said. "I suppose you might as well come in." He drew his weight off the doorframe and turned, opening the door wider to admit his guest. He led him into the same chamber where he'd chatted with the young lady and her friends, and with a swish of his hand, provided some simple refreshment. The visitor flipped his short cape, seated himself on the sofa against the outer wall, and stretched his long legs out in front, crossing them neatly at the ankle. His arms rested on the back of the sofa.

"You are all hospitality, as usual, Cousin." The pale man smiled.

"I am delighted you feel so at home, Golgathaur, as to not be compelled to wipe your boots on the mat as you enter," Kayme scolded mildly, indicating the dirt that had travelled in like parasites on the other fellow's footwear.

"So who were your recent guests? It's so nice to see you keeping company with real people once in a while."

"I'm sure you already know the answer, or you wouldn't bother asking the question." Kayme's tone was as frosty as the mug of beer he handed to Golgathaur. "What do you want, Cousin? Are you meddling on behalf of your tiresomely power-hungry commander-in-chief?" Kayme remained standing.

Golgathaur laughed. "Oh, dear me no. I give him what he wants, to be sure, but no, Cousin. I meddle only on behalf of myself."

"So what is it you're meddling in now?"

"Oh, it is such fun being me!" Golgathaur said airily. "Tell me: What did you think of the *strong female* presence in your home yesterday?"

"There was a female, yes. What would you like me to have thought about it?"

"She is unusual and I don't mind telling you that I am curious about her." Golgathaur got to his feet, his head nearly brushing the ceiling. Kayme raised it a few inches, just to be a polite host. "Thank you." Golgathaur was ever the polite guest. He moved about the room, taking long strides, not quite pacing, yet Kayme sensed that his cousin was trying not to look agitated. The scent of heliotrope wafted around him. "I have witnessed her actions once or twice now, and I know others who are curious about her. I find myself . . . fascinated. Did you not feel anything of that nature?"

Kayme gave him a quizzical look and shook his head. "I confess that I did not spend much time in their presence. I noted who they were, that is all. They asked for some information, and I chose not to give it to them. It was the young captain and the mage who did most of the talking on behalf of the party, so no, I cannot say she, in particular, stood out." He took a sip of his drink.

Golgathaur spread his arms out wide, and his beverage slopped out of his mug. Kayme glanced distastefully at the floor and wiped it away with a wave of his hand. "I cannot understand you sometimes, Cousin! How many years has it been since you saw anyone, spent time with anyone? How long has it been since you saw a woman, let alone made love to one?" Kayme's eyes darkened. "One such as she walks right up to you and you don't even notice her!"

"Are you suggesting I ought to have taken advantage of a female?"

"Naturally not, but you certainly have a few powers of persuasion in your little bag of tricks, do you not?"

Kayme finally sat. "Did you come here to rave about your fascination with a woman?"

"No, of course not, that was fancy only. No, I just need some information to help me with my meddling."

"Are you weary so soon with the trinkets I have given you already?" Kayme asked.

"This?" Golgathaur's fingers played with a chain around his neck. Kayme had seen a similar one only the night before. Golgathaur grinned. "This is very useful to my meddling. I would not have nearly so much fun without it. Why even now—"

"You know very well that I prefer to be kept out of all your activities," Kayme interrupted.

"Yes, as well as the activities of the continent in general."

"Of course. It has nothing to do with me, so I have nothing to do with it."

"Well, if that is the case, it can't be too much trouble for you to tell me where you sent the recent company of guests you entertained, among whom was a lovely young woman you did not bother to pay heed to because of your self-absorption." His grin widened as he returned to his sofa. "I jest, of course."

"Oh, of course," Kayme said sarcastically. He gazed at his younger cousin's tall, lean frame, and contemplated his personality. How a talent for magic could run in the family and pass him by completely had always been a mystery to Kayme. So while he had occasionally been willing to help his cousin, he guessed that Golgathaur had adapted, and learned his own way of approaching the world. That casual manner. The pale face that always appeared to be hiding something or teasing. He had the attitude of one who knows something but isn't willing to share it. Well, Kayme was certainly just as good at that as Golgathaur. And at least in his own case, it was almost always true. "Why do you want to know where they are headed?"

Golgathaur waved his fingers at Kayme. "Make up your mind. You don't want to have any involvement in the world outside your tower, and you definitely don't want to have anything to do with me, so why bother asking? If you are only on your own side, what do you care?"

He was right. Kayme shouldn't care. But now that the information had been requested, well, there was a niggling discomfort with telling him. An instinct to protect the young woman in question crept up his spine like spiders. Kayme did not know or want to know what his cousin was up to, and yet for some reason, he hesitated.

What concern did he have about Kyer? She had refused his offer. She did not care about him, so why should he care if his cousin interfered with her progress? He set aside his precautionary compulsion.

"They are headed to the Cold Fells."

"Ah. *Thank you*, dear Cousin." Rising, Golgathaur drained his mug. With a bow, he bade farewell to Kayme and took his leave.

When he was gone, Kayme looked around the room at the dirt, at the damp spot where he'd spilled his beer, at the spot where Golgathaur'd sat so blasted comfortably. He wished he had not said a word.

Too late now. He took himself to his chamber.

The wood elf had told Hunter that Valrayker's party had gone north, confirming Golgathaur's previous intelligence that their destination was Kayme's tower. Given this knowledge he would have thought their trail would be easy to trace. Instead his tracker had had no luck finding the path of their quarry. Along the trade route, it was understandable; many horses and carts travelled the roads at this time of year. But even back out here in the grassland, their trail could not be found. Hunter suspected magical intervention. He had to assume they were still the same two days behind. Nothing to do but press on. The gleam in Hunter's eye still flared in anticipation of his reunion with the woman.

"When we finally find them," he told his dozen companions as they ate and prepared to bed down, "the girl is mine. Do what you want with the rest of them, but leave her to me." They grunted their assent. These people were nothing to them. They looked forward to the kill but for them it was not personal.

"Funny you should say that." Hunter jumped at the all-too-familiar voice behind him.

"Must you do that?" he said grumpily. "Can't you at least . . . yodel or something to let a fellow know you're coming?"

Golgathaur's laugh rang out in the night. "You delight me! I tell you, you are much more fun than that snivelling Ronav. I will very likely keep you on."

"Marvellous." Hunter turned back to the fire, illustrating that he was in control and no longer nonplussed by the sudden arrival of his leader. Kep suddenly decided to look for more wood, and Mullin and Tigo needed to prepare their beds. Hew and Harley and the others carried on with their business, content that the pale figure's attention was not directed at them. Misty and Juggler stayed put, listening to every word with vague curiosity. "What is it you want this time?" Hunter demanded.

"Straight to the point. That is just what I like about you. I have for you two tidbits of information, both of which I am sure will delight you. First of all, to help you locate those you are pursuing, I have learned that they are headed for the Cold Fells. The second tidbit is a slight change of plan: I understand you have a personal grudge against the woman, Kyer."

Hunter took another bite of meat and didn't respond.

"The new instruction is quite interesting, I found. Let's see if you find it so: She is not to be harmed. What do you think about that?"

Hunter stopped chewing. He stood up and faced the lieutenant. "I don't like that at all. I want her dead. By my own hand."

Why was it that when Golgathaur sat, leaving him on his feet, Hunter did not feel larger or stronger, as if he'd risen in status? Instead he felt ridiculous. He would have sat as well, only Golgathaur had taken his rock.

"I'm afraid that is not to be, Chief." The pale man waved his cloak with a flourish as he drew it 'round himself. "We have a suspicion about her. One that was roused some time ago during an interview with your predecessor. We want proof. And we have finally figured out a way to get it."

"I don't care about your suspicion!" Hunter spat, his fists white-knuckling. "I want to kill her. You hear me? It's the only thing that's keeping me going."

"Oh dear. That is a problem."

"Yes! It's your problem because when I see her, I will *not* be in control of my actions."

Suddenly he was flanked by Misty and Juggler. He tried to break away, but their grip on each of his arms was uncannily strong.

Golgathaur's voice went low. It retained its cheerful tone as if speaking to a child, barely above a whisper. "You will not harm her." Fredric felt the tip of cold steel on his neck. "Do you imagine you are exempt from punishment?" Golgathaur rose and stepped closer, towering over him. Juggler's steel pressed. "Are you afraid of the dark, my dear *Hunter*?" Fredric shook his head, ever so slightly. "Ronav was. Did he ever tell you why?" Fredric's head quivered again. "You will not touch Kyer Halidan, my good Chief, unless you wish to discover what dwells in the darkness of my lord's deepest places."

Fredric was no fool; he acquiesced. He was seething and cursed his fear and trembling.

"You will take this girl, Kyer Halidan. Separate her from her friends, just for a while. Keep in mind that my last instructions still apply: Their mission must fail. She must stay alive. You will take her aside and repeat the following words to her." Here Golgathaur spoke a sentence in another language, one that was not the least bit familiar to the chief nor his followers. It was a short sentence, just a few words, and though the lieutenant made him repeat them a good many times so he would have the strange uvular pronunciation of the words perfect, he did not disclose their meaning.

"That's it?" Hunter's mouth was dry. "You want me to say that and then just let her go?"

"Yes, that," Golgathaur said, "with one important step missing. You say that to her and *watch her reaction*. Then you leave her and report back to me."

"How do I do that? You have this habit of appearing; it isn't as if I've ever asked you to show up."

"Ha ha," the other said. "That is true. You won't be seeing me for a while, my friends. I have some errands to run and important matters to attend to at my home. But when you are ready, take your tracing stone in your hand and call my name. I will find you as soon I can." And with that, he was off again, to wherever such a man called home.

Fredric cursed himself for the—well, he'd lost count of how many times he'd cursed himself. His one pleasure in all this had been taken from him. Turning, he unwillingly caught Misty's eye, and she winked at him as though they shared a pleasurable secret. He met her gaze coolly, though his insides smouldered, and he sat back down on his rock.

Eight

Their Only Chance

So far, so good, Kyer thought. Camp-time found them in the foothills of Mount Taymor, having headed up and over them, rather than going around. Tomorrow they would head down into the rolling grasslands and travel more directly northeast to the Cold Fells, where Kyer hoped to receive more detailed instruction from the wizard.

The westering sun warmed Kyer's back, though it beamed through the filter of haze on the horizon. Making sure she was still visible to Janak, she took a few steps further into the bushes. Even while collecting firewood, they had all agreed to avoid heading off alone anywhere. She had seen lots of promising dried, spindly twigs that would make excellent kindling. Just as she bent down to twist the dead sprigs off their mother plant, she heard a voice and froze because it came not from Janak, but from directly in front of her.

"Kyer." The urgent susurration was like a breeze in the bushes.

She looked up at the source of the voice, glanced back at Janak, then squinted into the bush. "Who said that?" she demanded in a whisper, though she did not call out to the dwarf.

"It is I. Have you so soon forgotten our previous meeting?"

Kyer's jaw slackened as she finally glimpsed a pale human face within the bushes. She clutched the spindly branches as though they would support her weight. It was the man from the alley in Shael, the one who had told her to go around the square. The hairs on her neck stood up. "How did you get here?"

"Quickly, there's no time to explain."

"Explain what?"

"You and your friends are in danger here," he said. "You must move deeper into the trees. A band of goblins is approaching from the northwest, about three hundred strong. If they maintain their current pace, they will emerge from the pass in about thirty minutes, and if they come across your party, you will surely be destroyed."

"Why are you telling me this, not Derry? He's our captain."

"I do not watch out for Derry; I watch out for you. I must go. Tell them. Tell them now." The man retreated into the bushes and was gone, leaving behind a vague scent of heliotrope.

Kyer stood dumbfounded for a moment or two. What was she supposed to do?

I can't tell them we have to move because a strange man in the bush told me so. It would be no less strange if she assured them she'd met him before. She figured *"I met him in the alley in Shael"* wouldn't fill her friends with confidence. She would just have to come up with something else.

"You talking to yourself over there?" Janak hollered.

Kyer collected herself and grabbed as many of the twigs as she could. "Uh, yeah, I was just thinking this stuff would be great for kindling." She joined the dwarf with her arms full, and they headed back to where the group was preparing camp on the edge of the forest. What to do?

Wait a moment. Why did she believe him? Why not see if he was for real?

An idea took shape in her mind as she dumped her wood contribution next to the ring of stones Skimnoddle had arranged. Their camp overlooked the plain and Kyer brushed stray strands of hair from her face as she stood watching the rippling waves of the grasses. Her gaze turned involuntarily toward the north a couple of times, and she wished she could see around the bluff. Finally she said, "I have to piss, I'll be back in a minute."

Once she lost sight of the camp over the rise, Kyer traded her casual stroll for a swift gait and trudged up the hillside. A little higher up now, she peered over an outcropping of heather-covered rocks and saw in the distance, as promised, a patrol of goblins, about three hundred strong, moving fast.

At once relieved and alarmed, Kyer fled back to the camp.

"Quickly, we've got to move." She hurried to gather things together.

"What is it?" Derry asked.

"Goblins, about three hundred of them. They'll be around that bluff in no more than twenty minutes, and we're in plain view."

They scurried around, assembling belongings. Skimnoddle scattered the campfire rocks; Janak tossed their wood back into the bushes; Derry and Phennil led the horses deeper into the forest and up the slope. Kyer gave the area a quick once-over to make sure they'd grabbed everything, and Jesqellan finished off by magically obliterating all signs of their temporary residence. Farther back and higher into the foothills, they found a suitable spot to stop. Phennil located an excellent vantage point down to the plain through a break in the trees, and they lay low and watched as the goblins marched by, not two furlongs from where the group had just departed.

Not until the last rank of foul things was a good mile beyond their place of concealment did they finally breathe easy.

"Where were they going, do you think?" Skimnoddle quivered.

"Any number of places." Derry continued to watch them through the bushes. "At that pace, they'll round the northern spur of the Grey Mountains in about three or four days. I would hate to suggest they were headed to Donnan. Perhaps they were even going to the Gulf of Tarash to get on a ship and head south, though I shudder to think it."

"Wow, Kyer, good thing you saw them." Phennil laid his head back on a bed of moss.

"How did you come to see them, Kyer?" Derry asked.

Kyer hesitated only slightly before answering. "Like I said, I had to piss, and then I saw the hillside beyond and thought I'd take a look. It sure was lucky I did."

Jesqellan placed his fingertips together and peered over them at her.

Derry took first watch that night while the others slept and Jesqellan meditated. The air was mild and a few stars showed themselves from behind the clouds once in a while. He stood facing the place where they'd seen the goblin army pass by and wondered why the wind always seemed to fall at night and rise again in the morning as if it needed rest like they did.

Usually Jesqellan went straight to bed after re-energising, but tonight when Derry heard him stir, the mage appeared at his side.

"Trouble?" the captain asked in a low voice.

"Nothing pressing," Jesqellan replied softly. "I wish to hear your opinion. What did you make of Kyer's announcement this afternoon?"

Derry thought for a moment, puzzled. "Do you mean about the goblins? I was tremendously relieved that she saw them, of course. We'd have been slaughtered."

"Hm, yes that's true." Jesqellan rocked forward on his feet. "I was referring more to the coincidence of her going up the hillside just at that time."

"Explain."

"Ever since we left Kayme, I have felt a hint of power surrounding her. I know about her medallion, which also emits a magic that I do not recognize, but I have grown accustomed to its . . . *aroma* might be an accurate enough descriptor for it, for a layperson. I sense something new, though, and I have come to wonder what else occurred between Kyer and Kayme that she does not share with us. I feel compelled to observe her behaviour and question anything I see as . . . suspicious."

"And it strikes you as suspicious that she saw the goblins?" Derry asked doubtfully.

"I watched her look in that direction prior to heading off that way. I sense that she knew there was danger coming. And I am not convinced she had time to both relieve herself, and casually go to admire the view."

Derry frowned. "What are you suggesting?"

"Please remember when I say this that we have known Kyer for only a short time. I see her as an unknown variable, which could be dangerous on our mission. She says she is not a magic-user, and yet magic surrounds her. I believe we must at least watch her closely for any other strange occurrences."

Derry considered Jesqellan's words. He thought the mage was perhaps overreacting, but it was his responsibility to listen to each of his companions and not brush them off. "Very well. Watch her. But let's give her the benefit of the doubt for now. Be careful how much you read into every little action," Derry warned him. "You may see things that aren't really there just because you are looking for them."

The party descended the hillside on the third morning and plunged into a sea of purple. Blueberry bushes carpeted the rolling landscape as far as the eye could see, and the riders dismounted to walk and pluck the plump, early-ripened fruit. They filled every vessel they carried, including mouths and bellies, and the horses nibbled the fruit and greenery.

All that day and two more they travelled northeast, and the air grew more and more chill. A dampness drifted down over them from the Talankang Mountains, and no amount of sunshine warmed the breeze. The biting wind was unstopped by her cloak, no matter how tightly Kyer drew it around herself. And it only got worse as they approached their destination. Finally, on the fifth afternoon out of Kayme's, the dismal view of the Cold Fells greeted them.

Kyer stared. "Aptly named."

Derry nodded grimly as they looked over the rocky hillocks that jutted out of the expanse of land before them. The grass ended just a few paces beyond the bottom of the slope on which the horses now paused, and the only green to be seen among the rocks was the lichen that clung stubbornly to the otherwise barren surface. Grey, grey for leagues. Rock, crag, escarpment, divided into sections by fissures. And wind. Chill wind, and fast, flew down between the peaks of Talankang to the north. Kyer huddled into her cloak to shield herself from its talons.

"This is summer. I wouldn't want to be here six months from now." Derry pulled his hood over his head against the frigid breeze.

"I don't think we ought to take the horses down there," Phennil called. Derry didn't respond. His face was locked in consternation.

"Gorgeous spot, this is," Janak pronounced from Kyer's right, and he wasn't being ironic. "I could stay here for days, wandering, searching for signs of whoever might have called this place home."

"We might just be here for days, at that," Derry finally said, though entirely without Janak's passion. He dismounted and scanned the area with narrowed brows. Kyer slid out of the saddle and stood in the shelter of Trig's body using him like a wind break. Phennil leaned over and rested his head on his arms across Leoht's neck. "What now, Captain?"

"Kyer, how do we even know where to begin?" Derry's tone was just as devoid of life as the landscape.

Kyer didn't want to give credence to his despairing tone. This was only their first step, after all. If they succeeded here, there would still be two more ingredients left to find. If they gave up this easily at the first step, then she didn't want to imagine how they would feel if things became truly dismal. "I don't know for sure. I expect if we just head down there, well, we'll eventually find something." She gave him a cheerful nod and took up the reins.

Derry spoke so everyone could hear. "I suggest we take the horses down the hill at least; they can graze on the bit of grass that's there, and it may be warmer. A little. Kyer, you and Phennil will venture into the eastern section, and Janak, you and Skimnoddle take the western. Jesqellan and I have less aptitude for this kind of terrain; we will remain with the horses." He started down the hill.

The two parties ventured into the crags and spread apart. If one found anything that looked remotely cavernous, they were to call Kyer. Or whistle. She wasn't really sure *how* they would get her attention in this howling wind. It didn't matter. She was quite certain she would be the one to find what she was looking for. She was meant to and she would. Kayme would have seen to that.

She and Phennil stayed within eyesight of each other and headed northeast. Dwarf and halfling headed northwest and were soon out of sight to the other two, hidden among the crags. Janak loved the place. He would be fine. But Kyer wondered how Skimnoddle would manage, walking among these sharp, unsteady rocks.

Phennil, not surprisingly, was light of foot and stepped along just as easily as if he were dancing a reel. She was astonished at her own ability. She found it much easier than she'd expected, that the rocks were sturdier than she'd anticipated, or it may just have been that she had keen enough eyes to spot safe footing. Climbing was a matter of using the cracks in the sides of the rock faces and step-two-three, she was up. Going down was only slightly trickier, squatting to look for the footholds, turn and down-two-three, she was there. As long as she turned to her right, to avoid catching her sword, she was fine. *Maybe I ought to take up dancing after all!*

Only once she slipped and came down hard on her backside. Phennil started toward her, but she waved him on. No damage. This land was obviously not a glacial creation; there was not a smooth rock in sight, let alone a valley smoothed out by the vast sheets of ice. It also couldn't have been a riverbed, or the stone would have been worn down by the water. It was all too jagged. *Earthquakes, I guess.*

She climbed and stood on the top of a hillock. The wind whistled through the rocks like so many flutes, all playing different pitches, the musicians refusing to cooperate. She pulled her cloak about her and glanced back to see if Derry was visible from here. He was. She could just see his torso in the distance. He must have been sitting astride Donnagill because that was all she could see. No Jesqellan, none of the other horses. For all their walking through the past hour, he was only about two furlongs away. How much farther could they have gone if they hadn't had to do all this up-and-down nonsense? She waved and he waved back.

But she remembered it wasn't distance that mattered. She was looking for something. Her dream had told her that the falander lined the walls of a cavern, so it was an entrance she sought. She caught Phennil's eye and held up her hand to call a halt. She didn't know what she was going to tell him just yet; she had to think for a moment. Shutting her eyes as she stood atop a crag, she let the wind buffet her face. The pale sun was to her right, though it gave no warmth. A sudden gust whipped her braid around, and her arms instinctively went up to help keep her balance. But it slowed again, and she was able to concentrate. Sure enough, she felt Kayme prompting her again. Whether he was communicating with her telepathically or he had planted these thoughts in her mind while she slept there, Kyer had no way of knowing. *Time-release dreams,* she mused, thoughts that had been placed but were allowed to surface only after a certain amount of time.

In her mind the wind was directly on her left cheek. She turned to make it so. In her mind she had to climb over four hills of rock. She opened her eyes and squatted to find the footholds, then turn, step-two-three, and she was down. Stepping and hopping due east, she clambered, leapt over a deep crack, walked, climbed, clambered some more, and waved Phennil over. Four rock hillocks later, and her mind told her to climb down and around an outcropping, which she found almost immediately. The elf followed her, awestruck into silence at whatever magic was helping Kyer find this place. Kyer didn't understand it either, but she mentally thanked Kayme.

"There." She pointed at a large granite boulder leaning against the wall. It was blissfully calm down here, out of the wind. The whistling could still be heard from above but fainter. "Good thing Janak didn't come with us." The gap behind the boulder was not very wide. The dwarf's bulk would never have managed to pass through.

"He might have been able to move the boulder out of the way," Phennil said helpfully.

"I don't suppose either of us thought to bring a torch?" Kyer peered behind the enormous rock.

"Well, I don't have a torch, but will this do?" Phennil put a hand inside his cloak and withdrew what looked like a simple stick. But when he held it out, she saw that it was actually a long, narrow tube with the slightest of S shapes to it.

"Gee, that's . . . remarkable, Phennil," Kyer said dryly. "I'm not sure a stick will be quite as useful as a torch would be right now, though. What the hell is it?"

He looked at her as if she'd just asked him what an arrow was. "It's a rod of light, of course. One of the simplest, and therefore least expensive, types of magic available. Which is the only reason I have it." He held it up again and peered into it. "It's easy to store to boot!" He then surprised her by sticking one end of it in his mouth. She felt her face crinkle into a grimace. He continued to stare at her, scratching his elbow, as though this was the most obvious way in the world to pass time while in a barren wasteland.

"This is fun." She rested her shoulder against the rock wall. He held up a finger for her to be patient. Tapping her foot, feeling nothing of the kind, she waited. Then she leaned forward. The stick began to glow, just faintly. The elf finally took it out of his mouth.

"It'll warm up in a moment or two. Shall we get moving, or are we going to just stay out here where everything is grey?"

A sarcastic remark came to Kyer's lips but didn't pass through. She merely smirked, and squeezed through the narrow opening, pressing her sword against her body to keep it out of the way. Phennil came right behind her, holding the rod of light aloft so she could see her way down the naturally rocky path.

The steep sloped passageway was too narrow for them to walk abreast. Ceiling, floor, and walls were straight, jagged, and smooth, as if they'd been hacked out with a massive chisel with no finishing work done. The pair had to tread carefully, the natural steps not following any pattern of regularity.

"How about handing me that light for a bit so I can see in front of me?" Kyer said. Phennil relinquished it without comment. She held it at shoulder height, out to the side so it would still light Phennil's way. The rod illuminated with a strong, steady radiance, not as intense as a torch, but certainly comparable to multiple candles. Its added bonuses were that it did not flicker, felt cool in her hand, and was smokeless—a particularly useful tool for exploring a narrow underground tunnel. After a few steps, the path wasn't as steep, but it angled left and right until neither of them had a notion of direction. Kyer put a hand up and brushed her palm along the low ceiling. Phennil occasionally stooped to avoid cracking his head.

"How far down are we d'you think? See any lichen by any chance?" Phennil asked hopefully. "This place is not exactly what I would call 'homey,' and I'd just as soon find what we're looking for and get out, if you don't mind."

"Don't get panicky on me now, Phennil. I have no control over any of this. Take your complaint up with Kayme. I'd just like to know why—in all the corners of Rydris—this is the only place to find falander."

Just then the tunnel levelled off and widened, and they found themselves in a small chamber. It was empty, with three doorways leading from it. *How stereotypical.* The ceiling was higher than in the tunnel, though, to Phennil's relief. Kyer held the light up. They stood in breathless awe. She used the rod to trace the angular stripes on the walls, formed by layer upon layer of rock. Natural decorations that manifested the innumerable centuries taken for the cavern's formation. Deep below the surface, not a note of the flutes could be heard.

"Who," Phennil whispered, afraid even his breath was a disturbance, "created this? The tunnel, the room?"

Kyer shook her head. "All I know is I'm looking for lichen," she whispered back. "And there isn't any here. Which passageway do you think?"

"I don't know. You're the one with the dreams."

She looked about them. "This seems almost like a foyer." She closed her eyes, hoping for another clue, but none was forthcoming. "Well, I've always had good feelings about the left."

The elf followed her obediently.

The level passage twisted and turned, and Kyer was grateful there were, so far, no other passages leading off it. She doubted even Phennil's tracking skills would be helpful in getting them out of here if they were lost. There was not a trace of dust for them to disturb, and their feet left no prints on the rock floor.

Kyer stumbled suddenly. There had been a shudder in the very solid rock. She was about to carry on walking, but Phennil touched her arm. "Kyer. I think that was a tremor."

"Possibly." She began walking again.

"But, Kyer, don't you think we ought not to stay down here?"

"What are you talking about? We haven't found the falander yet."

"But it was a *tremor*, Kyer."

"Very good, Phennil, you've done your studying." The passageway forked in front of them. "Left again, I think, don't you?"

"But—"

Phennil followed her. She had the light.

This passage was wider, and soon they came upon two doorways, one on each side. They entered one. A low slab lay in one corner, and a taller, narrow rock stood in another. A stone box, like a chest, sat up against the wall with the withered remains of a wooden lid. "A bedroom?" Kyer said. Bed, washstand, and a chest for belongings. Given the right adornments, this could be as comfortable as a chamber in Shael Castle.

Eight other almost identical rooms along the passage solidified their speculations. The slabs of rock were in different configurations, and the lids of the chests in varied condition of decomposition. Some rooms were larger, with larger stone slabs. For couples? The rooms were, not surprisingly, windowless, though the air quality wasn't too bad for underground. The stone chests were all empty.

"I sure do wonder who used to live here."

Phennil agreed. "And it's as if they left in an organized fashion too."

"How do you mean?"

"Well, observe. There are no remains of living creatures, so they didn't die here. They didn't leave anything behind, so they either didn't have much stuff or they had lots of time to pack. It doesn't seem like a hasty departure, that's all. It was planned."

The raising of the light to see farther down the hallway revealed that there were many more doorways lining the hall and not a feather of lichen to be seen.

"Shall we try the right-hand fork?" said Kyer.

It was as they turned back down the hall that they felt another tremor. Harder this time. They both touched the wall to steady themselves.

"Kyer, really, I think we should get out of here."

"Go ahead, then," she snapped, betraying her own nerves. "I'm not leaving without what we came for." Her stubborn side could win any argument with her nerves. "Listen," she said, more calmly, "tremors happen all the time in places like this. It doesn't mean there's danger. Look at all the people who lived here."

"You'll note it's decidedly unpopulated at the moment," the elf muttered as he followed her. She said nothing. "By the way, how many 'places like this' have you visited in your lifetime?"

Kyer went up the right-hand fork.

Several paces up the passage was a wide, arched doorway. The rod of light was not nearly bright enough to illuminate the whole room, but a few steps in each direction led them to believe fairly strongly that this was the rock-world equivalent of a great hall. No ornate stone pillars and arches as would be found in a dwarven hall, just practical simplicity. Jagged pillars held up the ceiling that was only twice as high as the ceilings in the bedrooms, none of the vastness of a dwarven hall either. Simple stone benches or stools lining stone slab tables, row upon row. And at the far end, they found the entrance to the kitchens. Phennil had forgotten his desire to trade places with Janak. "I can hardly wait to tell Janak about this." He grinned. "He'll go puce with envy!"

Kyer just grunted.

"What sort of industry kept them going, do you suppose?" Phennil asked.

Kyer had no means even to guess. She was getting fidgety. "This is all very nice, but where is the falander?" Her desire to get out to the relative safety of ground level intensified.

She pushed herself onward to look in the kitchens. As large as in Shael Castle, with two gigantic stone fireplaces that had steel spits fastened right into the rock. Countertops, tables, shelves for storage, all hewn out of stone.

A great gaping hole in the floor in one corner was not quite covered by a lid that used to be a thick round of oak but now was crumbling with decay. Phennil nudged it with a boot, and a few hunks of rotted wood tumbled into the hole. A second or two later, a splash met their ears, followed by a dank, wet smell.

Kyer moved farther in to view the back corners of the kitchen. She stopped short, holding up the rod to see that the ceiling had caved in. It had not happened recently, but Kyer was forced to recognize that something greater than a mild tremor had occurred at some point. Kyer rubbed her left shin with her right heel and bit her tongue. She looked at Phennil. He had seen it too, and his brow was creased with worry. They left the kitchens.

There were two other passages off this corridor. As they hurried past the first, they felt a lightness in the air, a breath of freshness that was unmistakably reminiscent of outside. Although it was nice to know where they could come if they needed an alternate exit, it was useless now without the falander. The other doorway led into a passageway that was blocked by fallen stone. They looked at each other again. There was really no point in saying anything.

They retraced their steps to the foyer, to try the right-hand doorway. Even Kyer stepped up her pace now. Her blood pulsed in her temples. Derry and the others had no idea where they were, only a vague notion of which direction they'd gone. Phennil glanced apprehensively, and wishfully, at the passage by which they had entered. "It's no good, Phennil."

"I know, I know, we can't leave until we've found what we came for."

They both questioned the wisdom of that when the next tremor came. Kyer was getting anxious. What if they didn't find the lichen? *No*, Kyer thought, *Kayme wouldn't do that*. She didn't try to answer the question, *Why not?*

The right-hand passage was long. About five minutes they stumbled along it, growing weary of the search, the exploration having lost its fascination.

Suddenly Phennil reached out his hand again. "Do you smell that?"

Kyer sniffed but could smell only dry ageless stone. She shook her head, and they kept on. "How long does the light last, anyway?" She wasn't sure she wanted the answer.

"Oh, it'll keep going strong for a long time yet. It's supposed to last a day."

"Hey, wait a minute, I smell it too!" Kyer picked up her pace.

Whatever it was, it smelled . . . organic.

They broke into a run, their nimble feet continuing the same dance they'd used above ground on the crags, missing any cracks or juts in the rock, until finally they reached yet another doorway. They burst into the room and held aloft the rod of light. It would have been obvious to anyone who'd ever entered a physicker's preparation room that this was one. Shelf upon tiny shelf, from floor to ten-foot ceiling, had at one time held all manner of items used for medicinal purposes. The room was large enough for more than one person to have worked here with adequate space. Every few feet along the wall, footholds like those of a ladder had been hewn into the rock, and handholds of iron had been sunken in higher up. The physickers, or healers, or alchemists for that matter, could easily access the upper storage areas. Beneath the counter space in the middle of the room, all around the outside, were tiny drawers, all carved out of stone. Apparently the stoneworkers didn't waste time in other areas of the underground village in order to use their skills more effectively here. In one corner was another, smaller well. Phennil opened a couple of drawers. Most were empty, but one low drawer was not.

"Look here." He held up a hawk's claw. "I guess they forgot this." He put it in his pocket just as Kyer gasped.

Clinging to the walls of this exquisite room was a yellowish lichen.

Kyer's only guess was that the evaporating water in the well triggered growth in whatever organic material was left either lying around or in the air after the residents had departed. Those bizarre growing conditions were surely rare, which would explain why, of all the corners of Rydris, Kayme had sent her here.

"Is this the right stuff?" Phennil asked.

"Well, of course." She opened her pouch. "It must be. I haven't seen any other lichen in the place. Have you?"

Then another tremor came, and this time, dust and pebbles fell from the ceiling.

"Quickly!" Kyer said, and they tore the coarse webs of the plant off the walls and stuffed them into their pouches.

"How much do we need?" Phennil asked.

"I don't know. Let's just take as much as we can fit."

Her pouch crammed, Kyer yanked on the drawstring just as a massive jolt threw them both to the stone floor.

They were making such good time. Sure, they'd ridden the horses harder than Hunter would usually have done, but these were unusual circumstances. And besides, after tomorrow, the horses could rest as long as they liked. If they started early and took short rests as they had been doing, they would reach the Cold Fells by late tomorrow afternoon. Hunter had never been to the Cold Fells, but from what he'd heard, if Kyer and company were looking for something, they would be there quite a while. On a peaceful mission, they would not anticipate any threat, so Hunter's band would take them by surprise.

His horse stumbled. Was that a tremor? Nothing to worry about; it had stopped.

We'll have to survey the situation, though. It's Kyer I'm supposed to take.

Then he pondered what to do with the others. Kill them? That would hinder their mission all right. But, damn it, if their mission failed, Alon would die. Fredric could not let that happen. How to make it look as if he were trying to thwart them without actually doing so?

A sudden jolt struck, and the horses whinnied in panic. Fredric was thrown and the animal galloped off amid the swaying land. His men clung to the grasses and cried out to the gods of their choice. Fredric whispered a silent thank-you for what was likely to cause a delay.

Kyer cried out and they tried to cling to the firmness of the floor as it rocked—not gently—from side to side. Kyer grasped all around her. There was nothing to hold on to and nowhere to find shelter. Anything she thought ought to be sturdy was not. "Phennil!" she screamed. Shaking, rumbling, and roaring. Who knew rock could roar like that? Like gigantic waves in a storm at sea. She was bounced and jounced along the floor until she was certain bruises would cover her entire body. And the crashing noise offered no comfort at all. Thundering crashes of rock outside in the corridor and splinters of rock falling all over her. Dust, pebbles, clouds of it coming in from out there. She buried her face in her elbow on the floor so she could breathe.

Then the swaying slowed. And stopped. The smell of dry, dry rock was heavy in the air. Where the world around them had roared deafeningly, it was now deadly quiet. At least thirty seconds it had been, and it was another thirty before the friends could look each other in the eye. Phennil's hair and eyelashes were sprinkled with dust and bits of stone, and his usually brilliantly blue eyes were cloudy. Kyer imagined that she looked no better.

"Is it over?" she whispered, afraid to make the shaking start again.

"I . . . think so," he replied, just as softly. They stared at each other, horrified.

"Are you okay?"

"I won't know until I move. You?"

"Same."

Finally they rose, gingerly, and examined themselves, brushing off dust. Kyer ensured that none of the precious falander had been lost in the chaos.

"We were lucky," he said. "Nothing fell onto us." Some of the drawers had jounced out of place and smashed to the floor around them. Kyer felt a pang of regret that the room had suffered damage.

"Luck is relative," she pointed out, wincing as she ran her hands over herself in search of lumps and bumps. "I'm not anxious to see how much or how little is left of the way out of here."

"Let's hurry." Phennil snatched up the rod of light, still glowing strongly, from where it had landed after being jolted out of Kyer's hand.

They went back the way they had come, holding their cloaks over their noses to filter the dust, though coughing could not be prevented entirely. They stepped carefully over fallen clumps of stone and avoided the sides of the passage for fear of loosening more of it. Their footfalls echoed dully in the hall. Around a bend they stopped short. The way was completely blocked. The corridor had imploded, the entire roof, all the way to the surface of the Cold Fells, had dropped and obliterated any sign of an underground village beyond this point.

"The only two ways out of here that we know of were beyond this mess. We couldn't possibly have arrived here yesterday," Kyer muttered, fear tightened across her shoulders.

Phennil sighed. "We'll have to go the other way and see what's at the other end of the passage, beyond the healer's room."

"You're awful calm all of a sudden," Kyer remarked.

Phennil chuckled softly. "I guess when you fear the worst, and then the worst happens . . . Well, there's nothing more to fear."

Kyer envied her friend's composure. Her pulse thrummed in her throat, and a trickle of sweat ran down her side. With furrowed brow, she took the light source from Phennil and walked deliberately the other way, limping from her bruised knees.

Phennil had long legs, and he needed them to keep up with her.

The corridor went on for what seemed like miles to the two weary explorers, with only a few small chambers along it. Possibly an infirmary area, possibly simple storage spaces. The rubble was hard to avoid in the inadequate light. Twice Kyer tripped over debris, one of those times taking her flat to the ground. Her palms were scraped as if she'd been climbing rope.

"What did these people do?" Kyer kicked a rock aside in frustration. "I mean, they must have had more than one way out of here, or else how would they get above ground? To get food, to hunt?" She thought with yearning of Jesqellan and the tunnelling spell he was working on, though he probably wasn't ready even if he knew where they were.

"It could very well be that there were other exits further along any of the other passages we went down besides this one," Phennil said reasonably. "We just didn't go far enough."

"Well, that's not much help now. Even if we had found them, we couldn't have left without the falander."

"I hate to point this out, Kyer, but if we don't get out of here, it won't do much good for us to have found the falander."

"Shut up, Phennil."

She stopped short at a fork in the corridor.

"What do you think? Do you have a coin we can flip?"

"No," he answered. "I mean, I have a coin, but see, that way is a narrower passage. This way looks a lot more like an entrance hall to me." He pointed to the right opening, which was, indeed, quite a bit wider.

"Too bad it never occurred to them to use signage," she murmured. "All right, that sounds logical to me." They hurried to the right.

About twenty paces later, their noses were bombarded with another smell. This time it was hot. And moist.

Steam came at them from somewhere farther on. Shortly thereafter, the corridor opened into a cavern. The rod of light could not penetrate its depth. Just past the entrance, some steps led downward, each step wider than the one above it, and the third one down was under water. The sound of trickling and dripping was eerie in the darkness. Phennil took the light from Kyer and held it as high as he could, allowing his elven eyes to pierce the misty murk.

"It's a hot spring." His voice was filled with wonder. "Can you see? Just let your eyes relax—"

"Yes, I can see."

"Oh. Hey, it looks like there's been some damage in here." He moved around on the narrow ledge surrounding the pool of steaming water.

Kyer went down a couple of steps. It was a bit slippery. She crouched and cupped her hand in the water. "Wow, that's beautiful. Time for a swim?" The water trickled through her fingers, and the echo of the falling drops offered a hint at the size of the cavern. "Hey, don't get too far away, it's awful dark over here!"

"Gods' breath," came Phennil's voice from twenty paces along the pool edge. "Look at this. There must have been another massive earthquake sometime. The rock makes nearly a wall over here, and it's obvious there was once another whole pool extending off that one. You can see the beginning of the curve."

Kyer's skin prickled as sweat seeped from her pores. "I wonder if this is what these people did?" she suggested. "I mean, a large physicking prep room, all those chambers along the corridor, and now a hot spring. Maybe people came here for healing."

As Phennil made his way back, she lowered herself to sit on the top step, careful not to slip on the moss that coated the rock. The light in Phennil's hand drew near. *Moss?* She looked up at Phennil, but her gaze moved past him, over his shoulder. Her eyes snapped open. *It's not moss at all.*

"Oh gods, Kayme," she moaned as she raised herself upright.

Phennil looked around. "Where?"

"We got the wrong one, Phennil." Her voice trembled with urgency. "Look on the walls." She clambered up the steps, afraid of losing her footing in the damp.

He held aloft the light that glittered softly on the moisture that coated the walls. Moisture from the condensation that trickled down among a soft, weblike lichen of a bluish-green colour.

"This lichen is the wrong one!" she said in a quiet squeal, pulling out her pouch and trying to undo the very secure knot. Her fingers fumbled.

"How do you know?" Phennil set down the light rod and did the same.

"I don't know. The moisture dripping down . . . this is not falander." She stopped a brief moment to point. "That is."

Then another tremor hit.

Not heavy enough to throw them off balance, just a low rumble. Just enough to stop hearts beating. Small amounts of debris fell in the entryway.

"Shit, shit, shit!" She finally got the pouch open and frantically tore lichen out of it. She cursed herself for packing it so full. "We still don't even know how to get out of here!" Lichen from both pouches fell, discarded, into the hot water. Fingers tore the new plant off the walls and stuffed it into the emptied sacks. "*This* is why Kayme sent me here," she cried. "These people were *healers*, and this stuff grows here in these perfect conditions so that they could use it for *healing* people. That other stuff was just a coincidence."

"Get as much as we can, and we have to get out of here," Phennil said. "There has got to be a way out farther along."

"There isn't a farther along, Phennil, the corridor ended here!" Her pouch was nearly full.

"Gods, you're right. Then back to that other passage; that's got to be it."

There was nothing more to say.

The pouches were full and tightened. Phennil grabbed the light rod and her hand.

The aftershock struck. Kyer and Phennil cried out as they tumbled backwards into the hot water. Kyer fought desperately to reach the surface hindered by her armour and weapons. The water had an unusual buoyancy to it, for which Kyer was eternally grateful, not least because she hadn't touched bottom. Rocks narrowly missed her as they splashed into the pool, and she didn't want to know where they had come from. She felt herself yanked, and it was Phennil, not as weighed down as she, dragging both of them toward the edge of the spring. She got both elbows up onto the ledge and held on madly.

"Phennil, you're bleeding." Kyer spoke through gasps, nodding in alarm at the dark smudge oozing from a gash on the side of his head.

He moved a hand up to wipe it out of his eye. "Oh. Thought it was jus' water." He sounded dreamy.

"Stop it," Kyer said sharply, frightened by his casual acceptance of the wound.

"Hey, look," Phennil said with bizarre cheerfulness. "The rod of light floats!" He rescued it from the water and held it up for her to see. "That's pretty lucky." He set it on the ledge in front of them.

"Well, like I said, luck is relative." She indicated over her shoulder to the entrance, which was, naturally, now nearly completely filled with stone. "Suppose we'd be able to move enough of those rocks to—" She turned back to Phennil in time to see his eyes roll into his head as he passed out. "No!" she screamed and just barely caught him under one arm before he could droop into the water. The extra weight pulled them both down, and she kicked desperately to raise them up so she could get a better hold on the slimy, slippery ledge. Again she thanked the buoyancy of the water. *Gods, if I could make it to the steps* . . . She kicked her feet to shift in that direction.

And the rod of light chose that moment to lose power.

"Hey!" Kyer cried. "No, no, no! Not now," she pleaded. But its glow grew fainter and fainter. And went out.

Utter, utter darkness. Dark as death must be.

Kyer was gripped by a terror she had never known. It clasped her heart with both hands and squeezed until she thought she might scream. "Shit god damn it, damn you, Kayme!" The words tumbled out, pushed from behind by panic. And the fact that their sound seemed to travel no farther than the wall to which she clung brought her close to tears. "Phennil," she whimpered, pleading, shaking the sodden, dead-weight elf.

The sound of trickling and dripping had been eerie before; now it was like harsh, devilish laughter echoing all around and taunting her. Kicking frantically and inching along with her elbow, she tried to move toward the steps, but in her blindness, she had no idea if she was gaining any ground. She slipped and lost hold, and both of them plunged again into the unimaginable depths. The cavern's only answer to Kyer's silent scream was a mouthful of water, and she came up coughing and spluttering, realizing that she couldn't tell if Phennil's head was above water.

Treading water for one in armour was bad enough. Trying to keep the two of them up was going to exhaust her sooner than she wanted to imagine. Extra buoyancy or not, they both wore armour and steel weapons. No amount of mineral salts could offset that. Her arm ached from holding his waterlogged body. Her other arm ached trying to keep hold of the wall. Her legs melted to jelly from kicking.

Oh god, oh god! She couldn't even decide which god to pray to.

Another tremor sent yet another sheaf of sharp rocks hailing onto them. Her stomach sent up a burst of terror that caught in her throat, constricting it so she had to force her breath through it.

Guerrin . . . Aidan . . . we have to get out of here! We have to get out!

Her head bobbed so water filled her ears and she pulled herself upward again.

Suddenly there appeared just next to Kyer in the water, a shimmering arch, like a doorway, its glow a welcome source of light that the terrified warrior could have kissed.

Kyer had seen it before. Only once. Seeing it again brought back the memory of what it was. She didn't know where it had come from, nor where it was leading them, but it was away from this place. And it was their only chance.

She adjusted her arm so it was under Phennil's shoulders. She took an enormous breath and shoved off the wall, dragging her friend with her. They plunged under water, and she gave a violent kick, propelling the two of them through the portal.

Nine

Call Me The Guardian

Thanks to the earthquake one of the horses was lame, and Hunter was glad it was only one. Harley had a sprained wrist and Mullin a broken ankle. Harley would be fine in a day or two, with the help of a mild healing potion, but Mullin was in considerable pain and, of course, could not walk. He could, with help, mount his horse and ride, but he complained of the difficulty in staying straight in his saddle with the use of only one stirrup. Also, understandably, searing pain shot through him as they rode. Hunter found him irritating as hell, but used the mood to pretend he was irked at being held up.

They'd lost a couple of hours' time in rounding up the scattered horses and tending to the two men's injuries, so tempers were already short. Hew fired an arrow through the neck of Kep's lame horse, and Kep rode with Harley.

We're losing time rapidly, Hunter said to himself.

"We'll have to stop to camp soon, Chief," Tigo said after a while. "Mullin'll need another pain draught."

Hunter grunted. "We'll start all the earlier in the morning. I want to catch them!"

Bianca Ardra dismounted and, drawing Marlyn along behind her, cleared the way through the underbrush, using the small scythe she had had the foresight to bring along. *Been a long time since anyone's come this way.* If anyone had ever come this way. She had purposely chosen a new route. A different path. A change.

There had been plenty of that in the village of Hreth. A quick review of the last three or four moons was enough to make her head spin. She could trace it back to the attack on her best friend.

Kyer had said over and over that it wasn't Bianca's fault, that Gar and company had been counting the days since they were kids, waiting for the right time to jump her again.

"If not last night, then next week," Kyer had said. "Anyway, I'm *fine*. Stop worrying."

No amount of denial from Kyer could convince Bianca. She should have been there. She knew something had been brewing for weeks. Yet Bianca had had her eye on Sten for months, so she allowed him to talk her into another drink, which had naturally evolved into more. Not only had it not been worth the wait, but the next day she had learned what was really going on. Sten had laughed in the morning.

"Thanks for the tumble, sweets." He tickled her neck and reached for his trousers. "I'm sure I had at least as much fun as Gar and the others."

Bianca sat up, pulling the blanket around her, suspicion nibbling at her skin like the chilly morning air. "What do you mean by that?"

"Somebody had to keep you occupied. Don't get me wrong." He reached for her, his hand on the back of her neck. "I'd been wanting to try that for a while." She pulled away. "Hey, I'm glad I did, don't be mad. The timing worked out perfect."

She didn't say anything right away, words stuck in her throat as she grappled with *don't be mad*, after hearing *Gar and the others*.

"What did they do?" she demanded.

"Better get your clothes on and go check on Kyer." His tunic on, he reached for his cloak. "See if she's lying in the mud somewhere." He rammed his foot into a boot, and fumbled about for the other, which had been hastily flung aside in the darkness. "Never understood why you're friends with that witch."

Bianca scrambled out of the blankets and started grabbing clothes. "You mean to tell me that you planned this? That tumbling with me was about beating up Kyer?"

He stood up. "I told you I enjoyed it," he said defensively, as if that was the only thing that mattered to her. "I'd even do it again."

Bianca had assured him she did not share his assessment of the experience, before dashing to Kyer's, expecting to find her laid up with broken bones and stab wounds.

Of course, she hadn't. Though Bianca and their other close friends, Tarqan and Adric, did not believe Kyer was a witch, as others did, their friend had always been a little bit frightening. Despite the odds, Kyer had bested her eight attackers, suffering only some cuts and bruises, whereas Gar and his friends . . . Well, they were relieved when Kyer had left a week later. Bianca, on the other hand, had lost her best friend, and despite Kyer's insistence that it wasn't her fault, had not forgiven herself for being taken in.

At least I got him out of my system. Whacking her scythe at the bushes helped, too, even though the memory was several months old now. She sang soothing words at Marlyn, who was tossing his head a little, and Bianca wondered if there was a mountain lion or something nearby.

Bianca had used what she now analysed as "poor judgement" several times lately, starting with that night she had been diverted, and allowed Kyer to be attacked. Not long after she'd lost her best friend, Dregor's army had invaded the village with senseless destruction. Their leader, not Dregor himself but some deputy, a tall fellow who ought to wear brighter colours to boost his pallor, had called all the young men and boys, even the littl'uns.

The littl'uns all the way up to the very rogues who still looked battered and beaten after their ill advised jumping of a *waepnian* trained fighter. The deputy had lined them all up and asked who among them had magical power, or magical devices. Ridiculous! Why? Why had he come to Hreth of all places, looking for such a thing? You couldn't get much more isolated and insignificant than Hreth, not if you covered every inch of Rydris. And when they couldn't give him the answer he wanted—of course they couldn't give him the answer he wanted! —he'd begun killing.

Three. One of Gar's mates, a lad barely thirteen, and a littl'un. Wee Tamiz, only four years old.

Tarqan stood in that line, unarmed, his eyes piercing her like darts, pleading for her to take some sort of action. Their friend, Adric, the fourth of Brendow's trainees, already lay dead where he had defended his family in the initial attack. They had destroyed sections of the peaceful village, and then left with, apparently, nothing.

And Bianca, the *waepnian* trained fighter, had done nothing.

She emerged from the trees, and the wind that scooted across the slope cooled the tears that moistened her face. Bianca wiped her cheeks with her sleeve.

Destruction for destruction's sake. Bianca did not share the common view that the timing of Kyer's departure was suspicious, that she had left knowing they were coming, nor did she believe Kyer had sent them. Kyer had been her friend since they were little, and there was simply no way the other woman was responsible. She'd been in Hreth since she was a littl'un. The accusation made no sense to Bianca. Yet there was one thing she was sure of.

"Kyer would never have done nothing," Bianca said to Marlyn as they stood on the edge of the forest. She had lost sight of the stream as they'd picked their way through the bushes, and she saw it now, just to the left of where they stood. She drew Marlyn along toward it.

The village was rebuilding. Folks had come together like never before and helped each other. Neighbours had taken each other in, even if it meant entire families sleeping on the floors. Everyone pitched in, including Lord Bartheylen's soldiers, and more than once Bianca left to fetch water, returning to find a house where nothing but rubble had stood moments before. Her biggest fear was that it wasn't enough.

Not that Bianca truly believed such a senseless attack would occur again. It was hard to imagine they would come back, but it was foolish to assume that it would be a one-time event.

And as with any time a terrible thing occurs, she would do anything in her power to make sure that terrible thing never happened again.

She loved Hreth and the people in it, and unlike Kyer, would not consider leaving it. But a village tended to feel smaller and closer as time went on, and Bianca's way of dealing with that was to take a few days away once in a while to . . . collect herself. Many a time she had packed her horse with her bedroll and enough food and supplies for a few days and headed into the mountain above Hreth. This time was different. This time she was searching. She needed to find a way past her recent failures. Especially now that she was preparing for something completely new. And that was why she had packed her horse and had taken a different direction.

She left Marlyn on the edge of the forest so he could nosh on some lovely dandelions while she looked for a decent place to camp. She trundled up the scree, following the stream toward a rocky outcropping, the morning sun warming her back. She turned around to gaze out across the valley to where the village of Hreth lay nestled, the farmlands stretching out along the river. The sun climbed the other side of the opposite mountain, its rays peering over the peaks to brush the tops of the new roofs below.

Rebuilding wasn't enough. To rebuild implied the new version of Hreth would be a duplicate of the old Hreth, and Bianca believed in her soul that a new version of the same Hreth was not good enough. They had received goods and support from other towns, and a lot of the villagers were content to accept the donations and return nothing but gratitude. Others agreed with Bianca that they must find a way to not only repay those generous offerings, but to stand on their own. And now she was responsible. People would look to her.

The new magistrate of Hreth could not return to her village feeling just as helpless as she felt in this moment.

Bianca sighed heavily, breathing in the pine scented forest on the light breeze, and . . . another smell. Something animalish. She looked back at Marlyn thirty paces away, contentedly chewing.

She breathed again. Just forest.

Bianca stepped carefully over the rocks, along the hill, scanning the area. Then the wind changed. There was definitely another smell that was distinctly not forest. A rock wobbled under her foot and she nearly fell. The morning sun caught a sparkle on the rock and she crouched, shifting the sword on her hip, and turned the rock over. Her eyes widened and her jaw went slack. The underside of the rock was pebbled with pale green gemstones, each one about the size of her thumb. She flipped over another rock. And another, excitement bubbling in her chest.

"Aidan's breath."

She drew her dagger and, with almost no effort, pried several chunks of green stones. She lifted her hand and the sunlight bathed the gems so her palm was a yellow-green glow. Bianca's hand trembled with excitement.

"This is peridot!"

Marlyn *hooshed* in agreement.

Peridot was known for its magical properties of harnessing the power of the sun. It was a charm against spells and evil, as well as giving the wearer courage, and it had many other attributes. Bianca would check with Brendow but she was pretty certain. And if she was right . . . This *might* solve some of Hreth's resource problems. She tucked the stones into her pouch. If they could gather it, sell it raw, or maybe some of Hreth's crafters could use it in jewellery, or tal—

She froze. Every hair on her body stood on end.

Marlyn, her beloved mount, was thirty paces back down and across the hillside. The *hooshing* sound, which she had, out of habit, *thought* was Marlyn, had come from *up* the hill. In the opposite direction from where she had left him.

It *hooshed* again. A wind ruffled her hair, echoed by a tremble all through her body.

Bianca stared down at the rocks. A mountain lion? She had to look up, she *had* to, but terror had seized every fibre of every muscle like she gripped her sword in a sparring match.

You're a swordfighter! she pleaded with herself. *Are you going to let it pounce on you without looking it in the eye?* No damn way.

She drew her weapon and whirled around to face it. It wasn't a mountain lion.

Five paces up the hill was a baby dragon.

She shrieked, and slid on the wobbly rocks beneath her boots, sending pebbles rolling and bouncing down into the trees. She slipped and landed ungracefully on her knees, then her belly, joining the rocks in sliding down the slope. Frantically she grabbed at rocks, and between her hand and her sword she finally slowed down. The rolling rocks stopped. She looked back up at the dragon from her prone position.

It bobbed its head, for all the world like it was laughing at her. Its wings were tucked in at its sides.

"Hello," Bianca said, as softly as the breeze. "Where'd you come from?"

It looked at her out of one eye, then twitched its head to observe her out of its other eye.

Bianca searched her memory for every story she had heard of human encounters with dragons. They were rare but not unheard of. Hreth had two elders, Brendow being one of them, who had each come in contact with a dragon in the wild. Both of those were decades ago, and not around these parts. Still, the stories were thrilling enough to be requested at community gatherings, and the concept of being courteous to a dragon was more or less common knowledge. It was one thing to hear stories. To meet one face to face was another thing altogether, and everything Bianca had heard seemed to have dropped out of her mind and bounced down the hillside with the pebbles.

Below, Marlyn stomped and whinnied, and Bianca willed him to calm down lest he aggravate the dragon. Unfortunately her powers of psionic communication were limited to nothing. The only way to calm him was to deal with the present situation.

Bianca strained to remember anything about dragon behaviour. Mostly she remembered they were one of the smartest creatures in existence. With that in mind she hoped she had shown, by laying there on the rocks, that she did not intend to attack it. Her initial engagement with sword in hand probably had not helped. The dragon hadn't pounced on her, anyway, which she took to be a good sign.

Dragons could sense mood and even understand human body language, she recalled Brendow saying. But that was an adult dragon. Were the rules different for a youngling? How would this littl'un have learned those things if it had never encountered a human before? Was it instinct? Or intelligence, such that it had the ability to learn quickly, to know that there was even something to learn here? Did it innately understand the difference between a friend and an enemy?

That would make it a lot smarter than humans, Bianca thought.

She couldn't lie here staring at it all day. She made up her mind. She began to sing, as she often did to Marlyn, tentatively at first, paying attention to the dragon's reaction, then with a bit more confidence. Still softly. It was a song about the morning, the first idea that came to her head. She couldn't tell if the dragon liked the song, but figured if it didn't like it, its feelings on the matter would be clear.

Bianca took her next risk. Still humming, she painstakingly drew her knee beneath her and pushed up. The dragon watched, its head cocked to the side. She lifted her knee again to place her foot carefully on the rocks. The last thing she needed was to try to get to a standing position only to lose her footing and startle the creature by falling again. At last she got herself upright, pausing each time the dragon shifted uncertainly, its feet almost as tentative on the rocks as her own. She straightened, and the dragon took a little hop backwards.

One more thing she recalled from Brendow's tale was how a swordwielder should show she didn't intend to use her weapon. Bianca carefully sheathed her sword. She stood with her arms straight, palms out, and raised them out to the side, halfway between vertical and horizontal, and bowed her head. She held the position, and stopped singing for a few slow breaths intended to portray calm, then carefully, hopefully, heart banging in her chest, looked up at it.

It opened its wings slightly, and bobbed its head at her.

Exhilaration was like lightning through her every limb. A funny thing happened. The dragon made some noises in its throat, like cooing, or purring. Or singing. Bianca sang another line of the song, a bit more strongly this time. The dragon purred again. All around them was silence, the slight breeze making its own music through the trees. She realized even Marlyn had been calmed by the song.

Her voice sonorous now, Bianca sang to the dragon, and slowly, slowly, like an insect's progress across a leaf, like a *waepnian* sword drill, she reached her hand toward the dragon. It hopped uphill, sending a few rocks rolling and bouncing. Bianca didn't move, but kept singing, her hand out as if to catch raindrops. The dragon steadied itself and cocked its head at her. She kept singing. It flapped its wings. It cooed and purred again. Bianca kept singing.

The dragon cooed, and in a gurgling sort of hum, began to sing with her. It had learned the melody and sang with her.

Bianca kept singing through a throat clenched with emotion. Her cheeks dampened by tears, she continued to sing with the dragon. It stretched out its neck until it could reach, and sniffed her hand.

In the back of her mind, behind this magical moment, she was aware that although she had just arrived on this mountainside, hadn't even found a spot to camp yet, she had found possible solutions to several of Hreth's problems: a supply of a valuable gem, and a dragon.

Bianca Ardra, the new magistrate of Hreth, would no longer do nothing.

Phennil clung to life like the lichen clung to the dripping walls, but within his unconscious state he submerged into memory.

The murky, mucky water surrounds him. Cold. Blind. Smashed into sucking mud. The force that pushed him in lifts its weight and moves off. He tries to kick, but his little foot is bound by . . . a weed? Like serpents and eels. The lake bottom is slimy and sludgy. He reaches down to unhook his foot. Misses. Chest constricts with panic, the need to breathe. Reaches down. The foot does not slide out of the slippery weed. Need to breathe! His head screams with fear, panic, demand. His hair is in his eyes, his nose, his mouth. Sees red . . . white . . . black, as life depletes. A desperate yank pulls the weed from the sludge's grip. He thrusts . . . Which way is up? Out? Out! Flailing arms.

Another yank—from above—grips his shirt. Pulling against the press of the water. Drawing him with a burst into . . . glorious, glorious air! Voices hollering. Rupi. And Paullin. Gasp. Cough. Gasp. Clutching the grass with small hands. Vowing never to return to Dionne's realm.

Kyer and Phennil landed, sopping wet, on the hard ground. Water spilled around them and rushed away. It steamed violently in the chill air. The doorway closed behind them, the rest of the water trapped in its lightless prison. The ground was grass, though sopped like after a full day's rain. Kyer rested her face on it, not caring where she was, only that she was no longer underground. The whistling wind blindsided her. It instantly annihilated any warmth leftover from the hot spring. Now she was just wet. Her drenched body turned to ice. Her left arm was still around Phennil, who lay facedown. The abrupt climate change had not brought him around, though she could now at least see the rise and fall of his chest. She gave his head a nudge so his nose and mouth weren't obstructed by grass.

She trembled with fear and cold.

This was not the first time she had been inexorably trapped in a terrifying circumstance and had escaped through a doorway that appeared when things couldn't possibly get any worse. The first time had not been all that long ago. And when she had described her experience, she had been greeted with suspicion, even accusation. She didn't want to imagine how Jesqellan would react if he knew the inconceivable had happened again. Could it have been Kayme? No. The wizard wasn't around the first time. *How in seven hells am I going to explain this?*

She shoved fear aside to deal with the here and now. A quick check on her and Phennil's pouches told her the knots were secure and none of the precious lichen had been lost. It had lived in a wet environment, so it could stand to stay wet, at least for a while, until it could be dried properly. A wave of intense relief flattened her to the ground again, and she permitted one sob to escape her chest.

A distraught whinny aroused her attention. She sat up and was immediately sorry for it as the wind smacked her square in the face. They were not far from where they had dismounted earlier that day. At least, she assumed it had been that day. The sun, blindingly bright after the blackness of the cavern, was a hair's breadth from the tops of the western mountains.

The horses had scattered after the quake but were finding each other again. Kyer braced herself and stood up. Her teeth clattered and every muscle vibrated with cold as she cast her eyes about for any sign of her companions. Derry and Jesqellan, who had remained behind, were nowhere to be seen. The horses appeared to be all right, could she assume her friends were unhurt as well? Presumably they were all off looking for her and Phennil. It occurred to her that Janak and Skimnoddle had been wandering on the rocks too. What had happened to them when the quake struck?

Kyer's fingers were stiff from trying to hold her soaked cloak close to her. She unfastened it and flung the garment to the ground. *Damn this wind!* she thought as it blasted her again. Though the wind was not as severe here as it had been out on the rocks, it hadn't died down since their departure from the surface of the world, and it mixed poorly with two saturated explorers. Kyer could hardly move with cold but she had to do something to alleviate their circumstances. Blankets were a must.

Donnagill was nearest and Trig and Leoht had sufficiently calmed themselves to munch on some grass beyond him. Skimnoddle's pony wasn't far away, and he was a wiser choice than the warhorse. Forcing herself to a bent standing position, she bade her legs to hasten. Their frigid, jerky movements were better than nothing, and she finally stumbled close enough to the creature to speak to him in as soothing a tone as her shivering voice could muster.

Her fingers were almost paralysed with cold, and her body shuddered uncontrollably, but she finally managed to unbuckle the straps holding the halfling's blanket and bedroll in place. She ran back to her friend. She rolled him onto dry ground and threw the blanket over him. It barely covered his upper half, but it was better than nothing while she took a moment to care for herself. She'd be much more useful to Phennil if she weren't suffering so. She squeezed water from her braid then shed armour and all upper clothing as well as her drenched boots. She took the blanket off Phennil and wrapped it around her shoulders. The white rose from Kayme was still in perfect, silken condition. She placed it carefully underneath her cloak, to be hidden until she could get some clothes on. Nakedness under the blanket was an astonishing improvement over wet clothes, and the shivering lessened.

Working quickly, Kyer laid the halfling's bedroll open on a dry section of grass, then yanked every stitch of wet clothing off Phennil. She rolled him up in the bedroll like he was filling for flatbread. His legs stuck out the bottom end, but she could fix that. She whistled to Trig, but the bay couldn't hear her in the wind, so she ran over to him. The run did her good, sending the blood pumping through her and warming her. She dug out her other tunic and threw it on before leading the horse back to Phennil, where she wrapped her blanket around his chilled feet and legs.

By this time, the sun had completely retreated below the edge of the world, and the sky was being overtaken by night in the east. It would not be too long before the darkness would stretch its canopy fully across to the west. But Kyer would never dread the mere darkness of night ever again.

She hoped the others were all right and would be back soon.

Kyer dug out her minimalistic physicking kit and knelt down to see what she could do about her friend's lumpy gash.

"What the hell?"

Phennil's voice. Weak, but conscious at last.

"Oh, Phennil, I'm so glad." Kyer leaned over to kiss him on the cheek.

"Wow, maybe my mother was right," Phennil said.

"About what?"

"Oh, nothing."

"Well, welcome back. In more ways than one." She smiled.

"But, Kyer, how in the name of the goddess did we—"

"Shh, take it easy. I think Kayme might have stepped in. I'll try to explain later. Right now, you've got a nasty cut here, and I'm not Derry, so you'd better hold still."

He winced in agreement as her cloth touched an especially tender spot.

"At least the spring water cleaned it for me," she murmured as she worked. "That's saved you even more pain."

"I'm an idiot, Kyer," he whispered.

She grinned. "Yeah, I know. Did you just figure that out?"

His eyes widened in intensity, and he gripped her arm. "No, Kyer, I mean it. I could have got us help sooner. My mother gave me a bell. If you ring it, the call can be heard for some distance, but only by friends. Here, let me show you—"

She stopped him. "Hold still. It doesn't matter. Your bell will be useful another time, and our friends will be back soon."

"Where is Derry, anyway?" Phennil asked. "And everyone else?"

She shifted her position, putting one knee up and the other down. Her trousers were still wet and clammy and heavy. She waved the cloth in the direction of the fells. "I imagine they're still out there somewhere." She resumed mopping.

He shut his eyes and squirmed under the blankets. "Oh, hell on earth, what a day."

"Speaking of 'a day,' Phennil," she said as she finished bandaging him, "that rod of light that was supposed to last a day? Apparently 'a day' means something different wherever it came from."

She patted his shoulder and stood up. And just then they both heard a cry. In the last traces of daylight, Derry stood on the rocks, waving back to the others before rushing to embrace the two lost friends. In spite of the cold, neither elf nor woman had ever received such a warm greeting.

Kyer finally changed into spare trousers, and after stuffing a rag down inside her boots, she laid out her and Phennil's wet things on the rocks so the wind could whip away the water. Derry checked Phennil's wound and praised Kyer for her treatment of it. There was no fuel for fire, so Jesqellan had to conjure one, and it was small; just enough to boil some water for tea for Kyer and the injured elf, and for some potatoes to bake in the embers. Thankfully as the daylight died, so did the wind, and warmth was not so scarce.

When the potatoes were done, Skimnoddle extracted them with tongs and handed them around. But he sat down to a hunk of bread and an apple himself.

Janak peered at his potato suspiciously. "What, did you do something to these?"

The halfling shook his head. "No. I hate potatoes."

Derry put his spoon down. "How can you hate potatoes? They're a staple."

"I assure you," Skimnoddle shuddered, "when it came time for the dispensation of these bulbous tubers, I was provided with a surfeit."

Kyer dug into hers with her knife and let the hot, flaky flesh crumble on her tongue as they talked. She had assured them all straight away that their sojourn underground had been successful, and they all agreed that the lichen should be divided between them, so that if for some reason they should become separated during their travels, some, at least, of the precious ingredient would find its way to Bartheylen Castle.

Skimnoddle and Janak had been out on the rocks when the tremors began. They had tried to return to the horses, but had made it only halfway when the earthquake struck. Both had tumbled and slipped, sustaining minor injuries, scratches and bruises mostly. When at last it was over and they finally reached Derry and Jesqellan, the four had set out again immediately to try to locate the other two.

"And I'm hoping now that you'll be able to tell us where you were and how you got out," Derry said. "We were all heartsick for quite a while there. With the way those rocks caved in over in the eastern area where you both were, well, we could hardly hope you had survived."

Phennil and Kyer took turns describing the subterranean village and the discovery of first one lichen and then the other. But when it came to the point where Phennil lost consciousness and all eyes were on Kyer to deliver the rest of the story, her heartbeat sped up with what she was about to say.

Before the others' return, while fetching blankets and so forth, she'd had plenty of time to come up with an answer. When she had "escaped" from Ronav Malachite in the same fashion, Jesqellan suspected that some wizard had been present and had taken pity on her and sent her back to her friends. Kyer had no other explanation to offer. The mage had spoken to her as if he was accusing her of . . . something. Of what, she didn't know. This time there was definitely no one else around to hand the responsibility to, and if she was honest with herself, it frightened her more than a little that twice now, something had happened that she had no control over.

She had no more answers to the inevitable questions this time than she'd had before. She didn't know how it had happened and didn't want to be treated like she was some sort of criminal for the rest of the journey. She did the best she could to come up with something plausible until she could work it out.

"I just went into 'automatic' mode. Adrenaline kicked in, you know?" Phennil's unconsciousness had given her plenty of room for flexibility. "The light rod lasted long enough for me to haul us both out of the water and into the passage." She went on to describe a faint glow of light that appeared once her eyes had acclimated to the darkness. "And then Kayme stepped in. He guided me in, and he guided me out. That last tremor worked in our favour,

Phennil: where an earlier one had blocked the path, that last one caved in the ceiling and opened a gap. I dragged you up the pile of rocks—sorry about any extra bruises—and hauled you out. Luckily it wasn't too far from here. I couldn't drag you any farther."

Phennil was moved to dumbness. He seemed about to speak but instead reached over and squeezed Kyer's arm.

Janak shook his furry head and gave Kyer a sidelong glance, which told her he was impressed.

"Such bravery! Such skill! Such determination, tenacity!" Skimnoddle boomed, as much as a halfling can boom. "It is just these characteristics, these demonstrations of strength of body and mind, that continue to draw me to you."

"Shut your trap," Kyer said with little feeling, appreciative of the darkness to hide her flush of guilt. She became aware of the captain's odd frown, the dullness in his eye, and had a suspicion he wasn't convinced. Nobody asked to see where she and Phennil had emerged from underground, for which Kyer was profoundly thankful.

"We're all just glad to have you back and that you found the lichen," he said.

A tremor of exhaustion shuddered through Kyer, and she raised her head from her knees long enough to say, "Skimnoddle, I've used your bedroll for Phennil, so if you want, you could use mine, rather than exchange everything around."

"Madam, I am both surprised and delighted by your suggestion," the halfling said, "and I accept your offer with the greatest pleasure!"

Kyer kicked herself for giving him such a golden opportunity. "I said use, not share."

Phennil came to her rescue. "I feel at least well enough to change from Skimnoddle's bed to my own. That is unless you want to share with me." He gave Kyer a sly wink. "I've bathed today."

Derry offered to keep the first watch. He wasn't all that tired and had some things on his mind, not the least of which was the white rose Kyer carried with her. He sat just outside the feeble light from the conjured fire and stared out into the deep night. A brushing sound drew his head around to see Jesqellan coming to join him.

"Everyone else asleep?" Derry said.

"Soundly." The mage gathered his robes around his knees and lowered himself gracefully cross-legged to the grass.

"Anything on your mind?"

The question hung in the dark for a moment. "Do you mean Kyer?"

Derry lay back on the grass. It was not like him to be this lax when it came to a night watch, but with all that had happened today, he had a hard time believing anyone was out there waiting to attack. Besides, who could be bothered to show up here in the Cold Fells? This soulless fragment of Rydris, uninhabitable, nothing living but grass. And Jesqellan was here now too, so between the two of them, they'd spot anything untoward. "Yes, I guess I do."

"Let me guess: You do not entirely believe her story of their escape, but you do not know how to broach the subject without calling her a liar?"

"You too, hunh?"

The Moabi nodded and clasped his hands, resting them on his ankles. "I am afraid there are still times that I just do not know what to make of our friend Kyer."

"You don't trust her?"

"It isn't that I mistrust her," Jesqellan explained. "Like I said, she is an unknown variable. She risked her life going down there with Phennil. They were successful in finding the falander. It took a deal of strength and courage

—all the things dear Skimnoddle listed—to get the both of them out."

"But her ending didn't sit well with you," Derry finished for him. "It was too glib. Something was missing from the story. I don't understand it. After everything we've done in the last few months, even since we left on this journey, why does she feel a need to keep things back from us?"

"Not to mention the water."

Derry looked at him sidelong then remembered the darkness. "What about the water?"

Jesqellan wrapped his arms around his knees. "If she dragged Phennil across the rocks and along the grass, why was there a patch of very wet grass in one localized spot?"

Derry shook his head. "I'm afraid I don't understand what you could be getting at."

"I checked. Perhaps I noticed it as we all moved about our camp because I am barefoot. I stepped in one small area where the grass was drenched. There was no other place that I could find where the grass was as wet."

"Then obviously they lay there long enough to— Look, Jesqellan, what are you suggesting? Are you saying she *didn't* drag Phennil out of the caverns?"

Jesqellan shrugged, waving his hand, as if embarrassed about bringing it up. "I do not know. It is probably nothing. But I find it does not become easier for me to get close to her. Perhaps you, Derry, can ask her more about it. You're the one she connects with mostly, out of all of us. You could find some polite way of finding out more."

Derry's eyebrows shot up doubtfully. "I don't know." He turned his gaze toward the west, as if looking for final vestiges of sunlight. "She seems to be closer to Phennil these days." He finally had voiced the thing that had occurred to him but he hadn't yet put into words.

"That's only natural considering what happened at his father's home," Jesqellan said reasonably.

Derry shrugged.

"It cannot hurt for you to approach the subject with her; she respects you."

Derry placed his hands on his belly. "Maybe. It's worth a try."

It was the cornfield dream again. Only this time the stalks went on and on, and Kyer couldn't reach the edge. She tripped and one of the plants fell onto her, its long narrow leaves wrapping around her face and shaking her. Her eyes opened to the dark of the Cold Fells and the face that stared down at her. She stiffened but she didn't yell because there was a hand over her mouth. The face that hovered just above hers was as nonthreatening as the whiff of lilacs surrounding it. It was smiling. Its eyes were uncommonly dark and were accentuated by the pallor of his skin, which was framed by even darker hair. The face was not unfamiliar. She had seen it once—no, twice, before.

This time the faint firelight flickered off him the way it would off a mirror. Strange that she should awaken from a deep sleep and not feel threatened by the man whose hand covered her mouth, but stranger things had happened to Kyer lately.

"Don't yell, please." He spoke so softly, she could hardly hear him. "I'll remove my hand, now, all right?"

Kyer found herself shrugging in agreement. *Why not?* He lifted his hand and beckoned for her to follow him. She checked who was on watch. How had this person come all the way into their camp without being noticed by anyone? Not even the horses? Voices murmured from the other side of the campfire. Derry and Jesqellan, if the empty beds were anything to go by. She stole out of her bed and silently went after him, though she grabbed her knife that still lay next to her blankets. *If he was a baddy, he could easily have taken it*, she reasoned.

She followed him almost to the rocks. He was also uncommonly tall.

"Who are you?" she asked.

He smiled pleasantly. "First of all, you might put the point of that dagger in another direction. If I'd wanted to hurt you, I'd have done so already. And I certainly would not have let you keep that."

She lowered the knife. "How'd you get into our camp?"

"Your friends are very busy chatting over there." He gestured toward the two they could not see at the other side of the fire. "I stayed away from where they were because they would have awakened the lot of you had I let them know I was here."

"That's the point of keeping watch. But what are you doing here?"

"You might call me The Guardian." He scratched his beardless chin. "*You* might call me *your* Guardian."

"What? Why? Why did you want to talk to me? How did you know about the goblins? And the explosion in Shael?" A thought struck her. "Was it you who opened—?"

"Too many questions," he perched on a low rock. She could hardly see him, his black clothes dissolving into the black night. Thankfully, *or weirdly*, as Kyer thought, his translucent complexion glowed even with the conjured fire so distant. "Now, the reason I came was to tell you that you would be wise not to linger in the Cold Fells."

"We didn't plan to."

"Of course not, you bright child. But I must warn you that you are being followed. Now, don't be alarmed. I am not sure if they intend to do you harm or even who they are. But I thought you should know. As you're on a peaceful mission, there really is no reason for anyone to desire contact with you. The earthquake has bought you some time, for they did not escape unscathed, but you should make haste."

"Why are you telling me this? What does it matter to you?"

The sound he made was like a whispered laugh. "Of course it matters to me." He leaned toward her, his breath like warm water. "The Good must prevail."

"How do you know all this?" Kyer trembled, both mystified and irritated by his charm. His voice had a low sibilance, his t's pronounced clearly but gently.

"How do I—oh, my dear, lovely girl, I know all about your mission and about you. Did I not say I am your Guardian?" He lowered his voice, and his eyes darkened. "You are Kyer Halidan. You are looking for the cure for Alon Maer. You killed Ronav Malachite in Nennia. What's more, you *enjoyed* it. It felt good to kill him. Until afterward."

Kyer's skin prickled. She had been alone in those woods when Ronav had died by her sword. She tried to speak but no sound came out.

"Need I tell you more?"

She could hardly breathe, and she was unable to back away.

"But I will tell you more. One thing more . . . a thing you possibly don't even know yourself. I know about a particular magical gift you have. Now, lovely, lovely girl." He reached out an index finger and stroked her cheek, sending shimmers down her body. "I must go. I leave it up to you to decide whether to tell your friends about our chat or not." He drew out from somewhere a white stone that fit in the palm of her hand. "Keep this with you, and I'll always be able to find you, rather than by trial and error. I say again, make haste."

And with that, he rose from his rock and faded into the night.

Kyer sank to the grass, clutching the stone. *A gift?*

She lost track of time, but it might have been a half hour later that Derry appeared in the firelight and noticed she was gone. Kyer forced herself to stir and hasten back, calling quietly. "I'm here." She told him she'd gone to relieve herself and volunteered to take the next watch. He and Jesqellan settled in bed at last and Kyer wandered around the outskirts of the camp, wondering what was the point in keeping watch when strange men can just walk right in with nobody noticing?

And what the hell did he mean by 'gift'?

Ten

What Have You Done Now?

K ien Bartheylen took Roman's recommendation—the most recent in a long string of them—and sought seclusion in his study. He poured himself a glass of wine and pulled out parchment and quill. Poised to write, the high elf could not erase his wife's strained face from his mind. A large mouthful of wine served the purpose of sending a breath of air to his taut muscles. He put quill to paper.

Val,

This letter will take several weeks to reach you, so the news will be that much older. Have you had any word from your company? Based on your last letter, nearly eight weeks have passed since they left you. Alon seems to have several days of stability, and then she worsens and even the best healer in Rydris cannot ease her. Her fever increases and subsides hourly. We are only able to dribble broth into her throat. No conventional medicines help. We are all exhausted, and grateful for the moments of respite that occur too infrequently, and are too short-lived.

By now the people of Shael must have elected a new mayor; I am confident that you and Governor Lyndon have everything running smoothly.

Yours,

KB

With any luck, Kien would see Valrayker in a few weeks' time.

There was no need for Kyer to urge her friends to leave the Cold Fells immediately the following morning. No one had slept well. The wind picked up as the sun rose, blowing the damp-rock smell of the nearby crags through their hair and making the place unbearable again. They'd found what they came here for, so why hang around?

They ate while packing up their belongings, too chilly to sit still, and eager to get away from this desolate place. With no warning of pursuers, fictitious or otherwise, necessary to get her friends moving, Kyer decided to hold off on telling anyone about her visitor of the night before. She scrutinized the white stone for any marks of identification, and finding none, she tucked it into her pocket. *I'll keep it for now, anyway.* The strange man had been truthful about the goblins; she had no reason not to trust him. For now.

As if some higher power had been listening to her thoughts, a cry from Jesqellan pierced through the whistling north wind. A dozen riders had approached from the south, their descent of the hill muffled by the gusts. *Okay, Guardian, you have my attention.* A chill that was not the wind raced up Kyer's spine.

"Do you suppose they're hostile?" Jesqellan hollered.

Kyer knew the answer to that. Phennil and Skimnoddle had already nocked arrows, and she grabbed her bow from its straps on Trig's side. "I think we should assume everyone's hostile."

"Why aren't they coming any closer?" Derry yelled, his cloak billowing around his legs. He was right. The riders had slowed, showing a bizarre lack of desperation to reach their quarry. And now they seemed to have come to a stop, horses rearing, about sixty yards from where Kyer stood.

Phennil leapt onto Leoht's back with agility in spite of his wound. "They can't come any further!" he cried triumphantly. "It looks like there's some sort of fissure in the ground." He dropped into the saddle. "Caused by the earthquake, I expect. Let's get going before they find a way around."

They hastily mounted and Jesqellan set a hurried pace to the northwest. Unheard over the wind, a volley of arrows flew by, sticking into the ground in an unrhythmic staccato. Pain shot through Kyer's left shoulder, and the reins slipped through her limp fingers. With a yell, she dropped forward and clung with her right arm to Trig's neck. *Yup, they're hostile.*

Hunter backhanded Troy, whose bow flew a few feet away.

"You fool!" he raged. "I said not to shoot." He hardly blinked as an enemy arrow, assisted by the direction of the wind, *thunked* into the soft underside of Baker's left arm. Baker fell and Harley ran to him. The chief stormed back and forth. "You idiots! I said *not* to shoot. I said not to touch the girl and what did you do? You hit no one *but* her!"

They'd travelled two-and-a-half leagues north since sunrise and had just reached the top of a slope and sighted their prey. Those who could, galloped forward in pursuit. Valrayker's company hadn't heard them coming, by mercy of a north wind. But the riders had stopped abruptly, horses rearing up, squealing. A section of the hillside had crumbled, leaving a rent across the path that extended in either direction. Arrows flew in spite of the chief's order. Now Hunter cursed as he watched Kyer and her friends dash away. From the distance, he couldn't tell how seriously the girl had been hurt. She was still horsed—that was a good sign—but they might be bluffing.

"I will kill you if she dies!" he growled, pointing a finger at Troy, who glowered as he retrieved his bow.

Chief Hunter rode a few paces in both directions, and was unable to see either end of the tear in the slope. At its narrowest, it was about eight feet across. "Tigo, you take your horse at a run and see if you can jump the crevice," he ordered.

Tigo snorted. "With all due respect, Chief, I'd like to see you try it first," he answered, to Hunter's shock. "I will not risk my mount's life, let alone my own."

Hunter gritted his teeth against a reply, admiring the man's pluck for saying the very thing he would have said himself. He marched forward. But as he neared the precipice, he found himself unwilling to do so in a standing position. He lay down and crawled ahead to peer over the side. A horse could likely jump it, but the animal would shy away from its depth and would risk breaking limbs on a downhill landing. He backed off before rising and kicking a notch in the grass. "Damn it!" he yelled. "We'll have to send scouts in either direction to find a narrow point in this crack, if not the end of it. My patience is being tried by fate." He glared around at his company. "I advise none of you to see how far I can be pushed."

"Somebody help me down if we're going to be here a while," said Mullin, whose broken ankle had kept him in the saddle throughout the exchange of arrows. "Ow!" he yelled at Kep, who positioned himself as if he were assisting a lady and guided the man's weight off the horse. "Watch it, you bastard! Take it slow." Kep said nothing but removed himself from Mullin's side as soon as he was down. "Hey, where do you think you're going? Just help me siddown, would you?"

A brief flash of silver startled them all, and suddenly Mullin was sprawled on the grass, having been separated from both the offending ankle and his head.

Juggler had already wiped and sheathed his shortswords by the time they all realized what had happened. His feet were planted evenly, hands hugging his elbows, a disgusted look on his face. He shrugged. "Hate whiners." They were the first words Hunter had ever heard him utter.

Hunter snapped his jaw shut and glared. *Mental note: don't ever offend Juggler.*

With a shudder hidden by a sigh of frustration, he sent Tigo to follow the crack to the northeast, and Harley to the southwest. They were to return as soon as they found a narrow and shallow enough place to cross, or after two hours, whichever came first.

More delays. Great.

Skimnoddle let an arrow fly back at their assailants. A rider went down.

"Good shot," Phennil said.

Derry whirled Donnagill around to come to Kyer's aid.

"Don't stop—yet," Kyer panted through the searing pain in her back. "Get out . . . of bow range."

"She's right. Ride on!" Derry called, though he rode next to her from there on. Jesqellan trotted along on his bare feet, achieving remarkable speed.

After half an hour, even Phennil could no longer see the strangers who had attacked them, whereupon Derry insisted they stop. The land rippled in swells and hollows, so Derry posted Phennil and Skimnoddle at the top of a rise to watch for their attackers while the others readied a rest spot in a hollow, where the wind was comparatively calm. Kyer had not said a word, but she tasted blood on her lips, she bit them so tightly. She clung to Trig's neck, her body bent double in the saddle, all her energy concentrated on staying there. The world had gone silent around her. She allowed Derry to ease her off her horse, giving him her full weight. She was beyond pain.

Facedown on her bedroll among the sagebrush, Kyer gritted her teeth while Derry unbuckled her cuirass to see how deeply the arrow was lodged in her shoulder. Sweat trickled down her face in spite of the wind, and she breathed the musty aroma of sage.

"Hold still, Kyer." Derry bent down to peer under the leather armour and padded jerkin without lifting them too much. She winced and sucked air through her teeth. "Okay, it's all right." He lowered the leather and sat up straight.

"You were lucky, Kyer," the physicker-adept said. "The head is only just under your skin." He illustrated with his fingers, holding them low enough so she could see. "It looks worse because it penetrated the leather and cloth, but somehow—and I have no idea how, which is why you're lucky—it made a much smaller puncture than I expected, given its velocity. I'll have to remove it before I can see what internal damage there is, if any. There's too much blood to see more."

He managed, with help from Jesqellan, who held the edge of her cuirass and jerkin, to pull out the arrowhead without tearing the open skin. Kyer held back a cry and felt relief as soon as the metal had been removed. Once it was out, Jesqellan broke the shaft and pulled both ends out of the layers. Then the mage helped Derry remove her armour completely so the physicker could clean the wound and assess the damage.

Derry's salve numbed the pain, and he gave Kyer a bitter leaf to chew, which took the edge off further while a healing potion worked its way into her system. She refused further treatment so they could get moving.

They rode due west, aiming for a pass that would lead them through the mountains to the eastern tip of the Sea of Khûn on the other side. By late afternoon, Kyer had regained close to full mobility of her arm with only minor pain. She'd have to work out the stiffness, but that was easier than healing a wound. They had at last outrun the chill winds and could no longer see the jagged stone of the Cold Fells. They also seemed to have left their pursuers far behind.

The mountains stretched from side to side as far as even Phennil's eye could see. And as they neared them over the next few days, the serrated spurs and textures of the hills began to distinguish themselves, looking like crazy tendrils of curls or spindly tree-covered insect legs. Clumps of snow stubbornly hung on to their solid form even in early summer, and Kyer thanked herself several times for bringing along a woolen hat and extra underclothes.

The horses laboured into the higher elevation. The going was slow, and Jesqellan was just as glad as the animals for the chance to rest his legs one midday.

"I hope your friend Kayme knows what he's talking about," Derry said.

"Of course he does," Kyer said. "Why do you doubt him?"

"Oh, I don't," Derry replied. "Yet. I can just picture him sitting in front of a crystal ball, laughing as he watches us struggle along on this wild journey."

"Why would you accuse him of that? He wishes for our success."

"We'll only know that once we are successful. How can you defend him so readily? Do you really know that?"

"He's a good man, Derry," Kyer insisted, irked by his odd mood. "I spent some time with him, remember?"

Derry harrumphed. "I remember."

Kyer smirked at him and was relieved to get moving again.

The trees were different from what she had seen before: yellow cedars with silvery trunks jutting skyward and mountain hemlocks with their bluish cones swollen with pollen. Low-hanging clouds coated their path in a mist that dripped softly off the trees and dampened Kyer's hair. The silence seemed to be more intense, and Kyer felt oddly jittery. It didn't help that she caught Jesqellan stealing glances at her every now and again.

The second night in the mountains, Kyer awoke from a disquieting dream and instinctively snatched up her sword. Jesqellan instantly appeared at her side.

"What is it?" he whispered.

"You didn't hear it?"

"It has been as still as ever." He slanted his head thoughtfully. "What ought I to have heard?"

Kyer shook her head. "I heard a voice. It was nothing, I guess. A dream."

"It is no matter. Rest easy now." The mage hesitated before moving away. "You did not happen, did you, to find any items while you were in the underground caverns? Items that could perchance be magical?"

Kyer bristled with alertness. "No. At least . . . Phennil found a hawk's claw. Why?"

She saw the silhouette of the mage's nod in the dim firelight. "I have not wished to alarm you, but I sense the presence of magic when I am near you. Have you any idea what might cause me to feel that way?"

His tone reminded her of her old schoolteacher and the way she would none-too-sweetly try to wheedle an admission of guilt out of her. "Um," she paused, "you've seen my medallion. Could that be it?"

"I have sensed that all along. I am feeling new sensations of late."

"Hm." Kyer shook her head in the dark. "No idea. I never picked anything up." That was true. Her Guardian had handed it right to her.

Jesqellan hesitated, as if expecting her to add something else, then left her.

Kyer lay down again. Her conscience kept her awake for a little while.

Late the next day, Kyer heard the voice again.

They plodded along a narrow path in a particularly dense mile or two of firs. Derry led with Phennil behind him, followed by Jesqellan on foot and Skimnoddle's pony. Janak brought up the rear behind Kyer. A bee buzzed around her head, and she nearly missed it the first time. The voice said, *Here.* An opening in the wall of trees caught her eye, but with the laziness of the travel, she disregarded it in the first instant. In the second instant, however, she was straight as a yellow cedar in her saddle.

Yes, here, said the voice in Kyer's head. She reined her horse in, and Janak had to stop suddenly to avoid running into Trig.

"What's the big idea?" Janak demanded, but Kyer was already on the ground striding back a few paces behind them. Phennil and Derry halted their horses and turned to see what the fuss was all about, and Jesqellan called out.

"Where are you going?"

Kyer kept walking. There was something she had seen, but only out of the corner of her eye. "Didn't you see the tunnel back here?" She walking and stared off to one side of the path between the trees. She didn't mention the voice.

"Tunnel?" Jesqellan joined her.

They had missed it because they were so intent on the path ahead, and it was obscured by heavy undergrowth, but she was right. Overhanging branches, twisted and gnarled, curved above them, forming not really a tunnel, more like an archway through the forest. If there had at one time been a path beneath it, it was now less discernible, covered with bracken and sword ferns and snowberry. Kyer reached out and touched one of the trees to find that it was smooth and felt as damp as it looked. It was as if their bark had been peeled off, revealing the unblemished wood beneath. Grey-green lichen hung in tendrils from above, and a soft mist curled around the plant life on the ground.

Phennil and Derry reached her and peered down the tunnel that curved a few paces in so they could not see where it headed, besides deeper into the forest.

Kyer turned back to the others. "Who wants to come with me?"

"Wait a minute." Derry put a restraining hand on her arm. "Is this one of Kayme's instructions?"

"No," she admitted.

"Why is this necessary, then? We're a little pressed for time, you might recall."

"Honestly, Derry, I'm surprised you don't have a taskmaster's whip in your hand." Then Kyer softened. "Look, why not? It won't take long, I promise."

"Kyer, my answer is no."

She smirked at him. "Good to know, in case I ever ask." He stiffened, eyebrows peaked. "Look, you go on ahead; I'll catch up. I won't be a minute. I have to just look."

The captain scowled at her. His lips worked over clenched teeth, as though he fought a desire to shackle her for insubordination. She smiled hopefully, acutely aware of manipulating him. Finally he yielded with a sigh. "Well, we can't all go." He raised his eyebrows at Jesqellan.

Jesqellan nodded. "I'll come with you, if only to be aware of magical presences or anything that might be potentially harmful." The mage gripped his staff. Kyer translated his comment to mean, *I'll come along because I don't trust that you won't get into trouble*, with a little bit of *I don't want to miss out on anything interesting* thrown in.

Skimnoddle's full voice rang through the trees. "To shield you from danger, I would stride fearlessly into the very conflagration of Dregor's dragons," he pronounced, "and yet, this time I feel my place is with your beast." Kyer hoped her relief was not too apparent.

"If you aren't back in half an hour, we'll come after you," Derry said by way of warning Kyer to be quick about it.

Kyer nodded and ducked her head under the strands of lichen.

The smooth, purplish archway was low enough that a taller person would have to watch their head, but Kyer and Jesqellan did not share this concern. They wisely paid attention to what their feet were doing, for the mist veiled their footing in cloudy swirls and they stumbled over occasional rocks and tree roots. The tunnel curved to the right then left and to the right again.

"How long do you suppose it's been since anyone walked on this path?" Kyer asked.

"I cannot say," Jesqellan replied. "I cannot see the ground well enough through this clingy mist," he added distastefully. "It may have been travelled yesterday, maybe a hundred years ago. Nor can I see signs on the trees. Perhaps if Phennil were here, he'd see something I cannot."

"It's unnerving." Kyer stepped over a protruding root. "Why is there even mist here? It doesn't make sense. And these trees. They look sort of like cottonwoods but not really. Look at all the colours in them. Brown, burgundy, violet, green, gold . . . Strange."

"A trick of the light, perhaps, as it filters down through the branches. Slow down, would you? How can you step so sure-footedly, Kyer, without tripping? I am stumbling with every other step." The mist had moistened the earth, and there were mosses under Jesqellan's feet to make his barefoot walking even more hazardous. Kyer slowed down. She could not explain her eagerness to follow the tunnel, nor the reason she didn't stumble on the path. She knew only that she had to follow it.

They walked for about ten minutes before the tunnel opened into a clearing the size of Hreth's village square. The trees stretched high, their tops curving overhead like a protective dome, with only a small patch of sky visible. Like the path, the floor of the clearing was blanketed with thick mist, white as snow and equally obscurant of the ground beneath. Kyer gazed in awe, her muscles twitching and alive, her very skin fine-tuned, listening to the energy that radiated all around. She stepped forward, about to plough through the fog, but Jesqellan grabbed her arm.

"Do not be foolish, Kyer. Let me see if I can detect any magic first. You do not know what lies hidden beneath the mist."

"Okay, okay! A little nervous, are we?"

He glared at her.

"Do your spell, then." She rested her left hand on the hilt of her sword as the mage bent his head to his staff, murmuring words in a sibilant tongue. *He's right*, she conceded and cast her eyes about the clearing. The mist might conceal a massive pit, for all she knew. A fresh, damp smell hung in the air.

Jesqellan finally lifted his head. "I can sense no animal presence, not alive anyway, and though I can detect a slight hint of magic, it is very faint. It is either far away, or it has been so long unused that it is dormant. I would still caution you to tread carefully, Kyer."

She nodded and, heeding his words about things hidden under the whiteness, she drew her sword to poke the ground in front of her as she walked. Spiraling inwards, in a counterclockwise direction, she stuck her sword tip into the mist every few feet, and the clouds curled and swirled coldly around her legs. *It has been a long time since anyone was here*, she thought. The coldness felt ancient. That was the only way to describe it.

Something caught her foot, and she fell headlong. The mist billowed around and over her. She heard Jesqellan cry out in alarm as her head disappeared under the opaque fog.

"I'm all right!" she called, but her voice simply came back to her, the fog playing a trick with the sound and enveloping it close to her body. She lifted her head and looked back. As her companion rushed to her aid from across the clearing, he halted in alarm. The mist undulated and rippled as if touched by a breeze. It surrounded the mage, and he shivered with the frigidity. The cloud of fog curled over itself, as wave after wave, it drifted up, out of the clearing and clung to the surrounding trees as if it grew there alongside the lichen.

Kyer found herself on hands and knees staring at the thing that had tripped her, and her hair stood on end. A cry of horror stuck in her chest.

She had tripped over a skeleton. And it was not the only one in the clearing. A dozen people had done battle here. A long time ago, for the bones were clean of flesh and the meagre assortment of armour they had worn was rotting into the ground. Kyer disguised a shudder by sitting back on her haunches. She looked over her shoulder to where Jesqellan stood transfixed, his staff held against himself like an amulet.

She swallowed. "How old do you suppose these are?"

Jesqellan frowned thoughtfully and shook his head. His voice trembled.

"It is difficult to estimate." With his staff, he poked at the unfortunate fellow nearest him. "I should not have thought they could last long out in the weather, not to mention the invasion of wild animals. It is one thing to preserve bones and such in a place out of the cold damp air and rain. They should not last so long out in the fog. Then again," he added, casting an uneasy glance up at the clouds hanging from the trees, "that was no ordinary fog. Their armour is old, though. Maybe several hundred years." He crouched to investigate the bodies near him.

Kyer had all but tuned the mage out. The man who had tripped her—at least, she assumed it was a man—was on his side, his arms splayed out above his head. One hand, though it was only white, weather-polished bones, still clutched the hilt of a sword. Even in this dim clearing, after several hundred years, it gleamed as brightly as Kayme's silver wine goblets. The two-handed hilt looked as new, the leather-bound ricasso was intact. Kyer wondered if this man had even tried to defend himself during the ancient battle, though if he had, she could not believe he could have been bested by any other weapon.

Yes, said the voice again and Kyer jumped. Jesqellan had moved to examine one of the fallen on the other side of the clearing. The mist still hugged the violet branches up above, but it had started its slow swirl again, and she wondered if she was on a time limit. She hastily returned her eyes to look hungrily at the sword, admiring its sheen, the smooth curve of the crossguard, and the deep red gem on the pommel. Slowly she reached out to touch the etchings in the silver. *Yes!* the voice insisted.

But this is burial ground; it shouldn't be disturbed, she told herself.

She felt, rather than heard, puzzlement from the voice.

She hesitantly changed her reasoning. *Is this why I was called to come here?*

Yes! the voice said. *Barakel.* The whirling mist had descended halfway back to the earth. Kyer looked into the sockets that once held a warrior's eyes.

"*Barakel.*" It was a good name for a sword. "Thank you, friend," she whispered and, heart pulsing in her ears, her hand gripped the hilt of the sword, drawing it swiftly to her. Her left hand joined her right to compensate for the length of the weapon, and it was upright in front of her. A quiver shot through her body, and Jesqellan suddenly cried out from across the clearing.

"Kyer, no!" He ran across the ground to her. "You must not touch it! That is the magic that I felt earlier. Be it evil or good, you have awakened it! You must put it down!" He stopped short in front of her.

She barely heard him, mesmerized by the feel of the weapon in her hand. The rightness of it. The three-and-a-half-foot blade, not much longer than her old bastard sword, shone curiously bright in the dull misty light, and its tip sparkled like a crystal. It weighed much less than she expected it to. It was as if she were meant to wield it.

Jesqellan's face was rigid with fear.

"Kyer, this is sacred ground, untouched for hundreds of years! What can you be thinking by removing that?"

She slowly lowered the silver tip to horizontal, her muscles easily compensating for its length, then raised her eyes to his. His gaze was equal portions of shock and fear. "It's all right." She smiled calmly. "He gave it to me." The first waves of mist plunged down around them again, and Kyer had to scramble to retrieve the warrior's baldric and scabbard. She fumbled blindly with the buckles, but in spite of the barrage of rebukes from her comrade, she was unhesitating. The sword was hers. The baldric came free, and she snatched it up, the bones of its previous owner *thunking* unceremoniously to the ground in her haste.

Jesqellan fled the clearing and cowered at the mouth of the tunnel when the tide of mist crashed over the battle ground. Kyer walked over to him, sliding the blade into its home. It was a bit longer than Brendow's; she'd have to practice. She slung the leather strap across her shoulder, adjusted and fastened the straps. Jesqellan turned his reproving stare away from her and entered the tunnel. Kyer followed and tried to think of something to say.

"Listen." She hurried to catch up with him. "I can't stand it that you're angry about this. I understand your feelings. Please, I don't know if I can explain it to you but I'll try."

Jesqellan waited, shifting his weight from one foot to the other, as if reluctant to spend another moment in that tunnel.

Complete honesty was best this time. "Call me crazy if you like, but I swear upon my life that the warrior spoke to me, telling me the sword is mine." She read doubt in his eyes, and her heart fell. "You have to trust me on this."

The mage did not respond.

"How else can you explain the mist?" she suggested. "It stayed up out of the way just long enough for me to find this, and then it fell again."

"That was caused by your movement," Jesqellan argued. "All mist swirls away when you step through it."

"And clears out a whole area like that? I don't think so, Jesqellan. You can't explain it any more than I can. Do you want to go back and try to make it happen again?"

"All right, then, I will." The mage stubbornly accepted the challenge. Kyer hoped he would be unsuccessful; she could think of no other way to convince him. They retraced their steps.

Jesqellan marched into the clearing, a challenge in his step. He spun around the ring trying to dissipate the fog. To no avail.

"Can't you see that what happened before was completely out of the ordinary?" Kyer stepped forward to call a truce. "I promise you, I would not have taken it if—"

She stopped short. The mist billowed around Kyer's feet, curling and swirling as before, retreating in waves to the trees. She froze and stared around her on the ground. They looked at each other in horror.

The skeletons, their armour, their weaponry, were gone. Every sign that a battle had ever taken place in this clearing had vanished.

Kyer's stomach lurched.

"How do you explain that?" Jesqellan said softly.

"I don't."

"Let's get out of here."

Neither of them had ever walked so quickly.

Her thoughts went back to Kayme and his offer of knowledge. If she had stayed with him, she would not have found this magnificent weapon. Still, the mist, the battle scene, the warrior's voice in her head . . . She finally forced herself to ask the question, *Did I make the right choice?*

Derry's expectant glances toward the tunnel entrance had become more frequent, and he was about to suggest that someone go after them when they came into view. Kyer's lips were pressed together and she held her chin up as though trying to appear unruffled, yet her furrowed brow told him her composure was feigned. Jesqellan looked downright alarmed. The captain opened his mouth to ask.

Jesqellan beat him to it. "Let's go," he said sharply, and they all scrambled onto horseback. The mage's glance told Derry he'd tell him later.

As Kyer put a foot in her stirrup and hoisted herself upward, the baldric across her chest, and a brilliant red jewel at her hip flashed at Derry like fireworks. He caught Kyer's eye and shot a question at her, but he was met with a stare that bespoke smugness and challenge.

He frowned. *What have you done now?*

Kyer rode in silence for a time, considering how to explain her choice to the others in a way they'd understand. She expected they would not, no matter how she approached it. Derry rode in brooding silence. The look on his face had said, "How dare you?" How could she possibly explain when he already thought her guilty of using terrible judgement? It was if he'd dug a hole and stuck her in it, and demanded she dig her way out. "I didn't do anything wrong," she had tried to convey with her wordless reply.

Kyer's body undulated along with Trig's, and she adjusted her baldric to make riding comfortable with the new weapon. Her left hand rested comfortably on the hilt, next to her old sword, and she felt a strange sense of completion.

"What's with you, Kyer?" Phennil piped up, laughing at her. "You look like someone just gave you a surprise gift."

"I do?" She couldn't argue with his assessment: she *had* been given a gift.

"You're grinning like you're dancing during Springrites!"

"Oh! I guess I am."

A short self-assessment confirmed a giddiness she hadn't been aware of. Instinct told her it was the sword. *Should I be worried?* she thought, but dismissed the concern almost instantly. The sword, she realized, was happy.

That was certainly not a thing she intended to speak aloud.

From behind her Derry said, "We need to camp soon. Travelling in the these mountains we lose the sunlight early. Given that we have lost an hour I am gratified that it wasn't a complete waste of all our time."

Stung, all Kyer could say was, "I'm glad you see it that way."

A while later, settled into their camp, Skimnoddle handed Kyer her share of the rabbit he had turned on the spit. She thanked him quietly, avoiding attracting more attention.

"Care to tell us more about your sidetrip into the woods?" Derry slid meat off a small bone.

"I'd be interested to hear how you knew to go that way," Janak said.

Kyer swallowed. "The answer won't satisfy you. It was really just a feeling I had. The place itself was eerie, wasn't it, Jesqellan?" She hoped he would elaborate and help her explain.

The mage was no help. "I did not like being there. Not one bit. I said we should leave. And then that mist rose." He broke off, and shuddered.

"It was the scene of an ancient battle." Kyer described what the two of them had seen. "We looked around, and left."

"Only after you took the weapon off a dead body."

"He wasn't using it anymore," she said, and instantly wished she hadn't. "Look, I can't explain it any better than I have. I had a feeling. It felt right. It still feels right. We lost a little bit of travel time. I'm sorry about that."

"The sword's a beauty," Phennil said.

"Twas only an hour." Skimnoddle dropped a bone onto his tin plate with a metallic *click*. "We shall make it up with ease in the coming days."

Phennil elbowed the mage. "Just hustle along a little faster, Jesqellan."

Kyer didn't think the mage found the comment funny.

The next day, they reached the edge of the dense forest and burst out into an alpine meadow where some great arm had swept the trees to one side and had spread a rainbow of coloured cloth across the empty bowl that remained. All manner of shades of green grasses and ferns were emblazoned with heather, lupines, buttercups, purple daisies, and trilliums. Wondrously bright in spite of the fog and mist. The continuing *drip-drip* sound was more like laughter than the rain it had resembled when they were within the trees. Now, too, it was accompanied by an orchestra of bumblebees skitting among the heather. A spiderweb clung to a bush, its every strand detailed by the dew. Two mountain goats grazed, and a grouse or pheasant fluttered into the air and descended again. A chickadee-filled tree was a chorus of chatterers. And all around the edge of the bowl, the yellow cedars spiked up like swords into the fog.

Out of the mist rode a solitary figure.

Hunter could think of no way to slow them down. After following the rent in the earth far to the west, it narrowed enough for the horses to clear it with ease and few jitters. Far from setting his little company behind on the trail of their quarry, Hunter bemoaned the nearness of the mountains. Kyer and her friends had gone into them, and though Hunter could not tell which spur they'd entered, Misty said it didn't matter.

"We know of another way, don't we Juggles?"

Juggler polished the sword that lived on his right hip and nodded without looking up.

"There is a trail not two leagues from this place," Misty went on in her satiny voice, "that will carry us into the hills and around close to the Sea of Khûn. If we hurry, we will skirt 'round our little party of heroes and likely reach it before they do." She grinned at Hunter—a sight that did not bring him mirth. "We can *surprise* them!" Misty giggled.

Hunter tried to find something interesting in a fir tree that clung stubbornly to the precarious hillside. "If you insist."

Huranan Danay hesitated before leaving the cover of the trees. Far across the alpine meadow, he saw riders. Six of them. They were travelling west, and he would likely intersect their path on his southward route unless he remained in the shelter of the giant yellow cedars and hemlocks, hidden from their view. His habit had always been to avoid conflict wherever possible. Then he considered that six was a ridiculously small group for Dregor to send on patrol; he did not seem to believe in groups smaller than one hundred head. Besides, Huranan was alone. A lone rider should not pose any threat to them, so why should they attack him? And if they did, well, he was the best swordsman in Rydris, and they would quickly feel the icy fire of his blade. He emerged from the forest and cantered down the hillside into the meadow of mist-dampened heather.

Heads turned and became aware of him. They rode until they were directly in his path before halting their horses. Slowing, he took them in before he was within distance to speak. A knight on a warhorse; a bald, dark-skinned man on foot (must be from a nomadic tribe); a dwarf; an elf (these were, indeed, friends not foes); a halfling (whatever for?); and the one in the middle . . . a woman. A motley party! He had nothing to fear here.

When he was within thirty paces, he raised a hand in peace and called, "Hail, friends!" Reining in his horse, he spoke to the woman, whose forest green cloak gave her eyes a dark glow. Her dew-dampened hair sparkled with the morning mist. "It is long since I saw friendly faces on my journeys. What brings folk of your sort hereabouts?" An easy enough question, though they seemed hesitant to answer. Did they not speak Rydrish?

The knight urged his warhorse a step forward, asserting himself as the leader of the group. "Hail in return, friend, though it appears we have an advantage, with six of us to your one. We would ask what brings *you* to these parts?" the knight replied. His tone was courteous, but Huranan's back stiffened. Was it the knight's words, or was it that the woman smirked when he spoke them?

"Huranan Danay is my name, and my travels take me from my home further in the north to the south where I hope to reunite with some acquaintances. I would hope that these lands are still free wherein peaceful people may travel without fear of threat?"

"Your fear is your own to do with what you wish," the knight said, his face stern. "The threat is the same throughout Rydris, fear or courage notwithstanding."

He felt his face flush, the familiar heat of anger flaring, and he opened his mouth to retort. The woman saved him. "Settle, Derry," she admonished quietly. "We're *friendly*, right?" The woman switched her pleasant gaze to Huranan, and he felt his blood quicken, though this time not in anger. "What he means is that as long as you're a friend to the Guarded Realm and foe to Lord Dregor, you are welcome to travel wherever you wish." She glanced back at the knight, who seemed to approve of her interpretation.

The rest of the party softened their demeanours upon her cordial reply; the nomad even raised his brow in . . . surprise? "I thank you for the translation, fair lady," Huranan said with a bow to her and a glaring glance at the blond knight, whose cool stare supported the evidence of the woman's reprimand that the man tended toward hasty judgments. Huranan wondered who had received this Derry's quick temper recently and what had happened to prompt the woman to alter his behaviour. The natural darkness of the woman's eyes was much more engaging than the mood-darkened gaze of the knight. Huranan had experience handling quick-tempered men, though. He ignored him and focussed his own pleasant smile upon the woman. "Foe I am, indeed, to Dregor. I am on my way to add the service of my sword to his destruction, for I believe his time has come." He could not lend meaning to the glint in her eye.

"Only now? Some have been of that mind for decades," the knight said pointedly. "Yet you seem sure of yourself. Why don't you go to him directly and save the rest of us the trouble?"

"Derry." The woman's voice was like a dart. It arrested the bubble of fury that tempted Huranan's sword hand. He swallowed deliberately and used the hand instead to wave his acknowledgement of the knight's comment.

"It is a valid concern." He breathed through the flare of his own temper. "Though I question your approach to expressing your doubt. We have met in a friendly capacity; I have done you no wrong, nor threatened you in any way. I would point out that you yourselves are heading away from the area where the allied armies are gathering, but it is not my place to take issue with your presence here."

"We are on a private mission," Derry said through gritted teeth.

This one is very prickly, indeed. Huranan bowed. "As am I. And I have not asked you to reveal your business to me." He felt a sense of triumph, however minor. "Now, although *my* reasons for only now stepping forward are my own, I will assure you, fair lady, that had I not been detained, I would certainly have lent my support sooner."

The knight sat in silence, but the woman said, "I'm sure that all who oppose Dregor can't help but be grateful for your assistance."

"I am glad to have come upon others of my way of thinking."

"Have you encountered many who are otherwise?" the nomad said. His voice was warm and vibrant. A cleric, likely.

"Only a few," he replied. "Those who tried to bar my way no longer pose a threat to anyone, so I hope I have cleared your passage." If this comment had impressed the lady, she made no sign. A hard nut to crack, then. Then she surprised him.

"Since we're heading northwest, not due north the way you've come, I'm afraid we won't feel the benefit of your gallantry." She was half smiling, and he wasn't sure if he detected a hint of sarcasm or not. He decided he hadn't.

The halfling spoke in a clear voice that would be suited to the stage. "What news can you tell us of the north?"

Huranan inhaled before speaking, and was cut short.

"If I may be so bold as to remind our party of the time of day," the cleric said, all politeness, with a glance at the knight. "It has been a pleasure meeting you, sir, but we must be on our way."

"Are you in such a hurry? I hope you are able to take the time to appreciate such beautiful land!" His gesture took in the meadow and the mist-covered mountain. She may as well know that he was not only an excellent warrior but a sensitive man who had an eye for beauty in all things.

"Our errand is urgent," the knight explained with less impatience than before, "and we cannot tarry here, awe-inspiring though the environment may be." He bowed. "We wish you a safe journey. Dima be with you, sir."

"And also with you," Huranan answered automatically, taken aback by the knight's abrupt dismissal. He looked to the woman again. She regarded him not unpleasantly, and he wondered what her relationship was with the stern knight. He hoped it was not a serious one. She shifted in her saddle, and he noticed what he hadn't before: the jewelled pommel of a sword at her hip. His heart jumped. Oh, his fortune was both good and ill today! To have met such a woman and yet have no chance to make her complete acquaintance. With a bow to her, he ventured to say, "Perhaps we shall meet again. And in the between time," he added, though he knew she wouldn't understand it, *"Fyn heorthe an wehrn, vun hlaefen."* But when he looked up, her head was tilted to one side. Their eyes met, and he thought he read . . . shock? Certainly not! He looked closer and, sure enough, it was just blank incomprehension. Still, he smiled at her, waved farewell to the strange party, and continued on his journey south to find Lord Valrayker.

Eleven

Someone Else Knew

The party watched the strange, dark-haired young man as he rode south through the alpine meadow. Kyer wiped away the strands of hair that mist had stuck to her cheek.

"What did he say to you, Kyer?" Skimnoddle asked after the odd young man had gone.

"How should I know?" Kyer replied crossly.

"What language was that?" the halfling went on.

"It is strange," Derry said thoughtfully. "It sounded familiar and yet not so. I could not place it."

To mask her discomfort at nearly giving herself away, Kyer said, "Why were you so rude to him, Derry? You told *me* to be patient and polite with people."

Her friend accepted the rebuke, though he scowled and half-turned in his saddle to watch the departing man. "I make no apologies. I didn't trust him," he said. "He rubbed me the wrong way; that is all. Such arrogance. A lone man riding out to us where he could have stayed hidden if he hadn't had some reason to find out who we were."

"Are you suggesting he was a spy?" Jesqellan asked.

Derry shrugged again. "I don't know, I just didn't feel right about him."

"That is a fair analysis," the mage said.

Kyer said nothing. She was struggling with bewilderment she could not speak about. No, the young man was not a spy. She knew it unequivocally but was unable to tell the others. It was a terrific challenge to pretend she did not understand those words the stranger had spoken just to her, so unexpectedly. And what in the world had he meant by it? Surely he couldn't have known she—no the look on his face afterward had shown her that he didn't think she had understood him.

And then there was Derry. Why had he been so stiff with the fellow? His reasoning was just and sensible, but she didn't believe he had been entirely truthful.

A pity she would never see the stranger again. She would be best to forget him. But how could she? It was not every day that a handsome warrior came upon her so suddenly and revealed an ability to speak Dark Elvish. She had always thought that Brendow and herself were the only non–dark elves who could speak the language. Unless . . . unless the stranger *was* dark elvish. Common knowledge said that Valrayker was the only one left; if this young man was proof to the contrary, Kyer could not tell. His height, were she able to guess at it as he sat on his horse, was no clue, as dark elves were on average no taller than humans. His facial features were just as easily human as elvish: oval face with a scar on the left cheek, tanned skin. The only feature that would have tipped her off would have been the man's ears, but for the fact that they were covered by long, thick black hair.

Whether it was his mother tongue or not, Huranan Danay had spoken to her in Dark Elvish, and there was no way anyone with close enough ties to the dark elves to know their language could possibly be a spy for Dregor. The two were incompatible concepts.

And the way the Dark Elvish words tumbled off his tongue! He must have learned from a master, his accent was so perfect. How mystical, musical, startling out a reaction she had been forced to repress. *My heart is yours, fair lady*, he had said. What a pity she would never see him again.

That night during his watch, Derry stood with his back to the fire. Hands clasped behind his back, they tapped a rhythm against each other. He stepped a few paces to the left and stared outward into the darkness again. He tried to listen for unwanted noise within the usual nighttime noises, but his thoughts drowned out all other sound.

Who did that handsome young wayfarer think he was, looking at Kyer that way, and speaking to her instead of him? And speaking such things to her too. Derry did not understand a word of it, but the man's implication was clear. The captain was all the more annoyed knowing how Kyer loved being singled out in that way. Oh, she feigned irritation, but he knew better.

Derry shut his eyes and shook his head to loosen the notions in his mind. *I shouldn't be angry about the sword.* It had nothing to do with him. But why did Kyer always get what she wanted? They stopped travelling at her insistence, losing an hour of travel time, and she wound up with a gorgeous new weapon. Stolen off a dead body, Jesqellan had said. Derry shuddered. Kyer hadn't a care. The disturbance of a corpse meant nothing to her.

Kyer was so . . . distracted these days. Derry had intended to chat with her at the earliest opportunity about her escape from the caverns. He wasn't sure anymore if there was a point. If he spoke to her she would only snap at him. Jesqellan had said she trusted and respected him. Derry was not convinced that was the case any longer.

The mountain stream turned Kyer's hands red with cold as she filled the last of the waterskins. The stream fed the Sea of Khûn at the east end, but the company intended to journey through the mountains to join the sea farther west. When the skin was plump with the clear, fresh water, she corked it and slung it onto her shoulder and up over her head. She now carried three on each side and tested her balance before Phennil handed her the full pails. She braced herself as he reloaded his arms with the wood he'd gathered. Each stick *clopped* noisily onto the pile he held in his left arm; then his right arm joined it underneath the pile and the two headed back to camp.

Kyer stopped short when she saw the man standing at the entrance to the path. With their arms full, neither of them had time to draw sword or bow before he had raised his hand in a gesture of peace.

"I'm sorry to have alarmed you, but it couldn't be helped. I only wish to speak," the light-brown-haired man said quietly. He looked to be about thirty and was clothed as a traveller. Only cloth armour showed between the folds of his brown cloak, yet a sword was poorly concealed at his hip. Kyer lowered the pails of water to the uneven, root-protruding ground.

"Why did you come upon us so discreetly, then?" she said.

"I can't help it if I walk quietly." He shrugged. "I didn't want to catch the attention of every living thing in the forest."

"You must have been aware of our whole group. Why not approach them or wait for us to get back there?" put in Phennil.

"Because I don't want to speak to the whole group. I only want to speak to you." He focussed on Kyer. "Our chief wants a word with you."

Kyer frowned. *I've heard* that *before.* "Why didn't he come himself, then?"

The messenger smiled patiently. "Oh, come on. We aren't children. You know that isn't how things work."

"Who's your chief?"

"It's not my position to say any more than I was instructed."

"Are you part of the group that attacked us in the Cold Fells?" Phennil unloaded his sticks again.

"I wouldn't call it an attack; it was meant to get your attention."

Kyer snorted. "That's ridiculous. Your aim was too good." She shifted the lingering stiffness in her shoulder muscles.

He shrugged. "That was poor aim. The man who hit you has been reprimanded." The man looked over his shoulder as if he'd heard something. He lowered his voice. "Look, I don't have time. I was sent to bring you—only you—for a short time. He has a message for you. No one of your group will be hurt if you come with me."

"You're a jackass," Kyer said. "We aren't children, remember?"

"Our chief can be very persistent. Half a dozen archers are waiting in the woods, poised to wipe out the rest of your company if you don't come along."

Kyer's stomach lurched, but she fixed her smile. *Shit.* "I think you're bluffing."

The messenger shrugged again. "Your choice."

Phennil stepped forward, about to speak, but Kyer held up a warning hand, her mind racing. He wanted only her. *What if he isn't bluffing?* They'd be slaughtered. "Why me?"

"Put it this way," the stranger said softly. "You killed our former chief. The new one wants to make an arrangement with an old friend. You have bargaining power."

Kyer stared at him.

Phennil whispered, "I don't buy it."

"I don't have all day." The messenger's tone hardened. "The archers are poised to fire on my signal."

Kyer stood dumbstruck. He was part of Ronav's band of cutthroats. Ronav had referred to them as his *council*. Even if she didn't know this man, he'd likely seen her before. Kyer shuddered to recollect how badly things had gone the last time she'd appeared among that group. No, going alone into that circle was not a good choice. Yet the instigator of that affair was good and dead. Who had taken Ronav's place and would want to bargain with *her*? What did "bargaining power" mean?

"What makes you—or him, for that matter—so sure I'd be in an all-fire hurry to get reacquainted with that bunch? Our last get-together wasn't exactly a party."

"No, not for you, anyway." He shook his head thoughtfully. "Believe me, the new chief has a few more smarts. And very different priorities." He sounded so disgusted at the comparison with Ronav that Kyer very nearly believed he was sincere.

Kyer saw Phennil's fingers twitching out of the corner of her eye. She held herself rigid as she struggled to choose the best course of action. Ronav was dead and so was another of their own who'd met an unfortunate end just prior to Kyer's dramatic exit. How likely were they to mess with her after *that*? She sized up her opponent and thought of her new weapon. How sure of herself did she feel?

"Well, never mind," the man went on. "If you don't want to bargain about Alon's life, the chief can just as easily tell his message to the other side. Then you can explain it all to your beloved Valrayker after Alon is dead." He raised his fingers to his mouth, about to whistle.

Phennil's sword whipped out of its sheath, but the other man was just as fast. He parried Phennil's swipe, and Kyer ducked away to avoid the swinging blades. Phennil's first choice was not his sword, but Kyer suspected swordplay was the messenger's second skill too. Phennil side-stepped and his opponent missed an overhead strike. The elf smashed the flat of his blade on the other's hand, loosening his grip so the man's sword fell to the ground. Only seconds after drawing his weapon, Phennil's sword tip was at the stranger's chest. The man shook out his numbed fingers.

"Wait!" Kyer held up her hands. "Wait." The messenger eyed her cautiously from his half-crouching position. She let out a breath.

"Prove it."

"Kyer, *what* are you—?" Phennil looked at her as if she were crazy.

And maybe she was. She stopped him with a glare.

The man tilted his head. "Do you think Dregor is unaware that his greatest enemy is fragile?" He spoke low and quickly. "If Alon's condition doesn't improve, the Bartheylen hold on Rydris will grow more tenuous, and Dregor will use his advantage. Now, do you want to hear the chief's message or don't you?"

Kyer frowned. It wasn't exactly proof, but . . . "Where are we going?"

He blinked. "A short walk. Let me warn you, though, that if your friends try to follow you now, we'll flatten them."

Damn. Were there really six archers? She had a good sword, knew how to use it, and if things got out of hand, well, *I'll think of something.* She had to find out what this chief knew about Alon Maer.

She also had to enlist the help of her friends without dooming them.

Phennil's flaming blue eyes flashed frantically at her. How to persuade him? "Phennil—"

"Kyer, don't do this. I've *got* him—"

"Phennil, I have to. Our party's in danger."

"You can't believe—"

"Listen. I need to go and hear what this man's chief has to say. It's important. I'll only be gone a short time."

Phennil shook his head slowly but lowered his sword. "I don't like it, Kyer."

"It's not my favourite idea either," she whispered. "I don't think we have a choice. Hurry back. Tell the others what's happening but be careful." She eyed the messenger cautiously as he slowly retrieved his weapon. She bobbed underneath the straps of the waterskins and laid them on the ground. "If he isn't lying about the snipers in the woods, you're all in danger. Sniff them out and track me as soon as you can." She fervently hoped it wouldn't take long.

"All right," Phennil said. "But I don't like it."

The man sheathed his sword, his eyes shifting from the elf to Kyer. He caught her expectant gaze and cocked his head in instruction for her to come along. Over her shoulder, she nodded encouragingly to Phennil as he watched her, his sword loose in his hand and his brow furrowed. She followed the young man as he plunged into the woods.

Phennil watched the bushes close in around Kyer. There had to have been a better way to handle this. He'd already bested the man. Two to one, they could have easily taken him prisoner. He sheathed his sword and hurried stealthily back through the woods, alert for any signs of said archers.

If he'd been more alert, he'd have heard the attacker earlier. If he hadn't been distracted, he'd have reacted quicker. Being an elf, he didn't completely fail to defend himself, he was just too slow.

"Do you have a name?" Kyer brushed aside huckleberry bushes as she plodded, stepping carefully on the downward sloping ground. "Or does your chief just say, 'Hey, average-height guy'?"

Her leader chuckled through his nose. "I'm Harley."

"Ah, Harley the Messenger, that's very nice."

"Are you always this sarcastic?"

"Pretty much." Kyer had an odd feeling that she could grow to like the fellow if given the chance. "You said it was a short walk to where your chief is?"

Harley pushed through a last stand of rowan into a clearing. "No, I didn't say that. It is, however, a short walk to my horse."

Kyer's heart dropped. *Damn.* All right. So they had to go a little farther away. Things were not out of hand. She still had her sword, and it was one on one. Two horses waited in the clearing.

"Nice of you to provide me with a magnificent steed," she said coolly.

He shook his head. "Sorry, you get to ride with me."

"Whose is that, then?" she said, just as the sound of twigs snapped through the bushes.

"I took care of the elf," said the lanky man who now joined them.

Kyer's heart sank lower. *What have I done?* "What do you mean by that?" she demanded and tried to break away back through the forest. Her path was blocked.

"Don't worry, girlie," said the skinny fellow. "He'll come 'round soon."

Not soon enough, damn it. She fixed Harley with a cold stare. So much for growing to like him. At least he wasn't as bad as Con.

"Do you prefer in front or in the rear of our magnificent steed?" Harley offered with a grandiose gesture. The mahogany animal raised its head and blinked in greeting.

"I prefer to ride alone," she said, increasingly conscious that she'd bungled things. "Why don't you two double up?"

Harley actually laughed.

Score one for me. "Fine. Since that option isn't open, I'll take the rear." That would at least keep her free to slip off and run. Prospects weren't too bleak yet.

Harley chirruped to the mare, and they were off, followed by the other horseman.

They hadn't been on the road more than three minutes when Kyer heard the whicker of horses from farther along. *Not from the direction of our camp.* She craned her neck around Harley's shoulder to see whom he was waving to.

"Success, boys," he called and abruptly veered the horse off the road onto a smaller path to the south, and as they changed direction, three other men on horseback who'd been waiting for Harley now wove into the procession.

"Nice day for a ride," she said flatly as she acknowledged she'd been duped.

They'd be able to cover quite a bit of ground before Phennil was found.

"What's taking them so long?" Derry was more impatient than concerned.

"Oh, it hasn't been that long," Jesqellan said. "Besides, you know what those two are like when they get talking."

Derry stopped his whetstone mid-swipe. *That's the trouble.* "We're in a forest for gods' sake. Why does it take so long to find wood?" His stomach growled audibly. He resumed his steady motion. "Skimnoddle, will you please go and tell Kyer and Phennil to hurry up?"

The halfling tottered off into the trees.

Back and forth they rode, on the switchback trail up the mountainside. No words were spoken between the men. Kyer's trust of Harley had plummeted, so she was unwilling to risk dialogue. But as if he'd read her mind, her escort spoke.

"It's all right, you know, I wasn't lying."

Kyer didn't respond.

"Hunter really does have a message for you. That's all it is."

"Really. Well, since you're unlikely to give me a hint what it's about, I suppose there's no sense in discussing it, is there?"

He laughed. "You weren't kidding about being sarcastic pretty much all the time."

"I take my sarcasm very seriously."

They'd reached the top of the switchback path where the sky opened as the trees thinned. Thick, rolling grey clouds hung low and heavy, compressing the air. The path now drew them due south. "I was only trying to reassure you."

"Gee, thanks. You threatened me with fictitious archers, you knocked out my friend, and you've taken me hostage. I feel very reassured."

He shrugged. "Fair enough." He smiled over his shoulder at her as he pulled up by an outcropping of granite flanked by hemlocks. "Here we are."

She slithered off the back of the mount, glancing uncertainly at the other men who'd joined them. Dust billowed around them as they dismounted. Kyer heard someone call, "Tell Hunter she's here." Kyer felt a tap on her arm. It was Harley, beckoning her to follow him.

"You're a weasel," she hurled at him.

"As I said before, we aren't children. You wouldn't have come with us if I'd just asked nicely."

"Did you leave some men behind to snag my friends when they come looking for me?"

"I've done what I was asked to do. I don't care a flying fart for your friends."

"Nice use of alliteration," Kyer muttered automatically. She heard Harley chuckle as they passed around the rock and the trees. They stepped down a slope that opened up before a tranquil lake dotted with yellow pond lilies and framed by low bushes and the reddish blooms of marsh cinquefoil. The water was still and black, reflecting the dark clouds and hills beyond without a ripple. Whiskeyjacks flitted about, expecting donations from the new arrivals, which told Kyer that the birds were not unaccustomed to seeing people around here.

About half a dozen armed travellers paused briefly in their business, long enough to give Kyer the feeling that not all of them understood her arrival. Two people in particular stood out: a man and a woman, so alike they must be siblings, both with short, curly hair the colour of coal and eyes to match. They sat side by side. The man offered no expression, but the woman smiled a little. Not a smile that gave Kyer any sense of welcome; not disdainful, for that required self-righteousness. Hers was a smile more of a humble, indifferent superiority, and Kyer was brushed by the briefest chill of fear.

Harley placed himself on a fallen log and opened a sack of nuts and raisins. He held the bag out to her but she declined. "Suit yourself." He dipped his fingers into the bag. Kyer relaxed slightly. She was in full control. Nobody seemed too concerned about her. She looked out over the lake and wondered how long she'd have to wait.

She turned at the sound of hoofbeats from around the corner of the lakeside. "He's coming," someone said, and suddenly Kyer felt her arms pinioned at her sides by unseen hands. "Hey!" she cried. She struggled against the force that held her, but it only tightened. She searched for Harley so she could bestow a "What the hell is going on here, you son of a bitch?" look on him.

"It's what Hunter asked for."

Shit. Where did Ronav's band get magic? And who in the group of rogues could wield it? No one was paying attention but Harley and the two siblings, who watched the proceedings with nothing more than mild curiosity. No one looked like a mage.

And damn it, she still couldn't help liking Harley as he sat there nonchalantly tossing raisins to the whiskeyjacks.

The horseman emerged from behind the bushes, and Kyer felt very little surprise at the identity of Hunter.

"Captain!"

Skimnoddle's voice sifted through the trees. Derry leapt to his feet and ran toward it, joined by Jesqellan. They soon came upon Skimnoddle supporting Phennil by the arm. Blood dripped down the elf's face, oozing from a wound on the forehead. He carried his sword clumsily in his other hand.

"Good god, Phennil, what happened?" said Derry. "Where is she?" They helped the pale, woozy elf into camp and lowered him to the ground. Derry fetched his kit and was at Phennil's side instantly.

"Skimnoddle, Janak, go find her," Derry said, checking Phennil's wound.

"No." Phennil waved his arm rather than shake his head. "Gone."

A series of images flashed through Derry's mind—Kayme's offer, Kyer's new sword, the mysterious words of the young stranger—and was shocked at how quickly he let himself jump to conclusions. Stopping himself before he could voice an accusation of her inconstancy, instead he said, "Who did this?" He mopped the blood and assessed the damage.

"Dunno. Some guy. I didn't see him. Kyer went with the other one." His eyes filled with alarm, and he tried to rise. His dizzy head forbade it. "Check the woods. He said . . . archers ready to shoot . . . if she didn't go."

"And you believed that?" Janak said.

"No, but Kyer did." Phennil's hands trembled, and he clutched them into fists. "He said his chief—" He pressed his fists to his cheeks.

"Who? What chief?" Derry grabbed the elf by his arms.

"A man appeared at the stream. He had a message for Kyer, that his chief wanted to speak to her alone." He repeated the threat about the snipers in the woods.

"I tried to reason with her," the elf said. "I had him at sword point. We could have taken him down." Phennil screwed his fists into his eyes. "She told me to come back and tell you and look for the snipers in case they were here and then track her. You know how persuasive she can be," he said defensively. "She said it was for the best." Phennil had heard his attacker approach and drew his sword but turned around only in time to receive a heavy stick in the head.

Derry's whole body sagged as he dropped his arms to his sides. "You little fool." Derry didn't really care that Phennil thought he was referring to him. Derry bandaged the gash. "This man was so convincing that Kyer believed him?" He sprinkled some powder into a cup of water and made Phennil drink it.

"It wasn't really that he was convincing," Phennil pleaded. "I think she honestly thought she was doing the right thing, that if she didn't go, they'd kill you."

Derry darted a look at Phennil and tossed his blanket and saddle up onto Donnagill's back. "I can't believe you didn't yell or something. I can't believe she didn't pull out that fancy new sword of hers." Phennil was too confused to protest, and Derry ploughed on. "I know you didn't intend to get hit in the head, but now she's been gone for ages. She could be d—" He stopped short. "What are you standing around for? You're coming with me. I don't know which way she went."

Phennil drained his cup and climbed bareback onto Leoht. Skimnoddle's cries of, "I shall save some dinner for all three of you!" echoed behind them.

The last time she saw him, he stood before his lord, pale and defeated as Kien Bartheylen set down his judgement.

Fredric lost everything: his sword, his knighthood, his rank, his home. Kien exiled him out of Shael. He'd left without a word to anyone, even his sister, Acadia.

The former captain of the Shael Guard galloped up and slid from the saddle barely after reining in. His swift smoothness would have been a delight for Kyer to watch had the circumstances been otherwise. But any favourable opinion she had of him had been as brief as a single spark from flint and steel, and equally unrecoverable. He strode purposefully toward her, drawing his sword.

Acadia didn't blame Kyer. She'd said so. But Fredric certainly did.

In spite of her efforts, her composure slipped. She drew her head back in retreat, and her eyes widened to see his weapon rise to horizontal and approach her throat like an arrow in slow motion. She read the vengeance in Fredric's face, sucked in her last breath, and believed she was about to die. The sword tip was an icicle against her throat, the trickle of blood running down like the tip of the shard of ice melting with the heat of her body. His fingers toyed with the hilt; she flinched at the slight movement. His hand trembled with desire to complete the motion.

He did not thrust. She blinked slowly, as if the flicker of her eyes would prompt him to make a sudden move. Her neck stiffened with the struggle to pull away; her legs were rooted to the spot, and the invisible hands were unyielding. Harley watched with interest. Fredric continued to pierce her with his glare. Although now she saw the wheels turning inside his head. He wanted to kill her; she knew that without a glimmer of doubt. But the fact that he hadn't already done so spoke volumes. She risked a breath.

"Lovely to see you too." She was sure she heard a snort from Harley.

Fredric's hackles rose, and she thought, *Oops, might have made a mistake there.* But he still did not kill her, so she tried again.

"So when did you change your name? Right away, there, after we last saw each other?"

This time his eyes registered defeat, and she knew that he would not kill her. Could not, even. *Under orders from someone?* He must be or else he could not have had any qualms about impaling her.

He lowered the sword, and her neck could finally relax.

"Cocky bitch," he growled. He hitched his head to one side, and as suddenly as her body had been immobilized, she was now released. Harley and the siblings moved away, stepping down the slope toward the lake and out of earshot. She was left alone with Fredric, fully armed. She shook her arms to make sure she could still move them. He removed his helm. His red hair was longer and looked like it might be a bit greyer since their parting.

"Careful about being so gentlemanly," she said. "They might start to guess you're not truly one of them." She used a rag from her pouch to stop the ooze of blood from the nick in her throat.

"They already know that," he snapped. Then he spoke more quietly. "But I don't make a habit of talking about it."

She wiped the blood where it had run down toward her chest. "So who are you working for these days?"

He looked at her sharply. "How did you—? I won't answer that. What brings you and your little friends to the Guarded Realm?"

She tucked the rag back into her pouch. He had asked casually enough, but since he had known where she was, she couldn't believe he didn't already know why she was there. She folded her arms across her chest. "Look, Fredric, we're in rather a hurry. You didn't bring me here to catch up. What do you want?"

"There's a message."

She scoffed. "Oh sure, I suppose you want me to send your regards to your sister . . . or to Kien. You already showed your regard for them."

The sword tip materialized at her throat again. She'd definitely made a mistake this time. She could have taken a step backward but didn't.

"You don't know a damned thing about my regard," he said in a voice so low, it might have been in her mind. She made a mental note of the comment. "You have no idea what you—" He cut himself off, breathing heavily, and moistened his lips. His voice came tight and hoarse. "Like I said, there's a message."

"Well, out with it, then, and quit wasting my time."

The guttering in his eyes showed her his struggle with the desire to kill her. With the sword still touching her throat, he spoke carefully and deliberately, the words he had memorized.

Kyer heard him speak the words. And for a brief moment, all she felt was confusion. She knew those words. But why were they coming from the mouth of Fredric Heyland? The confusion evolved into dizzying shock.

She knew those words. *But nowhere in her memory had they been used by anyone but herself.* For it was *her* language; the only tongue she spoke when she arrived in Hreth at the age of three. Nobody had ever used it but her. *How . . . ?*

All blood drained from her face. Her head felt both cold and hot and grew numb. Fredric's face was blurred by a sparkling redness in the air around her that changed quickly to black. "What did you say?" Her vision cleared enough to see Fredric staring at her intently. Her head whirled. A hush fell over her like a blanket of snow, and she noticed her sword was in her hands, but it was unsteady, either because she hadn't had a chance to practise with it or because Fredric had spoken in *her* language.

Then the woman with the black hair was before her. The hand the woman put on Kyer's forehead was neither warm nor cool. A sharp jolt went through her head, making her ears burn, and shot down her entire body. Her knees wobbled alarmingly, the earth rocked and there was nothing she could grasp to steady herself. Her legs gave way, knees smashing down, and she pitched to the ground, the dirt cool against her cheek.

Hunter had been told to take note of her reaction. He was astonished by the effect of his words. A smile spread across his face. This was what

Golgathaur was hoping for. Hunter had been successful in his first mission. Then the smile faded. This would probably mean he was still not allowed to kill her.

The sword she had drawn, though, what a beauty! He had never seen its like. Here was a little trinket he could take from her since he couldn't have her life. The red-jewelled pommel sparkled even in the diffused light of cloud cover. He looked over his shoulder to where Misty had rejoined her brother. Sheathing his own weapon, he crouched and slowly reached for Kyer's and withdrew it from where it had landed beneath her. The silver of the blade was startlingly bright—bright as moonlight reflected off glass. Two-handed, it was perfectly balanced, almost weightless as he rose and tried a few swings through the air. Noiselessly it sliced the humidity that hung around him.

A stabbing motion or two later, he felt it change. Perhaps he was experiencing his own reaction to the strain of the encounter with Kyer, but it was almost as if the sword were getting heavier. With a heave, he waved it again, and his arm ached with the effort of it.

In a matter of half a minute since picking it up and proclaiming it weightless, Hunter was nearly unable to wield the sword. It was all he could do to keep it off the ground. And what was that pain in his hand? He didn't want to give up, but the weight forced him to let the sword tip hit the earth; he simply could not lift it. And suddenly he yanked his hand away from the hilt, letting it clatter to the ground. The hilt, he finally realized, was flaming hot. His hand was already red and puffy.

In puzzlement and fear of Kyer and her mystifying weapon, he backed away and called to his company to prepare to leave. A spattering of rain drops hammered tiny craters in the dust, splashing her prone body with mud.

Harley stopped near where she lay and said, "Are we just going to—?" but Hunter growled at him. Harley shrugged and went to his horse for his kit. He slapped a quick salve on the burned hand and bound it, but when he asked how Hunter had acquired the injury, the chief hollered, "Don't ask so god-damned many questions!"

Hunter didn't need a new weapon after all.

As the swordfighter lay unconscious in the dust, the lake underwent a change. A storm wind stirred up a torrent of waves where Kyer had earlier admired its glasslike stillness. And raindrops as large as hazelnuts pelted into it. Any fish lurked in safety near the bottom.

After a time, the storm abated.

When Kyer awoke, her back was drenched, and she was very much alone in the silent wood. Fredric and his men and woman were long gone, and the air was fresh with a wet dirt smell. She looked up then sat up, head unsteady, absently noting the dusty ground where she had lain, surrounded by mud. The thick clouds filtered too much of the sunlight for her to tell how far it had moved. Fifteen minutes? Two hours? She couldn't tell. Long enough for a soaking rain to pour. She wondered about it for a millisecond before Fredric's words flooded her mind again.

Twenty years since she had walked out of a cornfield into the Halidans' farm; twenty years since she had spoken that tongue aloud, and she had never forgotten it, though it had faded to a distant memory. Sometimes she'd wondered if she hadn't made it up. Apparently not. Someone else spoke it too and had taught Fredric Heyland the single, but all too significant sentence: "We know who you are."

The implication of those words hit her like a tidal wave. Then the woman had done . . . something, and she'd collapsed. And now, fully awake again, the mere thought of it grabbed her by the throat and drew her up to standing. *Someone else knew her language.* And that someone, whoever it was, must know where it came from.

Knees wobbling still, confusion and irrational fury took over, shutting out all other thought. She retrieved her sword from the ground, wiped it off, and slammed it into its scabbard. *By hellfire, who taught him those words?* She darted up the hill to find a trace of which direction Fredric had gone. Their hoofprints were unmistakable on the southern trail into the woods. She tore along the path after them.

Twelve

Renewed Purpose

Phennil and Derry flew up the switchback, the trail of horses' hooves clear. The rain had not penetrated the canopy of conifers, but when they emerged onto the south path, the trail became mud. Eyes darting all around, they found the sloping opening that led down to the little clearing by the lake. Derry dismounted and slipped, dirt driven up into his left poleyn. Phennil gave him a hand up. The medicine had taken effect, and the elf was feeling much better.

"What do you think?" Derry shook out the muck as best he could.

The elf wandered around. "This may be of interest." He pointed out a distinctly Kyer-shaped dust pattern in the wet.

Derry hastened over. It was about her size, anyway. If it had been her she had lain here for the duration of the downpour. Water had run in rivulets all around and streamed into the lake, but dust remained where she had been.

Phennil quickly found her footprints, where she had gone to pick something up off the ground, and then she'd hightailed it up the path by which they'd come. The tracks of her captors had been washed away by the rain, at least until farther along the path that headed south.

Kyer's trail was easy to find. It carried on in the same direction the horsemen had taken. Not back to her friends. Derry stood in the middle of the path, puzzled.

"But what does this mean?" He had an idea himself, but it did not match what was sensible to him.

Phennil sighed and leaned against a tree. He shook his head slowly and shrugged. "I don't understand it. She was here. The tracks seem to indicate that they left her here. She lay on the ground for the entire rainstorm. And then she woke up and—well, I don't get it, but it looks like she followed them."

"Why would she do that?" Derry had drawn the same conclusion, and hoped for a logical explanation. "Did they take something of hers, maybe?"

"Maybe." A hopeful tone crept into Phennil's voice. "Maybe it had something to do with the message. Or maybe she was disoriented and thought she was going the right way."

Derry's gaze wandered farther down the trail. He wanted to believe that Phennil was right. But Kyer was too smart to follow the wrong path by mistake. Why would she have done it purposely, though? *What were you thinking, Kyer?* What was this message? What could have been so important that she'd do her utmost to convince Phennil that going with that man was the right thing to do? She'd told Phennil she didn't want to risk all their lives. Was there some other reason?

"What do we do now?" the elf asked.

Derry exhaled heavily. "It's getting late. We ought to go back. I hate to, in case she's in danger, but we have no supplies. All I can think is that if she left here on her own, then . . . maybe she's all right for now. We'd better risk it."

"It's getting dark," Phennil agreed. To ease their minds a little, the elf followed Kyer's trail a short distance, just to make sure she hadn't collapsed on the path nearby. When he returned he said, "At least we know which way she went. We can pick up the trail tomorrow."

Phennil looked upward through the branches to the grey sky. A vague recollection of his sword tip at the man's chest had materialized in his memory. "I'm sorry I let this happen, Derry."

"Never mind," the captain said stiffly. "You shouldn't have let her persuade you. But it's her own fault, I guess." He took one last look around. "Why do these things always happen to her?"

Derry climbed onto Donnagill's back again. It was true. Things *did* always seem to happen to Kyer. Being singled out by Kayme was where it began. And after that, well, the earthquake—Phennil had just had the rotten luck to be with her at the time—the arrow in the back when nobody else was touched, and now to be taken by the enemy, again. Derry recalled a certain white rose Kyer carried close to her heart.

"What do we tell the others?" Phennil asked.

Derry paused, lips pursed. "I think for now we should just say that we have discovered her trail. Let her answer for herself before we cast doubt on her."

The two horses turned down the switchback trail, and Derry's brooding thoughts twisted and gnarled. What had possessed her to go the wrong way?

Kyer took the trail at a run. The mountain climbed higher on her left and fell away on her right. The stream was down there somewhere, shielded from view by bushes, flowers, shrubs, berries, and fallen logs. It would have been lovely if she'd actually looked at it. The trail wound along the side of the mountain, up, down, around. Her throat stung with the chill air. She slowed down to catch her breath but sped up as soon as she was able—a purely physical reaction, not a conscious decision. The one and only thing on her mind was Fredric's words.

Or not *his* words. Someone else's words in Fredric's mouth. *Her* words, that was the thing about it. It was her language; she had a right to know who else knew it. Someone had taught those words to Fredric, and whoever it was knew more about her than she did. Just like Kayme. Somewhere in the back of her mind, Kyer was aware that she was afraid. Knowledge was power. And anybody who knew more about her than she did had power over her. Not a comforting thought.

On, on she sped, her footsteps light as a deer. She realized how long she'd been travelling only when she started having trouble seeing the path. She stopped and rested her hands on her knees, breathing deeply. Straightening, she looked up into the drops that plummeted off the trees, the aftermath of the storm. Hungry.

Her vision was decent in the subdued light, and she headed off the trail in pursuit of berries her eyes had registered as she'd run. A few handfuls of huckleberries later, and fatigue set in. She removed her baldric and sat next to it. Curling up against the bole of a red cedar, she drifted off into a busy sleep.

The man who called himself The Guardian—*her* Guardian—showed his glowing, milky face, saying, " . . . a magical gift you have. . . I know all about you! . . . The Good must prevail." His lean figure faded, to be replaced by Fredric Heyland, confessing his guilt to Kien Bartheylen. Kien demanding his sword and Fredric's pallor as his lord handed down his fate. Fredric rushing out of the great hall at Shael Castle. Fredric's face in the flickering firelight as they made love. Fredric's sword tip at her throat as he said, "We know who you are." Fredric laughing, laughing, laughing at her because he knew something she did not. Kayme . . . "When are you going to start focussing on what *you* want to do? . . . So you will admit you left Hreth to learn more? . . . Your friends do not need you so much on their journey."

And faintly, so distant she almost did not hear it, a voice she knew to be that of Alon Maer calling her, calling for help. *No, they can do it without me!* she cried. *I don't know you.* But still the plaintive voice wailed her name.

Kyer awoke in the deep darkness of the forest, alive with cricket chirps and the scritchings of small nocturnal creatures. The chill of night had seeped into her uncloaked body so she crept further under the ferns. She breathed in the soporific, cedary air, and fell asleep again.

My slippered feet pad softly along the brightly lit corridor. Those stone walls are familiar. I know the way. The swish of my shift against my legs is all I hear. In my hand is the gift for the lady, to be presented to her right away. Her door is . . . this one. I knock. Her clear voice answers and I enter.

Colour crept back into the forest as the grey dawn lifted the darkness from the trees, slowly, gradually, as if reluctant to awaken those sleeping within. More rain had fallen as she slept, and the *drip drip* of water all around her was like strange percussion music. It soon accompanied the trills and twitters of birds. The squirrels added their chatter to the cumulative tune until Kyer was fully roused. She felt exhausted, as though she'd been awake all night. Her body was stiff from sleeping in an odd position and tense with expectancy. She shivered in the cold morning air. Every sudden sound of bird or creature made her jump. Who was it? Was someone trying to find her? Did she want to be found?

Her fingers, all but fused to the hilt of her sword, they'd gripped it so tightly all night, ached as she pried them away. She flexed and shook them to get the feeling back and sheathed her weapon. She picked her way back to the trail and looked both ways along it. Which direction did she want to go? Which direction *should* she go? Her chest felt heavy, and she struggled to suck in air.

Kyer had always known what she wanted. In the past, whenever she'd had a decision to make, she'd had a point of reference: her goal had always been clear. Working for Valrayker had fit neatly into the pursuit of that goal.

Originally, the quest to save Alon had made sense too. But now it was all askew. She had never even met Alon. And she wasn't right for Valrayker anyway; Derry was constantly reminding her of it. After what she did to Ronav, Val wouldn't see her departure as much of a loss. The rest of them would understand why she needed to abandon the mission now. Phennil would explain it to them.

Whether they understand it or not is their problem.

Kyer hid her face in her hands. She'd left Hreth to learn who she was. Anything else was a mere distraction. She knew that now. She turned southward and followed the trail that Fredric, Harley, and the others had taken.

Derry awoke in the predawn light, brooding over Jesqellan's final words to him last night. The mage had again brought up the magic he sensed surrounding Kyer. He had felt a troubling change again in the past few days. He had assessed her new sword, and determined that it was magical, but he didn't think the weapon's magic was strong enough to fully account for it.

"Naturally I can block out magic I detect when I am around other mages," he said, "but I believe I am more sensitive to whatever magic Kyer is carrying simply because—well, not only is it unusual for a non–magic user to radiate such energy, but hers seems to have multiplied at an alarming rate."

"Could her medallion have changed somehow?" Derry suggested.

Jesqellan thought but shook his head. "I do not think so. I believe my sense of her medallion would simply have intensified, were that the case. This is something new."

Jesqellan had retired to bed then, leaving Derry to contemplate his remarks.

It was utter nonsense, of course, Derry told himself as he lay there staring up through the trees, silhouetted black against the paling sky. Kyer was no more a magic user than he was. It was too much to believe that she could leap from being magically impotent to radiating it after a matter of weeks. He listened to the wakeful birds and the morning chatter of squirrels. Skimnoddle quietly puttered over breakfast but he made no move to join the halfling.

Derry was more concerned with her disappearance than some perceived, probably imagined use of magic.

Kyer was no fool, he told himself. She could not have mistakenly chosen to follow the path of her captors. Then why? He dreaded broaching the subject with her. He'd felt the sting of her remarks before. No matter how he worded the question, she'd know they doubted her. Her vehement defence would only leave Derry with a figurative slap mark on his cheek. *Assuming we even find her.*

Was it too early to get up without looking overly eager? He was anxious to get going, to look for her, but he fought the desire. The captain had spent an inordinate amount of time worrying about Kyer lately. When she went off with Kayme, he'd fretted for nothing. When she and Phennil were stuck below ground in the earthquake, his concern over their fate had been brushed off with an unsatisfactory explanation. And he was starting to resent it. Unconsciously or not, Kyer had made a mockery of his distress.

And now this. He was worried about her, and would his fear be for naught again?

He remembered the easy conversations they'd had in weeks gone by, when they were first getting to know each other. When she'd needed his confidence and reassurance, he'd given it to her happily. She seemed to need him less and less these days. And she was more and more difficult to talk to.

Finally he joined Skimnoddle and roused the others. They ate and packed the camp in haste. The captain sighed heavily to himself as he rolled up Kyer's dew-dampened bedroll where it had lain all night near the fire. He tucked it in its place on his friend's horse, doubt weighing on his mind. *We'll ask her why she followed them, and what will she say?*

"Let's get going," he called to the others.

When they reached the mountain lake, they sped right past it and carried on along the trail they were certain Kyer had taken.

Kyer's footsteps were slower today. She trudged steadily but without the urgency and adrenaline that had carried her yesterday. Her mind was a mire of confusion. She felt stupid and childish, this soggy, mossy indecision. Well, she'd made a decision, but still she couldn't say she was right. An emotion akin to loneliness had taken root in her heart. Could her friends truly understand what it was like to not know who she was? She doubted it. But was that reason enough to leave them?

Besides, she was forced to come to grips with reality: she had no horse and no supplies.

Why? Why did Fredric say those words then run away?

Damn it, she wouldn't let him get away with it. Him, and whomever knew her language and used it to torment her. She trod deliberately on a flower that had fallen off its mother plant in the rain and picked up her pace.

Kyer's strength and self-assuredness had been inched aside by insecurity and weakness and it irked her. She'd left home to find answers. But this . . . being tossed little tidbits, little hints, yet nothing solid, this was not what she wanted. Kayme, the man who called himself the Guardian, and now Fredric, poking her, taunting her with, "We know something you don't know!" She frowned and took to a run.

In the still of the forest she picked up a rumbling vibration from behind. Hooves.

A band of panic seized her chest and cinched it tight. *No! I don't know yet!* She fled the path up the steep mountainside and found a place to hide: the concave underside of a fallen hemlock's root system, now almost vertical as the massive trunk stretched out horizontally and rested on a rock outcropping. Lichen dripped down from the roots and shielded Kyer from view. She unsheathed her longsword, crunched herself as small as she could against the roots, and waited. Who was it? Tension rang in her ears, and her thudding heart sent blood surging through her like little knives, cutting and biting at her. She clenched herself so the scream could not escape.

The hoofbeats approached. Slowed. *Go away!* Stopped. *I'm not ready!* Voices. Phennil's, Skimnoddle's—that blasted halfling—Janak's. Derry's. Tears prickled at the inside of her eyes.

Suddenly she wasn't sure if she feared being found or not being found. She breathed heavily but silently. Footsteps, climbing, nearing her place. The dam was about to break; she couldn't hold back her inner turbulence much longer.

They'd found where she had to have slept the night before. The trail of the horsemen was much older than hers. The fact that even in the morning she'd followed their trail rankled Derry. Had her senses taken leave of her? Now Phennil saw the unmistakable fresh path of someone crashing through the bushes up the hillside. He raised his hand in warning to the others, stopped, and dismounted.

"I think we may have found her," Phennil said softly.

"Oh, my lady is alive! I am overcome," Skimnoddle intoned.

"Knock it off, you imbecile, or I'll knock it for you," said Janak.

"Hush," Derry said. He nodded to Phennil.

"Kyer!" Phennil called softly. "Kyer, it's us."

The two gingerly stepped through the heather up the hillside, toward an uprooted hemlock. Whatever storm had been the catalyst for the tree's demise had been long ago, for the trunk was now a nursing log, a provider of life for new bushes and trees. Phennil reached out, placed a hand on an outstretched root—

A wildly vicious Kyer burst from behind the tree roots, brandishing that fearsome sword of hers, and threw Phennil head over heels, nearly taking Derry out with him.

"Get away from me!" she snarled. "Don't touch me! I won't go with you!"

Derry had instinctively reached for his sword at the sudden movement but drew his hand back when he saw it was Kyer.

"Of course we won't touch you, Kyer." He immediately recognized the need for calm. "It's us. Everything's all right now."

Her eyes locked on his for an instant. Then her face contorted in a mixture of fury, helplessness, and relief, and she crumpled to the forest floor.

Kyer rocked back and forth on her knees, her face in her hands. Her shoulders were taut in knots of anguish, and all she could say was, "I'm sorry. I'm sorry." She was sorry for causing them trouble, sorry for abandoning Alon Maer. Even if she had done it only temporarily, she had made a choice to desert them. But she said nothing else.

Derry dashed forward and sank down next to her. "It's all right; it doesn't matter now." He put his hands on her upper arms. "All that matters is that you're okay."

She let him raise her to her feet and lead her down the hill to the path.

The madness had dispersed at the sight of her friends, like a puff of steam erupting from a pot when the lid is lifted. These were not enemies stalking her, trying to make her do things she wasn't ready to do. She was horrified that she'd nearly run Phennil through with her sword. When she saw Derry, it was like hearing Kayme's harp again, bringing the chaos in her head into focus. It hit her that leaving her friends felt entirely wrong. These were the only friends she had. She should enlist their help, not turn her back on them. Derry led her to Trig, and she stroked the animal's neck, wondering if he forgave her. She felt the others' eyes on her but could not raise her own to meet them.

For all that Kyer could tell herself she didn't care what others thought of her, she knew better. She cared deeply what this group thought of her. She'd struggled hard to gain their respect. How could she have considered throwing that away? It had been temporary madness, brought on by the shock of Fredric's words. Chasing after Fredric was foolhardy. What would have greeted her at the end of that path? Anything that took her so by surprise was not to be trusted. Somebody else knew her language, and that was intriguing, to be sure, but it would not do to throw aside everything else she'd worked for. She nudged Trig into step behind Donnagill.

How to explain all this to her friends? The whole truth was out of the question. For one thing, she could not explain Fredric's use of an unidentifiable language without telling the whole story about her arrival in a corn field with no knowledge of how she got there. And that was not a story she desired to delve into in these circumstances. It would not fill them with confidence in her. And that was not the only issue.

I chose to abandon the mission, she thought, with no small measure of guilt. She did not think they would forgive her easily. She was especially concerned about Derry. As a knight, abandoning a commitment, for any reason, was just not part of his culture. He'd forgiven her mistakes in the past, but she didn't think he could forgive this one. At a loss for the right words, she said nothing to any of them, and they, assuming her ordeal had been traumatic, did not press her for information. Her eyes locked on the swish of Donnagill's tail. She let them make that assumption and considered what to tell them. It couldn't be the whole truth.

At the evening mealtime, coincidentally taken by the lakeshore where Fredric had spoken to her, she finally reached a decision about it. And if they didn't believe her? Well, she'd scale that cliff when she couldn't find the stairs. Swallowing her mouthful of tasteless cornmeal cake, she took the plunge.

"It was Fredric Heyland."

Mouths dropped open.

"I don't know who he's working for, but he's in league with someone." There, she'd given them news of the enemy, that ought to remind them that she's on their side, buy her some trust.

"The messenger said his chief wanted a word," Phennil said. "What did he say?"

Jesqellan leaned forward just a touch in anticipation of her answer. Derry, too, was all ears. She hesitated. It was as if they knew something she did not. "It was a warning: for us to keep out of the mission."

"So he knows about our mission?" Derry looked around at Jesqellan.

"Apparently."

"Why did he want to tell only you?" Jesqellan put in casually.

Kyer didn't care for his suspicious tone. Her mind raced to come up with credible answers and she hoped the mage wasn't a Perceptor.

"How should I know? You know our history. Maybe he wanted me to believe something that wasn't true, get me in trouble. He said I had an excuse not to be involved and should get out if I valued my life. I—told him I value her life too."

"What sort of excuse was he referring to?"

"Because I've never met Alon before; remember how Val questioned the same thing?" There. That was a point Derry couldn't dispute.

The whiskeyjacks fluttered from tree to tree, calling for handouts. Derry stirred his soup absently and didn't raise his eyes. "Did you escape or did they let you go?"

At least this was something she could be truthful about. Stick to the truth as much as possible. "Neither. They gave me a nasty knock on the head, and when I came to, they were gone."

Jesqellan cocked his head and seemed to be trying to word his question carefully. "Why would you follow them instead of coming back to us for help?"

The accusatory tone was getting to her. "Another in a string of bad decisions by Kyer Halidan. Obviously, I wanted more information." She was on a roll now. "If they don't want us to continue on the mission, maybe they know what's ailing Alon, how she became ill. I didn't know how much time had passed since they'd left me, and I thought I could catch up. And then of course I realized I didn't have any supplies with me, and it got to be too dark to carry on or go back."

She looked around at their faces; Phennil frowning apologetically, the halfling eager, Janak's one-eyed expression unreadable, Derry and Jesqellan not meeting her gaze at all. It was these last two she targeted.

"This is working out just great for Fredric, isn't it? I wanted more information because I knew you would ask all these questions and I wouldn't have satisfactory answers. What's the result? You're all looking at me like I'm the guilty one here."

"No!" Phennil jumped to her defence. "You're not to blame, Kyer."

"I thought he was bluffing about the snipers, but I couldn't be sure; that's why I went with him in the first place." She wasn't lying when she said, "I guess it was stupid of me to think I could handle it. And I was counting on Phennil to bring you all right behind me. Things just got out of control." From her spot on the same log Harley had sat on to feed the whiskeyjacks, she looked around at them as sincerely as possible. "I'm sorry."

"It's okay, Kyer. I'm sorry too," Phennil said, a bit quickly.

"We'll just have to travel that much quicker from here," Janak said, which she took as his way of forgiving her.

"Of course, we'll manage, dear lady," Skimnoddle's voice rang out. "We shall be like the gazelle! Fleet like the wind my feet shall be, merely beholding your fair countenance again."

"Uh, thanks," she said. "I suppose I'm feeling like a bit of an idiot."

Would they buy her explanation?

Phennil clapped her on the back. "That's okay. You're not the only one. I'm sorry I let you down."

He was trying awfully hard to brush it off, and Kyer didn't know why. Harley's words had intrigued her, and Kyer had wanted to go with him. She had convinced herself it was fear of the archers that made her do it, but that was another lie, one that she didn't regret, in spite of everything. That was definitely not something she was prepared to tell Derry.

When they left her to have a rock skipping contest on the lake, she remained where she sat. *Hellfire take the next person who speaks to me in a language foreign to everyone but me.* It was just too much to take.

Footsteps approached. Derry. "Maybe I should check your head where you got knocked."

She shrugged but let him examine her. He could find no evidence of a wound, certainly not one severe enough to put her out of consciousness. She tried to explain what had happened, but the memory was all shadows, nothing solid.

Derry was visibly puzzled. "You lay on the ground for the duration of the rainstorm; that had to have been for a reason," he said with a sigh, "but I'm damned if I can determine what happened. A spell?"

Kyer just shrugged. "I don't know."

Great. The one thing I'm absolutely honest about.

As Derry fell asleep that night, listening to the gentle lap, lap of the shiny water and watching the clouds scud across the half moon, he could not dismiss a strange suspicion that Kyer was lying. Jesqellan agreed with him. For one thing, the wallop on the head made no sense; there was no evidence of it, apart from a Kyer-shaped dry spot in the dirt. Derry could not begin to guess what had really happened between Kyer and Fredric, but one thing he was sure of: it wasn't as simple as his warning them off the mission. Something passed between them, something traumatic; only that would account for Kyer's behaviour when they found her on the mountainside that morning. And true to form, when she felt attacked, she attacked back. Derry rubbed his cheek. What he had yet to determine was whether that was a panicked reaction when she felt guilty. Did she wish they hadn't found her?

Whatever Fredric had said, Derry was certain it had, at least for a moment, become more important than Alon Maer.

"She was dumbstruck."

Golgathaur's eyebrows narrowed thoughtfully. "Oh yes?"

"Fell flat on her face. Well, with a little help from Misty. But she was speechless, which is saying a lot for Kyer." Hunter let a rock fly into the lake. This lake was larger than the one where he'd left Kyer.

"Hmm." Golgathaur slowly nodded. "Yes, that is quite favourable, isn't it?"

Hunter turned away. "Yeah, sure. It's great."

"How can I help you, Hunter?" Golgathaur placed himself on the fallen log, resting his hands in his lap. "You are looking particularly glum this morning."

"Really." Hunter flung another rock into the lake. It went farther than the last one. He was in no mood to humour a man who could probably just as easily snap his fingers and make him fizzle away into the misty air as he could flash that stupid, expectant grin at him. But the grin was there; Hunter wished he would snap his fingers instead.

"Yes, most definitely. I can't imagine why someone with all your skills, your talents and charms, not to mention gainful employment, might be as close as you appear to be to the depths of despair. Now, I want to help you—let it never be said that I do not offer support and all manner of encouragement to all my contractors—but dear me, I cannot possibly help you if you do not share your troubles with me."

Hunter ground his teeth and finally made contact with the red water lily fifty paces off the shore. He darted a resentful glance up at the pale, translucent skin of the otherwise dark man's face and was surprised to see that Golgathaur's expression had altered slightly but perceptibly. The playful condescension had been subtly replaced by serious interest. The smile was still there, but it had deepened to one of gentle concern. And the eyebrows had lowered from their cheerful peaks to a narrow valley. "You sound like a father," he said doubtfully.

"Do I?" the other replied, as if that were unlikely. He shrugged, an unusual gesture for him. "Well, whomever I coincidentally resemble, what is it that is causing you to sink to this mood?"

Fredric shifted uncomfortably. He looked off into the trees. "I'm surprised you even have to ask," he said, testing the ground. Would Golgathaur actually permit him complete, unexpurgated honesty?

The lieutenant nodded his encouragement.

Fredric plunged ahead. "Am I correct to assume that you'll still want her alive?"

The lieutenant nodded.

"Well, then. There you go. You have taken away my one pleasure. The one goal that gave meaning to my life." Once he'd begun, all Fredric's thoughts wanted to tumble out with the redoubling force of an avalanche.

"That girl, that . . . *bitch*—" he spat, "I don't even want to pronounce her name. She ruined my life. You know it. I don't know how you know, but you know it all. I am destroyed because of her. I had everything I desired. Everything I had worked for all my life. And everything I ever cared about was ripped out of my grasp. Because of her." Fredric's vehemence rang through the trees. "And since then all I've wanted is to find her and crush her. To clutch her by that throat that talks too damn much, that neck holding up the head that's too big for the body underneath it . . ." He paused to shake off the choking feeling that had risen to his voice.

"I want to feel that throat struggle for breath beneath my hands as I squeeze the life out of it. I want to laugh at the terror and panic on her face when she knows she's going down. I want to hear her gasp for that last breath. And before she dies, I want to tear that head off and fling it as far away as I can. Feel the bones and tendons stretch and give way as I pull. So she knows what it's like to have her life severed from her." The rock he threw was backed with the force of his words and flew farther than any other. With no more rocks in hand, he gave up the game. "I want her to know what my life is now."

Panting, Fredric recollected himself. He sat down as if he had nothing left. It felt supremely good to have spilled it all. Though now he would have to live with Golgathaur's taunts and jibes about the pathetic nature of his position.

Golgathaur was silent. After a few moments, the lieutenant adopted a helpful pose, resting both elbows on his knees and rubbing his chin with clasped knuckles. He cleared his throat.

"These are heavy frustrations indeed." He was all seriousness, to the great surprise of Fredric Heyland. "When I was a youngster, much younger than you are now, I was given a choice. My choice was to live under the hand of a most . . . oppressive father. Either that, or death. Not a difficult choice for a young person, though the consequences of such were not always pleasant. After a time, I realized that my position held certain . . . advantages, and I gave myself another choice: to continue to feel oppressed and trapped or to allow myself to live within the boundaries set for me. To create ambitions that fit. Again, the choice was an obvious one. You have the same option now."

Fredric was a soldier, not a philosopher, and had not caught the lieutenant's meaning. He looked at him quizzically.

Golgathaur took pity on him. "If you do not mind my saying so, your ultimate goal is misplaced." He raised a hand as Fredric tried to protest. "Pray, hear me out. Kyer Halidan ruined your life, you say. I have no doubt that your feelings are warranted. I am grieved to hear you express your dissatisfaction with your current position and must admit to a certain amount of sadness that you simply cannot feel pleasure or fulfillment in working for me. Perhaps that may change in time; I cannot say. That aside, you do feel unhappy with the current state of affairs. Kyer Halidan caused your accomplishments to be for naught, she precipitated the stripping of your previous position, redirecting your ambitions into the dust. You are, to put it mildly, angry with her, and rightfully so. I would be as well.

"If you were to kill Kyer Halidan, even in the violent and satisfying method you described, what would you have achieved? She would be dead, and you would still be here. I have heard it said that even when one is successful at revenge, it never brings finality. What would be left for you to live for?"

He paused, letting his words of reason seep through Fredric's mood until the younger man recognized their soundness. Fredric's hopeful glance asked for further details.

"Think of it!" Golgathaur leaned forward. "Would it not be better still to ruin her life the way she ruined yours? I have told you I need her alive and that will not change. Yet it need not stop you from finding some way of making her life as utterly miserable as yours is, unaccountable though that may be," he finished smugly.

Hunter became aware of the drumming in his chest. "But . . . what's in it for you? You want her alive—"

"Alive, yes. Needy would be even better." He waggled his eyebrows.

Hunter allowed a glimmer of hope to tickle the back of his mind.

"It would bring new meaning to your life, I believe. We all need something to live for. I found my meaning many years ago. It is time for you to locate yours."

"But what can I—?" Hunter was at a loss. "She's so much in control of herself."

"Moreso than you were a few months back?"

The sun rose on Fredric Heyland. The mist in his heart and head cleared, even if the air around him remained as damp and dismal as ever.

"Now, Hunter," said Golgathaur with a change of tone. "You must give some thought to what ruining the life of one such as she would entail. I have an idea of how I can be of assistance to you in this new ambition, but I must first go off and see—but never mind, I will return soon, hopefully with some new instructions that will please you. In the meantime, I suggest you stay close enough on the heels of your quarry that you do not lose them, but do not let them become aware of you. I have a feeling that soon your nearness to them will serve you well."

Golgathaur walked through his own private door and was gone, leaving Hunter with thoughts of renewed purpose.

Kyer Halidan was in control of her life. He had to wrest that control from her grasp. What did she want? To be a knight? She'd denied it but it must be so. And above all, Kyer certainly desired the good opinions of Kien and Valrayker.

Ah, now *that* was something he could work with.

Golgathaur swept past the wisteria vines that loaded the trellis alongside his front door. He paused to pluck a bloom and tuck it in his breast pocket. The aroma swirled around him, following him inside. Several corridors, staircases and doorways later, he knocked on a thick, solid wood door and entered.

"Good evening, my friend. May I call you 'friend?'"

The figure rose from an armchair, book in hand, and grimaced sardonically.

"Hardly the way *I* would define the word. To what do I owe the dubious pleasure this time?"

Golgathaur smiled warmly. "Only that I do believe you'd be interested to know what I have just learned."

The eyebrows raised in doubt. "Well then?"

"It would seem we have a mutual acquaintance."

"I don't think there's much likelihood of that."

Golgathaur clapped his hands, then clasped them loosely on his chest. "I didn't know it right away, but now that I observe more closely, there is a startling resemblance. Let's see if you can guess: female, early twenties, and—oddly enough—understands what I believe is her native tongue!"

The listener's reaction was to not react at all but remain quite still.

Golgathaur slapped his thighs and clapped again. "Well. Have yourself a nice day."

He closed the door behind himself and started down the stairs. Moments later he heard what he could only assume was the sound of a book being thrown to the floor with the force of rage.

Thirteen

The Only Plan that Matters

My slippered feet pad softly along the brightly lit corridor. Those stone walls are familiar. I know the way. The swish of my shift against my legs is all I hear. The little box in my hand is the gift for the lady, to be presented to her right away. Her door is . . . this one. I knock. Her clear voice answers and I enter. She sits in her armchair by the fire, reading.

"For you, my lady," I say. "It just arrived." I hold out the box.

"From whom?" she replies, receiving it from me.

"From his lordship, my lady."

She opens the small, leather case and traces the length of the necklace with her slender finger. "It's beautiful." She turns to me. "Do you know what this is, Misha?"

"No, m'lady."

She draws the snake out of its resting place. "The serpent is a symbol of undying love," she tells me. With a finger she gently brushes the snake's jewel fangs where they clench its own tail, and clasps the necklace behind her neck. "Do you like it?" she asks.

"Yes, m'lady," I assure her. "Is there anything else you need, m'lady?"

"Thank you, Misha, no. You may go."

I curtsey. As I reach for the door handle, I hear her say, "Dear Kien."

I am successful.

Kyer woke and could see no stars between the trees. She'd had a dream, but its vague memory drifted off as she recognized that the sky had become overcast. The dream had left an unpleasant feeling in her chest, so she rolled over and curled up, drawing the blanket around again.

In the morning, they retraced their steps down the switchback path to their intended route. Kyer's dream was forgotten, and she attributed the lingering unpleasant feeling to the troubles of yesterday. Nobody said a word about those events, for which Kyer was grateful, though she occasionally caught Derry looking morosely at her sidelong. She scowled at him, and he looked away.

They continued higher into the mountains on their westward journey, alert for the possible return of Fredric and his party. Kyer thought that perhaps it wasn't necessary: if Fredric's only task was to speak to her, he had completed it. But *caution is the first stage of preparation*, Brendow said, so she remained watchful.

The path they travelled was too narrow to be called a road. Growth of underbrush indicated it had not been travelled in many months. Grasses, clover, and buttercups had taken over, and the bushes to each side had encroached so that it was barely wide enough for two horses to travel abreast. An hour or so after the midday meal, made more palatable than usual by the discovery of a treasure trove of wild strawberries, they seemed to have reached the crest of the mountain. The horses, in reaction to the level ground after the slow and steady incline, got a second wind and wanted to pick up the pace. Out of consideration to Jesqellan, whose second wind had not caught up with him yet, they held the animals to a restrained walk.

Janak was the first to complain of stomach pains.

"Gotta stop," he said and did so, suddenly, to the surprise and annoyance of Leoht, who was directly behind the dwarf's pony and reared up in alarm. Janak was doubled over in the saddle. Derry leaned down to him from atop Donnagill, a worry line across his brow.

"What kind of pain, Janak, sharp? a dull ache? throbbing?"

He got no answer. The dwarf slid off his mount and disappeared into the bushes.

Kyer looked over at Phennil, whose eyes were fixed on Leoht's mane. After about ten minutes, Janak returned, a bit pale under his whiskers. His face and hands were scratched from the bushes.

"All right?" Derry asked.

Janak grunted. "The runs," he growled. "Better now."

All appeared well for about a half hour, when Kyer, going through all the Elvish words for various berries, got stuck on "huckleberry" and turned to Phennil to ask him. His eyebrows were furrowed, as if in concentration, and even as she looked at him, his face took on a greenish hue.

She called a halt and hastened to help him off his horse. The elf crumpled to the underbrush and threw up. Janak took the opportunity to enter the woods again. *The runs aren't gone yet, I guess.* Kyer massaged the back of Phennil's neck, looking up at Derry in alarm.

"Is there a point in going on today?" She simultaneously took stock of her own digestive system lest whatever ailed her friends was attacking her too. *Not so far.*

Derry shook his head.

The middle of the path was not an ideal location to camp, but it was all they had. They would simply have to trust that nobody else was likely to come along that day. The woods provided some shelter. They separated the horses, putting Trig and Donnagill at the south end of their designated camp and Leoht and the ponies at the north, opening a long, narrow space big enough for bedrolls and a fire. Janak's and Phennil's illnesses could take hours—even days—to pass through their systems.

Kyer laid out Phennil's bedroll and assisted him to lie down, where he promptly rolled onto his side and curled into a groaning, quaking ball. The rank odour of illness made a putrid combination with his poor hygiene.

While Jesqellan saw to the horses, Derry rooted through his saddlebag for his kit and other supplies. Skimnoddle gathered stones to surround a firepit and toddled off into the woods to collect kindling.

"How far to the stream, do you think?" Kyer asked.

"Too far," answered Derry. "We'll have to just use what we—Oh."

Jesqellan had sunk to his knees next to Trig and crawled to the side of the path to throw up. *How thoughtful of him not to puke right where someone might need to walk.* Kyer brushed the hair off her forehead, resigned to the new agenda for the day.

"What do you think it is? Flu?"

Derry opened his kit and reviewed its contents. "Could be. Could be food poisoning too, in which case we're probably all in for it."

As if on cue, Derry's hands began to vibrate. "How are you?" he asked her, his face going grey. He didn't wait for an answer but rose, clutching his belly, and staggered into the woods.

She let out a determined sigh and prepared the firepit using the rocks Skimnoddle had gathered. *How long does it take to get a few sticks?* she thought with a sinking feeling. It had been several minutes since the halfling disappeared into the brush. She followed his footsteps and soon found him, a heaving mass of brightly coloured cloth, quivering in a ball next to a pool of his own rank vomit. Probably Derry would have been able to analyse its contents and determine the source of the illness, but he was too busy producing his own purgings somewhere on the other side of the path.

In less than an hour since Janak's first eruption of symptoms, the entire party had been taken down, leaving Kyer—so long as she didn't fall sick herself—to fend and care for all of them.

"Come on, Skimnoddle." She tried to sound like any mildly sympathetic physicker. Holding her breath against the odour, she forced her hands under his clenched armpits to half drag him back to where his bedroll lay waiting for him. Dumping him unceremoniously onto it, she went back for the firewood. With an ample supply piled next to the firepit, she stood for a moment, at a loss of what to do. Jesqellan had found his bed, and both his and Phennil's bodies were overtaken by tremors.

What were you all thinking? she reprimanded them. *Derry's the physicker, not me. What am I supposed to do?*

Gritting her teeth, she left off bemoaning her predicament and set about caring for her charges, starting with a search for the two missing ones. She smelled Janak before she saw him. "Janak?" she called.

"Get away. Leave me be," he hollered back weakly. His voice had all but lost its snarly edge and was now pitiful to hear.

"Okay, just so long as I know where you are. There's a bed ready for you."

Derry wasn't far from Janak. He was given away by the burning, fetid odour that told her the captain was producing it at both ends. Kyer nearly vomited herself. Again she considered whether she felt ill or not and came up negative. Derry choked out, "I'll . . . be . . . all right in a . . . minute or two." She decided not to count on it and went back to build a fire, though she wasn't altogether sure what she'd use it for. *Damn Derry getting sick before he could tell me what to do.*

When she had a decent fire going, she erected Skimnoddle's fold-away grill and put a kettle on. Dampening a rag from her waterskin, she made rounds to her patients, bathing faces and necks in a sorry attempt to lower their fevers.

Skimnoddle's cramping prompted him to haul himself back into the woods, just as Derry staggered into the clearing and fell upon his bed. Kyer went over to him.

"Derry, you have to help me. I don't have a clue what to do," she implored apologetically. Sweat beaded on the captain's forehead in spite of his uncontrolled shivering, and he didn't respond. She remoistened the rag and swabbed his face and even squeezed a few drops of the water into his mouth.

She knew it wasn't necessarily a good idea to stop the body from spewing out whatever impurities had caused the sickness, but how long to let it go on before she should become concerned? Adding some fuel to the fire, she became aware of rumbling in her stomach. Alarmed, she sat back on her heels to analyse it. It rumbled again and she relaxed. *Hunger.* That's all it was. *At least I know how to treat that.*

Surrounded by moaning and the occasional disappearance of one or another of her patients into the woods, Kyer nibbled at hardtack and dried meat. She couldn't bring herself to make anything more interesting while her friends suffered. Eventually Janak crawled into the clearing and flopped on his bed.

Okay, Kyer, you always profess to not be an idiot; think! As she poked at her fire, she tried to remember what her mother used to give her as a sick child. More than a few times, she'd come down with some sort of flu and had lain on her bed feeling nearly as dreadful as her companions did. She remembered being ornery and protesting when Della urged her to sit up. But her mother was gently persistent and succeeded in getting Kyer upright so she could sip—what was it? Something hot and not actually unpleasant but for its association with feeling sick. Ah, that was it. Ginger.

Well, she didn't know what to do for the runs, but she could make some ginger tea from Skimnoddle's supply of the root and spoon-feed it to her charges. Maybe if his stomach felt better, Derry would be able to give her some other advice. Looking over at him, her heart sank. He was quaking with chills; she couldn't see him being of much assistance today.

Speaking of day . . . Kyer glanced up at the deepening shadows between the trees, the stretched-out look of the diffused light. Her fingers curled around the ginger root in Skimnoddle's bag. It would be a dark night and not altogether warm either. She slivered some of the ginger into the boiling water and moved it aside to keep it down to a simmer. She considered cool compresses to lower the fevers of her patients but didn't want to stop their bodies' natural battle against the infection—or whatever it was. *Damn it, Derry, you can't leave this up to me!* She decided to monitor their condition and treat the fever if it peaked.

Kyer had come to the conclusion that if she weren't sick already, she wouldn't get it. For some reason, the illness was passing her by. Instead she felt worry lines etched into her forehead, stiff shoulders, and a depressing feeling of inadequacy. When her brew had simmered long enough, she made her rounds, checking foreheads, adjusting blankets, spoon-feeding some of the ginger tea down each of their throats, imploring them to keep it down.

Janak took her arm in an alarmingly feeble grip. "Y'take . . . take care," he managed to whisper.

"I'll be all right. You just get better."

She was exhausted, but fearful for her friends' condition, so she fought her need for sleep. One of them might need her help. She would be hard-pressed to defend them all should an intruder show up, but that was no excuse to give up on protecting them altogether. Yet as the darkness of night deepened she could not keep her eyes open and her legs began to wilt beneath her. She made her rounds once more before settling down by the fire to get some rest. *Just a short one.* Wrapped in only her cloak, she shivered but eventually fell asleep.

My slippered feet pad softly across the floor, through the doorway and up the stairs. I walk along the brightly lit corridor, with their flower baskets and candelabra evenly spaced along them; this isn't the first time I've come here,

and I know the way. The swish of my navy shift against my legs is all I hear. An open door on my right. I pass by. The little box in my hand is the gift for the lady, to be presented to her right away. Her door is ... this one. I knock. Her clear voice answers and I enter. She sits in her wing-backed armchair by the fire, reading. Her dark hair gleams brown, red, gold.

"For you, my lady," I say. "It just arrived." I hold out the box.

"From whom?" she replies, receiving it from me.

"From his lordship, my lady."

She opens the box and pulls out the small, leather case. Opening it, she traces the length of the blue, gem-inlaid serpent-shape necklace with her slender finger. "It's beautiful." She turns to me. "Do you know what this is, Misha?"

"No, m'lady."

She draws the snake out of its resting place. "The serpent is a symbol of undying love," she tells me. With a finger she gently brushes the snake's jewel fangs where they clench its own tail, and clasps the necklace behind her neck. "Do you like it?" she asks.

"Yes, m'lady," I assure her. "Is there anything else you need, m'lady?" The remains of her tea things are on the table next to her chair.

"Thank you, Misha, no. You may go." She doesn't look at me but smiles at the space in the air in front of her, still lightly fingering the trinket.

She doesn't ask me to take the tea things so I don't. I curtsey and move toward the door. As I reach for the polished brass handle, I hear her say, "Dear Kien."

I am successful. I feel triumphant as I close the door.

Kyer woke up, feeling jittery. At once she attributed the nerves to her worry about her friends and stood up, clutching her cloak around herself. They all slept soundly enough.

As she added sticks to the fire, and it burst anew with warmth, the dream came back to her. The familiarity of it was startling, now that she began to think about it. She had dreamed the same dream just a few nights ago. She was in Bartheylen Castle, in that way that one's dream self knows a location, and that was most definitely Alon Maer. But she didn't look sick. *Now, why would I dream about Alon Maer when I've only ever seen her in a portrait?* Alon wasn't sick in the dream, but there was something very disturbing about that gift, that necklace. A snake. *A symbol of undying love.* Kyer shuddered.

She repeated her rounds at least once each hour that night, catching a few moments of rest in between. There was no fear of falling too soundly into sleep; her companions' moaning and dragging themselves to the bushes to purge their already empty bellies and bowels was just as effective as the morning crowing of the rooster. At least they wouldn't dehydrate if she could keep a few sips of tea down them.

All the next day, Kyer tended to her friends, cleaning the dried vomit off their faces, bathing foreheads and the backs of necks. She persisted with the tea, which seemed to settle their stomachs a little. They drifted in and out of sleep and dreams, sometimes begging a sip of water or another blanket. Wiping Derry's face brought him around for a moment, and he opened his bleary eyes.

"You're all right?" he whispered hoarsely.

She nodded.

"Blueberry decoction." His eyes burned with earnestness, or fever.

"Hunh?"

"Blueberries. No seeds. Simmer twenty minutes."

His eyes closed again. *Okay,* she thought. *I'll see if I can figure that out.* They'd passed through a blueberry field only days ago and had gathered some. Derry must have been puzzling through this in his fever-beleaguered mind.

She emptied a waterskin into a saucepan. Only about half a cup of water squeezed out, and the skin was empty. She scrambled around, checking all the waterskins. *Shit.* She had put off a trek to find a stream as long as she could, loathe though she was to leave her friends unattended.

"Derry," she said into his ear, hoping he'd hear her through his stupor. "I'm going to look for water. Be back soon." After assuring herself that each man was as comfortable as possible, she saddled Trig, put every last water vessel into her saddlebags, and set out. Her cloak was her only shield against the cool mountain air; she'd put her bedroll over top of Phennil, and Skimnoddle was curled up under her blanket as well as his own.

She rode west because they'd come from the east, and no water lay in that direction. She urged Trig along, keeping a watchful eye on the sun. She would allow herself an hour to ride away and an hour to return. Water or not, she could not leave her friends alone into the night. Kyer tuned her eyes and ears to detect sight or sound of water. Once or twice Kyer thought she heard a trickle or a hush of a stream, but whenever she slowed to listen, it was nothing but the wind in the bushes. Being alone was making her jumpy.

The shadows lengthened and the sun's light only barely reached woman and horse on the mountain path.

There's nothing, she thought in despair. *I have to go back.* She'd have to try again in the morning. But giving up was hard for Kyer. *Just one bend more . . .*

She slowed Trig as they rounded one last bend in the path.

Kyer was looking for water. She did not expect what she saw. She shrieked in alarm. Trig reared up with a whinny.

The tall man in black stood in the centre of the path.

Heart thudding, Kyer wrested her mount back under control.

"Blood and death!" Kyer yelled. "What the hell are you doing here, and what do you mean by standing there—? You bastard, you did that on purpose! You knew I was coming and stood there like a gods-damned— Shit, I don't know what." Kyer dropped her head onto Trig's neck and exhaled completely, calming both herself and the animal.

The Guardian laughed softly, which infuriated her.

She dismounted and her still-trembling fingers fumbled in her pocket for the white stone he had given her. "It's this, isn't it?" she demanded. "This is how you find me, isn't it?" At his nod, she grasped the stone threateningly in her right hand. "If you *ever* sneak up on me like that again, I will fling this thing as far from me as I can get it. You understand me?"

He bowed apologetically. "I did check to see that it was safe for me to come to you, you know." His smooth voice was all too reminiscent of Kayme's.

"How did you find me before you gave me the stone?"

"Simple trial and error. I had a vague idea of your direction, and Gated to places I had been."

She leaned in and stroked Trig's neck. It calmed her jitters. "That sounds like a lot of jumping about."

He gave a small bow. "Once I can see another destination in the distance, I am able to open a Gate to it. I assure you it was worth the effort. The stone *does* save time." He smiled as if thanking her for granting him the privilege.

Kyer looked at the stone again and sighed. *Fine.* She excused his carelessness on account of his fear for her safety. She tucked it back in her pocket.

"I confess to a certain amount of concern to find you alone on this darkening path."

"Why were you looking for me?"

"I am not merely looking for you, but looking *out* for you, if you grasp the distinction."

She shrugged, a bit embarrassed that someone would care for her like her mother.

"Are you in some kind of trouble? Is there something I can help you with?"

All at once Kyer was overcome by a desire to tell him everything that had happened in the past few days, her abduction by Fredric, his words to her, her dream about Alon Maer. But it was getting so dark now. "It's Derry and the others. They're all sick. I need to find water. But I have to go back now; I've been away from them for too long." She endeavoured to keep the high-pitched, frantic tone from her voice.

The Guardian took a single step, and he was close to her. She could feel his warmth and smell his strange scent of mild lavender, jasmine, and traces of wisteria. She breathed in slowly as she watched him raise his hand. Warmth radiated from his palm, warmer than mere body heat. Her eyes closed, waiting to feel his soft fingertips touch her cheek. But they didn't. Opening her eyes again, Kyer saw his hand there, poised, but hesitating. With an odd disappointment, she looked into his dark eyes, and the compassion that glowed there almost melted her. She found she was holding her breath. With a small shudder, she realized she'd felt something similar before. Kayme. But in the Guardian's company, the memory of Kayme faded like the dream of Alon Maer. The Guardian was fascinating as fire. But without the glimmer of danger. With the Guardian, she felt the fire's heat; she felt . . . well, safe.

"My dear."

She felt a smile overtake and ease her tense facial muscles.

"You have endured much these last few days. I can see it. I can feel it pouring out of your very skin. Let me help you. Give me your water bottles and go. I will come to you once I have filled them. Return to your companions. Care for them and yourself."

Kyer gave in immediately. It was the best plan she'd heard all day. She gave him every container she had brought and headed back on the trail. Once he'd been out of sight for ten minutes, it occurred to her to wonder if she could trust him.

Nothing much had changed in the little sick camp. Her friends all slept, much more easily than they had in the past two days. Kyer had to fumble about in the dark to start a fire but managed it and checked each of her charges in its light. She sat down to eat something and to wait for the Guardian to show up with her water.

She hardly had time to worry if he would come when he appeared. She received all the water containers from him and filled the teakettle, refusing his help and insisting that he stay back in the shadows, lest one of her companions awoke. While the water heated, she approached him where he sat next to Trig.

"Thank you," she said.

"Easier for me than it is for you."

"I suppose so."

"Sit, my dear, and chat with me."

Kyer observed the pale face, faintly glowing in the meagre firelight. It looked open and welcoming, honest, even. But it had an austerity, an agelessness that she couldn't relate to, and she thought again of Kayme. Cautious of both the Guardian and her own suspicion, she crouched down and came to a sitting position, facing him. *What should I say?*

"Now," he said gently. "How is it that you managed to stay well with all your friends becoming so ill?"

Kyer was startled. She had wondered about that but had been too busy to dwell on it. "I don't know. Don't you have an answer for that one?"

He merely shrugged. "My suggestion is that you accept it; it is not necessary to question everything."

"I don't question everything, just the things that don't make sense. For instance, why do you keep popping up out of nowhere?"

"That is definitely something not to question."

"So I'm supposed to think it's normal?" Her desperation came out in a squeak, and she lowered her voice. "If that's normal, then so is everything else, the fog and the voices and the fact that people—" she stopped herself. For some reason she didn't quite feel ready to talk to him about Fredric's words. "Oh, never mind."

He smiled gently in the shadows and brushed her hair with his hand. "Don't forget, I'm here to help you." His words held a peculiar fondness that implied a longstanding relationship with her. It was almost patronising but not enough to protest.

What does he want? It seemed lately that everyone wanted something, even in the name of helping. Kayme said there was a price for everything. Derry, who truly believed in his code of ethics, still wanted something. His dedication to helping Alon Maer was without question, but in the end, he wanted his knighthood. Kyer herself wanted something. Less conventional, perhaps, certainly less tangible, but she, too, would get her reward if they saved Alon's life: a mentor, a role model, maybe a friend?

And if everyone desired some sort of personal gain, did it work both ways? Did it also mean that everyone could be bought if the right price were met? Where did loyalty and integrity fit into a theory like that? What would it take for Kyer to give up the mission?

Wait. *I nearly did it already.* A flush crept up her neck. *I already ran away.* If the price had been a bit more tempting, would she have stayed away? Indeed, if she'd had her horse and supplies . . . A wave of guilt flowed down her body.

One of her companions shifted on his bedroll.

"What do you get?" she asked.

"I beg your pardon?"

"This 'help' you're giving me. What do you get in return?"

He looked puzzled, if not slightly hurt.

"I mean, why now?" she pressed. "I needed help a couple of months ago, and you didn't turn up. Why am I suddenly in such need of your assistance if I wasn't then?"

The Guardian took a moment to think.

"Let us say that others needed my assistance more than you at that time.

Now you need it more than anyone else."

"Oh?" Kyer was sceptical.

"The fact that you are unaware of the danger makes it no less prevalent. All manner of forces are at work here. But as for what I get, there is no fixed return on my efforts. If you choose to recompense me, then that is your decision. You will never hear me say that I expect something from you in exchange for my aid." He leaned forward, placing his hand on her knee. He left it there for several heartbeats before drawing it away again. The contact, then the release, sent a shiver through Kyer.

Whatever the reason, he was here. And he had helped her by warning her about the explosion in the square and again about the goblins. He had brought water for her sick companions. And he asked nothing in return.

He had told her he knew all about her. Was he the source of information she'd been searching for? Unlike Kayme, whose offer of knowledge was entrammelled in obligation, she could ask the Guardian anything. She could ask him about Fredric's words, who Fredric was working for. Or better yet . . .

"What do you know about me?"

She felt his body straighten. "Right to the point, as always."

"Well?" she insisted. "You say you know all about me. Tell me."

"It's not that easy."

"Thanks for coming. Bye." She started to get up but he held her.

"Dark forces are at work." His tone brought her back to her sitting position. "If the people you trust haven't told you more, it's because now is not the time."

Kyer rolled her eyes and scoffed.

"I need you to trust me." He put a hand on her arm.

She pulled her knees up and her head dropped onto her arms. A deep sigh eased her frustration. Now wasn't a good time, anyway. Any new thing he told her would probably prompt her to leave again, and she didn't want to do that.

There was, however, something her guardian might be able to help her with.

"All right. But let me tell you about a strange thing," she began, her voice barely above a whisper in the darkness. "A dream I had last night. And I realized then I had dreamt it a few nights ago as well, though I didn't pay attention to it at the time."

"Oh?"

"I was a chambermaid for Alon Maer. I knew the castle; I knew the corridor. I took something to her. A box. I told her it was a gift from Kien, but I was lying. It was a necklace in the shape of a jewelled snake. She told me the serpent is a symbol of undying love. And when she put it on, I was overwhelmed by—the only thing I can think of to describe it is *glee*. But sort of . . . malicious glee. What can you make of that?"

The Guardian shifted, crossing his ankles at the end of his long legs. "Very interesting indeed. And it was very vivid, then?"

"Yes, I swear I could give you the directions to her chamber, and yet I've never set foot anywhere near Bartheylen Castle. Do you know if Alon has a necklace like that?"

"I do not know. But I will learn it if you want me to."

"Well, if it isn't too much trouble. I can't help but think it has something to do with her illness."

"Then I will do it. And now your water is boiling." The Guardian rose and extended his hand to help her up. She surprised herself by accepting it. His hand felt cool and soft in her rough one. It pulled her to standing, and she found herself quite close to him again. Again a thrill of excitement played up her spine. But this time she couldn't bring herself to look up into his ink-black eyes. They were too deep, too cavernous, too full of history and knowledge.

"Thank you," she said. "For helping me."

His fingers touched her chin with a feather-light brush, and she tipped her head up in response. Her eyes remained averted.

"Kyer," he whispered and melted away into the blackness of the forest.

Kyer let the blueberry decoction simmer, and as she made her rounds, she could still feel the butterfly touch of his fingertips.

The firelight danced with contrary delightedness, filling Hunter with irritation. When Golgathaur appeared this time, Hunter didn't jump nearly as violently, in spite of the darkness of the night. The thin, lofty man was grinning broadly. Hunter held his reaction in check; he was never sure whether to fear the lieutenant's good moods. Golgathaur gestured to Hunter, and the two walked a few paces away from the others.

"It is as I thought," the lieutenant said. "I have spoken with my lord. His plans have changed, and things are now in your favour. He no longer requires the Lady Alon Maer's death."

Hunter slumped visibly. "Am I permitted to be relieved by that?"

Golgathaur laughed heartily and thumped him on the back. "Of course. Insomuch as the lady is not our enemy. I do caution you, however, that I, and the Lord Dregor, still require your loyalty. But with that in mind, dear fellow, you may celebrate as you'd like." At the reminder of his forced commitment to Dregor, Hunter clenched his teeth, his disparate emotions still dissatisfied.

Golgathaur changed his tone. "But you have other reason to celebrate, my friend."

Friend? Hunter thought.

"I have certain information for you that, if you use it as I advise, will ensure both your other goals are met: finding peace with Kien Bartheylen, and bringing about the disgrace of one Kyer Halidan."

Hunter leaned forward, eagerness flitting across his features. Suddenly Golgathaur had become a highly appealing figure.

"Now sit down and listen, dear Hunter. I have a story to tell you. What would you say if I told you how Kyer Halidan possessed the capability of killing the Lady Alon Maer?"

Hunter stood before his company with rekindled confidence and purpose. He felt like a new man, now that his commitment to Golgathaur was no longer at odds with the loyalty that was ingrained into his soul. The plan developing in his mind had generated energy and drive that he had not known for weeks. And at the end, he would have achieved his two goals: forgiveness, with the chance for a new beginning with his lord, and the downfall of Kyer Halidan. No longer did he desire her death. *Let her suffer at my doing as I have done at hers.* Her brief career as that dark elf's treasure was over.

"People." Hunter spoke with such exuberance he had all their attention immediately. Even Misty and Juggler stopped their whisperings and were all ears.

"I want to thank you all for your commitment to this mission. Lieutenant Golgathaur has informed me of a change of plan, and as a result, we will adjust our strategies. New knowledge has come to my attention, the result of which is a natural conclusion as to the identity of the one who is even now trying to kill Lady Alon Maer."

Murmurs circulated around the clearing. Misty and Juggler looked at each other with dead eyes.

Misty took off the opal ring that transmitted her communication to the lieutenant and shoved it back in her pouch. The rest of the company was asleep, except for Juggler, with whom she always shared watch. She pulled an object out of her saddlebag. It was oblong, flat, about the length of her forearm, and wrapped in black cloth. She unwrapped it and caressed the gold etchings on the back, the pearls inlaid in the handle, and the initials *AMB* engraved in stylized lettering. Turning it over, she admired her thin, precise mouth and high cheekbones. She tipped her head back, tilting it from side to side, toying with the way the firelight shone on her skin's iridescence. *Like amethyst.*

She reached for a brush and ran it through her black curls. When Golgathaur finally responded to her call and appeared on the edge of the camp, she carefully finished her task before rewrapping the hand mirror and replacing it in her saddlebag.

"What's that you have there?" Golgathaur asked.

"A souvenir," she said, as if it were none of his affair.

"I see. Now then, you called?"

She stood before the tall man with feet apart defiantly. "What are you playing at?" she demanded politely. Juggler stood behind and off to the side, whetting his blade, glancing up from time to time.

Golgathaur folded his arms on his chest. "I wondered what you might think of that little announcement," he said with a crooked smile.

"We could not believe our ears, could we, Juggles?"

Juggler looked up and shook his head at Golgathaur.

"We are of a mind to ignore the new plan," Misty said.

Golgathaur looked at her dryly. "I would advise you to rethink that."

"On what grounds?"

"Patience, my dear Misty, patience. All will come out right in the end."

"We don't like the way this is going, do we Juggles?"

Juggler looked up and shook his head at Golgathaur.

"We don't like to leave jobs unfinished."

"Exactly." Golgathaur adopted a stern expression and shared it with both twins. "You can't have it both ways," he said in a low voice. "You can't work for me and for yourselves. You began this and committed to me to finish it." He smiled at Misty's glacial face. "You are not privy to the plan. Nor will you be. But suffice it to say that if you don't follow my directions, you may run into . . . problems." He vanished.

Misty remained standing, staring coolly at the spot where Golgathaur had been.

"We are privy to the only plan that matters." She turned her chin to Juggler. "Aren't we Juggles?"

Derry was impressed by Kyer's decoction. His head was still woozy, but he was feeling much better. When she came over to give him some broth, Derry asked, "Were you talking to someone last night?"

A stricken look flashed across her face before she adopted a wide-eyed expression of confusion. "No."

He gave her a sidelong glance. "Are you sure? I heard your voice and a man's."

She emitted a humourless laugh. "You must have been having a fever dream. Or it might have been one of the others," she suggested.

Derry allowed that it could, and he *had* been drifting in and out of feverish sleep. But he was confident he'd have been able to identify any of their friends' voices. Her eyes veiled challenge as she turned away. *She's holding something back. Again.*

Fourteen

Dangerous Times

Another full day passed before the invalids were well enough for travel, and even then, they had to take it slowly. An all-encompassing weariness had set in as their bodies recovered. They loped through a marshy area and saw moose tracks, though none of those shy creatures themselves.

Janak eyed some ducks paddling on the marsh. "Those critters are making me hungry."

"I'm famished," Derry agreed.

Birds of a multitude of varieties swooped and twittered their displeasure at being disturbed by the travellers, but Skimnoddle gave them what for, and since they all felt hungry again, proved his point by cooking up a feast of duck. The birds were greasy, smelled heavenly and felt surprisingly good in their hitherto dissatisfied stomachs.

When they descended the westward slope of the Black Mountains, they found themselves in the relative shelter of a forest that brushed the southern edge of the Sea of Khûn. There still had been no sign of Fredric and his party, though Kyer figured there had to be more than one route through the mountains. And the illness of her friends had delayed them by three days. Fredric and company could be as near or far away as they wished to be.

Throughout the journey, they all kept their eyes open for a tiny white flower in the shape of a trefoil. Kayme's instructions said it could be found in this area, near the Sea of Khûn. But they had seen nothing, not even when any one of them had taken short excursions off the trail. They were losing hope.

"Your friend is leading us on quite a chase," Derry said with quiet sarcasm.

"My *friend* is helping us save Alon Maer's life," Kyer snapped.

"Uh-hunh." Derry didn't have to roll his eyes for Kyer to know what he thought.

Come on, Kayme, where is it? Perhaps if Kyer said it often enough, the wizard would hear her across the distance and help them. It was getting harder to defend him.

More than a week after Kyer's run-in with Fredric, in the early afternoon, the company trickled out of the forest of pine, spruce, and fir trees to find themselves overlooking the southern outskirts of a town. The low buildings and houses with slanting roofs had popped up like mushrooms on a promontory jutting on an angle into the southwest corner of the Sea of Khûn. The town perched on a plateau, framed on three sides by the water, and the slope plunged into the sea. Whitecaps topped the waves like frosting on little cakes. Kyer approved of the town's position well above the potentially hazardous waters. She pulled her hood up against the wind that raked its fingers through her hair.

Shading her eyes against the glare of the water, she peered westward across the narrow stretch of sea to the dark line on the horizon. It must be the Rank Meres, if she remembered her geography correctly. To look past the town to the north rewarded her with a sense of awe. This was as close as she ever had been to open water. In the near distance, the water was dotted with boats. Beyond, the sea stretched far to the north. Geography lessons had taught her that there were northern lands beyond the sea, but they were several days' sail away, entirely invisible to her naked eye from this corner. The vast emptiness made her feel lonely, and it was with relief that she looked across the eastern bay to the rocky shore.

The green of the shore pines and firs was speckled with bright green, white, and red of a tree Kyer had never seen before. It had bright green leaves, and its spiny branches gave it a wind-blown look. The red bark was peeling like bits of dry skin off the smooth, golden inner surface, and clusters of white, drooping flowers seemed to be the source of a honey fragrance on the sea breeze.

"Are those the flowers we're looking for, Kyer?" Phennil asked.

She frowned thoughtfully. "I don't think so, but we can take a closer look. Like when we found the real falander, I think I'll *know* when I see it."

"I don't know the name of this place. Anyone?" Derry asked.

"I have been cogitating on the matter of our whereabouts for some days now," announced Skimnoddle from beneath his hood. "I have, in my youth, spent some time in the northwestern quadrant of the Guarded Realm. In this moment, nothing would give me greater gratification—excepting, of course, one kiss from my beloved's sweet lips"—Kyer held back a growl —"than to procure a satisfying conclusion to your disquietude."

"Well, I would hardly call it disquietude, but in any event . . ." Derry murmured.

"Out with it, Skimnoddle! I'm going grey over here," Janak said.

Skimnoddle bowed with one hand on his breast. "Your premature senescence would cause me ineffable sorrow, my good dwarf." Then, righting himself again, he flourished with his arm. "I give you the Portal to the Sea, the imaginatively labelled town of . . . Seaview."

The group was silent for a moment. Then Kyer said to Janak, "Do you think maybe we don't pay enough attention to him?" Janak snorted.

"Seaview," Derry said thoughtfully. "Friendly to our cause?"

Skimnoddle apparently had purged himself of his desire to orate. "So far as I know, Captain."

"Do you suppose someone there might know where we can find the elusive tahleema?" Derry asked.

"I'm sure there will be a herbalist who can help us," Kyer answered dryly.

"Well, it'll be a relief to spend the evening among civilized folk once again, wouldn't you say?" Phennil grinned, sitting up jauntily in his saddle.

"All right," Derry decided. "We'll settle ourselves at an inn and then do some scouting to find an herbalist. Finding the tahleema is our first priority. Hopefully we can get some in time to enjoy ourselves this evening."

"And we should also try to learn what we can of the area south of here," put in Jesqellan, "so we know how to find the Indyn Caves."

Derry nodded. "Let's remember we want help from these people. Try to be polite."

Was he purposefully avoiding Kyer's eye?

"Yeah, polite like you were with Huranan Danay," she blurted. Derry shot a toxic look at her. She had cut him. She didn't care. The captain's behaviour in the past couple of weeks had been disagreeable, to say the least. And now here he was, dragging up her behaviour in Plicatha again. She thought they'd left that far behind. It was in bad taste. And had the captain already forgotten how she'd spent three days nursing them all while they puked? Without even a thank-you.

Fine. I'll show him polite. How about downright friendly?

The group descended the hill and entered the town by way of the heavily travelled road from the south. The breeze less strong, here, Kyer let her hood fall back. The air off the sea smelled fresh, yet carried hints of the pleasantly musty, earthy smell of coal smoke from the town's chimneys. Kyer had heard others say the smell of coal made their nose hairs curl, but she loved it. It reminded her vaguely of Shael Castle and, more strongly, of home. She breathed it deeply and automatically liked Seaview. A youth intersected their path as he burst out of a shop.

"You there, lad," Derry called.

He halted his course and removed his cap with a little bow. "At your service, sir."

"Do we have the pleasure of entering the town of Seaview?"

The boy confirmed this. He had a naïve look about his face that made Kyer judge him to be about sixteen or seventeen years of age.

"My friends and I are unfamiliar with this town," Derry went on. "Can you direct us to a reputable inn with both lodgings and decent fair?"

"Well, I'd hate to disappoint you, sir, but it'll be hard to find lodgings what with the festival and all. Inns are all a bit crowded. You might try the Trout. Or the Odds and Suds." He pointed down the road to the left.

"Thank you for that."

"What festival is it that you speak of?" Jesqellan asked.

"It's the Annual Fish Fry. Folks come from all over to join in. There's cookin' all over the town square and dancing and lots of places to sit and drink beer too. You'd all be welcome." He bobbed his head again, making eye contact with each of them.

"And is there an herbalist in town?"

"Yessir. Bodkin's, just opposite the chandlery."

"Thank you, young man," Jesqellan said.

"Yessir, and if you need any errands run, just ask for Tod. People know me."

The group trotted ahead. Tod waited for them to pass, and Kyer observed the way he noted their armour and weaponry. He dashed off as soon as they'd gone by.

Two figures watched the exchange between the teen and the newcomers to the town. They sat nonchalantly, inconspicuously, on the grass under a large aspen in front of a house on the second corner of the street. As soon as the lad disengaged from the company and headed in their direction, the woman nudged the man.

"Ask him." The man got to his feet. "Be friendly," she advised as he pulled one of his swords partway out. He resheathed it and grinned at her. "Save it." She nodded.

The man stepped out of the trees just in time to startle the boy as he hurried by. "Hello, sir." The boy's hand slapped his heart. "I didn't see you there; you gave me quite a turn."

"Nice day," said the man.

"Yessir, perfect," returned the boy.

"Those folks you were talking to." The man cocked his head in the direction of Valrayker's company as they turned down the other street. "They after a place to stay?"

"Yup. Are you? Town's nearly full up."

"Already have a spot. Where'd you send them?"

"The Trout or the Odds. Why, do you have room where you are? I could go after them," the boy offered.

"Naw, we'll find 'em there. Old friends."

"Oh, well, they were going to find the herbalist as well, so if you can't find them at the inn, you could try there."

"'Preciate your time." The man tossed the lad a silver coin.

"Thank you, sir! Good day to you, sir." And the lad was off again.

The subdued *clock clock* of the reed windchimes alerted Bodkin that a customer had entered his shop. He tied string around a bunch of little flowers and hung them on a hook on the wall and turned to the lady, resting his palms on the counter. "What can I do you for?"

"Nothing for me. It's about what you can't do for someone else."

"Beg pardon, miss?"

"A party of an odd assortment of folk will be here soon." She leaned her elbows on the counter. One hand held her chin, and the other traced invisible shapes on the shiny maple countertop. "Six of them. One is a woman, with a knight, a dwarf, an elf, and a couple of others."

The herbalist grimaced. "That certainly is an interesting group."

"The bottom line, Mr. Bodkin, is that you do not have what they want."

He looked confused. "How do you know? What do they want?"

"I don't know and it doesn't matter." Her hushed tone made Bodkin shiver involuntarily. "What matters is that whatever it is, you do not have it." She produced from thin air a gold coin. "This is for you for saying so. And this," suddenly visible in her other hand was a dagger with one keen edge and the other jagged with tiny asplike teeth. "This is what I have for you if you do not."

Bodkin paled. His condition did not improve to observe the two bright swords hanging on either side of the woman's companion. He gulped.

"Which is it going to be?"

"Uh," he whispered and cleared his throat. "Uh, that should be no trouble at all, miss, I can help you with that." He accepted the coin with a smile. "Easy as herb tea, as I always say. Can't be too careful with all these strange sorts going about, don't you know."

He babbled on until the two very unnerving people left his shop.

Not a room was to be found at either of the inns the lad had recommended.

"All full up, sirs," said the angular fellow at the Odds and Suds. "I daresay you'll find it the same everywhere."

"What about your common room?" Derry asked hopefully.

"We-ell." He glanced over his shoulder and peered into the dim room beyond the desk. "I've already got about eighteen folk in there. I could maybe squeeze a couple of yous in there, but I can't take all of ye. And ye'll have to pay in advance."

In the end, they divided into pairs. Kyer and Derry left their belongings at the Odds and Suds—they went as a pair out of habit, all the while putting on an excellent show for the others of being amicable. The other four tossed between the Trout and the Happy Beerbarrel.

"That was exhausting," Kyer said when they had finally all taken possession of mats on the floor of the three different inns and the horses were stabled. "I'm ready to eat." Her gaze stuck to the tray of meals drifting by on their way to a table, but Phennil dragged her away.

"We have to find the herbalist first," he reminded her. "We can come back after and have a snack, right, Derry?"

The captain nodded. "But we don't want to fill up; there's a fish fry tonight."

She groaned but allowed herself to be pulled outside by the elbow.

The streets were a bustle of folk setting up for the festival, positioning themselves for a good view and arriving from out of town to partake in the merriment. Bushel baskets of potatoes next to women with tubs of water and scrub brushes, scrubbing potatoes and tossing them into another bushel basket on the other side. More women chipping the clean potatoes and dumping them into tubs of water so they wouldn't turn brown. Men suspending iron pots from chains above fire pits. Still more men erecting grills large enough to cook many pieces of meat at once. Children dashing about, setting up chairs, chasing each other among them and knocking them down, being yelled at by adults. Humans, dwarves, halflings, on foot, on horseback or ponies, in wagons and buggies. Ponies and donkeys pulling carloads of fish up the hill from the pier, this being the Portal to the Sea.

The folk walking alongside the fish carts were clad in bright colours made even cheerier by the early summer sun. They wore the wind-blown hair of a recent boat trip and cheeks rosy as if they'd been rubbed with rough wool. Cries erupted as townsfolk of Seaview greeted their friends from the ships. Musicians, succumbing to the festive excitement, had already struck up spontaneous performances on street corners. The air of mirth and camaraderie was contagious, and Kyer struggled to stay focussed on their task. *Once we have the tahleema, we can reward ourselves*, she told herself.

They asked for directions only once and soon found themselves at the door of Bodkin, the herbalist. The rattle of reed windchimes announced their arrival as the six of them crowded into the small space. The dark and cool shop maintained the perfect condition for herb storage and preservation. Mingling aromas hung motionless in the air, a musty bouquet of pungent, sweet, spicy, even fungal. These were woven with the soft aroma of beeswax and the tinge of alcohol. Kyer was reminded all too vividly of medicine powders and herbal remedies of her childhood. *You'd have to really like your job to work in a place like this*, she thought with distaste.

Row upon row of bundles of flowers hung from the ceiling and more along one wall. A floor-to-ceiling shelf behind the counter was jammed with glass vials and clay bottles of tinctures, ointments, creams, salves, syrups, vinegars, and oils. Some were labelled, some were not, and Kyer mused that an herbalist would have to know their trade very well to keep them all straight. Shelves all around them held jars of dried herbs and barks for use in infusions, decoctions, aromatic waters, herbal baths, compresses, and poultices. Everything on the customer side of the counter was labelled neatly with all capital letters. Familiar names such as licorice, feverfew, passionflower, and chamomile whirled by Kyer's glance, as well as more obscure products such as valerian, meadowsweet, baptisia, and comfrey. Kyer pointed to a jar marked astragalus and tugged Derry's elbow. "Isn't that one of the things in the tea you make?"

He nodded as a short, scrawny man bloomed out from a back room.

"So sorry to keep you waiting, I was grinding—" He stopped as he saw the group crammed into his shop and quailed. Kyer got the sense that he was counting them or sizing them up individually.

Derry glanced around at them. "I suppose there are a lot of us; Phennil, Janak, Skimnoddle?" He nodded at them. The selected three went outside to wait so as not to intimidate the herbalist.

"Not necessary, but I appreciate your courtesy," he said, a bit stiffly, Kyer thought. "I'm Tavi Bodkin. Are you in town for the festival?" His fingers drummed the countertop lightly.

"By mere chance only," Derry said. The muscles in Bodkin's neck did not relax with Derry's smile. "We are actually looking—My name is Derry Moraunt, by the way. My friends and I work for Lord Dunvehran."

Kyer was stunned by Bodkin's reaction to this. Rather than appearing impressed, as most people would, the little herbalist's colour drained, the eyes widened, shoulders and jaw sagged. It was an ever-so-brief reaction, and he then resumed his attitude of composure, but Kyer had seen it. *There's something going on here.*

"What—?" Bodkin whispered then cleared his throat. "What is it you're looking for?"

Kyer spoke up, stepping to the counter, behind which the man seemed to cower. "We need a certain flower." Her fingers came together and drew the shape of it. "A tiny, white trefoil called tahleema. Do you know of it?" She observed his face and saw a brush of confusion mixed with something that resembled relief. She did not know what to make of it, but she stored the memory away for future discussion.

He shook his head. "I . . . I'm sorry, but I don't have any of that."

Derry and Jesqellan looked at each other meaningfully. "We can afford to pay you whatever it's worth," Derry said pointedly.

"You're wasting your time; I don't have any."

Jesqellan took a step forward as if to confide in him. "We are perfectly prepared to pay anything you ask. We are that much in need of it."

The fellow hesitated, nervously fiddling with the button on his waistcoat. "Ah, but you see," he said with determination that Kyer thought might be just a tad forced, "were you to pay me a thousand nobles, I still would have none to give you."

"You don't have such a useful plant as tahleema?" Jesqellan said doubtfully.

"In all my years of study, I have not heard that tahleema had any unusual or . . . or useful properties."

"Do you know where we could *find* some?" the mage said, unsuccessful at masking his own desperation. "Anywhere. Fresh would suit. Derry, here, is a physicker-adept; he knows about harvesting herbs. If you could just direct us to where we might find it. In a field perhaps?"

"No. I'm sorry but no, I can't. Even if I could I—I don't think it blooms at this time of year. Is there anything else I can get for you? Primrose and cowslip make an excellent soporific. And honeysuckle, galingale, and spikenard are an effective aphrodisiac, should you so desire."

"Thank you, no," Derry said quickly. "The tahleema is all we came for. A good day to you, sir."

"You sure have a huge assortment here," Kyer said suddenly. Derry and Jesqellan looked askance at her and at each other. She kept her eyes glued to Bodkin.

"Why yes, miss. I find I'm able to help the townspeople with most of their ailments."

"We recently helped a group of villagers who'd been poisoned with amorin over a period of several months," she went on. "Once we found the source of the poison, we stopped it, but had to let the poison just dissipate from their bodies. Would you have had any suggestions of antidotes or remedies?"

"Ooh well now, comfrey can be used to draw out poison." He looked up thoughtfully at the bunches of flowers on the ceiling, and Kyer saw her chance to give a wink to Derry as if to say, *Bear with me.* "Poppy, St. John's wort, ta—" he halted in his list and paled visibly. "That is to say, uh, tongue of adder—"

"Yes," interrupted Derry, pretending he hadn't caught the slip, "I've used tongue of adder in my own salve. It's more of an ointment, really," he added modestly.

"Really? What does it consist of?" Bodkin asked.

And Derry went into a detailed explanation of his ingredients while Kyer sidled closer to the counter to peer idly over and look for what only she would recognize, with Kayme's help. Jesqellan kept an eye on her progress and popped his own question or two into the herbalist's conversation with Derry, buying her as much time as she needed.

Her keen eyes rapidly scanned all the vials and bottles on the back shelf.

Her efforts paid off. One corked vial, three shelves up from the floor. Nothing on that shelf was labelled, but she identified it as immediately as she recognized the correct lichen in the damp caverns of the Cold Fells. Tiny blossoms, the petals separated. It was as if Kayme were occupying her mind, seeing the bottle and identifying the herb through her eyes. A warmth glazed across her face as she felt the wizard's presence, but then Jesqellan's voice carried through.

". . . and it certainly has helped my friends suffer through their injuries."

Kyer snapped back to attention, hoping Bodkin hadn't noticed where she'd been looking. "Yes, it sure has. I might be getting addicted to the stuff."

"Well, thank you for your time," Derry said.

"It was my pleasure. I'm sorry I couldn't help you. Enjoy the festival."

The bell jingled behind them, and the company casually walked back up the road.

"Any luck, then?" Phennil asked, falling into step with Jesqellan.

"He doesn't have it," Jesqellan said.

"Doesn't have it?" the elf exclaimed. "But what do we do now?"

"Thanks for picking up my signal, Derry," Kyer said quietly.

"Of course, but what was that about?"

"Are you kidding me?" She stopped short next to a rack of textile samples at a weaver's shop. "Didn't you see his face?"

"No," said Derry.

"What?" Jesqellan asked.

She addressed them all, except Skimnoddle who lagged behind. "He was terrified of something. I can't believe you didn't see it. He was lying about the tahleema."

"And did you find it?" Jesqellan asked.

"As a matter of fact, I did," she said. "A glass vial of it."

Skimnoddle finally caught up. "Which he just poured into a blue clay bottle and put in his vest pocket, or I'm a hill giant." All eyes turned to the halfling. He shrugged. "The keyhole is my friend."

"Damn," Kyer said. "There goes the idea of stealing it."

"Stealing?" Derry said. "I would not approve of stealing it."

"What would have been your suggestion, then? Sending Phennil in there disguised as a woman to buy some?" Kyer demanded.

"I don't know." Derry shook his head and started walking again.

"The main thing is, how are we going to get it now?" Janak said.

Derry's brow furrowed. "I don't know that either."

"Let's talk about it over some food," Phennil suggested, and they headed back toward the Happy Beerbarrel.

Skimnoddle, however, excused himself. "I have some things I'd like to do." He scuttled off in another direction.

Bodkin locked up early, leaving by way of the back door. He hurried down the alley, right hand over his left breast pocket inside the cloak drawn 'round him. He darted glances this way and that, though he hadn't really thought about what he was looking for. Had it occurred to him that he might be followed, he might have gone in some neighbouring building and snuck out another back door in an effort to lose his pursuer. But it didn't and he didn't, and so the one following the skinny herbalist did so with no difficulty, for he was very good at following unnoticed.

When the herbalist drew near to the square, he turned left by the basket weaver's, so as to avoid the crowds of the festival. He nearly fainted when a man caught up with him and grabbed him from behind, presenting a silver knife in between his eyes.

"Where are you off to, Mr. Bodkin, in such a hurry?"

The skinny fellow stammered and stuttered, finally producing the word, "Home."

"And what's that you're hiding, Mr. Bodkin?"

"It's what they asked for, sir! Tahleema." He pulled out the bottle and held it up so his captor could see. "I don't want any trouble. I brought it with me to keep it safe." The pitch of his voice rose with fear, as did his body temperature. Sweat beaded on his wrinkled brow.

"Are you sure you weren't going to give it to them?"

The herbalist quaked. "I never even thought of that! I swear it!"

The bottle was snatched from his hand by a newcomer. She held it up and turned it 'round and 'round. "I daresay he didn't think of it. Let him go." The man's body went limp with relief as the clutching arm and the knife were drawn away. "How about we take it off your mind," she suggested in a smooth voice. "If you don't have it, there's no chance of you being either tempted to give it to them or of any physical harm coming to your person.

"Pay the man for his goods, Juggles; it's his livelihood, after all." She was an assassin but a reasonable one.

Juggler tossed the herbalist a noble, and they left him, the woman secreting the blue clay bottle away in a lambskin pouch at her left side.

The herbalist stood shivering in the road for several moments before going home. "We are living in dangerous times," he quavered to his wife. "Dangerous times, indeed."

Only after he'd gone did the one who had been following him step out from behind the stack of baskets. Having viewed and heard the entire scene, Skimnoddle was satisfied that he knew not only who now had the bottle but exactly what the bottle looked like. He leapt up and clicked his heels as he returned to the inn to meet his friends.

When the halfling joined them at the table in the inn, he had fetched his pack from the common room where he and Phennil were to stay. He sat down and eagerly helped himself to some tidbits from the elf's and the mage's plates. They were too stunned and downhearted to be offended by his effrontery. Skimnoddle smacked his lips and licked his fingers before leaning down to produce his square of canvas and the soft-bristled brush. He said nothing and the others watched him curiously. He took Kyer's clay mug, emptied it into his own throat—to her annoyance—and set it on its side on the table before him.

Humming to himself, he looked around the room, saw what he was looking for and skittered over to a table against the wall, speaking in uncharacteristic undertones to the patrons there who were digging into their plate of bread and cheese and a bottle of wine. When he returned, he placed a cork on the table next to the mug. He removed the cloth napkin from Derry's lap and laid it over top of the two objects.

Skimnoddle's companions had stopped eating by now and watched the halfling's actions intently. "Illusions," he said, "are everywhere." He looked around the table and reached over for Phennil's cup of water and finally sat down. Spreading the canvas square on his lap, he dipped the brush in the water and began to paint. Even Kyer, who was next to him, couldn't see what he was painting. He took a great deal of care with his artwork, pausing often to squeeze his eyes shut, playing with the end of the brush handle in his mouth.

Finally he put the brush down and laid the cloth on top of the napkin with the mug and the cork underneath. As he waved it from side to side, the water-picture evaporated, and Skimnoddle rolled up the canvas. He passed it to Kyer, who took it without comment. Five pairs of eyes were locked on the napkin as he drew it aside.

And five pairs of eyes looked bewildered as Skimnoddle revealed his creation: a clay bottle with a cork stopper.

"Yes!" he exclaimed in a subdued tone.

"What?" asked Phennil.

The clouds cleared from Kyer's face as it dawned on her. "It's the bottle he poured the tahleema into!"

Skimnoddle stretched to his full, unimpressive height and clapped his hand to his heart. "Dear lady, you reaffirm my profound adoration for you; I maintain my partiality not without reason." He bowed.

"Yeah whatever, but what are you going to do with it?" she asked.

"You haven't created the tahleema inside there, have you?" Phennil piped in excitedly.

"Sadly, no, my dear elf," Skimnoddle said.

"I suppose you would not be able to produce the precise properties of the plant?" Derry put in.

Janak thumped the halfling on the back, nearly buckling him. "You are a creature full of surprises, not discounting where you choose to aim your affections. What's your plan?"

"Ah!" Skimnoddle said. "If my scheme is not self-evident, then I will ask you to rely upon me: Before this night is out and the sun's rays glint across the eastern skyline, I shall have attained that which we seek."

Having completed his oration, he gathered up his belongings and departed.

It was obvious that Skimnoddle knew more about the whereabouts of the herb than the rest of them, so most of the others resolved to leave him to it. Derry felt uneasy but the others convinced him that it could do no harm to try to enjoy the evening. Skimnoddle would undoubtedly find a way of reaching them if he ran into trouble.

"I just want to sit, eat, drink beer, and watch the dancing all night," Janak said with an enthusiastic growl.

"We'd better get going, or all the good spots will be taken," Phennil said.

They stepped out into the twilight and joined the river of townspeople headed for the square.

They had only minimal trouble securing an excellent placement. Indeed, there wasn't any such thing as a poor placement. Tables and chairs had been brought out from every establishment surrounding the square—which was rectangular—and placed around the perimeter, leaving plenty of room for dancing in the centre. Seaview's town square was a flat area in the hillside. During market time, vendors and their carts followed the road, which was a low-grade hill, but advantage had been taken of the higher levels.

A series of wide terraced steps had been paved with cobbles on the higher edge of the square, one not quite a foot above the other. Each level had ample room for tables and chairs, and they all had a perfect view of the dancing area. They also provided an excellent view of the platform erected at the far side of the square upon which the band had already begun to play. On the second of these levels, Phennil scouted out a table with three chairs and darted ahead to snag it just before a halfling and her family. Phennil stuck his tongue out playfully at them but then assisted them in securing a table by asking two couples if they might share.

"Now everyone's happy," Phennil exclaimed as the halfling laughingly joined her children at their table.

Derry, in the meantime, had found two more chairs for himself and Jesqellan, though he twisted his head 'round looking for the mage.

"Where's Jesqellan?" he asked. Nobody had seen him follow them.

The elf sat next to Janak and Kyer just as Jesqellan strolled up looking as if he'd seen someone he knew and didn't want to be recognized. Kyer wondered what he'd been up to.

The mage didn't try to join the others right away. He had to catch his breath first, not to mention organize his thoughts and steady his mind. He'd nearly jumped out of his skin when the server addressed him, but now that he'd read the note she gave him, his head was a jumble. Who would be giving him a message, here in this ratty little town with its sorry excuse for a celebration?

I have information of use to your party, the note read, *though not for all ears. Meet me behind The Trout Inn at moonrise.*

He'd looked around the room for a possible sender. The other patrons were all occupied by their drinking, laughing, and making merry, far too occupied to be sending notes. But he shook his head. Whoever had sent it would have made sure he—or she—was not around to be detected.

There was nothing to do but wait until moonrise. *Not so*, he contradicted himself. *I must think on things.* Should he tell the others about this? Should he even attend the assignation?

These questions could be pondered over a mug of beer. He hastened after his friends.

Fifteen

Her Motive was Assurance

When Jesqellan finally joined them at their table Kyer asked, "Did you lose us by accident or on purpose?"

"Hm? Oh, yes, well, I was assuring myself of the safety of my appointed bed in the common room. I do not wish to return tonight to some drunken oaf occupying my prepaid accommodation."

"I'm sure you would have no problem kicking him off it," Kyer replied.

The group's light snack had chinked the cracks in their bellies, but none of them was satiated; there remained plenty of room for the fare of the festival. The smell of deep-frying potatoes and grilling fish coaxed droplets to their mouths. The queue couldn't move fast enough for any of them.

Kyer eyed the selection and turned to Phennil. "You'll need a tray."

"These ones are wet." He shook one off and handed it to her.

For a few coppers, they loaded their plates with grilled cod and potatoes, and another two coppers got them a beer for each hand. Kyer arranged her tray and carried it over to the table, where Derry and Janak were already tucking in.

"I think this is my favourite place yet." Kyer set down her burden.

Derry raised his mug. "Best wishes to Skimnoddle; may he find what we're looking for." They all joined in the toast. "Let's enjoy ourselves tonight but meet at breakfast to discuss our next move. Or," he added, "what we'll do if he didn't find it."

The fish hadn't cooled much in the short trip from grill to table, and Kyer blew on her fingerful before popping the sweet, flaky flesh into her mouth.

"The food is nearly as good as the halfling's cooking, though it would bring a sharp pain to my ribs to tell him so," Janak said.

"I'll be sure to pass that on to him." Kyer laughed.

"I knew I could count on you," he replied sarcastically.

A mild breeze fluttered in off the sea in the darkening evening, but most of the revellers shed their wool cloaks as they were warmed by food and flushed by drinking and dancing. Two pipers, a lutist, a fiddler, and a drummer turned out reel after two-step after polka. The audience joined in the singing wherever possible. Kyer and her friends ate and drank and kept their eyes open for Skimnoddle.

"I believe I will venture into the throng; I feel like dancing," said Derry, standing up and eyeing the crowd for a potential partner. He looked down at Kyer. "You have made it plain in the past that you don't care for this pastime, so I won't force an embarrassing decline from you." He didn't make it clear which of them would be more embarrassed. With a short bow, he disappeared among the observers.

Kyer felt a pang of regret. It was true she had told him that dancing didn't interest her, but that was ages ago, a couple of months at least. Although she hadn't given him any reason to believe she had changed her mind, she had been giving it some thought. Dancers always looked breathlessly happy. Kyer liked music but she had never allowed herself the freedom to lose herself in it, to surrender control and feel the music through her body, to the point where it flashed out of feet, toes, arms, fingers, and even flew out the eyes and smile. Maybe, just maybe, it would be good for her to let go like that.

No, she could never make such a fool of herself. She smiled inwardly at the thought of her friends having a good laugh as she awkwardly counted out time while looking down to see what she ought to be doing instead of tripping over her partner's feet. She would never hear the end of it. And come to think of it, Derry was so moody lately, she didn't feel as comfortable approaching him as she might have in the past. That in itself gave her another pang of regret.

She chuckled along with the others at something Janak said and took a swig of her beer. Phennil left the group to find a partner of his own, and Kyer was left with Janak and Jesqellan. Soon the two of them were caught up in a discussion about whether they preferred beer over ale, and Kyer didn't feel like joining in. She suddenly felt melancholy. The party throbbed around her, but she lost herself inside.

This was the best time of her life. Everything she was doing now, everything that had happened over the past couple of months, both the good and the bad, was all exactly what she'd wanted. This was why she'd left Hreth. All the other little tiny people who inhabited her home village were probably still living their little tiny lives, closing their minds to anything or anyone who was different. Ignoring the threat posed by the vast world beyond their undefended borders. She swigged her beer that wasn't nearly as good as at the inn where she first met Valrayker. Yes, this was the best time of her life. Yet she felt that things weren't quite right.

"Come dance with me, pretty girl," said a voice, and she looked up to see a young man with curly blond hair. He reached for her hand.

"No, thanks," she said, not unkindly but without a smile.

He shrugged and left.

"I can't believe you turned him down," Janak said with a snort. "He's been staring at you for ten minutes. I didn't think it was your style to ignore men who looked at you."

Kyer didn't even feel like rising to the bait. "I never noticed him." Her friends seemed genuinely disappointed that she wasn't provoked, but they went back to their beer.

Phennil returned, hardly out of breath, and downed the last of his drink. Kyer pretended to amuse herself by gazing through the crowd, but her heart wasn't in it. It jumped just a little, though, when she saw Derry swirl through the dancers with a dark-curled blossom in his arms. Her brow creased. She had seen Derry dance before, when he was carefree and untroubled. Now, although his movements were smooth as ever, something was missing. Derry was obviously not happy. Was he unhappy with her, or was he just, as always, so preoccupied and concerned about their mission that he couldn't feel any other emotions than those associated with it? That was probably it. *And even if he is mad at me*, she thought, *it's his problem. I've apologized as best I can; I don't know what else he wants from me.* Kyer didn't even know why it bothered her so much. She heard his voice say, *Try to be polite.* Tiny flecks of anger sparked inside her. She hadn't exactly been polite to the young man who'd asked her to dance. This was no good at all.

Time to go! she thought, though she had no idea where. She set her mug on the table and slapped her knees decisively.

"Well, friends, I'd love to stay and discuss this critical issue further, but the fact is that, much as I love ale and beer, I like whisky and elvish wine even better. I'm off."

"Where are you going?" Jesqellan asked.

"Oh, you know me, I have to go stir up trouble somewhere."

A mild whoop emitted from her companion. "Oh yeah, and there are plenty of nice samples of trouble all around us." Janak glanced at the young men at the next table and giving Phennil a nudge that nearly set him on the floor.

"Just do not forget that we agreed to meet at the Odds and Suds first thing in the morning to discuss our plans," Jesqellan said.

"Oh stop." She wrinkled her nose at him. "You're starting to sound like Derry. Of course I'll be there." And with that, she plunged into the crowd.

Misty fluttered her lashes at the tall, lanky thing at the table next to her. His eyes cruised over her up and down. She stood. He stood. "Buy me a beer?" she asked him in her low-timbre, sing-song voice.

Nearly drooling from her attentions, he said, "Sure thing, me lovely." He hailed a passing server and paid for two brimming mugs. "Where would you like to sit?"

She smiled salaciously at him and took both mugs. "Right here suits me." She abruptly gave him her back and sat down across from Juggler.

"Hey!" the man said, putting an indignant hand on her shoulder.

She smiled at him. "Touch me again, and we'll see if you can count as high as five before you die." He gulped and retreated.

Misty and Juggler drank their beer and shared a plate of chipped potatoes with grilled trout. A pleasant vinegary smell rose from the plate, mingling gently with the lemon that Juggler had drizzled over the fish. Misty insisted on a small pot of ketchup for her chips, which Juggler couldn't stand, so there was no need for her to share. Juggler laid his fork down to lift his pint mug of beer when suddenly a small shape came hurtling toward him, a cry of surprise emanating from its throat. Juggler's chair did not quite tip over, but he was covered in his own beer as well as the creature's and had to thrash about to extricate himself from the thing's cloak, amid its muffled cries of, "I'm so terribly sorry!" As soon as he had achieved liberation, Juggler thrust the thing onto the cobblestones and stuck his blade at its neck, effectively shutting it up.

"What do you mean, throwing yourself at me?" he demanded.

The creature, which appeared to be a halfling of largish nose, asserted himself from underneath a broad-brimmed cloth hat.

"Back off, human! I can protect myself!" he announced, to the surprise of Juggler, who was not accustomed to having his swordwork opposed verbally. The funny little man fumbled through his beer-soaked cloak and drew out a small knife with a four-inch blade and held it out in front of him, more like an amulet than a weapon. "I have a blade, and I know how to use it too." He swished it back and forth with a dramatic flourish.

Juggler's face was fixed with puzzlement. Misty smiled nonchalantly and dipped a chip in ketchup. Her twin grunted, sheathed his sword, grasped the halfling by his cloak, and hauled him up to standing. Now that his life was no longer under serious threat, the halfling rustled through the yards of cloth to replace his knife in its home, speaking earnestly the whole time.

"Oh, my dear sir, thank you for your assistance, and I do beg of you to excuse me! So clumsy of me. Tripped, you see, over that cobble just there—" he indicated the stone in question, "—and I am terribly sorry if I frightened you, either with my initial lunge or with my self-defence. As you can see, I have suffered the same humiliation as yourself." He brushed beer off his cloak with a dryer section of the garment. That done, he bent down to pick up the bits of broken mug that had been his beer. "I took lessons, you know."

"Hunh?" said Juggler, who was finding it hard to follow the creature's babble.

"Self-defence," the halfling explained. "A travelling trainer came through my village a number of years ago, and several of us were fortunate enough to benefit from his skills. A wonderful man by the name of Billis. Do you know of him? If you ever have a chance to work with him, I highly recommend that you do so. Even someone like yourself, with no great deal of experience, could learn much from him in only a few weeks."

Juggler was dumbfounded and said nothing. Misty's eyebrows had nearly reached her hairline, but a twist of amusement hung in the corner of her mouth.

"And now, I do wish you would allow me to recompense you for the loss of your beverage by replacing it with another. Oh, miss!" he called to a passing server with a full tray. He glanced to see what Misty was drinking and held up three fingers then pulled out a drawstring pouch, bulging with coins. Misty and Juggler exchanged glances. Here was a naïve little fellow, out to have a good time this evening. Well, Juggler was not one to disappoint him. He turned to a man at the table behind him.

"Give me your chair."

The man stared in shock. "But I—"

"I said, give it to me." Juggler drew his sword. "I need it more than you do. I've been under a lot of *strain* lately."

The man relinquished the chair gladly.

Juggler pushed the halfling into it and drew it up to the table.

"Now suppose you tell me your name, little fellow."

"I'm not exactly 'little' you know," the halfling clarified. "I'm actually quite tall among halflings." He held up a hand. "But no need to apologize, I know it was said out of ignorance but kindly meant."

Juggler's face grew hot with the "ignorance" comment but cooled again at the end. Had he meant it kindly? He supposed so—but before he could think on it more, the halfling said, "Hector."

And Juggler said, "What?"

"Well, sir, you asked my name a moment ago, and that's what it is. It's Hector." He bowed to Misty and said, "And now, lovely lady, how may I address you?"

"Misty here's my sister." Juggler's blood was heating up again. "And if you say one disrespectful thing to her, I'll shave the skin right off your body one layer at a time."

"Really?" Hector said, incredulous. "Can they do that nowadays? I had not heard that it was possible. I've heard of shaved faces, shaved heads, even shaved ham, but *that* is truly something new. Thank you for the offer, and I know who to find when I'm ready to consider it. Now, would you care for a game of Dice? It is one of my favourite games and a delightful way to pass an evening, for we can still absorb the environment and the music. I am not much for dancing, for larger people *will* tread on me, but I do so love the *music*, don't you?"

Juggler was quite bewildered by the little man. He caught Misty's eye, though, and knew that look. She didn't trust him.

Meanwhile, Hector produced his bag of dice and, as he opened it, dumped them on the ground and had to plunge underneath the table to locate them, the whole time muttering, "Oh *dear*, oh dear me!" The little wooden cubes had rolled under the table and chairs, and Hector spent several moments crawling around and plucking them off the cobbles. He finally climbed back into his seat, shaking his head in self-deprecation. "I tell you, after three pints of beer, I become an absolute slithery-fingered mess!"

Three pints? Juggler thought. *How much can a small person take?*

Misty declined to play, but she and Juggler continued to eat while Hector taught them the finer points of Dice. They offered him some food, but he just said, "Thank you, no; I hate potatoes," and carried on.

"Now I do like to throw a little wager on a game like this, don't you? Makes it that much more exciting. Don't worry, we'll keep it low," he added reassuringly.

"Why not?" Juggler said; he always preferred low stakes.

They each put a noble in the ante. On his third turn, Juggler reached a thousand points, and carried on to 2,500 before calling it quits. Hector did not reach a thousand until Juggler was already at 5,750, but then he caught up to within a thousand points. Juggler won the first game by 3,200 points and was ahead by two nobles.

"Ooh, well done, lad." Hector shook his head in admiration. "I shall have to rethink my strategy next time." The first part of his strategy was evidently to order more beer. "But I say." He leaned forward conspiratorially. "How 'bout we start with a noble again but raise the stakes with each turn?"

Juggler shrugged and looked over at Misty, who reassured him that she'd advise him along the way. Her shrewd eyes were on the halfling, for which Juggler was thankful, but Hector continued to smile that innocent, friendly smile.

They played three more games, by the end of which Juggler was up about fifteen nobles, the halfling being too tipsy to bet sensibly. Juggler wasn't about to caution him.

"You certainly have the luck, Mr. . . . uh . . . Why, I do believe I never did get your name. Ah well, not to worry, and as it happens, I've just recalled that when I so rudely descended upon you—quite literally, and I do apologize again for my carelessness—but you see, I was on my way to meet another friend who is equally lucky with his game as you seem to be. Don't consider for a moment the fact that I will not have the opportunity to regain my pregame position; there is no reason whatever to feel any remorse. It is a fair price to pay for an entertaining evening such as this, and I'm just as likely to lose twice as much again when I get to my friend's!" Hector gathered the dice together as he spoke and swiped them off the table into the sack. He stood up, swaying gently, like a fir sapling, though with a decidedly different fragrance, and bowed to each of them with the grandeur of a courtly gentleman.

As he passed around Misty, he swayed a bit further than he could without losing his balance and bumped into her shoulder. She stiffened and helped him regain uprightedness before pushing him along.

"I'm glad he's gone," she said. "It was fun, but he was wearing on my nerves. I don't trust someone that friendly." She patted her pouch to double-check that the bottle of tahleema was still there. Reassured, she tightened it again.

"What do you suppose Hunter will say when he finds out we stopped them from getting what they were after?"

Juggler shrugged. "I just dare him to express disapproval."

"All the same, we'd better keep our eyes on Valrayker's band and make sure they leave here."

Juggler nodded and turned to watch some of the dancers. "Where do you suppose I could get me some o' them dice?"

Janak was listening to the music. Derry and Phennil were off dancing. Skimnoddle was executing his plan to secure the tahleema, and Kyer had gone to seek whatever sort of companionship a girl like her looked for.

Jesqellan watched for the moon.

The mage decided not to tell the dwarf about the note. He would attend the rendezvous then share what news he learned with the captain and the others.

Ah, there it was. The four-day-old full frog moon, the first moon of summer, was just peeking over the treetops in the east when Jesqellan pleaded a need to meditate and told Janak he'd find him again later. The dwarf grunted and gave him a wave, his attention absorbed by the band who was playing a stirring rendition of "The Ghost of the Darkling Mere." They were just coming up to his favourite line about *cowering I, between the rushes, saw it rise, face of transparent moonlight, sleeves of dripping algae.*

Leaving Janak to shiver with delight at the words, the mage darted between tables and skirted along the outer edge of the road toward the Trout Inn. He saw only one or two people, but still he was relieved that the darkness of his Moabi robes kept him unobtrusive. Ah, across the street was the inn. Jesqellan intersected the road and slid down the side of the building. The Trout Inn backed onto an alley with a washing line and a compost heap. And a back porch from which a young maid dumped a bin of dishwashing water before scooting back in through the rectangle of light amid shouts of, "Tena, have you taken that tray up to Fer Dumin's—" The door closed behind her, and the mage was immersed in darkness again.

"On second thought," said a quiet voice from the shadow next to the porch, and Jesqellan jumped for the second time that evening, "perhaps this is not quite private enough for my business." The man beckoned to the mage, and the two headed down the alley away from the town square. Jesqellan could just make out the sign *Trout Inn Stable* as they passed it. He made the finger sign for a simple Guard spell, which would at least warn him of anyone coming within ten feet on all sides. The flickering presence of his host confirmed that the spell had been successful. A few buildings later, they stopped at the back of a small shed behind some place of business, closed for the evening.

"This is better for me. Does it suit you?" The man's voice was oddly familiar.

"It's fine. What do you want to tell me?" The spell told him there was no one inside the shed or around the corner about to ambush them.

In the bright moonlight, the man pulled the hood off his red hair.

Kyer's only plan thus far had been to separate herself from her friends; nothing wrong with needing a break from the people she'd been travelling with for several months. She let her feet take her somewhere without letting her brain take over.

Oddly enough, her feet took her to the edge of the party where the crowd was thinner and she could see Derry perfectly. She leaned against a post that prevented the roof of the milliner's shop from landing on its porch and watched him idly as he dipped and wheeled with his newest dark-haired, creamy cheeked partner; naturally he had no difficulty in securing another. In fact, several other young women were pointing him out and claiming him for themselves as they adjusted their bodices and their curls. Kyer shook her head in annoyance at these silly girls. Was that all they had to think about? Looking nice so they could snatch the right dance partner? She sighed. *Maybe Derry likes women who look pretty all the time and don't embroil themselves in the affairs of the world.* She brushed a hand over her own hair, smoothing out the frayed braid, and stole a glance at her trousers and leather armour. She couldn't fail to observe the contrast.

A compulsion hit her. What if she asked Derry to teach her to dance? Privately, of course; she wouldn't have any of her friends knowing about it. If there was anybody with the patience to teach her, it was Derry, and if anybody could be discreet, it was Derry. The perfect combination. And maybe it would do something for his mood to see her trying to be pleasant. She caught his eye just then and gave him a nod. He paused in his dialogue with the girl and her dimples just long enough to toss Kyer a smile. His partner turned her head, and Kyer read the next words from girl's lips. "Who's *that?*"

Kyer drew her weight away from the post and steeled her resolve to go down the steps and interrupt Derry before he could be caught by the golden skinned girl with plenty of cleavage. She'd made up her mind to do this, and didn't want to lose the moment.

"Oh, I'm so glad to find you here," said a cheerful voice behind her.

Kyer arrested an annoyed, "Don't bother me," and was dismayed to find the lad who had so kindly greeted them upon their arrival. Though she regretted missing her opportunity, she was glad she hadn't told him off—one point for Kyer in her Don't Raise Anyone's Ire campaign. She glanced at Derry, who seemed to be watching her (*no doubt making sure I'm not about to kill anybody; I hope he noticed that*), and forced a smile.

"You're glad to find me here? What for?"

"Are you enjoying the party?" He bobbed his head. Clearly it was important to get the politenesses out of the way before getting to the meat of anything.

"Uh, yeah, it's great." She shrugged. "I like the music." *Which has started again, and Derry's dancing. I'll catch him next time.*

"Tod, remember?"

She was about to say, "Pardon?" when he added, "Tod Shelling," and she understood what he meant.

"Kyer Halidan." She shook his hand, and when he didn't let go right away, she masked her alarm. *I guess I didn't look busy enough.* Not wanting to miss her chance to speak to Derry, she got back to the point. "Why is it you're glad to find me?"

Tod let go her hand and ran his through the back of his hair. "I know you must be very busy, but you see—your swords. You didn't leave them at your inn?" His earnestness puzzled her.

"Of course not," she answered automatically. "They'd walk faster than you if I did that. Why do you ask?"

"Well, I saw that you have two, and, well, my grandda . . ." He looked idly over her shoulder.

Kyer peered around to catch his eye again. Apparently he had become distracted by some activity over on the next porch. "Your grandfather?" Kyer prodded with a fleeting look back at Derry, who, in spite of the dance steps, always seemed to be facing her whenever she looked at him. *Boy, he's pretty intent on keeping an eye on me.*

"My grandda loves swords. He's built up a collection of them over the years. I think he might like to look at yours, and see if, well, also if you could tell him anything about his."

She shook her head regretfully. "I'm afraid I don't know all that much about swords. I did read some weapon history texts, but I don't know how useful that information would be in this situation; I mean, I doubt if I could match a weapon with its era, or creator, or anything like that."

"Do you think you could pay him a visit, all the same? It couldn't hurt. I guess you're very busy." Tod shrugged apologetically and started to back away. Kyer stopped him with a hand, relenting.

"No, wait." She glanced disappointedly at Derry. *Maybe I can make it quick and get back here.* "I would be happy to come and meet your grandfather. Even if I can't tell him anything about them, I'd be really interested to see his collection."

Tod's boyish face lit up. "Oh, thanks!"

She turned again to Derry, who was giving her that expressionless look again, warning her to behave herself. She grinned and shrugged as if to say, "Look at me being friendly! I haven't even touched my hilt yet."

"Grandda'll be pleased," Tod went on. With his arm, he directed her which way to go, and she moved to follow. Uncertainty and inspiration hit her simultaneously and she stopped.

"Hold on a minute, all right? I've got to talk to someone before I go with you. Let him know where I'm going because looking at your grandfather's swords or whatever could take a while." She could also just let Derry know she wanted to speak to him later about dancing. He'd be pleased. She scanned the crowd for Derry's blond head.

It took a moment to find him because he wasn't anywhere near where he had been before. And the sight that met her eyes made her thudding heart sink. Derry was leaving the square on the far side. With a girl on his arm. A redhead. He was smiling down at her shining upturned face.

Kyer's lips tightened. She crossed one leg in front of the other and leaned against the post. *It's okay. He'd probably laugh at me anyway.*

"Can you see him?"

Kyer had forgotten the youth was even there.

She shook her head and sighed deeply. "No. I don't think it's all that important after all."

Scowling, she stomped down the steps again and headed at a springing lion's pace back toward Tod's cottage until she remembered she didn't know the way. She let the lad take the lead. She was strangely irked by what she had seen and did not lose the ferocity in her steps until they arrived on the cottage doorstep.

Once inside, though, she forgot everything else.

"Oh, it's you," Jesqellan said.

"Does that mean you're happy to see me?" Fredric asked wryly.

"You can't blame me for mistrusting you."

Fredric leaned against the shed. "But let me ask you this: Why should you not, in truth? The actions that led to my banishment were ... indiscretions. I used bad judgement. And I've paid for it; I *am* paying for it. Jesqellan, I did nothing that could ever be seen as disloyal. Lord Kien chose to see my mistakes as personal insults, and for that I am banished, but I did not—" His throat constricted with emotion, and he spoke to the shed wall. "I never have and never will commit any act in direct opposition to him." He sought the moon's assistance in controlling himself. "I still—I still love and honour him, Jesqellan. You have to believe me."

Jesqellan considered his words in spite of himself. The shaman had heard more than one confession and expression of regret; it was part of his duty, helping those who had erred return to their right and true path. Fredric sounded no different from other transgressors he'd known, who were truly repentant. It occurred to Jesqellan now that Fredric had just as much right to seek redemption, and that if Kien Bartheylen were any kind of lord worthy of respect, he would honour the attempt of this man who had served him loyally for so long. He remained cautious.

"We were taken by surprise by your urgent need to speak to Kyer a few days ago. Why not present yourself?"

"Surely you must understand that there are those among you who will not be altogether ... pleased to see me. I needed to talk to Kyer alone, I had reasons for it, so I thought to just bring her to me.”

“And finish your meeting with a knock on her head and abandoning her?”

Fredric shrugged. “Regrettable but necessary. I couldn’t have her rushing back to bring the rest of you.”

“Why was it necessary to separate her from the rest of us just to warn her off our mission?”

Fredric shifted, making Jesqellan’s spell quiver. “Is that what she told you? Interesting.”

“Isn’t that what you said to her?”

A pause. Then Fredric answered. “Now, Jesqellan, I had words for her and her alone; I would hardly repeat them here. However, the result of our exchange is partly why I need to speak with you.”

The tension emanated from the soldier like an aura of static electricity. “Her response merely confirmed my suspicions. She’s been found out. That she has not done as I advised tells me she thought I was bluffing.”

Jesqellan looked up at the taller man squarely. “You have my attention.”

“Thank you.” He bowed and the spell wavered.

“Still, why me? Derry is the captain of our party, why not share this information with him or one of the others?”

Fredric shrugged again. “It’s quite simple: what I have to say involves some . . . less-than-favourable news about Kyer. I’m sure you’d agree that there are several in your party who have a . . . biased sense of admiration for her. I think I’m not being unfair when I say that they wouldn’t accept what I have to tell with an open mind. You, on the other hand, are a shaman. I believe you have that clarity your friends lack and will be able to hear what I have to say and choose the right course of action.”

Jesqellan thought carefully. Fredric’s answer made sense, and it had been a long time since the mage’s particular attributes had been truly appreciated by his companions. Phennil and Skimnoddle were plainly of a mind that

Kyer could do no wrong. Even Janak had a peculiar fondness for her, in spite of his pretence that it was otherwise. Though Derry had confided in Jesqellan his own concerns about Kyer's level of commitment, the young captain undeniably had strong feelings of friendship for the other fighter. Only he had the experience at putting all prejudices aside to analyse a situation with—Fredric had put it well—clarity.

"Have I assessed the situation accurately?" Fredric smiled.

"Yes, yes you have. I can see that, in spite of the recent past, you are still a man of integrity. So, what news do you have for me?"

In the moon's glow, Jesqellan could just make out Fredric's nod of approval. In a low voice, the red-headed man spoke.

"I have reason to believe that Kyer's motive for coming on this mission was not one of kindness and generosity. Her motive was assurance."

"Assurance?"

"She wants to be certain that she finishes what she started."

"What are you saying?" Jesqellan's mind raced through a list of alarming scenarios.

Fredric's voice was a whisper, barely audible over the sound of the rising moon. "Kyer Halidan was the one who gave the Lady Alon Maer the magical device that is killing her."

Blood rushed through the mage's head like crashing waves. Still, he held his reaction in check. It would not do to agree or disagree hastily. He studied the other man. "That is a heavy charge."

"It started before you met her." Fredric's voice was full of heavy sadness. "Disguised as a maid, she got herself a post at Bartheylen Castle. Then one day a package arrived from someone she was familiar with and she delivered it to the lady, compliments of my lord. It contained a pendant in the shape of a blue, jewelled snake. The lady is wearing it even as we speak."

Jesqellan raised a sceptical eyebrow.

"The snake is a symbol of undying love," Fredric explained. "That *particular* snake is a cursed artifact: a *Malison*."

Jesqellan's dinner undulated in his belly.

"The curse secretes into Alon's body both through her skin and her breath. As long as she wears the snake, she will ingest more of its dark magic. Kyer stayed in her post long enough to ensure that the *Malison* took effect, and then she . . . travelled to where her correspondents had told her she could find Lord Valrayker. She joined with him, and the rest, you know."

The mage frowned in the darkness, his heartbeat quickening. "That all sounds . . . plausible, but why would she do it?"

"Isn't it obvious? I mean, while you were on your previous mission; Kyer's first assignment for Valrayker, remember, she was in contact more than once with a known Dregor loyalist."

"Ronav?" Jesqellan said doubtfully. "His men tried to kill her more than once."

"Maybe for not following orders?"

Jesqellan checked his protest. Kyer did have a tendency to act in her own interest. *Taking that sword, for instance.* And more than once, she had resisted Derry's leadership. "But when Ronav took her, she was beaten very badly," Jesqellan pointed out. "They flogged her. She was cut and bruised and had a broken rib."

Fredric waved a shadowy hand. "They made their point, didn't they? And who ever sustained long-term damage from cuts and bruises?"

Kyer in league with Ronav . . . *Kyer knew goblins were coming; the presence of magic on her has intensified; she becomes unreasonably cross when her actions are questioned . . .* Fredric's suggestions trickled into the pool of suspicions Jesqellan had harboured over these past few weeks. A grim doubt slithered along the bottom of his thoughts.

"There's something else." Fredric leaned back against the shed with an air of nonchalance. "I don't know if you've ever seen her vanish or suddenly materialize, as if out of nowhere?"

The pace of Jesqellan's heart had caught up with his mind. He knew exactly what Fredric was referring to, and he did not like where this was going.

"Kyer Halidan," Fredric said, "has the ability to Gate."

Flames leapt in Jesqellan's gut. That was the fear he had struggled for days to quash. *Impossible!* "It's not possible. She has no magical ability whatsoever." The words sounded weak even to himself.

He had not been satisfied with her story of her and Phennil's escape from the earthquake. That was the second time she'd appeared virtually out of thin air at their fireside, and he'd never forgotten the unease he felt the first time, upon her return from her "visit" with Ronav.

A Gate was a powerful spell. Creating a doorway to another location required a level of skill that, in spite of years of commitment and training, remained well and truly out of Jesqellan's reach. Yet Jesqellan had guessed, and now he knew, that such a spell was in the hands of this cocky young upstart. Kyer Halidan could Gate. Jesqellan could not. He shivered with the chill of his blood, and his head whirled.

But why would she hold back something like this from me? he thought. Unfortunately the answer was obvious. His heart thudded double-time.

Fredric's soft voice rang like a dinner gong through Jesqellan's tumultuous thoughts. "I can tell you don't like what you're hearing. I understand that," he said gently. His throat tightened with his next words. "And I can't tell you how . . . *debased* I feel. I was *intimate* with the woman who may very well succeed at taking the life of a dear friend, the wife of my lord." He leaned his head against the shed as if to ease the weight of his pain. "I find myself admitting that Lord Kien was right to banish me after all. If I didn't truly deserve it for the reasons he gave, I sure deserve it for falling for the enemy."

Jesqellan's heart warmed. He breathed deeply of the night air to calm and caution himself. It was still not proof that she had given Alon Maer a

Malison. Though he acknowledged that, it was clear this man had been through much in these recent months. His new humility had led him to openly admit his guilt, which was the first step in achieving redemption and forgiveness. The least the shaman could do was accept the steps Fredric was taking. *He was right to choose someone as capable as I of objectivity.*

Golgathaur stood outside Misty and Juggler's room at the inn a few blocks from the square. He hesitated only because he did *so* hate to breach societal codes of conduct. He shook his head and *tsked*. There was nothing for it. For the good of a cause, sometimes one had to do things one was not proud of. *Sacrifices*, some people called them. He assumed the undignified position known as a *crouch* and peered through the keyhole, eyeing his destination.

Given enough information, he waggled his fingers just so and stepped through. He saw immediately what he was looking for. He flipped open the flap of Misty's saddlebag and removed an object, flat, about the length of Misty's forearm, and wrapped in black cloth. He secreted it away inside his cloak and left the room the same way he entered.

She's far too vain for her own good.

Skimnoddle returned the broad-brimmed hat to its owner and slipped in an extra noble over and above the agreed-on price. *Success*, he signed in Thieves' Argot. "There'll be one less hungry child in town tonight," he said.

"My compliments to the chef," the other halfling replied. "That's some nifty boots you got there."

"My regards to your father next time you see him." Skimnoddle tipped his now hatless head and took his leave. The spoken form of Thieves' Argot came less automatically to him since he'd had no one to practice with of late.

On his way back to Phennil and the others, he picked a couple of pockets to make up for what he'd lost in his game with the assassin. He patted the hidden spot in his waistcoat where he'd tucked a little bluish clay bottle that bore an uncanny resemblance to the one in Misty's pouch. The difference was the contents. Misty's contained a few cherry blossoms, and the one Skimnoddle now had was brimming with tiny, white, trefoil-shaped petals. Having accomplished what he'd set out to do by dropping the dice on the ground, the games that followed had been truly pleasurable. He almost felt guilty for taking such delight in the evening when the others thought he was working.

Sixteen

I Must Plead Again for Your Secrecy

Jesqellan could not bring himself to return to the revelry right away. His brain teemed with activity. Suspicion, self-doubt, confusion, anger, and resentment surged through him like bolts of electricity. If he admitted it to himself, there was an undercurrent of envy. *Kyer Halidan can Gate.*

Fredric was correct to suggest that Jesqellan keep his eyes and ears open. Over a mug of beer, Jesqellan had wished for more evidence.

"She'll slip up," Fredric had said. "Deceitful people always do."

On his way back to the Happy Beerbarrel, Jesqellan found himself sympathising with Fredric Heyland's plight. Here was a man who had dedicated a lifetime of service to his lord and had been dismissed—plucked and discarded, all because of some minor breaches of protocol. The man's love and respect for Kien after such treatment said much about his character, and his vehement support of the mission to find Alon's cure was touching, to say the least. Jesqellan felt honoured that the former captain had trusted him enough to share his burden. *Poor fellow. I will certainly vouch on his behalf to Kien.*

There was a lot of truth behind his words, especially about Kyer's headstrong nature and the way she successfully hid her true motives beneath a short-tempered personality: If she were always abrasive and tight-lipped, she had a ready shield for the truth.

Back at the inn, Jesqellan asked the chambermaid for a bath. She trotted off to prepare it. As he fetched his belongings from the common room, Jesqellan's mind was a swarm of thought and emotion. Kyer was a willful, impulsive girl, who acted in her own best interests most of the time. If anyone challenged her on any of her choices, she became irate. She clearly had violent tendencies. She had volunteered to come on this mission without ever having met Alon Maer. Why would she do that if not for reasons of her own that she preferred to keep to herself? Not to mention the fact that she could Gate and denied it. Her arrogance was deplorable.

Ten minutes later, as he poured a pot of hot water over his head, the mage still sifted through his thoughts. Kyer had lied about what Fredric said to her. She'd lied about a lot of things.

She followed Fredric on the mountain path; all doubt of that had vanished. But why? Fredric had warned her to clear out of the mission. He'd accused her and found out the details of how she'd given Alon the *Malison*. Jesqellan was well aware of Kyer's temper as well as her ability to kill with cold calculation when she thought it necessary. Had she followed Fredric to kill him? Then they'd caught up with her. That would explain her crazed, distraught reaction to their appearance.

Jesqellan felt very uneasy. *I will be watching her closely.*

Misty reached into her saddlebag. When her slender fingers did not close around the cloth-wrapped package she expected to find, she arrested a curse. Instead she breathed out slowly, calmly, and thought things through.

Only one person besides Juggler knew about her souvenir. Misty didn't know how he did these things, but one thing she was sure of: he liked to play games.

Ah, but Misty had her own games. She liked to pick and choose which ones she participated in. She did not like being provoked. In this way he was trying to goad her into playing a game only he could possibly control.

She smiled. She would not play.

For the first time, Fredric did not jump out of his skin when Golgathaur appeared in his room.

"My, aren't we relaxed this evening," the tall man said archly.

"That went way better than I expected," Fredric said with real eagerness. "You were right. The mage was ready to hear anything against her, especially after I mentioned the Gate. I thought his eyes would pop out of his head."

"So the seed has been sown."

Fredric leaned against the wall. "I think it was already sown. I think we actually fertilized it a bit." He smiled, not least because of his comfort using the word "we."

"Well done." Golgathaur put out his hand.

Fredric hesitated, his smile altering subtly. Golgathaur was on his side.

Fredric shook Golgathaur's hand.

Soren Lowey's collection of weapons was nothing short of awe inspiring to a young warrior like Kyer. It was the reason he and his grandson shared a larger home than most of the townspeople. One whole room was dedicated to it: shelf upon shelf lined the stone walls, and some were free-standing in the middle of the room—*Like a library*, Kyer thought—custom made to fit the various sizes of boxes, cases, and sheaths, for he did not leave them all out on display.

"It's a collection, not a museum," the old man explained. With his lean, six-foot frame, he reached with ease up to a top shelf and gently lifted down a leather case, about four feet long. "I know what is in every container on every shelf, and if you asked to see a certain item, I'd be able to get it straight away. And I love them all." He opened the case, revealing a leaf-bladed short sword with a simple ball pommel and wooden grip. Holding the box in one hand, he grasped the hilt in the other and raised it to shoulder height, peering down its length. Kyer recognized instantly that Soren Lowey was not a mere collector: he was a swordfighter. It may have been a former self, but Kyer could tell he would still be deadly if he wished. He lowered the weapon, grinned with boyish eagerness, and handed it, hilt first, over to her.

"How did you come by them all?" Kyer grasped the featherweight weapon in one hand and eyed the blade for straightness, unconsciously mimicking the old man's pose. Before he could answer, she said, "Isn't this from the Pre-Luntiff era? Maybe from Shona?" She was surprised at how the information from the history texts came flooding back to her.

For several incredibly swift hours, she talked weapons history and origin with Soren and tested balance, craftsmanship, metalwork, blade quality, material choice, design, and style of sword, dagger, axe, morningstar, shuriken. Pieces dated from as far back as 800 years, long before Kien's and Valrayker's time, way back when the world was subdivided into infinite numbers of provinces and territories. Soren was somewhat of an archaeologist, having travelled extensively in his youth to learn more about the histories he had studied. Some weapons he'd found, some he'd bought, some had been gifts. Kyer continued to recall her own studies and learned new information from Soren while Tod sat by and watched and listened, and when their voices began to sound tired, he finally announced that he'd made a meal that waited in the other room.

Kyer was shocked that she was so hungry, considering the amount of fish and potatoes she'd belted back at dinner. She gratefully accepted the cool mug of beer from Tod and took several great long swallows. Falling into a wing-backed chair, she caught sight of the moon peeking through the shutters on the westward window on its way down to the horizon. "Death spirit, it can't be that late!"

"It most certainly can. We've been talking about my collection for nearly six hours," Soren said, his gravelly voice revived by his beer.

She shook her head with a grin of joyful disbelief and chomped into the large hunk of spicy cake, still warm from the oven.

"Tod, were you baking all this while we were talking?" She waved a hand at the low table laden with cookies, cake, cheese, and biscuits, amazed at how quickly the time had passed and how unaware she had been of the lad's activities. "I feel so rude, like we ignored you."

He brushed off her concerns with a shy smile. "I don't mind it," he said. "I was happy to see Grandda with someone to share all his stuff with. Anyway, we almost always have a snack this time o' night, don't we, Grandda?"

Kyer laughed, nearly spitting out crumbs. "You call this a snack? And at the second hour after midnight?"

Soren leaned over and took a piece of cheese and an oatcake. "Well, we don't have much else to do, do we, Tod?" The old man's silver hair shone amber in the firelight. "We keep to ourselves, mostly. Tod's a message runner for anyone who needs him, and I toddle in the garden by day. He visits his Mam and sister every day but lives with me so I'm not alone. We take care of each other, our family."

Kyer thought of fireside nights with Della knitting and singing, Gareth reading or playing his cittern, and herself frowning and griping through her homework. The slightest hint of homesickness crept into her smile. But she would never have been content, like Tod, to remain at home just for the sake of being with someone, family or not.

"You'd probably be interested to see my sword," Kyer said suddenly, as if to banish the topic in her head. She fetched her newly acquired scabbard and her weapon belt from the corner by the door. She half-hoped Soren might be able to identify the sword for her. She set Brendow's on the floor at her feet, keeping the longsword in hand. "Interesting story about this one." Sitting in the chair, she held it upright, the point end resting on the plank floor in front of her, and wondered what to tell them. How would Soren receive the truth of her "stealing" from the dead?

"I found it in a clearing, way off the beaten track." Kyer told them about the path and the compulsion she had to follow it. She tried to describe the eeriness of the mist and the wonder she and Jesqellan had felt at the scene of the age-old battle. When she talked about the voice, she hesitated, for a moment losing her courage. The story didn't sound credible at all. "The sword drew me toward it, as if it were calling to me. That probably sounds pretty weird to you." She looked at the two of them sheepishly.

"Not at all," Soren said. "Many of my weapons seemed to find me the same way. Let's see it," he added with youthful intensity in his voice and twinkling blue eyes.

She slowly drew her prized possession from its concealment and found herself oddly reluctant to make eye contact with her hosts until they reacted. Instead she was spellbound for the umpteenth time by the beauty of it, the way the blade reflected with perfection the light from the fire, captivating her with its flawlessness. The brilliant, glowing pommel and the absolute *rightness* of the way the hilt felt in her palm. Kyer suddenly realized the room had been breathlessly silent for some time. She looked up, embarrassed. Both men were enraptured, their faces shining with awe. "Have you ever seen the like of it?"

Soren held out his hand, and she passed it to him. He did not respond right away. Tod went down on hands and knees on the floor and rubbed his finger over the place where the pin-sharp tip, even resting so lightly, had bored a small hole in the wood. "No," the grandfather said slowly. "I can honestly say I have never laid eyes on such a weapon." She searched his eye and was puzzled by the expression in it. He directed his gaze at her again and threw a mask over whatever he had been thinking. "I can tell by the way you look at it, you are drawn to it still." He raised the tip until it was parallel with the floor and ran a keen eye down its edge. Kyer shrugged and nodded, leaning back in the chair nonchalantly. "I believe you when you say you were compelled to pick this up." He paused ever so slightly. "No matter whose hands were on it when you found it."

Kyer looked at him, startled, and tried to alter her expression to one of confusion or misunderstanding. His smile relaxed her. "I only meant that its aura must be very strong, and you would have had to take it under any circumstances. I have felt that way about some weapons too. You did right. Tod, refill Kyer's mug, will you please?"

"Does the name . . . *Barakel* mean anything to you?" she asked.

"*Barakel?*" He looked surprised, or baffled. "Now, where did you hear that name?"

Kyer shrugged. "I heard someone say it and wondered if it had some historical significance."

Soren stroked the flat side of the blade and studied it like he might an ancient text. "I think Barakel might be a Dark Elven name." He passed the sword back to her. "Unfortunately I can't enlighten you."

She observed his face. His words had held a tone of wonder, maybe even surprise. With the quick tempo of his denial, she didn't believe him. However, a man of his experience must have his reasons. She sheathed the sword and laid it on the floor, and picked up Brendow's. "This one is nice too, and mostly of interest because of whom it belonged to." She passed it, sheath and all, to Soren, nodding her thanks to Tod for the refill.

"Oh?" Soren examined the lines and trefoils on the sheath before drawing the weapon. He admired the delicate strength of the hilt, and Kyer was proud to notice that even after all it had been through, the blade was still perfect.

"It belonged to my trainer. He gave it to me just before I left Hreth. I don't think he's famous or anything, but he is a *Wæmniar*, so you know it must be a good sword."

Soren's gaze was focussed on the blade. He didn't respond directly. Testing its grip in both hands, he looked pensive, like he was trying to think of a tactful assessment. Finally he said, "You're right, it's a beauty."

They talked awhile longer, but Kyer began to fade and was uncertain what to do. It was too late to bother finding her way back to the inn, but she could hardly stay here. Tod solved the problem.

"Grandda, I think it would be unkind to make Kyer pay for such a partial night at an inn, why don't we let her stay here?"

"Actually, I had to prepay because of the rooms all being full."

"Still, it would be foolish make your way back at this hour," Tod said.

"Oh, that's all right, really," Kyer protested mildly. Truth be told, she could have slept on top of the woodpile at that moment. Underneath the woodpile, even.

"Of course she should stay here," Soren agreed. "She'll take your bed, and you can sleep in here."

Kyer did protest at that. She wouldn't have her host put himself out to that extent. In the end, Tod brought several blankets, and she made herself comfortable on the floor in front of the fire, on which he piled a few more pieces of coal before retiring himself. She fell into a deep slumber almost immediately, and so was completely unaware of the old man who returned to sit by the fire for a while to study her sleeping face.

Derry knew he was scowling, and that it was unbecoming to a man of his supposed training and experience. How could he help it? Why did Kyer have to so persistently anger him this way? To be fair—attempt fairness anyhow—maybe she wasn't doing it on purpose. *It sure comes naturally to her*, he fumed. He had escorted the redhead home, upon her request. How could he refuse? When he'd said good night at her door, she was clearly annoyed about something. Her "thank you" was anything but heartfelt. He guessed he just wasn't meant to understand women. *I need a drink before I'll ever sleep*, he thought and wove through the revellers back toward the square.

Kyer had obviously stood there on the porch because it was so close to the dancing area; a great place to meet men, turn them down as dance partners, but think of something else to do.

Oh stop it, he scolded himself. He decided not to join the others at the Happy Beerbarrel but carry on to his own inn, the Odds and Suds. An adroit move to avoid talking with them about the same old things. They probably had found more interesting activities anyway. The door of the Odds and Suds burst open, and Derry sidestepped nimbly to avoid a collision with a geezer whose walk had more back-and-forth movement than the tide. The captain went in, and the pickled timbre of the drunk's singing faded as the door closed.

A whisky in each hand, Derry smouldered at the bar. Why did Kyer frustrate him so much? She availed herself of every opportunity to take a jab at him. Even under the guise of being nice, she rubbed him the wrong way. These young things he'd whirled about with all evening hung on every word of his stories of valour and danger. To them he was important, a man to admire. Not only was Kyer not impressed with such things—she had her own stories—but it didn't even seem to cross her mind that he deserved respect, even deference, because he was the captain. She had her own views about everything, challenged his authority, and was constantly itching for a fight. She took liberties with him that the other company members wouldn't dream of, and he could never find it in himself to put her in her place. He felt powerless to do anything but let her get away with it.

The last straw was when he saw her with that youth. He was, what, maybe sixteen? Seventeen at most? She held his hand longer than necessary. She glanced Derry's way as she talked to the young man. So defiant! *Look at me doing whatever I want!* she was saying, practically *daring* him to stop her. And then she had the nerve to give him that little shrug and grin, as if to say, "It's just so easy for me!"

Damn it. He was supposed to be taking the night off. Derry tossed back both shots of whisky to forget his frustration. Even the news of Skimnoddle's success was insufficient to edge his troubles out of his mind. Overreacting again, he supposed. *But why am I the only one who notices how easily she separates herself from the task at hand?* He sighed. *Does she even remember why we're here?*

Derry settled up and hauled himself to the well to rehydrate before retiring to bed. She had not returned to the inn. More than once throughout the long night, he awoke to see she still was not there. A familiar ingot of black lead tumbled and swelled in the pit of his stomach like a snowball rolling down a hillside.

My slippered feet pad softly across the floor, through the doorway and up the stairs. I'm in the brightly lit corridor. The straw mats warm the floor. The baskets of flowers and candelabra evenly spaced along the stone walls make this a more homey corridor than any other in the castle. The door to the library is open on my right. I pass by. The smooth, varnished little wooden box in my hand is the gift for the lady. It's urgent that I give it to her, but I have no concern that I'll fail. Her door is . . . this one. I straighten my apron and knock. Her clear voice answers and I enter. She sits with legs crossed in her wing-backed armchair by the fire, reading. It's in High Elvish, so I can't read the title. Her dark hair gleams brown, red, gold, and her deep burgundy blouse looks good on her, the drawstring at the top hanging loosely open. It's a pity,

really, but I carry on.

"For you, my lady," I say. "It just arrived." I hold out the box. I can't help but smile.

"From whom?" she replies, receiving it from me.

"From his lordship, my lady." Eyes are steady. Heartbeat too.

She opens the box and pulls out the small, leather case. She lifts the lid, and with her slender finger, she traces the length of the blue and gold, gem-inlaid serpent-shape necklace where it lies on the deep red velvet, a red that matches her blouse. "It's beautiful." She turns to me. "Do you know what this is, Misha?"

"No, m'lady," I lie with sincerity.

She draws the snake out of its resting place. "The serpent is a symbol of undying love," she tells me. The word "undying" is ironic to me. She clasps the necklace behind her neck. "Do you like it?" she asks. She adjusts the position slightly, so the blue serpent lies centred on her chest. "Please get my looking glass off that table, Misha."

I fetch the glass and hold it up for her. "Do you like it?" she asks.

"Yes, m'lady," I assure her. "Is there anything else you need, m'lady?" I put the glass beside the remains of her tea things on the table next to her chair.

"Thank you, Misha, no. You may go." She smiles at the space in the air in front of her, still lightly fingering the trinket.

She doesn't ask me to take the tea things so I don't. I won't do anything more than I have to. I curtsey and move toward the door. As I reach for the polished brass handle, I hear her say, "Dear Kien."

I am successful. I feel triumphant as I close the door. I must share the news, so I run down the corridor.

Kyer awoke gasping and sat up. Blankets, fireplace, wing-backed armchairs, sliced-tree-trunk table, swords on the floor next to her, all the signs of familiarity served to dissipate the tightness in her throat. Once she was certain it was gone, she crawled out of bed and padded to the bucket to get a dipperful of water. Her shaking finally stopped with a series of deep breaths. Returning to her bed on the floor, she sat on it and dug her knuckles into her eyes. *Who am I in that dream?* she demanded of no one. *Why am I dreaming it?*

Kyer knew one thing unequivocally: that necklace, if it truly existed, was no gift of love from Kien.

Kyer slept soundly after that.

Too soundly. The sun was up when her eyes opened. She blinked a few times before she remembered she was supposed to be meeting with the others first thing this morning. She let out a small yelp and hurriedly folded her bedding.

"Can I offer you a warm drink to start your day?" Soren said.

"No, thank you so much, but I have to get back."

"Where is it you and your friends are off to?" Soren asked.

Kyer hesitated but decided that someone as well travelled and educated in history would likely take an interest in their destination. In fact, he might even know something of them. "We're going to the Indyn Caves."

"Ah." He sat down in the same chair he'd occupied last night. He didn't have the air of someone about to show a guest out. Kyer finished folding, trying to look hurried. Soren tapped the arms of his chair and looked as if he were going to whistle but didn't. "The Indyn Caves?" he said. "Haven't heard anybody mention them in years, let alone going there."

"No, I suppose not." Kyer secured her weapon belt around her waist, and reached for her baldric. She slung it over her shoulder, and stopped when Soren spoke again.

"Don't go there."

"Pardon? What do you mean?" she said with impatient perplexity.

"I mean, you shouldn't go there," Soren said firmly.

"We *have* to—"

"Not straight there, anyway."

She looked at the door, at the all-too-bright sunlight telling her how late she was. She planted her feet to keep from tapping them. "Um, why not?"

"Do you know how to enter?"

A pit opened in her stomach. "No."

"Sit down." Soren moved to the counter and scooped a coarse, deep brown powder into a cylindrical jug. Kyer sat heavily and took a breath to calm her impatience. She couldn't leave without hearing him out. She would just have to accept the scolding when it came. Soren carried the jug to the fire and poured water into it from the kettle that Kyer had not noticed hanging on the hook.

"My grandson is good to me. He always puts the water on before he leaves. He knows how much I enjoy my *qahwa* in the morning."

Ah, that answered Kyer's next question. She couldn't imagine Tod missing out on a chat like the one they were about to embark on. Soren set the jug on the little table, which had been cleared of last night's snack items, and went back to put a few things on a tray, including two mugs. It was obvious the old man had no intention of speaking further until he'd finished his deliberate preparations. Kyer gulped down the anxiety that swelled in her throat. The tray finally was set upon the table, and Soren lowered his long frame into the chair. When he spoke, he did not look at her, but put a heaping scoop of what looked like maple sugar into each mug.

"As I'm sure you are aware, it is sometimes difficult deciding who to trust. I have met a good many people in my time and would choose to trust only a handful of them." He poured a liberal amount of cream on top of the sugar in the mugs. "I have reasons for choosing you, yet I will not share those reasons with you."

Kyer wordlessly accepted Soren's decision, aware of the honour he was conferring upon her.

"What I am about to tell you," he said, "is not common knowledge. If it became known, all kinds of people—with all manner of intentions—would come flocking to the Indyn Caves. Curiosity seekers, vandals. Or worse. Here is the trickiest part: If it became known that someone gave you this information, certain people—with more specific intentions—would come flocking here. To this very house. And that must be avoided at whatever cost. Do you understand me?"

Kyer had a good enough imagination to picture what those specific intentions might be. She nodded.

"That being the case, I must ask you not only to not reveal who told you this, but not to reveal that *anybody* told you *anything*. I cannot tell you how to solve this problem because obviously you will be required to share the information with your travelling companions. I can only hope that they trust you enough to accept your information without much explanation. I beg your discretion as to where and with whom you spent the evening."

"I'll come up with something. You have my confidence."

"Thank you." He seemed to breathe easier at her assurance. "What do you know about the caves?"

Kyer shook her head. "Nothing, really. Derry knows roughly where they are, but I'd never heard of them. We're looking—"

"I'm not surprised. That you hadn't heard of them is intentional. The Indyn Caves were discovered, or created, no one is entirely sure, by dark elves about a thousand years ago. I'm sure you are also aware of the dark elves' notorious secrecy."

"I've heard it referred to as 'privacy,' but yes, I know what you mean."

Here Soren paused again, and Kyer thought she might squeal. *Please just get on with it!* He took up a long, thin wooden stick, on one end of which was a disc, pierced with tiny holes and covered with a circle of muslin. He placed the disc on top of the jug, and Kyer saw that it was just smaller than the inside of the jug, so it scraped the inside as Soren slowly pushed it down. She half expected the steaming water to spill out the top, but realized he was pushing slowly enough that the water came through the mesh of the fabric. When he had pushed it down as far as it would go, Soren lifted the jug and poured some of what was now a rich brown liquid into a mug, added another liberal dollop of cream, and passed it to her. It smelled like hickory, a pungent, pleasant smell that felt warm and alive. So this was *qahwa*. She'd heard of it but had never had occasion to try it. "You might want to give it a stir. Here." He passed her a spoon.

"The Indyn Caves," he went on, as if there had been no gap, "were one of their strongholds. The tales—and that's about all I know of it—say that the caves were the main dwelling of the highest families, the setting for a good many gatherings of the elders; tunnel upon tunnel, room upon room for ritual, magic, perhaps even tombs. I have heard that the caves were the main connecting centre for their travel and telepathic communications with the Cymrion people."

Kyer laughed in spite of herself. "The Cymrion?" Her denial faded into mere scepticism as she beheld his unchanged expression. "You can't be serious."

He looked at her darkly. "Oh, but I am."

She shook her head doubtfully. "There's no such thing, though. The Cymrion aren't . . . *real*."

"Because you've never met one?"

Kyer felt her face go blank. "The Cymrion are just . . . stuff of legend. Ghost stories that made you squeal, but you never really *believed* them."

"Stories, legends, have to come from somewhere, do they not? Tell a story over and over enough times, and the truth of it is bound to bend a bit, but it is still in there. The Cymrion have ceased their connection with our world, but that does not mean they never existed. Do you believe in dark elves?"

"Of course!"

"They vanished, too."

Kyer was sceptical but it was hard to argue with someone like this.

Soren went on. "The Cymrion and dark elves were always closely associated. The Cymrion were a quiet people, trying to avoid drawing attention to themselves. The stories started the same way most folk tales begin: someone has an experience, perhaps sees something they can't explain, makes up a story about it. The tale gets shared around the fire along with all the songs and stories that are told, and with repeated telling, it grows, changes, evolves. The Cymrion began to be victims of persecution as a result of these stories, and they slowly but surely retreated into their own society, associating less and less with the outside world. Much like the dark elves. Dregor took up the war against them all, taking both dark elves and Cymrion prisoner, burning down their villages . . . there was torture. Many speculate that he was searching for the secret of their magic. He was trying for an all-out genocide. What would you have done in their position?"

Kyer didn't need long to come up with an answer. "I would leave."

Soren nodded. "A generation ago, the dark elves and Cymrion did just that."

Kyer was too busy sitting dumbly to ask any of the many questions that had popped into her mind. Instead she sipped her drink and was pleasantly surprised by its rich flavour. The late hour was unimportant for the moment.

"More sugar?"

Kyer shook her head.

"Mainly because of their connection with the Cymrion, but for other reasons as well, the dark elves did not want uninvited guests, tourists, or explorers like you, if you must know," he added sardonically. "Few people ever knew about the caves' existence, and that number has dwindled to near nothing. Even now, if any of the remaining dark elves knew you were going there, they would not be too happy about it."

Here, Kyer kept her smile cloaked. She doubted that. But Soren went on. "The caves are, in effect, locked."

"Locked?" She hadn't really assumed they would be open-air caves that they could just walk into, but she hadn't given it much thought. She wondered if anyone else had. "Well, couldn't someone just come along and pick the lock? Or even magic it open?" She thought of the magic key Valrayker had given her.

"No, it can't be broken, picked, hewn, magicked, or even blown open with a blasting spell. It is dark elvish and has a dark elvish method of entry." He took a long swallow of *qahwa* and sighed contentedly. "Can't imagine a day starting without some of this."

"It's very good. I've never had it before." She took another sip. "So what exactly is a dark elvish method of entry?"

Soren tapped his foot against the leg of his armchair, as if questioning the wisdom of answering her. He glanced out the window. If the old man did not have such an air of self-assuredness, Kyer might have thought he was nervous. *Please tell me.* His voice, when he finally spoke, was low and secretive. "There is a key." Now that he'd uttered those words, the rest rushed out like pigs escaping their pen. "Not a conventional key, nothing you would recognize as such. I was told by its keeper, or else I would not have guessed. It is a disc," he illustrated with his fingers, "made of rock. One side is virtually covered in an intricate pattern of runes. I was told that entry is absolutely impossible without it."

"How—?" Kyer cleared her throat. "Where do I find the keeper?"

"You can't. She's gone."

"Gone?" Kyer's heart sank.

"But she no longer has it."

"Who does?" Kyer asked anxiously and was afraid she might sound in too much of a hurry. But Soren didn't seem to notice.

"She gave it to me, asking me to deliver it. Certain . . . dangers made me believe I was not a suitable courier. I passed it on, and I'm not sure it was the right thing to do. It's been a long time, and I don't even know if he'll still have it, but you must try if you're going to access the caves."

Perched on the edge of her seat, Kyer thought she might scream with impatience. *Come on, just out with it!*

"There is an outpost southeast of here, a garrison of the Realm Guard. They are positioned there ostensibly to prevent north-south movement by Dregor and to cover the west flank of the Tree of Life. The commanding officer is one Colonel Greenburg. He's a half-elf and understands the dire need for its protection. I placed the key in his care a number of years ago, suggesting that with the army, it would be safer than in my possession. I asked that he transport it further south at some point. It may be he has already done so, though," Soren spread out his hands, "I doubt he has taken the time. Moreover, he believed it made sense for it to remain near the caves. I don't disagree." The old man shrugged. "Still, I'm not fully at ease about it. Speak to him, convince him of your need." He paused and bit his lip.

"What *is* your need? What takes you to the caves?"

"An errand. Kien Bartheylen's wife is ill, and we've been told one of the ingredients for her cure can be found there."

Soren looked stricken but swallowed more *qahwa* and his face cleared. "You know Kien." He crossed one leg over the other. "Which means—" He looked down at his cup and held it in both palms, as if warming them. "You might suggest to Colonel Greenburg that you could transport the key south."

Dark elvish key. Kyer's mind was abuzz but something clicked. "The key needs to go to Dunvehran."

Soren slowly nodded his head.

Kyer sighed. It was obvious. The key would be safest in the hands of a dark elf. Valrayker was the only one left. Unless . . . Kyer thought briefly of the one they'd met in an alpine meadow weeks ago. Huranan Danay. Was he really a dark elf? And if so, were there more wherever he came from?

"And you don't want the key to be traced back to you . . ."

"For"—Soren's face clouded—"several reasons, not the least of which is that the enemy must never gain access to the Indyn Caves. I must plead again for your secrecy."

"You have it," she said. "Maybe the colonel will let us transport the key. At the very least, we could borrow it, and then we can tell Val where it is." Soren looked relieved at the prospect. Kyer gulped down some *qahwa* and heaved a sigh. "Well, that will save us all kinds of time in the long run. I'm deeply grateful to you."

She was. What would have happened if they'd gone straight to the caves, only to discover they could not enter? Would even Kayme have been able to help in this? And Soren was not exaggerating his fear of discovery. Kyer sensed it, rather than requiring proof. He was a swordsman. And something told her that there was more history to him than just that comprised in his weapon collection. No, she couldn't doubt him if she tried.

"Well, I guess it's rather fortuitous that we met."

He smiled. "You might say that."

Without even thinking, Kyer stood up and unbuckled her weapon belt. She deftly slid the carved leather sheath of Brendow's bastard sword off the end. "Here, this is for you." She held it out to him.

Soren's jaw slackened. His back straightened. A new brightness shone in his eyes. "For me?"

She nodded vehemently. "Yes. Absolutely. I can't thank you enough for entrusting me with that information. And I know how reluctant you are to give yourself away. It's all I have, but I can't think of anyone who would appreciate it more."

Soren stared at her in disbelief. She nodded at him and took a step closer, and he finally believed her. He set his mug on the table and rose to accept it.

"This . . . is . . . I am overcome." Thank you. Your gift is of immense value to you; I am well aware of that. And yet you give it to me?"

As he gently lifted it out of her hand, she was stung by a pain in her heart. But she also felt the rightness of what she was doing.

"You can't imagine the gratitude that will be felt by . . . well, a lot of people." She strapped the belt back on and was struck by the emptiness at her left side. In an effort to fill it, she adjusted the straps of her baldric, so the longsword hung lower, and rested her hand on the hilt, appreciating the feeling of it at her side.

The swordfighter held out her hand with a sober expression. "Thank you, Soren Lowey, for a fascinating evening and an informative morning."

"You are most welcome. You will always be welcome in our home, Kyer . . . Halidan. And thank you again. For this. And," he let his eyes twinkle, "I will no longer worry about your incurring the wrath of the dark elves as you enter the caves."

With that, she left the stone house and tore through the town back to the admonishment that undoubtedly awaited her. *What in seven hells am I going to tell them?*

Seventeen

Especially When They're Lying

Kyer burst through the door of the inn. Five heads turned simultaneously to watch her. Phennil's spoon didn't stop scraping up the second to last bite of porridge, which had been served with some kind of berries. Janak licked his fingers as he shoved the last corner of toast into his mouth. As she casually approached the table, she calmed her breathing and smelled the salty aroma of sausage, which made her drool. Adjusting her scabbard, she appraised the mood of the company. Jesqellan, a notoriously slow eater had only half an egg left on his plate. Skimnoddle had a nearly full plate, which he was scarfing as if he hadn't eaten in weeks. *Probably his second helping.* Derry played with the handle on his teacup. She pulled out the nearest chair and sat between Skimnoddle and Jesqellan.

"And it isn't even midday yet," Janak muttered, apparently in response to something she'd missed.

She looked levelly across the table at the captain.

"Be sure to hang on to that rigid stare, Derry. I wouldn't want your finely chiseled features to lose any of their sharpness."

Derry's body swelled perceptibly, but he said nothing, instead tearing his eyes away from her and taking a large sip of tea. He finally spoke with deliberate control. "Sarcasm does not become you."

"Oh, come on, Derry, of course it does! This is me, remember?" She grinned around at the group, most of whom were inclined to agree with her. "Look, I'm sorry I'm late, okay? Does that make you feel better?"

"Much," Derry said.

She leaned back in her chair and opened her hands to the ceiling. "Honestly, you make it difficult for me to feel at all remorseful. I come in here and you're already hostile, without even knowing where I've been and why I'm late. It's as if you don't think there can possibly be a good reason, and you've made up your mind to be angry. I might have been attacked or something."

"You? Attacked?" Janak said.

"Oh," Skimnoddle snorted. "Can't imagine *you* getting into a *fight*!"

"With your sweet temper?" Janak said.

Kyer smiled at them appreciatively, but Phennil looked at Derry anxiously.

She turned to the captain again. "Really, Derry, this accusatory stance is unbecoming of you."

The captain shot her a look that suggested an effort to send her to the fires of hell. She blinked at him and watched him regain control of himself.

"I apologize," he said slowly, through a very tight jaw.

"Accepted," she said with sincerity then winked at Phennil, directly across from her. "Now, first things first. Skimnoddle, how did it go for you?"

Derry dropped his spoon on the table with a clatter and an impatient frown.

"My lady, I humbly beg leave to express, withholding any tones that may be misconstrued as arrogance or self-satisfaction—character traits which I am sure you, dearheart, would not tolerate in a partner, and by the heavens, I am dedicated to the continuance of my suit for your affections—"

"Oh, knock it off. Did you get it or not?" she said.

"I did." He bowed at her resulting grin, and pulled out the bottle. He opened it, and Kyer confirmed that it was tahleema.

The innkeeper arrived then to collect the rest of the empty dishes, and she ordered some sausage and toast. Her feet bounced on her toes, as if she were jittery. She quickly quelled it. All her limbs had taken on a strange restlessness, similar to light-headedness. The *qahwa* was tasty, but it had a weird effect.

Derry sulked, as if he had come to some sort of conclusion about her. Why could he not just ask her straight out where she'd been? He assumed that she'd been up to no good, and her cheeks stung with resentment. Not only that, she had to find a way to impart the news about the rune pattern without giving Soren away.

"How was your evening, Kyer?" Phennil asked cheerfully.

"Fascinating." This was not a lie.

"Young Tod make for good company, then?" Janak said, with a nudge at Skimnoddle, who smirked. She just smiled, letting them interpret that as they may, and glanced at Derry. *So he told them who I left with, hunh? Nice guy.* But perhaps that would be the best way to avoid mentioning Soren. She recalled the sight of the handsome captain leaving the party with an adoring girl on his arm. "How was your evening, Derry?" she said softly. His peevishness fed her ill behaviour. Derry brought the worst out in her, just with his attitude.

"Not nearly as interesting as yours, it would seem," came the reply.

"I don't know; you appeared to have attracted more than your fair share of attention," she remarked.

"I was *dancing*," he clarified. "I walked a young lady home and returned here."

Jesqellan turned to Kyer as the innkeeper set a plate of food before her. "You did not return to the inn?" he asked rhetorically.

"There really wasn't a point," she said. "Not much left of the night by the time we were through what we were doing." Again leaving things open to interpretation. *I'm not lying; I'm just omitting certain truths.*

Derry poured himself some more tea.

"Now perhaps we can begin the discussion we ought to have started some time ago." The captain looked purposefully away from Kyer and toward Janak and Phennil. "With our deepest thanks to Skimnoddle, we have achieved what we came here to do. So where do we go from here? Which is the best route to the Indyn Caves?"

"We can't go straight there, " Kyer blurted through a mouthful of sausage before anyone else could speak.

Derry turned to her with some annoyance. "What are you talking about?" he snapped. Kyer reached for her cup of water, and her hand shook.

"What is the matter, Kyer?" Jesqellan said.

"I'm all right." She took a long draught. "I had a hot drink called *qahwa* this morning. I think that's all this is."

"*Qahwa?*" Jesqellan said. "Does that not come from Hamara? How did your young host come by it?" He asked with somewhat exaggerated curiosity that irritated Kyer. Why were these two reacting like this? Was lateness such a heinous crime?

A haughty tone crept into her voice. "He is a very worldly man, as it turns out." *Soren was my host, after all.*

"Very *well*, then." Derry was trying to regain control of the discussion. "What were you going to say, Kyer? About the caves."

She swallowed her bite before speaking this time and checked around their table for unwanted attention. In a low voice, she said, "Only that I was told we need a certain key to gain entry to the caves. The doors are essentially locked, and without the key, we won't get in."

"What sort of key? What does it look like?" Jesqellan asked.

"It's a pattern of runes on a stone. I was told it might be in the possession of a Colonel Greenburg at the army garrison stationed about two days southeast of here."

"Who told you?" Skimnoddle said. "Lightning strike me through my heart if I should ever hold your words in any doubt, fairest lady, but for the good of our responsibility to our mission, I ask if the source is a reliable one? Any loss of time could, as you well know, prove disastrous."

"Yes, and we've already lost time along the way because of interruptions."

She let Derry's insinuation bypass her. She had only then realized her mistake. She should not have said she was *told* anything. If whomever Soren feared learned that there was someone in Seaview who knew about the rune pattern, regardless of whether she revealed his identity, Soren would be tracked down. She had vowed to not expose his existence. Thinking quickly, she said, "I had another dream last night." Silence. Would they believe her? It was not so unlikely a story.

"How does this key work? It doesn't sound like a regular key," Janak said.

Kyer swallowed. *Shit! He never told me.* She hoped her sudden attack of panic wasn't plastered all over her face. He had probably meant to tell her but got sidetracked when he learned she knew Valrayker. Now it was too late. "Maybe," she faltered, "maybe it'll be clear when we get there. Like the other things have been." Could she sneak back to his house?

Derry turned his tea cup round and round. "Well, that settles it. We go southeast. And to make up for the delay, we'd better leave as soon as we are able."

"There's one further question," Janak piped in with a grimace at Kyer.

"And that is?" said Derry.

"Why *were* you late this morning, Kyer? Tod keeping you busy?" He was grinning wickedly, but certain others at the table clearly wanted the answer.

Kyer hesitated. On the one hand, it pleased her to be asked a straight question. On the other, she hadn't managed to come up with an answer that wouldn't give Soren away. Finally she decided to brave the worst and take the blow herself. With a shrug, she adopted a look of guilty embarrassment.

"Yup, that's pretty much it, if you must know every detail of my private life. Tod was . . . well, he's young and, uh, you know, insatiable." She gave Derry a wink and said coyly, "Sorry to have kept you all waiting." Better that Derry be angry with her than she break her vow to Soren.

Suddenly Tod rushed into the room, panting and red faced. He found her among the patrons and hastened over. She leapt to her feet.

"I'm so glad you haven't left yet," he said. She glared a warning at him. *Don't ruin anything!* Her companions eyed the situation with keen interest, and Kyer felt heat rush from her neck to her scalp.

"I have one more thing to say to you before you go." Tod lifted his chin proudly.

"Wait!" Kyer grabbed his arm. "Let's take this outside, shall we?" She guided him out the door. "I've been muffing my way through keeping my visit with your grandfather a secret."

He nodded. "Grandda will appreciate it, I guess. But he forgot to tell you this, he said."

"All right."

Tod recited:

"Breathtaking to behold
Vision alone will win your day
I touch you only with my eyes
Red light will point your way."

"What's that supposed to mean?"

He shrugged. "He didn't tell me. He said you'd understand."

Great, she said to herself. *Riddles.* "Thanks for telling me."

With a short bow, he was about to leave.

"Wait." Kyer put a hand on his arm. "Do me a favour. Hug me."

The boy looked puzzled but nodded. He reached out and they put their arms around each other. She kissed him on the cheek. He left hurriedly. She lingered just a moment before heading back through the door, where her friends were, as she predicted, watching her through the window. She strode to the table.

"What?" she demanded.

"Well, that's true love, all right," Janak snorted, and she grinned, more from relief than anything. Meeting Phennil's eye, Kyer was puzzled by the look on his face.

The captain's ice-cold glare she ignored as she turned and left the dining room.

Kyer was a colourful blend of emotions as she retrieved her things. Relieved that she'd covered her slip-up. Grateful that Tod hadn't said anything to expose Soren. But terrifically confused about Tod's words. Something to do with the key? A dismayingly cryptic message. Oh well, she had two days to figure it out.

She was also confused about Derry. Derry was angry but there was nothing she could do about it. Upon learning he had spent the evening alone, she'd been flooded with a bizarre uplifting feeling, and yet, recalling the sting of the captain's remarks this morning, she was glad she hadn't made a fool of herself by asking him to teach her to dance.

"Tod, my grandson," said Soren Lowey that evening as the two settled into their armchairs to have their tea. The gift from the young warrior lay across his lap, and he stroked the carved sheath thoughtfully.

"Yes, Grandda?"

"It's time I went on a trip."

"A trip, Grandda?"

"Yes. To see an old friend, to whom a visit is long overdue. I think it's time. Now that I know where to find him. I will leave day after tomorrow."

"All right."

"Look after your mam and sister, and the collection."

"Of course."

I am anxious to see his reaction when I show him his sword! The old man chuckled softly to himself.

The journey over rolling grasslands might have been pleasant on a warm day. The sun that had blinded Kyer as she awakened in Soren Lowey's front room had been eclipsed by savage coal grey clouds. A chill wind off the sea ushered the party out of town, and as if to make it clear they should be on their way, the saturated clouds began to purge themselves. Within an hour of their departure the travellers were equally saturated, and there was no sign of those ominous vessels being depleted. The lanolin in their woollen cloaks did much to withhold the moisture, but the liquid won in the end, coming as it did from all sides, splashing up from the ground, off horses' hooves, running down manes, streaming on leather equipment.

"I'm reminded of the last time we left Wanaka," Janak shouted above the drops pounding against the hard ground.

Kyer had to twist her entire upper body to look at him from within her hood. "You're just lucky you didn't have to fight four people in the dark and this kind of rain like Derry and I did, eh, Derry?"

Derry merely grunted. *Boy, is he ever in a mood.* Kyer scowled. She nudged Trig in the sides, and together they trotted up to see over the next rise. At the crest, a dark shape darted across the path, and Trig was startled by a shriek and a hiss. He stopped suddenly, throwing Kyer over his neck. She landed with a soppy thud on the wet ground and half slid, half rolled down the slope. The badger flattened itself out, hissed again at Trig, who, to Kyer's relief, had remained at the top of the hillock, unharmed. The badger scampered off to its den in the hillside.

"Kyer!" Phennil called. "Are you all right?"

Kyer checked herself over before struggling to her feet in the muck. "Just some bruises, I think." She shook out her wet cloak. The others led their horses around the side to a less steep slope.

Derry did not dismount but asked in his best physicker's tone, "Okay, then?"

She nodded. "Nothing worse than a little mortification."

"You were lucky," he remarked and moved on.

Kyer double-checked Trig's legs to make sure he had suffered no damage. She mounted and followed the group.

Phennil was puzzled about a few things as he held Leoht to a trot behind Skimnoddle's pony. He sensed the tension in the party as well as anybody else. Jesqellan, preoccupied about something, was even quieter than usual, and his eye had honed in on Kyer off and on all morning. The sparks between Kyer and Derry were about as subtle as fireworks, and the rain hadn't snuffed them. It was a relationship Phennil was having a hard time figuring out.

It was tricky to look at it objectively, though. Phennil was fond of Kyer and not so fond of Derry. That lack of fondness was reciprocal, Phennil knew well. Derry tolerated him and Phennil did his best to avoid aggravating the proud captain whose expectations were so high. The more he tried to perform to Derry's exacting standards, the worse things became, and the elf was aware of every impatient glance and suppressed sigh of frustration precipitated by him. However, between Kyer and Derry, things were decidedly different.

On one hand, the captain seemed to lose patience with Kyer more quickly than with anyone else in the party. Yet on the other hand, Phennil observed that Derry put up with a whole lot more nonsense from Kyer than he did from anyone else. Nobody minded, nor even appeared to notice except him, but the elf knew that he himself would never have gotten away with berating the captain so boldly, especially in front of the rest of the group. Phennil couldn't fathom what was going on there, but he had a foreboding feeling that something would ignite soon.

As for Kyer herself, there were some inconsistencies in her story this morning, which didn't make sense to him. He could not imagine that Kyer would outright *lie* but the elf could see no other explanation. First of all, she had been more than an hour and a half late. Entirely unlike her. Even if she had been occupied with Tod, Phennil could not bring himself to believe that she would be so enraptured with the youth that she'd disregard a meeting such as that. For her to be late, she had to have been doing something of much greater import than she had admitted to, and he had no clue what it could be, or why she would not reveal it. Derry hadn't noticed this inconsistency with her character. *Hadn't noticed or had chosen to ignore?*

Secondly, Phennil and Derry had arrived early for breakfast. Clearly Derry had forgotten, but Tod had come into the Happy Beerbarrel with a note for the innkeeper shortly after they'd ordered their tea. The lad had even waved to them, too out of breath from dashing through the streets to speak. So how could he and Kyer have been . . . ?

No, she was definitely not truthful about what had kept her this morning. Someone worldly who had given her *qahwa* and held her attention with something of great importance for an hour and a half.

The third thing was what happened at breakfast. Even if Kyer and Tod had spent all that time together, which Phennil didn't believe, why would Kyer's face have flooded with fear when the youth came through the door? *Puzzling.*

And the strangest thing of all was the absence of a particular item that normally hung at her left side.

He decided to say nothing about it for now or risk being told off.

"In a hollow we'll drown," said Phennil.

"On a high point we'll be seen far and wide," argued Jesqellan.

"If we're that visible, then whoever wants to see us has been watching us all day." Derry's tone was far drier than the land, and it was agreed. They set up a dismal little camp on the crest of a wave in the grassy sea.

Everything from the ground up was drenched. The very air presented a danger of drowning. There would be no fire here, not even a conjured one. The rain had alternated between "heavy" and "downpour" throughout the day and had at no point relented. The sleeping quarters, with no trees around to fashion tent poles for the tent cloth, were a choice of "wet" or "sopping." Supper was whatever cold bits they had in their saddlebags.

Seated on her bedroll, in the relative shelter provided by Trig, Kyer puzzled over what she could have done to get Derry so riled up. For the life of her, she could think of nothing. Yes, she was late for breakfast, but she arrived with important news. He might still be thinking of her taking the wrong direction after the incident with Fredric, though she thought it had been explained well enough. Going to get the sword? Surely he wouldn't be so bothered by that. Of course her initial blunder in Plicatha was what started it all.

Still, she did not understand his behaviour. Perhaps she ought to ask him straight out. *Why are you being so moody with me?* No, that would just put him on the defensive. *Is there something you'd like to tell me or ask me?* Closer, but she'd probably louse up the delivery and sound all accusatory, and he'd get defensive again. *There's something very wrong with our communication.* She gave it up. It would come out sometime; these things always did. Though admittedly, it was never pleasant.

"Well, I sure know that Jesqellan doesn't much care for slugs, particularly giant ones," Phennil was saying. "For myself, I'd have to say it has to be making a mistake that turns out to be fatal." He glanced at Kyer as he said this, and since she was clearly supposed to understand what he meant, she gave him a knowing smile and struggled to guess the topic of their conversation.

"My biggest fear in all this is finding everything we need but arriving at Bartheylen Castle a day too late," Derry said, and this time his remark did not seem to be aimed at Kyer. She risked a response.

"That won't happen. We have to keep believing that."

He said nothing more.

"What about wolves?" Janak said. "The chilling howl of wolves at night has always given me shivers."

"Not I," Jesqellan said. "You might say I have an affinity with wolves."

"Ah, of course," Janak said as if the two of them shared a secret.

"For me," Skimnoddle announced, "I fear no other than being spurned by my deepest love."

Kyer groaned. "You live that every day of your life."

"Crushed! Oh, I am slain, virtually." The halfling tipped over on his blanket.

"I've never been keen on ticks," Phennil put in.

"My mother faints if she sees a frog," said Kyer.

"Grizzlies," Derry said sensibly.

"Snakes," Janak said.

"The snake is a symbol of undying love," Kyer said.

She couldn't have ended the conversation more abruptly if she'd whipped out her sword and sliced someone's head off.

Jesqellan leapt to his feet, staring at her, the whites of his eyes bright in the dusk. The wind swooping around them drew their attention to the fact that the rain had finally stopped. The ensuing silence quivered.

"What did you say?" The mage gaped at her as if she'd called his mother a whore.

Puzzlement and disbelief rushing through her, Kyer waited for something to hit her in the dark. "The snake . . . it's . . . apparently . . . a symbol of undying love. You know, the snake holds its tail in its teeth, making a perfect circle." When nothing struck her, she carried on. "I heard it somewhere. What's it to you?"

All eyes were on Jesqellan—*for a change*, Kyer thought—and he gathered his robes into his arms and shook out the dampness. In the dark it was hard to tell, but Kyer thought he might be doing so to make it appear as if that was why he'd jumped up.

"Um, it's . . . an interesting concept," he said. "Surprising. In my experience, the snake has always been associated with evil. I'm going to give it some thought."

He whirled around and walked off, leaving the rest of them to wonder what had shocked him.

Kyer wished she hadn't said anything.

Late afternoon on the third day since leaving Seaview, the hills rolled them within view of the northwest encampment of the Realm Guard. It was laid out in a neat quadrilateral pattern with a defensive ditch surrounding the perimeter. There were mostly tents, some large, some small, and a few more permanent structures. A couple of hundred head of horses grazed in the northeast corner by some makeshift stables, beyond that some men worked in a garden large enough to supply the camp. Outside the western gate, a grid of tiny white posts indicated a graveyard. Kyer's inexpert guess was that the camp housed several hundred soldiers.

Now that they were here, Kyer was starting to worry about Soren's message; she was no nearer to solving the riddle and could only hope that seeing the key would bring something to mind. As they approached the encampment, they discussed their arrival.

"Let us storm them!" Skimnoddle said dramatically.

"You know, I'm certain you just say stuff to get a reaction," Kyer said.

"We will simply ride in and ask to meet with the commanding officer," Derry said. "This is a peaceful mission, and I can think of no reason why they would deny us what we ask, so there is no need for aggression on our part."

"Actually, Derry," Kyer said softly, "the key is somewhat of a secret. He may very well deny us. Maybe I should do the talking since I know what we're looking for?"

He didn't meet her eye. "No, thank you. I know how to employ the necessary diplomacy."

Kyer clamped her teeth shut. *Stubborn fool.*

They rode their mounts slowly down the hill with Jesqellan walking swiftly alongside Janak. Flags bearing the Guarded Realm insignia waved non-committally from poles on either side of the entrance to the compound. Sentries bustled to position, upon seeing the approaching riders. Kyer surmised that visitors here in the bleak north must be few and far between.

When they were about twenty paces away, they dismounted and approached on foot. A guard hailed the party.

"Who comes?"

"We are emissaries from the Dukes Kien Bartheylen and Valrayker of Equart, on a mission of the utmost importance. We would speak to your commanding officer," Derry said in a polite yet authoritative voice.

The sentry gestured to a soldier who departed down the main aisle of tents at a fast walk. They waited patiently for several minutes while the message was sent to its recipient. When the soldier returned, he spoke in a low voice to the sentry. The sentry addressed Derry again. "Major Gilvray will see you."

Gilvray? Kyer thought with a small measure of concern. *What about Greenburg?*

The sentry turned to another guard. "Please take our guests' mounts and stable them."

"Perhaps it would be wiser to leave our horses here at the gate," Derry suggested. "Our errand is but short, and we do not intend to tarry." The guard gestured for them to follow him. Four more of the guards fell in step behind Kyer and Phennil.

They were led through the makeshift gateway and down the path through the centre of the camp. Large tents flanked the path with a series of smaller tents erected around and behind these. Some of the tents had been replaced with thatch-roofed huts in an effort to give an air of permanence and comfort. Mud had overtaken the grass in the duration of the garrison's sojourn in this location, though it was still lush around the tents where traffic was infrequent. The mud, refreshed by the recent downpours, squelched under Kyer's boots, and she wondered, not for the first time, how Jesqellan could stand going constantly barefoot.

A long, low hut skulked in roughly the centre of the encampment: a well was directly outside. *The kitchen?* Kyer guessed. The Guarded Realm colours peeked out frequently from among the huts, brightening the dingy green and brown of the structures. *They must do all they can to stay cheerful.*

Just beyond the dining hut, the party made an abrupt turn to the left and passed a few more of the smaller tents before stopping in front of a small log cabin. The banner of the Guarded Realm hung limply from the roof, its silver tree dulled to a moody grey on a faded green field. Another hint of the duration of the army's posting. A polished brass bell hung on a hook just beside the wooden door.

Their escort knocked, opened the door, and entered.

"The emissaries from the south, sir." He held the door open for the guests to pass through. They followed Derry into the cabin. The four extra guards waited outside.

The ceiling was high enough for even Derry and Phennil to stand upright. Oiled sheepskin on the windows dimmed the light, but her eyes adjusted quickly as Kyer positioned herself on the left end of her group. Before them in the left corner was a table that doubled as a desk, littered with sheets of parchment, quills and ink, penknife, and a stack of mail awaiting attention. Rising and coming around from behind the desk was a man, human, a few years beyond forty, with jagged, greying dark hair and his hand extended. His beard was neat and peppered with a few grey whiskers. His high, black infantry boots made little sound as he stepped across the thickly woven straw mats that gave the illusion of a floor.

"I am Major Ryerson Gilvray. Welcome." He spoke with the lilting accent of the northern region. A little shorter than Derry, though of larger build, with an oblong face that was friendly yet weather worn and hardened by his cause to defend the north. A chain mail coat hung out from below his dark green sleeveless tabard emblazoned with the Tree of Life. A dagger poked out of its sheath next to a fist-sized, flat pouch at his waist. His left side held his sword, its leather-covered grip looking as if it had recently been freshly restored. A man who cared about his weapon, then, and took the time to maintain its condition in spite of his somewhat isolated posting. Kyer pictured him donning his weapon belt in honour of their arrival. His eyes were dark and curious, but he was smiling, as if glad for the novelty of visitors from the southern, civilized regions.

Derry shook his hand, introducing himself, then stated the names of the other five. The officer shook each hand, scrutinizing each face. Kyer guessed that in spite of his friendly appearance, this was not a man who would be an easy target of duplicity. When Derry announced her name, Major Gilvray's face lit up in surprise as he took her hand.

"Well, I must apologize. I did not notice until now that you are a woman."

Studying him, Kyer saw something more. A kind of hunger. How long had he been posted up here? Retrieving her hand, she said, "No apology necessary. I'm a warrior like any other and need no special consideration."

He bowed. "Well met, all the same." His eyes rested on her a moment longer before he moved to his desk. Shifting his quills and ink bottle, he made room to lean on the front of it, next to what looked to Kyer like a picture frame. With its back to her, she could not see whose portrait it displayed.

Derry's emotionless gaze was on Kyer, and he shifted his feet. She looked at him blankly. *It's not my fault.*

Major Gilvray waved away the two guards before he spoke again. "I have not enough chairs to offer one to each of you. Please accept my apologies for the lack of hospitality."

There wasn't enough room for more chairs. One behind the desk, one right in front of her. Army cot with tick mattress in the far corner. Chest, wardrobe, brazier with dead coals. Washstand between bed and desk. At least the army gave him nice curtains.

Derry waved his hand. "I'm sure you rarely receive visitors."

"True enough. Most people don't venture into such lands as these. And usually our guests are military men or councilmen. Not nearly as … colourful as your party." His face was glued to Derry's with such a look of concentration that Kyer got the feeling he was fighting to avoid passing another glance over the guests, herself included.

"We have been directed to speak to Colonel Greenburg," Derry said. "Is he here?"

"Colonel Greenburg has been away these five weeks," Gilvray replied.

Oh no! Kyer chewed on the inside of her cheek.

Gilvray continued. "He is travelling to meet with other commanding officers for a war council. I am commander here in his stead. I hope I might be able to help you?"

Kyer watched the major's face closely as Derry outlined the circumstances of Alon's illness, fulfilling his promise of diplomacy. Gilvray listened attentively.

"One of the ingredients we need for the antidote," Derry said, "is a dust that we are told can be found in the ancient Indyn Caves."

At this, the major's brows lifted slightly.

"Our sources," Derry went on, "tell us that we cannot simply enter the caves; we require a certain key. It is a pity Colonel Greenburg is not here, as we were given to believe he might be in possession of it. Of course, as his second in command, you must know of it. Please will you allow us its use for a short time, so we may obtain the ingredient necessary to save Alon Maer's life?"

A strange frown flitted over the officer's face, gravity edged with what Kyer perceived to be a hint of uncertainty in his creased brow. He drummed his fingers lightly on the table.

"I must tell you that I am perplexed. I have heard of these caves through myth and legend. Or so I thought. I have certainly never seen them. Who is this source who told you of their existence with such certainty?"

"The wizard Kayme gave us the recipe for the antidote, and we have no reason to doubt his knowledge," Derry said.

"Yes, I suppose." The major folded his arms on his chest. "If he is right —and I say, if—there must be considerable magic empowered in them. I would be apprehensive to even seek them out, would not you?"

"We know of the potential danger, Major, and I beg of you not to be concerned on our account," Derry assured him. "Our greater fear lies in the consequence of our not securing the substance we require." His tone was a strong reminder of their urgency. "What of the key?"

The major shifted his position. "You are braver folk than I," he said with a smile. "Yet I regret that I cannot help you. Someone has told you that I have possession of this key. Sadly, your source has misled you. I know of no such item."

Kyer had to enter the conversation. "It's not something you would recognize as a key," she told him. "It's a stone disc covered with runes in a complex pattern. Are you sure this doesn't sound familiar?" She observed his reaction intently.

Phennil snatched Gilvray's attention before he was forced to respond. "What about Colonel Greenburg," the elf put in hopefully. "Does he know of the runes?"

"No more than I, good elf," was the response. "I possess the same knowledge as does my commander, or else how could I possibly hope to be an effective leader while he is absent? My duty is to protect the North from the forces of Dregor, and regrettably, that does not involve the pastime of exploring mythological sites. I am not an archaeologist." He chuckled.

Kyer frowned. The others shifted uneasily in the confused silence. Derry couldn't have made it plainer that this was the only way to save Alon Maer's life, so if he knew of the runes, surely he would say so. *He seems awfully keen to deny the caves' existence.*

"Has the colonel *never* mentioned the key to you?" Kyer asked cautiously. "He would have acquired it a few years ago." Derry peered at her.

"Kien and Valrayker are your allies," Janak reminded him. "What about supporting the other duchies that cover the lines to the south?"

"Kien and Valrayker do a fine job, good dwarf," Major Gilvray said sternly. "However, my first responsibility is not to them, but to the Tree of Life and the Indyn Hills."

"Why protect the Indyn Hills so vigilantly if the caves don't exist?" Kyer muttered.

The major shot a startled look her way but recovered quickly. She felt the chill of Derry's frozen glare without even glancing at him. "I am the commander of five hundred men, young lady," Gilvray replied. "We have been in this vicinity for five years, fighting armies of orcs and madmen who are commanded by the maddest of them all. I hardly am under obligation to justify myself to you."

Clanging swords from a battle practice some distance away reverberated through the camp.

Gilvray broke the stillness. "My friends, this is getting you nowhere. My thoughts and best wishes go with you for the lady's recovery, but I am sadly unable to produce the item you're looking for. I am no alchemist, or I'd produce something from nothing."

Derry was nothing if not a diplomat. "We are warriors, Major, all too familiar with the type of work you are doing here in the North, and we thank you for your continued efforts to thwart enemy forces." His soft voice was filled with emotion. Kyer felt his sorrow at their failure and what it would mean for his lord's best friends. "We will trouble you no further on this matter. I only hope that we are able to find another source of the ingredient we need to complete the mixture. There are two lives at stake, and one of them is the only heir to Kien's throne." He bowed and turned to leave the cabin. The others followed him. Major Gilvray put his hand on Kyer's arm as she took a step. She stopped and her green eyes pierced into his like over-bright flames. He flinched.

"Dear lady, I sincerely regret that I cannot help you," he said. "I am sorry."

Kyer's voice was like the chilly rain of yesterday. "I don't know why you're apologizing to me. I'm not Kien Bartheylen. Nor am I his dying wife."

"Still—" He hesitated before completing the thought. "I wish we might have met under . . . alternate circumstances."

With a curt nod, she exited. Her friends awaited her with sober faces.

The major followed her out. "My friends, it approaches evening. Please set up your camp for the night near to ours and feel free to avail yourselves of our food and water . . . and anything else we can provide you."

Derry bowed and thanked him, accepting the gesture. The party returned to the horses and rode a short distance south of the encampment to set up their own camp for the night. Only when they were safely separated from the soldiers did they comment on the meeting.

"Well, Derry, we did the best we could," Phennil said tentatively as he wiped down Leoht's coat. "I mean, you were polite and said everything that had to be said and didn't get angry or anything. You didn't even sound as if you were begging! I don't think I could have said any of it better myself."

"That's for sure." Janak had an all new reason to glower.

"I do not understand it," Jesqellan said. "How could Kayme have been wrong when he's been right about everything else? Are you sure you interpreted the dream correctly, Kyer?"

Derry, who had suppressed his new anger at Kyer, let it spill over. "And once again, Kyer, you—why can you not hold your tongue?" He shook his grooming brush at her. "We do not want Gilvray and his *entire army* as our enemies! People don't take kindly to having their word doubted."

"Most especially when they're lying," Kyer snapped, and Derry looked as though she'd slapped him in the face. "I have not misinterpreted the dream. Kayme is not wrong," Kyer said with finality. "Major Gilvray is hiding something."

Derry puffed out his exasperation. "How can you say that, Kyer? What reason can he possibly have for giving false information?"

"All kinds of reasons. Honestly, don't you people have *eyes*? Couldn't you see the wheels turning in his head when I described the key? He was obviously wary. And that line about alchemy? Bet he felt pretty clever over that one. He's full of shit."

Eighteen

This Burning Betrayal

Jesqellan did not understand it and could not block out his puzzlement, though he was supposed to be meditating. Kyer had revealed herself when she told them about the snake's symbolism. To his dismay, Fredric was right, and yet . . . why was she still working so hard to cover up? Accusing Gilvray of lying instead of accepting his word? That would have been more characteristic of someone trying to prevent the success of the mission. Still . . . she'd slipped up last night, as Fredric had said she would. Maybe she was attempting to cover her mistake by representing their side so vehemently. *I think now is the time to discuss this with the captain*, he decided. *I don't think I'll tell him about the Gating. Not yet.* He would put off that humiliation as long as possible.

The wind was picking up. It already bore an unpleasant resemblance to the Cold Fells. The fire provided warmth, but the meagre promise of a meal from their rations gave little comfort to empty bellies. The mood of the group was weird. Kyer could describe it no other way. Derry sat hunched as though he were simmering inside. Janak painted his battle axe with his Oil of Unbreaking while grumbling about every notion that popped into his head.

Even after his meditation, Jesqellan was as nervous as a grasshopper. Phennil, the one who could usually be counted on for his good cheer, slumped like someone who'd been swindled out of his horse and all his belongings. Skimnoddle's odd muteness didn't help either. Kyer herself was preoccupied trying to decipher the riddle. *Breathtaking to behold, Vision alone will win your day, I touch you only with my eyes, Red light will point your way.* None of it made sense. What was so breathtaking that would win her day? Something about how the key worked, of course, it had to be, but there weren't any decent verbs in the poem to tell her what to do. She gave it up and unbuckled her baldric and laid it on her bed.

Her own frustration and impatience were of no help to the mood. "I'm going to take Gilvray up on his offer of food." Hastily she slung all the waterskins across her shoulders and bolted before anyone could offer to help her. She hoped the group would be too inattentive to be offended that she needed to get away from them. The short walk back to the army camp increased her blood circulation too, a handy side effect in this wind.

The guard at the south entrance let her pass after she explained her errand, and she walked along the path looking for the well and the mess tent. The layout of the camp from the south entrance was a different configuration from what she'd seen when they'd entered from the north end earlier. The sun had sunk too, and the minimal torchlight only exaggerated the labyrinthine effect of the greenish canvas and wood.

A few soldiers milled about, unsurprised at the presence of a stranger, though Kyer felt the touch of their passing gazes. Word of the major's visitors must have spread. Kyer turned down the aisle where she thought she had seen the well earlier, but she was wrong. She took a few more corners around tents, keeping to the more worn paths. *All these damn tents look identical.* By the time she realized she was lost, everyone had disappeared. *Must be mealtime.*

Suddenly she heard low voices from around the next tent.

She could have approached and asked the whereabouts of the well, but some instinct forbade her. Perhaps it was the hushed tones. Instead she crept closer, her footfalls inaudible in the grass. Glancing through the dim twilight to ensure that she was not being watched, Kyer put the waterskins down and lowered herself to the ground. She peered around the corner and was surprised to see Major Gilvray sitting on a stool. His broad shoulders blocked Kyer's view of the blue-capped officer to whom he spoke. The latter held a lantern in one hand, and the two were gazing intently at a small, flat object in the major's fingers. With their backs to the tent that shielded Kyer and their complete focus on the object, she was undetected. For the moment.

As she listened to their words, her surprise turned to amazement. Then to gratification.

"I never looked at it very closely before." Gilvray was speaking. "The colonel told me to keep it safe, but that was all. I never gave it much thought. Look at these intricate patterns! It's breathtaking."

"Does this correspond to some of the runes on the door, then?" Blue Cap asked.

"Yes, I guess so. It must. You've seen the doors; it would be next to impossible to pick the right fragment without it."

Lying bastard! Kyer thought triumphantly. *He has too seen the caves.*

"Why'd the colonel leave it with you?"

"I guess he thought it would be safer here than on him if he were waylaid." Gilvray's voice quivered with excitement, his well-defined cheekbone lifting as he smiled. "I'd more or less forgotten about it, but then these people arrived and described this very thing. It must be the key they're after."

He didn't even know what he had till I told him.

The younger man shrugged. "Why not give it to the emissaries, then?"

The major paused and gave a sigh. "I didn't trust them," he said pensively, as if he were thinking about it for the first time. "Not many people know about the caves. Suddenly along come half a dozen people saying they are from Duke Bartheylen, speaking of the caves as if they're common knowledge *and* asking for a certain key, which almost nobody knows about. I didn't even know about it.

"They say they got the information from Kayme. Even if that's true, since when did an association with Kayme ever make anyone trustworthy, with his reputation? Besides, what if it wasn't true? Perhaps they heard the story from some other source? Some evil source. Who's to say these people aren't working for Dregor and are after the magic that is reputedly contained in the caves?"

Gilvray is not a bad man, Kyer told herself. *He's just sadly misguided.*

"Why not go with them?"

Gilvray gave a grunt that sounded like consideration. "I could have, but think about it: We arrive at the caves, and then what? Let's say they somehow managed to get in. Do I allow them to roam freely around inside a place I've never been to? That to my knowledge, nobody's ever been to, not even the colonel? All for some sort of . . . dust. No, I can't imagine any good coming of it."

"Not worth the risk, I guess."

"No, this is my last chance, thanks to my less-than-stellar performance in the Black Mountains."

"Those raiders had some sort of magic on them," Blue Cap said. "'How else could they have escaped without even leaving footprints in the snow?"

"I know it and truly Colonel Greenburg did too, which is why I'm getting a second chance at all. It was still my mission and my responsibility. I've got this command for three more weeks. If I botch it up in any way, the colonel will send me north of the Sea of Khûn and I won't get home for another six months. I had to choose between risking the wrath of the colonel and risking that some southern duke's pregnant wife may or may not be sick. Which do you think is closer to my heart?"

From her concealed position, Kyer fumed.

The two men were silent for a moment, studying the stone disc.

"Do you touch this to the section on the door, then?" Blue Cap asked.

"Well, that makes sense. Like fitting a regular key into a lock." Gilvray stared at the rune pattern thoughtfully for another moment; then he tucked it in the flat pouch that was attached to his belt.

Blue Cap lowered his voice. "You should try it before the colonel gets back."

Kyer had heard and seen enough. She was already in danger of discovery by wandering sentries. Shifting slowly backward, she picked up the waterskins again and hastened away. She couldn't wait to tell Derry she was right about Gilvray.

She'd happened upon the exact location of the key. Now, how to get hold of it? The final vestiges of sunlight had faded completely now. She trotted along the torchless path, peeking down alleys in search of the well and the kitchen. A shriek nearly escaped her as she collided with a large form in dark blue. She was still trembling with the excitement at what she had just learned. The soldier grabbed her arm with one big hand and drew a dagger with the other.

"Who are you and what are you doing here?" he growled.

"I am a guest of Major Gilvray," she said confidently.

"Oh? And why then are you skulking around in the dark like a frightened rabbit?'

"I was . . . looking for the well." She grinned sheepishly and indicated the several waterskins over her shoulders. "I got lost and I confess I was a little nervous in the dark." She shuddered at the self-deprecating lie, but she could hardly tell him the real reason she was in a hurry.

He looked her over and with the dagger, drew aside her cloak to see the way she was dressed. She wore no sword, but he saw her leather armour and dagger. He grimaced, clearly concluding that she was no threat. "Oh, you're the female that came along with Duke Bartheylen's men!" His round face scrunched into a leer. Kyer seethed, clenching and unclenching her fists to restrain herself from any form of self-defence. This was not the time or place to prove her worth as a warrior.

"Yes, I . . . came along with them." The muscles in her back twitched and she instructed her hand not to go for her weapon. The oaf just chuckled and put his arm around her, guiding her toward the well, which she now saw was only a few paces away. She pasted on a girlish smile and thanked him. "Major Gilvray has offered us some food as well," she added. "Do you think you could help me out with that?"

"Sure, girly, I'll get you some supper for your men."

He patted her cheek, and she bristled but maintained her smile. He lumbered off toward the mess tent. She made a face at his back as she hauled the bucket up from the depths of the well. By the time she had filled all the skins, the big fellow was back, and this time he had brought a blond-haired friend. They each carried a sack of foodstuffs.

"Here you go, little lady. Can you carry all that?" Round Face said. Blondie was no better.

"Better hurry back now. All your men will be wondering where their supper is!"

"How do you manage to keep them all warm at once, honey? You must have one big tent!"

Kyer didn't bother thanking them for all their help and wasn't surprised when they didn't notice that she wasn't feeble, having hoisted the sacks easily. She stomped away as swiftly as her dignity would allow and let the continued stream of suggestive comments and laughter that followed her drift off into the night.

Now how to get that stone from Major Gilvray? She hurried to the camp, anxious to tell the others what she had learned.

Jesqellan's voice broke Derry out of his troubled thoughts. "Derry, a moment?"

"I think I can spare several moments if you like," Derry said wryly, poking at the fire with a stick. The other three were seated facing each other, playing some sort of word game. Laughter erupted from them periodically, but Derry wasn't paying attention.

"I see our fire is getting low. Shall we fetch more wood?"

Derry rose and followed him.

The army's woodpile was easily accessible and they had already availed themselves of a small portion of it. They would indeed need more to get them through the sharp chill of the night.

Jesqellan gathered his robes about himself and spoke into the chill air as they walked. "We began a conversation a while back about Kyer, how I don't know what to make of her, the magic I sense on her."

Derry thanked the gathering dusk for concealing the roll of his eyes at Kyer's name. It was unbecoming of a captain, but *this* captain was at the end of his rope where that woman was concerned. And the rope was beginning to fray. *I am sure most knights in training don't have to deal with anyone like Kyer.* "What else?" he said. "More breaches of conduct to add to her list of irresponsible actions?"

"To tell you the truth, I am relieved that you are in this frame of mind." The mage collected his thoughts over the next few steps. "What I have to tell you will be hard to accept, but I believe you will be more open to it now than you would have before."

Derry sighed, preparing for the worst. "Yes?"

Jesqellan plunged ahead. "I know why Kyer met with Fredric."

As they picked up firewood, Jesqellan talked. About Fredric's integrity and love for Kien, about the blue snake necklace that was really a *Malison,* about Kyer's dedication to the mission for the purpose of seeing her own carried out. Derry listened wordlessly, his head teeming with contradictory thoughts. Blood swirled through his body like a series of whirlpools, conflicting emotions battering against the walls of his insides. Kyer the one who cursed Alon Maer?

"No, Jesqellan, I just can't believe that of her. She's made some questionable choices, without a doubt, but *that*?" He shook his head and pressed it into his free palm.

"Think on it, Derry, she went willingly to speak to Fredric, and you know as well as I do that she has not been truthful about what happened there. We were all ill, yet she was not. Have you noticed that? And while we were ill, she left us for some period of time. I noticed that, even if you did not —"

"I wasn't aware of that, but I did hear her talking to someone."

Jesqellan stopped. "Oh?"

"She denied it, of course."

"Just as she still has not told us where she was the morning we left Seaview."

"She was with that boy, which is bad enough—"

Jesqellan's voice went quieter. "You do not know that she was with him the whole night. She might have met with anyone in that time."

Derry suppressed a groan. "And then she said that thing about the snake. Right? That's what set you off."

The Moabi nodded his bald head. "I think she slipped and regretted saying it. I don't know what to do about this, whether it is too soon to confront her. I thought you should know. I told Fredric to continue to track us, and we would speak with him later once I had informed you. In the meantime, if there are two of us watching her, it will be harder—"

"Why would she work so hard to find the ingredients?" Derry asked reasonably. "Why help at all if she could just as easily ignore it and let Alon die?"

"How do you know that isn't what she's doing?" Jesqellan leaned toward the captain as if he'd thought the same thing. "She could be leading us on a merry tour of the Guarded Realm. Or collecting ingredients for something altogether different."

Derry added a couple more sticks to his armload, and the two headed back to their camp. "You're right that I am not prepared to confront her about this," he said. "Not yet. Her other actions have been troubling me much more of late, and I need to deal with that first. I hear what you have said to me, and I am not discounting it, but it is too soon. I—" He exhaled and compressed his lips. "I—will keep it in mind as I continue to observe."

They replenished their woodpile, and Jesqellan left the captain to his thoughts.

Stormy thoughts. *I don't want to believe it. I* don't *believe it.* If she hadn't been so peculiar in these past few weeks, it would be easy for him to argue in her favour. With so many odd occurrences . . . Why *had* she not become ill? And on top of her speaking with someone while they suffered on their sickbeds, Jesqellan said she'd left them alone. Why would she have done that? Yet if he asked her, she would snap his head off. Why did she insist on behaving like such a stubborn, spoiled child? Heedless of the effect she had on others. Self-centred. Was that it?

If we have suspicions, she's brought them on herself.

And now, she'd been gone much longer than necessary to just get water and a few bits of food. Major Gilvray's face came into his view. His profile, as he looked *that way* at Kyer. Derry's jaw ached from clenching it.

"I hope you all appreciate what I had to go through to get this stuff." Kyer laughed wryly as Phennil, Janak, and Skimnoddle fell on the sacks of food. Derry and Jesqellan ambled over to help sort out and divide the bread, cold meat, cheese, fruit, and vegetables. There were also two bottles of wine. Kyer told them of the "kindness" she had received from the two soldiers.

"I've been wondering, Kyer," Skimnoddle said in mock seriousness as he munched on a carrot, "when *are* you going to come and keep me warm?" She threw a hunk of cauliflower at him.

"Yeah." Janak laughed. "Come and sleep with us tonight, Kyer!"

"I'll share your bed the day Phennil bathes of his own volition," she said with narrow eyes and a crooked smile.

"I bet Tod bathes." Skimnoddle nudged Janak.

"Ha," she said. "Really, the good news—"

"What, does *Gilvray* bathe?"

Kyer looked up into the eyes of the one who had spoken. Derry's eyes were just as astonished, as if something had involuntarily slipped out. Funny how the truth came out when one let one's guard down.

She turned away hastily. "I wouldn't know." It was a sorry excuse for a comeback, but she'd been taken by surprise.

Janak hooted. "That got her! Have you ever known Kyer to be speechless?" He whacked Derry on the shoulder and was joined in laughter only by the elf and the halfling. "Hats off to you, Captain."

Derry glowered.

Too much living in each other's pockets, she thought. *Knowing each other's business. Or thinking we do.*

The others had apparently forgotten that she had mentioned good news, and though a vague awareness told her it was juvenile of her, she no longer felt like sharing it.

Sparse conversation accompanied the meal.

"We need a plan," Jesqellan said afterward, when they were all wrapped in cloaks and seated as close to the fire as they dared. Skimnoddle pulled out one of his dice and practiced making it disappear and reappear in odd places.

It seemed to help him think. "If there is no rune pattern, we need another way to get the dust. If indeed the major was lying, we must learn where he keeps the key. Obviously the next step is to determine a way to get it from him. Could we send in a spy?"

Kyer continued to be petulantly silent. She'd already done the spy work. She already had the answer to the first problem.

Derry continued to be petulantly ill-humoured. "The entire army is likely aware of our presence by now."

Something clicked in Kyer's head. *Aware of our presence*, she thought, and the answer to the second problem began to formulate.

"Skimnoddle had great success the other night; he's small enough to hide in the shadows," Phennil suggested.

"What, he's going to *juggle* the rune pattern out of him?" Janak said.

They've already seen me, thought Kyer.

Skimnoddle leapt to his feet and mimed his actions. "We could surround his tent, one of us could enter and put a sword to his throat."

It might not even come as much of a surprise, she mused.

"Do you honestly think all six of us would get past the guards?" Derry wasn't putting up with ridiculous ideas.

She drifted off as the plan materialized. Their words went unheard by her. Her limbs tingled with energy as her excitement grew. She almost wished she could tell them, but it was impossible. If she told them what she had overheard she would have to also reveal her idea, and there was no way they would agree to it. It was a good plan, one that did not involve spies or hostages. She was certain it would work. She drifted back.

"Taking a hostage is preposterous," Jesqellan said disdainfully. "They would follow us and likely sacrifice the hostage to prevent us from reaching the caves. They are soldiers after all."

"Illusions," Skimnoddle said, puffing the die into the smoke of the fire, "are everywhere. The truth can be hidden right before your eyes." He leaned over and drew the die out of Jesqellan's sandwich.

"That's helpful." Phennil stared scornfully at the halfling.

"All I meant is that he's sure to have them hidden in his quarters. I could go in and just steal the runes if only we knew where they were," Skimnoddle explained.

Derry poked Kyer's boot with a stick. "Any ideas? You've been awfully quiet."

She smiled. "Maybe I'll go steal the runes."

"Come on, be serious. You're as bad as Skimnoddle."

For a fraction of a moment she thought of telling him. Then she recalled the way he'd spoken to her earlier, and over the last couple of days.

Kyer stretched. "You know? I haven't the foggiest idea. I'm bored." She stood up. "Listen, you guys don't need me for this. I'll see you later. What I need right now are some 'alternate circumstances.'" She wrapped her cloak about herself. "Who knows? Maybe with some new . . . inspiration I'll get a clearer set of instructions from Kayme." She strode off toward the encampment. Guilt nibbled at her for deserting them, though they would forgive her in the morning. Besides, she and Skimnoddle had literally just told them. If any of them had half a brain they'd figure it out.

Kyer held her cloak tighter around herself. She'd never get used to these chilly northern winds. *And it's summer.* As she trudged she looked up and watched the clouds scudding across the sky, blotting out the stars and in turn revealing them again. The moon waged war with the clouds, so she couldn't rely on it for light. Accustomed by now to the darkness, she could easily make out any large grass patches or pits to avoid. The muddy ground had hardened, still her footsteps made hardly a sound as she nodded to the sentry at the gate and proceeded into the rows of tents. A mouse scurried across her path on its way home with dinner.

She fingered the links of the chain around her neck. Lifting it over her head, she tucked the medallion deep into her pocket, and thought about what she would say to him. He might be alarmed at her return, yet he couldn't know she had overheard his conversation, so there was no need for him to suspect her true purpose. She had not forgotten the way Ryerson Gilvray had looked at her. His desire had been unmistakable. How long had it been since he'd had the company of a woman? That desire, that hunger, would be very useful to her tonight. They would each get something they wanted this evening. It would be a fair exchange.

Gilvray was good-looking enough. Yes, he would do. Kyer couldn't suppress an anticipatory smile. The runes were a convenient excuse, really. Who said she wasn't allowed to enjoy her work?

Kyer had more or less figured out the layout of the camp and she found the major's hut easily. A guard stood outside, light from the lantern above him casting his shadow onto the straw mat on which his feet were planted. With bent knees, he pressed his back up against the wall. *Stretching a sore back?* His hands hung at his sides. With closed eyes his head was tipped to one side, so that Kyer thought he might be asleep, but with a short breath he then tipped it to the other side. *Neck stretching as well.* So absorbed was he that he did not hear Kyer's footfalls until she was right in front of him. His eyes opened and he quickly pulled himself to attention.

"Halt!" he commanded, blushing and flustered.

"I already have," Kyer pointed out with quiet amusement. "Tell your major he has a guest, but don't say who it is. You may thank me later for giving you and your sore back the evening off."

Derry stared after her, dumbfounded, stunned into silence along with the others. Being an hour and a half late was one thing, but walking out in the middle of a discussion was unheard of. Derry was angry, and did not bother to conceal it.

He stood up. "Hellfire take her!" His voice rose with indignation. "I ought to go after her and bring her back. Tie her down, if necessary."

"Oh, never mind, Derry. Maybe a breath of fresh air would help us all come up with ideas," Janak said, his voice hoarse.

"She's not *going* for fresh air. You heard her. You should all be able to guess where she's going."

"Perhaps she has a guilty conscience so she's going to apologize to Gilvray," Skimnoddle suggested.

"'Apologize' . . . is that what they're calling it nowadays?" Janak snorted.

"She certainly ought to have a guilty conscience, but it has nothing to do with Gilvray," Derry said, louder. His whole body was a storm about to break.

Jesqellan pointedly kept his mouth shut.

Phennil was typically forgiving. "Look, Derry, it was a disappointing day."

"Yes, it was," Derry agreed, "but it was the same for all of us! Why is Kyer the only one allowed to feel it?"

"Maybe she isn't the only one," Janak snapped, his eyes gleaming the reflection of the flames.

"Why do you all insist on sticking up for her at the expense of the mission?"

"Why do you insist on thinking ill of her all the time?" Skimnoddle said.

Derry whirled to face the halfling who had never spoken with such defiance. His anger flared with heat, though his tone cooled. "Because she keeps adding evidence to my suspicions!"

"What suspicions?" Janak asked. "That she's a woman and likes her pleasure? Well, I'm a dwarf and I like mine, too. I hooked up with a partner in Seaview, didn't you?"

The captain fervently hoped the firelight disguised his blush. He straightened, and dropped his chin, shaking with the effort to control his temper. "We took the night off. You weren't late for a meeting, nor did you just walk out of what might be the most important discussion of this mission for the sole purpose of seeking pleasure."

"Maybe she truly felt that a break would give her some ideas," Phennil pleaded.

"Maybe she's going to encourage him," Janak chuckled.

"Mayhap she *is* going to steal the runes," Skimnoddle said quietly.

Derry scoffed with impatience at such ridiculous notions. He looked round at their expectant faces, and couldn't keep it to himself any longer. Fed up with hearing them defend her, Derry blurted, "I am questioning her dedication to this mission, and therefore her loyalty to Dunvehran and Kien." There. They might as well know.

They stared at him.

"Are you mad?" Phennil said.

"No, I am not. Her behaviour has been puzzling at best since quite some time ago. She has been untruthful, she's avoided discussion. We have not received direct answers to questions about her whereabouts. For instance how she got you out of the Cold Fells, Phennil—"

"She saved my life, Derry."

"Yes, so she says, but she won't tell us how. And as to why she followed after Fredric . . . well, Jesqellan has some new information about that. Look, how convenient is it that only she knows what exactly we're looking for? We don't even know that the stuff we're running all across the Guarded Realm for isn't just the recipe for some new kind of skin cream. And now, she has deserted us a total of three . . . no *four* times: looking for a sword, following Fredric, in Seaview and now this. As Captain, representing my Lord, I can no longer let it go."

"I really think you're wrong, Derry," Janak said.

"What are you going to do?" Phennil asked.

"I will speak to her when she returns." Derry sighed, his arms falling to his sides now that he'd decided a course of action. "I think it would be better if it came from me. I'm sure she would rather hear it from a friend than for me to tell Dunvehran and have him give her a formal rebuke."

Janak grunted. "Well. You can just leave me out of it. I'm going to bed."

Phennil rose. "Be careful where you tread with this, Derry. You had better be absolutely certain, or you'll regret it." If looks could kill Derry would have done some damage to the elf's back as he walked away. The damned elf was deluded because Kyer "saved his life." *He's getting just as mouthy as she is.*

When Skimnoddle had retired, Derry slumped down next to Jesqellan. "Do you think I'm overreacting?"

Jesqellan shrugged. "We have information the others don't have. I think you were right at this point not to draw attention to what I told you earlier. Let us just see how Kyer responds to your comments. You must at least pose these questions to her. You are Dunvehran's voice out here in the wilderness. She needs to be brought back into line."

Derry nodded. Jesqellan placed a hand on his arm before retiring to his own bed and leaving the captain to plan his conversation.

Once alone, Derry could finally hear himself think. He took a walk around their camp. That blackness ached in his stomach again. It must be his conscience manifesting itself in a strange way. His own loyalty to his Lord was insulted by Kyer's disrespect. She had agreed to this mission, and was openly flouting the responsibility that came with it. It was this sort of errant behaviour that had already cost him his knighthood. He was damned if he'd let it happen again.

If she'd gone to see one of the soldiers who had teased her earlier, he'd likely feel equal frustration, but not this burning betrayal blackening his spirit. He recollected the few extra moments it had taken her to emerge from Major Gilvray's hut and knew it wasn't so. His every muscle tightened. Derry swung his arms back and forth as if he were warming up for a sparring session. She had never had the tendency to go with underlings.

Having completed one revolution of the camp he turned and went back in the other direction. He pressed his fingers against his forehead. *How could she?* Sleeping with the man who was essentially the enemy. He was right to point out her indiscretions and give her a dressing-down. He regretted having to enforce the chain of command, but it had to be done. This was not the time to introduce the notion of her cursing Alon without further proof, in spite of Jesqellan's certainty. He was glad Jesqellan was of the same mind. He rubbed his face with his hands. He had to, at the very least, call attention to the fact that her letting the company down was becoming a habit. He stopped and planted his feet.

The group has come to look up to you for your energy, enthusiasm—no, that was not a good idea. Better to stick to the facts. She would feel pain for a while until she came to realize that he was right; then she would be grateful. There was no doubt in his mind.

Nineteen

Why Don't You Trust Me?

Ryerson Gilvray had things on his mind. He had been trying since supper to write up a report of the day's events. He'd slogged his way through the departure of troops to the Black Mountains after breakfast, citing details of Leaders, Captains and troop numbers. He sighed heavily as he wrote *Correspondence: reply to Colonel Greenburg regarding status on Indyn Lake outpost.* No further details necessary. They'd been logged yesterday. That brought him to the arrival of the so-called emissaries from Valrayker. Were they for real?

He still believed he'd made the right choice. Better to be safe than sorry. His responsibilities were the Tree of Life and the Indyn Caves, not Kien Bartheylen's wife.

Nor am I his dying wife, said that woman as she'd left. What a beauty! He sighed. He allowed his men short jaunts up to Seaview to "View the Sea" as it were. It kept his men happy, but he couldn't afford such luxuries. When the Colonel returned he'd only have two more weeks before his own long-term leave, and he'd be out of this desolate place and back home to Prost in no time. He ran a finger down the fair cheek of the lady in the framed sketch on his desk.

Emissaries arrived to ask about Caves, he wrote. A short knock startled him and ink ran a spidery trail across the page. He swore.

"Yes, yes, what is it?" he snapped. The door opened.

The guard hesitated in the doorway. "Uh, sir, you have a visitor, sir."

"What are you rattling on about? I'm busy. I am expecting no one!"

"But sir, there's—"

The door was pushed open and in stepped the one person he had hoped, but never imagined he'd actually see at his door at night. He practically leapt to his feet, reassembling his face to cover a mixture of suspicion and shock.

"Are you alright, Major Gilvray?" Kyer Halidan teased unlaughingly. "Has it been so long since you've seen a woman that you don't know what to do? If you like, I could come back later, say, in about six months time." Her words were a light-hearted challenge. She was all but daring him to send her away, and she must be fairly certain of how he would respond.

"No, no, of course I'd—" He moved out from behind the desk, thankful that he no longer wore his mail coat and tabard. His wife had told him how muscular he looked clad in a simple tunic and breeches. He cleared his throat. "Please, come in." He had recovered from the initial reaction. "Is this . . . a business errand?"

She met his gaze levelly and paused significantly before replying, "Not at all."

This was so unexpected—and yet just as he had been fantasizing all afternoon—that Gilvray was perplexed. The chilly breeze followed Kyer through the door like a toddler clinging to his mother's knees. "Eldon, bring in the bell, and you may have the rest of the evening off." Eldon looked at Kyer in suspicious surprise, as though she had correctly prophesied the end of the world.

"Told you," she said with a wink. Eldon took the bell down from its hook outside the door and set it on the small table just inside. "Try some ginger tea for your stiff back," she advised and gave him a friendly pat on the shoulder before closing the door behind him. Gilvray stared at her in amazement.

"Does ginger tea really work for stiff muscles?" he asked.

"I have no idea," was the amused reply, as she faced him. "It can't hurt."

The major was mildly confused, but made an effort to match her confidence.

"Please, uh, would you like to hang up your cloak—or were you here just on a short errand?" he added as a protective measure, just in case she wasn't here for the reason he hoped.

She did as he suggested. "That's up to you."

A pulse in his temple thudded against his skull. "Oh." He picked up his cup from where it had sat on the table. He drained it. "Would you like a drink?"

"That would be splendid," she said quite cheerfully.

He fetched another cup from inside the trunk and poured the deep orange liquid into it, refilling his own cup as well. His thoughts raced. Had he slipped up and told her something? Why was she here? *No, I didn't tell her anything. She must actually be here to see me.* Though he was inclined not to believe it, it seemed the only possible answer. The cold air had been chased out by an uncanny warmth.

They raised their glasses and she held his gaze until he felt sweat trickling down his arm. He adopted an air of nonchalance as he took a drink and gestured to the chair near the glowing brazier. Carelessly studying her face he tried to determine her age. Early twenties? *I'm old enough to be her father.* He drank, and let the liquid slide down his throat and dispell the doubt that she might find him attractive. *Well why not?* he thought. *I'm twenty years more experienced; maybe she likes that.* He drank again.

He moved his desk chair around to join her at the fire, and remembered his suspicion that she was not working for either of the dukes. Should he fear her? She would obviously be no match for him physically, but would Dregor have provided his envoys with other powers? He sat and hoped to be convinced otherwise.

The woman breathed deeply of the whisky vapours as if she had had nothing like it in a long while.

"This is good."

"I'm glad you like it. I save it for special guests," he said.

"Why thank you." She smiled coyly.

She seemed to enjoy the awkwardness of the situation. He tried to give in to this strangely welcome fantasy, but had to concentrate too hard on not appearing desperate. He didn't want this moment to vanish like a soap bubble. He leaned back and crossed one leg over the other, still half expecting her to start talking business.

"So, Major, is that your wife?" She gestured to the frame on his desk.

He nearly jumped out of his skin. "Uh, yes." His voice cracked uncomfortably. He cleared his throat again. "Yes it is."

"She's lovely," Kyer said with sincerity. "How long has it been since you've seen her?" Her tone was conversational, yet he felt suspicious again.

"It's been . . . nearly five months." He fingered the ring on his left hand.

She nodded sympathetically. "It's been nearly that long since I left home."

Ah, really? That was good to know.

She downed her drink in one gulp. He smiled, followed suit and poured again.

Kyer got up and took a few steps over to the bed, looking around the room. She moved with a grace and fluidity that reminded him more of a dancer than a warrior.

"This seems comfortable enough."

"It is." He rose as well, out of sheer agitation, and searched frantically for a reason to have done so. She was looking at him again, with those penetrating eyes. What did they see? His breath came in short puffs. "What *did* you come here for?"

Kyer didn't take her eyes off him. "Come now, you must have some idea."

He shook his head, puzzled. "I—don't have the key. If such a thing exists," he added hastily.

"So you said."

"So why are you here?"

"Oh, my dear man." She took a few steps toward him. Her fierce determination reminded him of a panther about to spring. He was almost inclined to retreat. Almost. "*Alternate circumstances*, you said, remember? You must know what I want. And I know you want it too."

"Oh? And how would you know that?" He was unable to hide the redness that crept up his neck. She was right of course, but he couldn't let her know it.

She slowly licked her lips and formed them into a smile. "I saw the way you looked at me today. I like that look. Besides, if you thought for a moment that I posed a threat to you, you would not have sent your guard away."

The flickering light from the lamp shone on her hair, and the contrasting light and shadow increased the depth of her eyes. *She's so beautiful.* "Why are you here with me instead of with your travelling companions?" He really wanted to know the answer to this. Surely that young captain . . . but he didn't want to think about that.

"I'm tired of them," she said. "I see them every day. And none of them does to me what you do.

"Now." She lowered her voice to offer one more challenge. "Would you prefer to keep this formal, or shall I remove my armour?"

Gilvray leaned against his desk, afraid for a moment that he might tremble. She was dangerous and beautiful in the firelight, and he wanted her. To avoid sounding greedy about his preference, he mumbled, "Uh, please, make yourself comfortable." He drained his cup again and turned to place it on the table, glad to shift, and hoping to hide the signs of his growing intrigue with these new circumstances. The tension in the cabin was explosive; if someone had opened the door Gilvray felt as if he might be sucked outside.

She unbuckled her breastplate.

His jaw slackened. *She's taking it off.* He watched hungrily. Such forthrightness was new to him. His heart pounded with a touch of fear. Soon she stood in front of her host, clad only in tunic and breeches.

"Why are you so nervous?" She licked her lips.

"Nervous?" He breathed for the first time in several moments. "Why would you think I am nervous?"

"Yes, of course," she nodded. "You are 'the commander of five hundred men;' you're all that stands between Dregor and the Tree of Life. You have to be ready for battle at a moment's notice. You're accustomed to facing much more formidable foes than a lone woman." Her cup was not empty but she set it on the chair she had vacated. "Still, I get the feeling that you don't trust me."

She was right again. He didn't trust her. In fact he found that he was afraid of this, as she had put it, lone woman, who flung his own words back at him. Alone or not, she was dangerous and he didn't know why.

"Who the hell are you?"

"What difference does it make?" She reached up and grabbed the back of his neck and pulled his face down to hers. Her mouth was already open as she attacked his lips, and he instantly lost all desire to resist. He let her tongue enter and welcomed it with his own, the taste of whisky lingering there. Her other hand kneaded his back, and his arms encircled her, discovering this stranger's body, which was far less delicate than he had assumed. His hands moved up and down, feeling the muscles in her back, her shoulders, her arms. His left hand found her breast and experimented with its firmness. Her left hand found the protuberance in the front of his trousers and he stifled a gasp. All this time their mouths feasted on each others lips, faces, necks, ears.

"I wanted you from the first moment I saw you," he said.

"I know." She pulled him with her to the floor and he fumbled with the string on her tunic.

Bodies shining in the meagre light, relieved to be released from their confining coverings, their hands pleasured in exploration. She pushed him gently onto his back and sat astride his abdomen. Though her breasts tantalized him, they were not all that drew his attention. He stared up at her battle-scarred torso and gently brushed the healed wounds with his fingertips. *Incredible power*, he marvelled, *I had no idea.*

She put one hand on the floor on each side of his head and leaned down to him, just looking into his eyes. His hands reached up of their own accord and cupped her breasts.

"Your eyes," he murmured. "So . . . captivating."

Taking her long braid in one hand she used the tuft at the end of it to softly trace the outline of his torso. Across his chest, back and forth, up and down from his throat to his navel. Breathlessly he took her face in both hands and drew it down to his.

He kissed her long and hard. And then she began to kiss her way slowly downward. His lips. His ear. His neck. His throat. His chest. His breastbone. "Does your wife do this for you?" she whispered. His navel.

He gasped, "No." His abdomen. And lower. Her mouth did some more exploring on its own. He pictured his wife's dark curls, her wave and smile as he rode away, and missed her. Though if there had to be a substitute . . . .

She came up again and grabbed his shoulders, pulling him over on top of her. They kissed again. And again.

"You sure know what you want," he whispered during a pause.

"Yes," she said. "And I usually get it too." *I have no doubt!* he sighed as she guided his head down her body. He was more than happy to oblige. She smelled of leather and sweat. Desire rippled through him. *It is not only her upper body that is muscular*, he discovered.

Finally she stopped him and they rolled over once more. In a moment of utter ecstasy he plunged inward. They both cried out with joy.

They took turns at being the leader, both proving and enjoying each other's strength. Gilvray delighted in Kyer's natural tendency to take charge. He had never experienced such a demanding woman. With aggression that thrilled him, she would pull him toward her, on top of her, away so she could change position, always guiding him to where she wanted him to be. Roughness was intermingled with exquisite moments of soft, slow intimacy. If this woman fought half as intensely as she made love, she was a great warrior indeed.

It was her very strength and energy that fuelled his own. He could not help but feel that he was the greater of the two; she was powerful, yet he was conquering her.

The fire was warm, and they were even warmer. They never did reach the bed. They continued on and on, caressing, stroking, hands, mouths, arms, shoulders, thighs. He was intoxicated by her and the alcohol he had consumed. At long last, bodies glistening, they reached a rapturous zenith. They held it for several breaths before collapsing in a heap on the straw mat, so still that someone entering may have wanted to check for signs of life. But he would have found that both hearts were racing.

Gilvray was spent. With supernatural strength he traced the shape of her face with his index finger, then let his hand drop. Overcome by the exhaustion that accompanies satiated longing, compounded by liquor consumption, he felt himself drift away. The dark curls he usually dreamed of were eclipsed by dark green eyes and a long braid.

Kyer had finished only half of what she had come for. *Well that's done,* she thought as she rose. The pleasure part of the evening was through. For the most part it had been pleasurable, though the man had been a bit desperate, and it had taken considerable power of mind over matter to ignore his breath. If anyone were to ask her she would not have recommended a straw mat trodden on by countless dirty boots as a good surface for lovemaking. Before doing anything else she grabbed Gilvray's discarded shirt and gave herself a hasty brush off. *Now time for business.* She took a pillow and blanket off of Gilvray's bed and made him a bit more comfortable where he lay dead to the world on the mat by the brazier. She swiftly donned her tunic and trousers and went over to the table, where she had seen upon her entrance the belt with the pouch on it laying waiting for her.

She spared one moment to peek again at the framed pretty, round-faced woman with thick dark hair. She looked about ten years younger than her husband. Kyer's gaze passed grimly over the prostrate form of the worthy major. *Sorry lady. You can have him back now.*

Opening the pouch, she held her breath as she drew out the flat round stone that held the secret to the last stage of their mission. She lightly fingered the five coloured gems that decorated the outside edge. She studied the intricacy of the swirling, criss-crossing pattern of ancient symbols. Only then was she suddenly horror-stricken. This was the one part of her plan she had not thought out. *What am I going to do with it?*

She couldn't take the stone. Gilvray would notice immediately, and know who had it. The army would overtake them in no time and the six of them would be no match for Gilvray's men. Heart in her mouth, she plunked down onto Gilvray's chair as she felt her mind seize up. *I can't think.* Panic and despair welled in her chest. *Shit! I should have at least talked to Derry. He would have had some idea. Shit.*

Soren's message was no help, either. She had no idea what the old man was talking about. Dismayed she leaned both elbows on the desk and stared at the intricate intersecting curved, straight, curly-cued lines. Gilvray was right about one thing: the runes were breathtaking to behol—

That's it. It wasn't Gilvray but *Soren* who'd said "breathtaking to behold." That was the meaning of the first line. He wasn't speaking of the key itself, but the *runes*! He wanted her to focus on the pattern, not the stone. Heart picking up speed, the hairs on Kyer's arms spiked as she bent her mind toward the rest of the puzzle. *Vision, vision something.* "Vision alone" and touching only with her eyes. She stared at the pattern. *Think!* With a hasty glance she confirmed that Gilvray was still out for the count. What had his companion said? About touch... Touch the key to the matching section on the door, or something. She tapped her fingers excitedly on the edges of the stone. *Touch only with my eyes...* What if... what if it wasn't the stone disc that was the key. What if it was only the runes? What if the disc didn't have to come anywhere near the door? It wasn't a conventional key, like for a lock. If the pattern was more like an *answer key...?* Kyer allowed herself a few deeps breaths to steady her heart. She was certain she was on to something.

If the pattern was an answer key, maybe ... maybe she didn't need the *key* at all. *I only need the runes.*

Gilvray moaned and rolled over, his arm flailing, looking for her.

Kyer was instantly at his side, lay down and stroked his cheek, turning her face into the blanket, so its lanolin and coal smell masked his pong.

"Where're you?" he murmured.

She fervently hoped he couldn't hear her heart beating. To her ears it could have awakened the dead. "Was cold," she slurred, pretending to be half-asleep.

He shifted his body toward her. "I'll keep you warm, lover," and she kissed him, long, slow, and deep, staving off a shudder as he shared the taste of whatever he had eaten for the last few days. She let her hands travel where they naturally would. She turned over and snuggled against him. He spooned around her and caressed her breast. Feeling repulsed, she let him, and he fell into slumber again.

Kyer thanked Aidan that Gilvray hadn't noticed the tautness of her body. She waited nearly forever until he rolled over. With as much stealth as she'd ever used, she slipped back over to her project. *Ok, I only need the runes.* So what to do, then? She didn't have much time. How long would it be before Gilvray woke up and wanted to move to his bed?

She stared at the pattern again, a frown etched deeply into her forehead and mouth. She didn't actually need the stone, but there was no way she could hope to sit here and memorize the pattern. Too complicated. Her mind dashed through her options. She could copy it, though onto what? Gilvray would undoubtedly notice if she used some of his parchment, a precious commodity in times of war. She would also run the risk of spilling ink everywhere, making it equally obvious what she had done.

She flitted her gaze about the place, thinking rapidly. Then Kyer's eyes fell on the penknife that lay on the table among the quills, ink bottle, sandpot and seal, and was struck with an idea. She hurried over to where her belt had been dumped during their desperate undressing and buckled it on. Untying her smallest leather pouch, she transferred its contents to another one. Moving the lamp closer, she sat down at the table and opened the drawstring fully so the pouch could lay completely flat. She picked up Gilvray's knife and scrutinized the runes once more. The leather drawstring pouch was extremely soft and supple, making it simple to scratch, and the knife was small and sharp, easy to make tiny, accurate markings. Holding her breath she worked, meticulously carving a replica.

So deep was her concentration that she only barely heard the crunching of footsteps approaching. *Shit!* Horror stricken at the prospect of discovery, she stuck the stone back in its pouch, just as a soft knock came at the door. She whipped her tunic off and snatched up the sheet off the bed, throwing it around her shoulders for effect.

She opened the door a crack.

"Sir, I stopped by to see—" The guard looked surprised and embarrassed.

"The major can't come to the door right now," she said secretively. She peered over her shoulder at Gilvray, allowing the soldier a brief glimpse.

"That's . . . that's fine," he whispered. "I only wanted to make sure he was all right."

Kyer hated herself for the role she was playing, but made the sacrifice for her cause. She let the sheet slip a little. "I assure you he's very good, indeed."

The young guard's eyes widened, and his overlong peek at her female contours slackened his jaw. "S—sorry to have . . . interrupted you. Good night."

She closed the door and leaned against it, squeezing her eyes shut. *What was that I thought earlier about enjoying my work?*

Clothed again, she finally picked up where she left off. The knife became not only an extension of her hand, but a direct link from her mind as it took in the rune pattern and released it onto the leather. When she thought she was finished she refused to trust herself and checked her work repeatedly. Two lives depended on her precision.

At last Kyer had to conclude that she had done the best she could, and turning the pouch inside out to hide the drawing, she returned it to her belt. Exhausted, she set the knife back where she had found it and swiftly replaced the stone to its hiding spot. She took care to ensure that Gilvray's desk appeared untouched so he would suspect nothing.

Only then could she take a deep breath. If Gilvray awoke now he would see only that she was preparing to leave him. He did not awaken. When she was back in her armour and had thrown her cloak over her shoulders, she knelt next to him. Leaning over, she kissed him softly on the mouth one last time. He stirred and opened his eyes drowsily.

"Thank you," she whispered, "for everything." He smiled wearily in response. "Goodbye, Major."

"'Bye, Kyer." He took her hand and pressed it to his lips before she withdrew it and turned away. His eyes were closed again.

She picked up her cup off the chair where she had left it, and, looking back over at the man she had conquered, drained it in one mouthful. Then she slipped out the door.

Not until she'd said "Good night" to the guard at the south entrance, and was well beyond the boundaries of the encampment did she sigh with relief. It was only phase one. She couldn't even stake her life that her interpretation of the riddle was correct. And she still hadn't a clue about the red light. Still, she felt certain she was worthy of self-congratulation. *I did it*, she grinned, and felt light enough to skip like a schoolgirl.

The half-moon was high as Kyer walked back to their small camp. She'd been gone for several hours. The wind had died down, though it left a lingering chill and a lonely silence. A figure sat by the fire. The straight, slim form was easily recognizable as that of Derry, and she picked up her pace, anxious to share her success. Maybe it would cheer him out of this funk he'd been in. If they'd come up with a plan, they didn't need it any longer.

Hearing her soft footfalls as she neared the area, Derry looked up. His expression was unfamiliar to her and she slowed her pace. He did not smile, nor did he appear to have been worried about her whereabouts. The others were all asleep, or pretending to be.

"It looks like you had a nice evening," he said. Kyer heard his sarcasm and felt her back stiffen. From across the fire her excitement rapidly disintegrated, vanishing in the night air like the smoke.

"Why, yes I did, thank you," she replied in a tired voice. She went to her saddlebag and dug out a small pouch, from which she pulled out a tiny, serrated leaf.

He shifted his position slightly. "We missed you around here."

The little voice of reason in her head whispered that she did owe him an apology for that. An explanation, too. Unfortunately she had never been good at listening to that voice. And she resented his tone. "Really?" she responded lightly, sticking the leaf in her mouth and chewing. "I'd have thought one less voice would speed up the process. 'Too many cooks,' and all that." A swallow of water washed down the bitterness, and she nearly spilled out the story of her evening.

His frown and the proud straightness of his head told her he was simmering inside. He had something else on his mind.

Derry got to his feet. "Will you walk with me, please?" Without waiting for an answer he strode past the horses and away from the camp. Setting her teeth, she inhaled and held it. Then she sighed and followed him through the knee-high grasses, picking her way so she didn't stumble. Finally he descended a low hill and stopped, and when Kyer turned around she could see their fire between the legs of a horse about thirty paces away. She stood a few feet from him and waited.

He took a deep breath. "Please don't think this is easy." He spoke in his Captain voice, and stood tall as if about to make a report to Valrayker. He had brought her downwind of camp, so their voices wouldn't carry. She stepped toward him huddled inside her cloak and braced herself for a tribunal. She could barely make out his form, but she felt his gaze and met it levelly. "As your captain it is my duty, however unpleasant it is, to discuss with you when I feel your efforts on the mission are not what they should be. I have observed that you have not been fully open with respect to actions and information that affect the mission."

Heat crept up Kyer's skin. "What do you mean, 'my efforts are not what they should be'?" Surely she had been working as hard as any of them, lack of communication notwithstanding.

He spoke with quiet intensity, thinking about each word. "I am concerned about your apparent selfishness, and I emphasize the word *apparent*—"

"What?" Of all the things he could have said, this was unexpected. "My *selfishness?*"

"More than once in the last week or so we have had the impression that your own needs have been more pressing than those of the mission."

"My needs? What needs?"

He spread his arms with a jerky movement that betrayed the ire he struggled to repress. "You tell me. You have to admit we've missed you several times on this journey."

She glared at him through the darkness, that little voice of reason silenced entirely by fury at his insinuation. She folded her arms and turned to let the breeze brush her hair out of her face. "I think you'd better be more specific."

"You are making this as difficult for me as you possibly can."

She rolled her eyes. "Oh, pardon my lack of sympathy while you throw accusations at me, *Captain*. If it's your duty, just bloody-well get on with it."

He sucked air in and looked away. "You once told me I could be counted on to do what is right; therefore, I will now do what I feel is right." He turned to her again, and his face was as cold as the half-moon's pale light.

"You don't talk to anyone anymore. You disappear on your own, you come out with announcements about goblin armies and rune patterns, yet you never say where this information is coming from."

"What difference does it make, if it's true?"

"You're missing the point."

"No, *you* are. You're the one standing there telling me I'm selfish and lazy—"

"That isn't what I said!"

"Oh no, you put it much more eloquently, Captain. Still, the intimation is there: just because I haven't given you a detailed account of my every movement you figure I'm not pulling my weight."

"And wasting our time!" Derry had stopped trying to keep his voice down. "Here we are, losing three days on a wild romp to an army encampment who cannot, or will not help us. Alon Maer is on her deathbed, waiting for us to save her life and where are you? Off having clandestine conversations with Fredric Heyland. Off physically indulging yourself, the other day with some doltish boy entirely beneath you—"

Her jaw dropped. "You *really* believed that's what I was doing?"

"You gave no other explanation! You've never told us a damned thing about what you were doing. Ever."

"Maybe that's because it was none of your damn business." Kyer clutched her arms to her chest, denying her instinct to draw a weapon.

"None of my business why you were an *hour and a half* late? And that's not all." He fumed, the words tumbling out like an avalanche. "I'm talking about you not telling me how you escaped after the earthquake, you holding us up while you steal a sword from a dead body, you not being truthful about what happened with Fredric, you miraculously not getting sick and going off by yourself while the rest of us lay there like dying animals—"

"You're *mad!*"

"You only *ever* give us part of the story! And face it, you already have a reputation for disobeying direct orders."

She could not speak. This last blow was the lowest of them all. Fury and utter shock blocked her thoughts from forming into words. The captain took it as an invitation to carry on.

"Every move we make *must* be for the good of our cause! Yet, the satisfaction of your own desires has, on more than one occasion, preceded the needs of our company, and as a result you neglect the rest of us who count on your involvement. Not least of whom is Alon Maer herself."

Her feet fixed evenly on the uneven ground, Kyer stared at his star-framed silhouette, open mouthed. Her guts were hollow liked they'd been scooped out. She wasn't sure whether to laugh at him or be outraged.

"And now tonight, you were with some man who has more good looks than good sense—"

"Oh, he definitely has plenty of the former," Kyer interrupted between taut lips. Derry truly brought out the worst in her.

"You insult us, Dunvehran, Kien, and especially Alon Maer with your flagrant neglect of our mission. To go off and sleep with him, *rewarding* the very man who stands in the way of our goal. It's . . . it's unfathomable!"

She bit her tongue. Clenched and unclenched her teeth. Did the darkness make it easier for him to speak these hateful words to her? She thrust aside an image of sinking her fingertips into his throat. Her voice was frost. "It's awfully generous of you to say it was rewarding for him."

His body tightened. "Dunvehran would be very disappointed to learn that you weren't interested in taking part in our discussion this evening."

The blood drained from her face. Kyer felt sick. "Is that a threat?"

Derry adjusted his footing. "I thought it would be easier for you coming from a friend. But you're just as bloody . . . obdurate as ever. Have you *nothing* to say?"

He wanted her to apologize, but she was well beyond that. Derry had practically called her a whore. Countless possible responses swam in her head, but only one thought emerged.

"So. That's what you think." She nodded slowly. "After all this time, *that* is what you think of me." She took a couple of steps away, and could not check the emotion from creeping into her voice. "Gods' blood, Derry! All we've been through, all we've accomplished, and *that's* the kind of person you think I am?"

His silence was response enough. She glanced to where Trig stood and made a decision. She whirled around and started back to the camp, her pounding footfalls muted in the grass.

Derry followed, an acerbic tone refusing to give her the last word. "You don't deny that you slept with him tonight."

That's all he cares about! A steely voice answered. "No. I do not." Kyer stopped walking. "Though I wouldn't quite call it sleeping." Her words were like icicles driving into his heart. She hustled back to camp, vaguely aware of Derry's footsteps behind her. She retrieved her sword from her bed and slung it around her shoulder, adjusting it at her hip with trembling fingers.

The rest of the group slept soundly, undisturbed by the argument that Derry had purposely removed from their hearing. Kyer wondered if they knew about the captain's feelings. If they shared them. Her eyes stung as she threw her saddle onto Trig's back and strapped her saddlebags in place.

Derry watched her wordlessly. His mouth opened and closed as if frantically trying to say something, but he couldn't force the words out. Kyer fetched her own waterskin from the heap next to the fire and tightened Trig's straps. She put her left foot in the stirrup and threw her right leg over the horse's back.

"Where—" his voice stuck in his throat. "Where do you think you're going?

Seated, her fingers quivered with rage as she fought to untie the pouch from her belt. "I don't know," she replied idly, in contrast to the wrath that burned inside her. "Maybe I ought to go back and stay with Kayme. Like you said, I'll take care of my own needs. What do you think?"

He squeezed his fists at his sides. "Kyer, what are you holding back?" His face looked as though an arrow was stuck in his back. "Why don't you trust me?"

She shook her head, hurt and disbelief whirled inside it. She managed only a whisper. "Because you don't trust me."

His face went blank with surprise.

"Do you know why I killed Ronav? No, obviously you don't." Trig pranced, anxious to move. "Had it just been the villagers, and Sasha? Had it only been about what he did to me, the flogging, the decision to cut off my thumbs and give me to his henchman as a toy? I'd have been able to arrest him, as you ordered. It was because of *you*. I saw what he had done to you. So

I killed him."

She tossed the pouch to him and his hand snatched it out of the air automatically. "Don't say I never did anything for you. My *friend*."

Derry winced at the word.

"By your own rules," she said softly, "I ought to kill you. But I'm not going to, because I'd far rather you had a good long time to think about how utterly absurd you've been." She pierced him with a glare and leaned down. "Something has seriously botched up your judgement, Derry. What kind of a *knight* lets that happen?"

Kyer gave the bay a gentle kick and rode off.

One backward glance showed her she couldn't have chosen more hurtful words. Horror flowed along every line of his face and seeped out through every pore. Oh yes, she had just as much to say to Dunvehran as Derry had about her.

Derry stood and stared after her into the endless darkness that stretched out before him. How much time had passed since she'd gone out of sight he could not guess.

His entire body vibrated with fury. Outside and in. He wanted to scream. He wanted to throw himself on the ground, or kick everything in sight. Hateful words came to his lips, all descriptors for the hateful, manipulative, spoiled girl who had just flown off. He said nothing. He did nothing. He just stood, toes twitching inside his boots, and watched the thin clouds that scuttled across the sky.

Confusion numbed his mind. The conversation had not gone according to plan at all. Kyer was the one who was guilty of wrongdoing, wasn't she? And he had been right to bring it to her attention, hadn't he? How was it that he now felt as if his accusations had been unjustified? *How dare she turn this around on me?* Again.

Horrible insults she'd thrown at him, when all he'd done was his job. And then to add insult to injury she'd tossed him her empty pouch. The symbolism enraged him. *You are worth nothing to me,* that's what she was saying. After all they'd been through. He turned and held Kyer's final gift to him over the fire.

Shit! Jesqellan believed Kyer had cursed Alon. And now she was gone. *Her work here is done . . .* Somehow, Jesqellan's idea no longer sounded so ludicrous.

To be continued . . .

Dear Reader: Reviews go a long way to helping authors reach more readers. If you enjoyed Gatekeeper's Deception I - Deceiver, I would be thrilled if you would leave a friendly review on Goodreads, and/or the site where you purchased it. Thank you so much.

Please visit my website to learn more.

https://kristawallace.com

Turn the page for a sneak peek at my next novel,
Gatekeeper's Deception II – Deceived

Gatekeeper's Deception II

Deceived

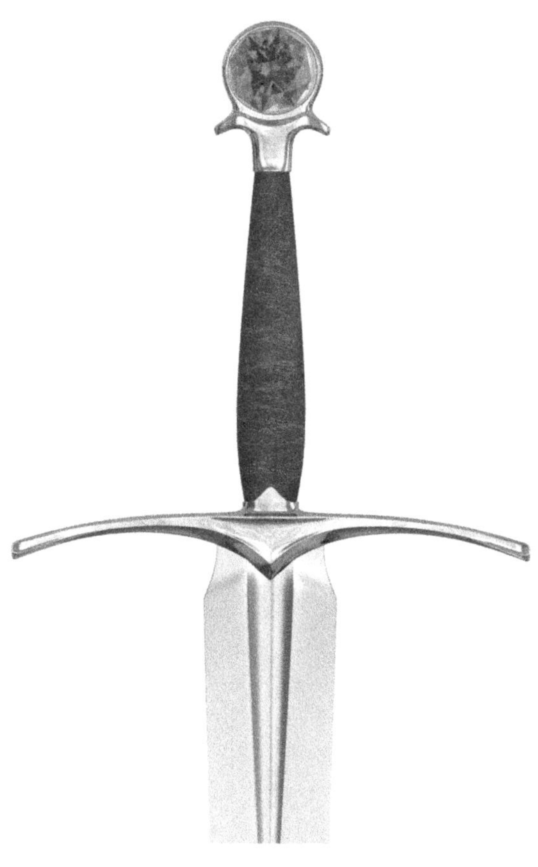

Twenty

On Proving Herself

Kyer rode northeast, Kayme's tower vaguely in her mind. For a long time, she didn't pay attention to where she was headed. Her focus had been stolen by Derry's accusations, and they replayed over and over in her head.

As your captain, it is my duty . . . The satisfaction of your own desires has preceded the needs of our company . . . You only ever give us part of the story . . . your flagrant neglect of our mission . . . some doltish boy entirely beneath you . . . just as bloody obdurate as ever . . . Have you nothing to say?

"That bastard," she told Trig.

Wind whistled in her ears. She drew her hood up, but it just blew off again. She left it.

You once told me I could be counted on to do what is right. That was true: she had told him so, but she never dreamed he would use it against her.

You insult us, Dunvehran, Kien, and especially Alon Maer with your flagrant neglect of our mission. Blood churned through her body so that she had to remind herself to breathe. Piercing cold air sucked into her lungs when she did.

A good league after taking off, she came to a sparsely wooded area. There was no path to speak of, so she dismounted to lead Trig through the stands of pines and balsams. Layer upon layer of needles cushioned her footfalls. The ground was springy beneath her boots, which crunched with the occasional pinecone. The cold, clear light of Frog moon peeked down between the branches, its pure white shafts ghostly and unnatural. Kyer breathed deeply of the aromatic trees, and only after several such breaths did she realize she had been stomping through the woods. Fury still coursed through her.

"Hold a while, Trig." She dropped the reins to the ground with a soft plop. She drew her sword—*steal a sword from a dead body*—and stepped away from her horse into a more or less open space. Swinging her weapon a hard left and right, she parried an unseen enemy's slashes. Up and overhead, then it crashed down into the spongy ground, and up again, horizontally, to block. An imaginary enemy screamed in agony as she cut him to ribbons. She hacked its head off. Kyer dismembered several orcs in this manner, and with a long, deep exhale, she flopped to the needle-strewn earth, only now realizing that she'd left her bedroll back at the camp. *At least the ground isn't so wet now.* Lying on her back she glared up at the shadows of tree tops.

Her body was shattered with fatigue, and though it still vibrated with anger, her mind had cleared a bit. She had never felt such rage. Certainly not aimed at someone who was supposed to be her friend. Friends were supposed to give each other the benefit of the doubt, weren't they? Somewhere along the way, Derry had stopped doing so. He had started reading into her actions, looking for things to find fault with. *If you trust somebody completely, that doesn't happen.* So what was his problem?

Two months ago, Derry would have known there was some reason she was late for breakfast, something important that she couldn't share. He would not have questioned it. She truly had not expected him to believe that she'd slept with—what had he called Tod? *Some doltish boy entirely beneath you.* And honestly, she didn't ever say that's what she had done. She simply didn't deny that she had. Necessary repression of the full truth.

But could she really blame Derry for his anger at her lateness? *You gave no other explanation*, he said. That was true. Should she at least have explained that she could not tell him and asked him to trust her?

That was the trouble. She didn't like to have to ask. Kyer pursed her lips in a stubborn pout.

Alon Maer is on her deathbed, waiting for us to save her life, and where are you? Off physically indulging yourself . . . Well, yes, she couldn't deny that she'd had her own pleasure in mind, but by the gods, she was doing it for a reason. She wouldn't have gone at all if it hadn't been for the runes. But she hadn't explained why she was walking out on them. Sure, she'd told herself she couldn't tell them or they'd not let her go, but how much of it was just a tiny bit of enjoyment at needling Derry?

The stars, peering out from the clouds that wisped across them, blinked down at her through the open-armed pines. She *had* been obdurate; there was no denying it. But did he have to be such a prig? She snorted.

And he'd accused her of neglecting Alon. She couldn't believe his nerve. *I was the first one to volunteer for this mission, and she's never left my mind.*

A sharp pain prodded her in the back of the head, and she sat up. *That's not true.*

Kyer felt like sinking into the chill-hardened ground, glad no one was there to witness the flush that passed across her face. She *had* denied Alon, in those brief moments of weakness after her encounter with Fredric. She had chosen to follow Fredric. Her own personal mission had taken precedence. Even when they'd found her, it took her quite some time to decide whether she was happy about it or not. She recalled her jumbled mixture of relief at being discovered and longing to be left on her own.

Derry couldn't possibly know that. Could he? And she'd made up for it. Hadn't she? She'd tried to. She pulled her knees up to her chest and dropped her forehead on them.

Even if Derry didn't know, Kyer did. How could she blame him for thinking she had deserted the mission when that's exactly what she had done? Her eyes stung.

So long she had worked to prove herself as a swordfighter, as a vital addition to the group. She thought she had achieved acceptance, finally. And now it had come to this. How many others in the party shared Derry's opinion? Kyer wished she'd spoken to Valrayker before she'd come away. *You already have a reputation for disobeying direct orders.* The dark elf would have dismissed her, and then none of this would have happened.

An unfamiliar sensation gnawed at her. It seemed to stab at her heart, forming an ache in her chest and throat, something she didn't remember feeling for years.

The woman whom Kyer called mother, Della, was highly regarded for her knitting. She raised the sheep, sheared them, cleaned and carded the wool. She dyed the soft, lanolin-smelling fibres all sorts of rich colours and spun it into beautiful yarn. After all the preparation, Della either sold the wool or neighbours chose their yarn and she would knit it for them. Kyer remembered being thirteen. Della had knitted her a sweater from a deep red soft wool. It was a yarn that had just won Della first prize at the fair for its quality and fine texture. Kyer wore the sweater to school, not trying to impress, which was not her way, but because she loved it. And wearing it, she felt proud to display Della's superb product and just a bit smug. Her sweater could be compared to those worn by her classmates without coming up short. There was no way anyone could make a sneering comment this time.

Sheska Bolen proved Kyer wrong. The pretty and popular blonde girl took one look at the sweater and sniffed. "Too bad. Even in that sweater, you still just look like a big mistake. Why don't you go back to your cornfield?"

Kyer had had enough experience with Sheska to not really be surprised. Her pride had been ripped away and trampled on, and her throat and chest ached. Kyer hadn't thought of that event for years, but the similarity to her current situation had reawakened those emotions. Her satisfaction at procuring the runes had turned to dust. Derry's unjust words had quashed the triumph she ought to have felt as she placed the pouch in his hand. His just words pierced her with their truth and reason. He'd called her negligent. He'd all but called her a whore. She was terribly angry at Derry for saying those things. Still, there was something else.

Hurt? Dreadful hurt. An unusual emotion for Kyer. Why could she not just let it go, as she had in the past? Sheska Bolen had tried to hurt Kyer countless times, and Kyer couldn't be bothered to spare any emotion for her. Probably because she could so easily take revenge on Sheska. Two days after the incident, she'd sneaked into Sheska's yard and shredded all her dresses hanging on the clothesline with her knife. But Kyer hated Sheska; it was easy to take revenge on her. This was different. This time there would be no such purging of feeling.

She had begun to see Derry's point of view, to understand why he'd thought those things about her. No, she couldn't bring herself to hate Derry.

Moreover, she didn't want to hate Derry. Her final words to him echoed in her head, and she knew she'd hurt him as much as he'd hurt her. Possibly more.

He was right about something else too. Something that hadn't occurred to her until he'd said it. *Why don't you trust me?* She'd accused him of the same thing more than once in these past few weeks. When—*how* had it broken down? Derry had been, not all that long ago, the one person in whom she had complete faith. Somehow her trust of him had eroded. As had his of her. Was one the result of the other? Which had come first?

Kyer cupped her chin in her hands and wondered what to do now.

She couldn't stay here. She couldn't, and didn't want to, go back to a group of people who were preoccupied with watching her every move, waiting for her to screw up again. She could give up. Go home.

Not a chance.

Kyer straightened. Memory carried her back to Gilvray's cabin, sitting at his desk, carefully cutting the rune pattern into her pouch. Etching it into her mind at the same time. The pattern stood out in her memory, vivid as if it were in the palm of her hand.

You're a fool, Kyer, if you let this go. It was time she took her share of the blame for the terrible misunderstanding that had arisen between her and her friend. It was not too late to make it up. Swinging up onto Trig's back, she nudged him west. The Indyn Caves lay somewhere in that direction.

Plus, her fatigue-crazed mind had come up with an interesting thought about red lights.

To be continued...

Acknowledgements

With each book the list of people to whom I am grateful gets longer and longer. Myst DeVana, Jonathan Lyster, and Brenda Carre: you three are supporters extraordinaire, and the English language is not adequate to express my gratitude. Also an enormous thank you to Elizabeth Stricker, Rob Smith, Stuart Hollet, Colleen Condit, Andrea Howe, and the late John Pitts.

Special thanks to the Original Six (Rob, Dougie, Matt, Brian, Phil and Garnet), to all my [totallyfantastictitle] podcast listeners, especially Paula, John, Teresa, Edwin and Chari.

Thanks Brian Rathbone and Brayden Fengler for your Photoshop expertise, and to Peter Andersen for the serpent photo on the cover.

And to my family: Matt, David & Heather, and Maggie, without whom I would be a slathery mess on the floor. You are freakin' brilliant.

Who is Krista Wallace?

Krista started out as a singer, studied Theatre and got her degree in Acting at UVic, then eventually added writing to her creative endeavours. She has sung classical, musical theatre, rock, R&B and jazz. She has been the vocalist for FAT Jazz for something like 427 years, and is half of a jazz duo called The Itty Bitty Big Band. She writes primarily fantasy, but dabbles in other genres, in both short and long fiction. Combining all her artistic exploits, she took on audiobook narration, and producing a podcast, [Totally Fantastic Title], which then branched into the production of her own audiobooks, which she is publishing in paperback and ebook. Krista grew up in the Port Coquitlam vortex, and so was naturally pulled back there after her time away.

To be continued . . .

www.ingramcontent.com/pod-product-compliance
Lightning Source LLC
Chambersburg PA
CBHW061053210726
48294CB00001B/128